Running Wild

Raven's Story, A sequel to Wild Thing

A novel by:

Peggy Poe Stern

Moody Valley
Boone, North Carolina

Published by:
Moody Valley
475 Church Hollow Road
Boone, N. C. 28607
moodyvalley@skybest.com

Cover painting: Peggy Poe Stern
Cover design: David Kenneth Stern
Edited September, 2009 by: Pamela Baldwin
Edited 10-15-10

Library of Congress Control Number
ISBN: 978-1-59513-043-3

Dedicated to:

Elva Buchanan

Known by many of us who love her as **Granny**

Chapter 1

Raven knew she could cause a rockslide by moving the keystone, but she never intended to cause such a large one. When the pole she was using as fulcrum did the job of unbalancing the big rock, the ground gave way along with the rocks and started sliding the earth from under her bare feet almost causing her to go down the mountain with the tumbling stones and dirt. If her muscles had not been strong and her reaction fast, she couldn't have leaped the distance to safety.

At the same time, the near loss of her life didn't concern her, or hardly entered her mind. Much like the wild animals that surrounded her, she was alive or she was not. Her death was something that would happen, not something she feared. The possibility of her being dead was entirely different from her losing her mother and then Aggie. She couldn't mourn for herself.

Once the billows of dirt from the slide had settled, she stood on solid ground and looked down the mountain where the tent still stood upright. Both relief and disappointment touched her, confused her as to what she really felt toward the man whose clothes she wore. She hadn't wanted to kill him in the slide anymore than she had wanted to kill herself. Her intent was to block the entrance to her cave so the man could not return.

That is what she had done. It would take a mountain goat to climb the rocks from his tent to where she stood. A slight touch of sadness stirred inside her chest at the realization of what she had done because a small part of her longed for the man's closeness, the smell of him, the warmth of his hand, the care he had given her after the snakebite. Something was surely wrong with her mind for her to be thinking in such a manner. She concluded it was guilt at coming so close to smashing his tent.

Yet, deep down inside, the companionship of another human was something she longed for, but could not put into words or entirely understand. Lu's and then Aggie's death had left a gaping emptiness inside her. There was an aching loneliness for her own kind without her knowing how to fill it.

Dog nuzzled against her leg and pushed his head into her hand. Her fingers absently petted his huge square head as she evaluated her situation and the events that had taken place and tried to decide what should happen next.

She continued patting his head as she looked out over the land of mountains, rocks, and the valley of Sodom that had always been her home. The place that was her home wasn't the same. Time had changed everything and she had added to the change. Regardless of how much she longed to put things back the way they once were, she could not bring back life as she had once known it, anymore than she could put the rockslide back.

She let a regretful breath escape and tried to force her mind to make decisions. Oh, if she could only be sure of what lay beyond those ridges, beyond the valleys, beyond all the people that lived in all the valleys. If only she knew what that far mountain held in store for her, but she didn't know. All she had to go on was her instinct, and her instinct told her it was time to pack her meager belongings and leave Aggie's cave. She was much like a little bird that had to fly away from its fouled nest.

She knew without doubt that the rockslide would not be enough to give her the protection she longed for. The man would surely come after her, and if he didn't find her, he would continue to come, and sooner or later, along with him would come other men.

She turned her gaze to the spot where she had buried her mother. Neither animal nor man could dig up her bones now. The grave was twenty feet beneath the rockslide. *"Mother, you need never be afraid again,"* Raven thought as she turned away from the rockslide. *"No man can reach you, nor will one ever catch me."* She made a silent vow to herself and willed her mother's spirit not to fret over her. She was a woman now and could take care of herself.

Mitch Kenilworth stood at the edge of the rockslide, a fearfully short distance from his campsite, looking at the mountain of rocks that had come sliding down toward him. It caused a tight feeling in his chest and a weak feeling in his knees. Had the timing of the slide been a little different, and the force of the slide a little more powerful, his tent would now be buried under rock, and most likely, he would have been in it. He wondered if that had been the wild girl's intent. Had she wanted him dead, even after he had cared for her when she was snake-bitten?

As he thought of the girl, a strange kind of emotion shot through him, one he seldom experienced. It was a mixture of anger, determination, and need. He was angry at the girl, not only for the rockslide, but for running away from him after he had bathed, clothed, fed, and cared for her after she was snake-bitten. He was determined to find her and make her talk to him. Perhaps she should even thank him. Also, there was a kind of need burning inside him and he didn't know exactly what to call it.

It made him think of times when he was a small boy and told both his parents and Santa Claus what he wanted for Christmas. He would spend weeks anticipating the day the gift would be his, only for Christmas to arrive and he get nothing but school clothes.

He hurriedly pushed that memory from his mind and assured himself his death was not what the girl wanted. She and that big dog could have killed him anytime he was in the cave and no one would have ever known. It would have been a simple case of a man's disappearance, and the Forest Service would have accepted that resolution. The government did not like human complications to interfere with their rules and regulations.

Once word got out he had not returned to his tent or his old pick-up truck, he would have become a man killed while doing his job. Surveying of mountainous terrain had more risks than anyone realized. Falls from cliffs or attacks from wild animals were always a possibility. Chances were no one would have searched for him, at least not more than casually, for there was no one who cared if he existed, only an ex-wife who never wanted to see or hear from him. Why should she? She already had everything of value that he once owned.

This morning the slide had settled and the silt from all the falling dirt and rocks no longer filled the air. The sun had risen just as it had every morning, and the birds were singing as though the side of the mountain had never collapsed. Life was continuing just as it should, while the rockslide could have been in place forever.

"I see it didn't get you," said Don Donavan.

Mitch turned and faced the old man. If Don had been concerned about him, he would have shown up the evening before.

"You weren't too worried about me, were you?" Mitch said.

"Not about you," Don admitted. "Pete Jenkins saw you right after the slide. Knew you were all right. No need for an old man to run all the way here and investigate until the dust settled."

Mitch accepted that and his hard feelings toward Don eased.

"Came too close for my comfort," Mitch admitted. "See all these big rocks lying around? They came down that mountain with a mighty force behind them. It sounded as though the world had broken apart and was coming down right on top of me. I don't mind admitting it scared ten years off my life."

Don shook his head in wonderment as he gazed at the sight. "I reckon the storm must have loosened those rocks enough to cause them to give way."

Mitch considered what and how much he was going to tell the old man. Actually, he could see nothing wrong with the bold-faced truth. He never was the sneaky sort. "I was watching through my instrument scope when the slide started."

Don's eyes widened and his gray brows went up with interest. "What did you see?"

"What do you think I saw?"

"Is this a guessing game?" Don asked none too pleasantly.

"It's no game." Mitch said. "Tell me what you know about the girl, and I'll tell you what I saw."

"Girl?" Don questioned with an old man's ability at fake naivety. "So, you're back to that again?"

"So are you, if you'll admit it. You not only came here to find out what I know about the slide, you want to know about the girl," Mitch told him in an easy conversational tone of voice. "Why do you refuse to talk about the girl when you and I both know she lives on that mountain? What is it about the girl you are trying to hide?"

"I know nothing about a girl," Don's eyes squinted as he looked toward the top of the mountain. "Those rocks were treacherous. Always was mighty dangerous to travel up that path. Reckon nobody will be climbing onto ole Ruffian now."

"I plan to," Mitch told him.

Don shook his grizzled head in irritation. "You can't do it. A goat would have trouble climbing up those rocks."

"I'm not going up this side. I'll go around."

"Don't know if it can be done."

"It can be done and we both know it. It'll just take a little longer than the path people used to take."

"Most likely you'd fall of a rock cliff and kill yourself if you tried."

"I don't think I'll fall."

"You still have to survey it for the Forest Service? Hain't you finished yet?"

"That's not why I'm climbing that mountain."

Don made a disgruntled sound.

Mitch watched the old man's face closely. "I want to see if the girl is still there. I found her cave yesterday."

Don's adams apple went up and down. Concern showed on his wrinkled face and his fists clinched. "If there was ever a girl on that mountain, chances are she's buried under that rock slide."

Mitch debated on what he would say next and how he should say it. He wanted to see the old man's reaction. He was tired of him playing his cat and mouse games.

"I was watching her through my scope. She caused the rockslide."

Surprise came, and then disbelief.

"She knew what she was doing," Mitch informed him. "She caused that slide to happen.

"A girl couldn't do that," Don insisted.

"She did."

"How?"

"It was near that steep place, where the ledge was narrowest. She was standing on the highest rocks. She had a long pole in her hands and appeared to be prying at something, most likely trying to make a large rock give-way. I saw one rock come tumbling down the side of the mountain, and then all the others followed until it seemed the entire mountain was coming straight at me."

Don recalled the very place he was talking about. He'd always thought those rocks were dangerously positioned. The girl must have thought the same. He was just surprised she would know enough to cause the slide to happen. Maybe she had more intelligence than he gave her credit for having. Aggie claimed she was smart, but considering the life she led and who her mother was, her intelligence was mighty questionable.

"Did the slide take her down with the rocks?" Don asked.

"I don't know. Once the slide started, the clouds of dirt blocked out all visibility. That's why I have to go back to the cave. I was up there yesterday when the storm hit and was forced to take shelter in her cave. I know she was further back in there for I saw her fresh tracks along with the dog's tracks going into the cave but not coming out."

"You only saw one set of human tracks, those belonging to the girl?"

"Should there have been others?"

Don swallowed back questions about a woman with bowed legs whose tracks would have been distinctively

different. "Hunters with dogs are always going up there on
that mountain. Could have been their tracks"

"Barefooted?" Mitch asked.

A great sadness came to Don's face as he looked at the
slide again. He knew what only one set of tracks told.
Aggie was no longer among the living.

"Tell me about her," Mitch requested. "I have the right
to know about the girl who tried to bury me under a
rockslide."

The old man forced the sadness to disappear until he no
longer showed emotion of any kind as he said, "You're
lucky to be alive. That slide could of got you. Came danged
close, if you ask me."

"She was still wearing my clothes," Mitch told him.

"What nonsense are you talking now?"

"I'm still talking about the girl you're pretending not to
be curious about. I put my clothes on her when she was
snake-bit and she was still wearing them when I watched
her through my scope."

The old man was obviously troubled enough to let his
emotions show, regardless of how hard he tried to act
different. "Son, if there is a wild girl, and I'm still saying
there's not, she would need a mighty powerful reason for
living like she does. Humans don't stay away from their
own kind without a reason."

"I know, and I think I know what that reason might be."

"Do you now?"

"Iva Dean told me the story about Aggie being her half
sister."

"What did she tell you?" Don could not hide the
eagerness in his voice.

Mitch considered withholding the story and swapping
information bit by bit, but he gave in and told Don
everything Iva Dean Stewart Grearity had told him as they

stood there staring at the tangle of rocks, dirt, and tumbled roots.

"Where does the girl come into that Grearity woman's story?" Don wanted to know.

"I'm not sure," Mitch admitted. "She left that part out, but I concluded the girl must be Aggie's daughter. Is that right?"

There was no way Don would answer that. "If this crazy story Grearity has told you is real, and there is an Aggie and a girl, why can't you leave them alone?"

Mitch's eyes drifted from the old man to the rockslide and onward to the mountain's top. "Let's just say I want my clothes back."

Don's steps were slow and troubled as he walked back to his house. His heart was resting heavy in his chest. He ran through his mind what Mitch Kenilworth had told him and he needed time to think things over and put them in their proper place. He knew one thing for certain, Aggie had to be dead if the girl deliberately blocked off the mountain pass. Aggie would not have let the girl do it if she had been alive. Aggie had never been entirely able to shut off her connections with other humans. Also, Aggie needed the pass so she could leave the mountain and go into the valley where she gathered food for her and the girl's survival. Not to mention Aggie had begged him to care for the girl if something happened to her.

He would need that path to bring the girl off the mountain.

Yes, Don was certain Aggie was no longer with the living.

That was it! That was why the girl closed the path. She wanted to make sure no one would come after her, try to make her live with her own kind. Only a foolish, young girl would close off her main supply route, a foolish young girl who had strong legs and a strong back, one who was afraid of a man who had found her cave.

"What in this world is wrong to make you look so whipped?" Betsy asked as he stepped onto the porch. "What damage did that rockslide do? Did it get that feisty surveyor after all?"

"It didn't get him, but it closed off the pass to Ruffian mountain."

"So?"

"So Aggie can never go up or down the mountain again, if she and the girl are still alive, which I doubt."

"I see," said Betsy. "That poor woman is trapped up there and so is the girl." Betsy frowned. "Why do you doubt they're still alive?"

"According to Mitch, it was the girl who caused the rockslide." He sank down in his chair and leaned its back against the wall.

"Surely not?"

"Mitch Kenilworth said he was watching the girl through his telescope and saw her cause the slide."

"A girl could do that? Impossible. How could she do a thing like that?"

"She did it. There's little doubt about it."

"Why?"

"I think Aggie died and the girl is left to survive on her own. You remember Aggie said the girl's mother was crazy along with being mortally afraid of men. I think she passed those traits on to the girl. When Mitch found her cave yesterday, the girl panicked and closed off the path leading up the mountain."

"Mitch Kenilworth found her cave?" Betsy's eyes narrowed.

"He said he did."

"How old did you say the girl is?"

"According to Aggie, she's fifteen, or thereabout."

"She's too young for Mitch to be interested in her physically," Betsy seemed relieved. "Can you imagine what it's like to be a child left alone in the wilderness to survive all by yourself?"

"Yeah, I've imagined it for years. At least she's better off than Aggie was. Raven has a strong back and a good set of legs."

"We did it," Raven said to the big black dog mainly to hear the sound of her own voice. She hadn't heard another human voice in some time and her words echoed strange in the deep woods. The unwelcome noise stopped the singing of birds and the scattering of squirrels. Human voices didn't belong in these mountains and she was glad of it.

"Good," she said. "It's good we go."

Yet, there was fear inside her as well, a fear threatening to discredit her decision of blocking the path to the rock cliff, a fear of running away. Hastily she assured herself she had done the right thing for no man belonged in Aggie's cave. No man belonged on ground where her mother's feet had trod.

Men were her mother's enemy; now they were hers as well. It was a sacrilege for another human to walk upon the ground Aggie and her mother had walked, even worse if their feet happened to touch their graves.

Many times, she had thought about leaving Ruffian Mountain, but now she was overwhelmed by having done so. For years, she had questioned whether she could leave the place she were born and raised, not sure she could go beyond what she had always known. What she had known was that Aggie could never leave the mountain.

She still found it unbelievable what moving a few rocks could do. It blocked off a path she had taken all her life – a path that had been part of Aggie, Lu, and her existence. Moving those rocks had covered her mother's grave until no wild animal could dig up her bones. She tried not to think about it for Lu and Aggie were gone to her. She could not reach out and touch them during a long and lonely night; nor would she see their loving faces, have them beside her, caring for her when she needed them.

Gone.

The word vibrated in her mind like a hateful echo, but she could not say it out loud for it would make their death too real, hurt her too deeply.

Her known way of life was gone. She might as well face it, her life, as it had been, ended today.

She had never been one to cry, but her eyes burned and her chest tightened. She forced the stinging tears back, telling herself that she was a grown woman now, fifteen years old, and mistress of her own world. She could take care of herself, her and Dog. They had each other and that was enough.

She stopped, dropped the straps from her shoulders, and let the travois sit still as she stretched her back muscles and aching shoulders. Her travois was packed and heavy, for it contained most of her worldly goods. But her worldly goods were not heavy, the bags of dog food were. Dog needed a lot to eat, more than she needed, since he outweighed her hundred pounds by a good bit. The life she led kept her wiry and tough as a greenberry briar

It was not easy pulling the travois through thick woods where the laurel hells grew in a tangle, but she was strong. She could carry anything, do anything, survive anything as long as she and Dog were together, she reassured herself. They could survive away from Ruffian Mountain.

What tormented her most was that *he* had found her cave. Even a wild animal cleared out once its den had been invaded. She had cleared out and left *him*, her enemy, the man that had destroy her way of life, at the bottom of the rockslide. *He* would never be able to find her again, never tell others about her.

Dog was at her side looking at her as though asking why she stopped. She had been traveling for hours, dragging the travois, but only her shoulders and back felt the strain of the straps. Her legs had not tired nor her breathing grown faster.

From where she stood, she could see through the woods to what appeared a natural bald. Aggie had told her many stories about natural balds and their rare beauty, but this was the first one she had ever seen. She did not want to go into the open space and yet it interested her for there could be berries growing. This high up, strawberries would be ripening late and a belly full would give her pleasure and ease her emptiness.

She stood behind a tree observing her surroundings. She hadn't seen a house for hours, but that didn't mean there weren't houses on the far side of the bald. She lifted her head, turned it sideways so her ears could catch sound better. She heard only the wind blowing through the trees, nothing more. She drew the air deep into her nose, held it there, testing it for smells. Plant-scents were swirling about as the sun warmed the vegetation. Animal scents were rising from the soil, the manure of cattle, dung from foxes, but nothing made by humans – nothing that alerted her to fear.

Dog winded the air along with her. Hair raised on the scruff of his neck for a moment before it settled down. He twitched his short tail showing no alarm. Raven knew it was safe to continue on. She looped the straps over her shoulders again, and left the shelter of the woods.

The grass wasn't tall and weeds weren't plentiful on the windy bald. She tried to remember what Aggie had told her about balds, plus what she had read in the books Aggie had obtained for her. From Aggie's descriptions, she believed this was one of the natural balds, places where trees never grew, places high up where the mountain winds always blew.

She found strawberries in a sheltered dip and ate all she could find. The taste of them made her hungry. She looked around for food, anything edible, but the bald had little growing other than those few berries and sparse grass that was as course as horsehair. She went to her pack, took out a handful of dog food, and gave it to Dog. She found a handful of corn stored in a jar, put a grain in her mouth to chew on as she looked about her.

The tall mountain she was heading toward was still in the distance, a beacon calling her onward. She knew such a mountain, where the morning sun hit, had to have caves deep and long. These caves would surely be warmer in winter than the one she was leaving behind. The tall mountain was where the sun rose and bathed it in beautiful colors every morning. The mountain was surely a blessed place.

She looked away from the far mountain to see valleys with creeks running way down below her in what looked like narrow gullies from the high distance of the bald, but she didn't see houses. Something inside her longed to leave the bald and walk those valleys, but she never would go down there willingly. She didn't belong in the valleys. She belonged high on the mountains.

The only times she would walk in the valleys was when forced to search for food. Even Aggie had to go to the hated valleys when hunger struck and gathering food became necessary.

She left the bald on the opposite side and pulled her load into the edge of the woods. She heard a snort and peered into the shadows of the tall trees. Cattle were lying on the ground chewing their cuds in peaceful contentment. She thought of the milk that Aggie used to bring her and longed for a drink of that life-giving fluid. She moved closer to the cattle.

The snort came again. She turned. Behind her, next to a huge hemlock tree, stood the largest bull she had ever seen. Its coloring was burnished copper with a broad, curly red head above a face of white hair. He lowered his massive head, shook it, and pawed up clots of dirt, hitting his under belly with the clots, obviously angered by her intrusion. The huge bull's body muscles quivered, his shoulders rippled as his hooves pawed faster. He appeared aggressive, eager for a fight, any fight.

She couldn't pull her travois without turning her back to the bull, nor did she dare run and leave all she possessed behind, and yet she couldn't just stand there waiting for the bull to attack.

Slowly, she moved forward, her neck craned backward where she could watch the bull from the corners of her eyes. *"If I move slowly,"* she thought, *"he might ignore me, might let me pass on by him."*

He snorted and dug up more clots of dirt. His head began swaying back and forth while slobber drooled from the sides of his mouth with each snort. Raven knew he was ready to charge her and so did Dog.

"Wait," she ordered the big black. "Come."

A warning growl rumbled from Dog as he came to her side, his body leaning against her legs in a protective manner. They both knew trouble was in the making – big trouble. Raven wanted to get close to a large tree with low hanging limbs or at least find a weapon, like a strong limb that had fallen from a tree, to fight the bull with. Surely, among the old-wood forest there would be deadfall, but she saw only small limbs lying on the ground.

Suddenly, like a powerful streak of erupting copper, the massive bull charged straight at her. Dog intercepted the bull's charge and sank his teeth into the bull's hind leg. The huge bovine skidded in the dirt as he whirled to face Dog. Raven dropped the straps and ran for a tree, leaving her travois behind.

She was afraid for her big black. He had never fought with a bull, didn't know how to anticipate a bull's movements. This was to the bull's advantage for he fought with everything that dared come near his herd. His massive head caught Dog in the side and tumbled him over. The bull bellowed his rage, pawed the ground, and bowed his body up as his powerful strength gathered for a killing attack. He charged. Dog dodged the head by inches, leaped upward, sinking his teeth into an ear.

The bull's massive head jerked upward, tossing Dog up onto his shoulders. Dog's powerful teeth held fast and a section of the ear tore loose. Dog tumbled to the ground with the ear still in his mouth. Blood squirted from the bull's ear. Dog gained his feet and backed off, watching, waiting for the next charge. It came, but Dog was ready and sidestepped the raging bull. Dog whirled and leaped for the injured ear. He caught it closer the head and ripped out another chunk of the sensitive ear.

Wild with pain, the bull allowed anger to overrule his caution. He charged straight at Dog. The big black veered sideways only enough to allow him to clamp his teeth in the bull's nose. The soft flesh gave way leaving a bloody gap where half the nose should have been.

The big black had the taste of blood in his mouth and now he was anxious to continue the fight. His animal instincts were pumping strong and the Rottweiler's killing need was hot. He circled the bull, his growls loud, furious, challenging the bull to attack. The bull lifted his head high and backed up. His action encouraged Dog and he grew brave as he charged straight at the bull. His teeth sank into the bull's throat and his jaws locked tight on the hold. This tissue didn't give as easily as the nose, allowing the bull to go into a slinging, whirling fit, until finally, he flung Dog aside, hitting the ground with a thump. Dog didn't act hurt for he was still in a killing rage where pain didn't exist. Carelessly, he went for the bull's side. His teeth bit and tore hide but he didn't get a good enough hold on the tough hide to latch on.

The bull swung around to face the dog and took a step backward as though ready to turn tail and run. Dog lunged for his head, but didn't try to bite. The bull backed up as Dog continued his aggressive charge.

Raven realized what Dog intended. He was driving the bull away from her.

Several cows were on their feet. Others were getting up. Unexpectedly, Dog sprang at a calf. The calf's tail went straight up in the air as it bounded through the woods to escape. The mother bellowed and followed at a run. Other cows and calves followed.

The bull saw an opening and charged, but dog was quick, for he was watching the bull. He got the bull in the fleshy dawdle between the foreleg and belly. The bull roared. Pain and anger were now both rulers of the bull.

Anger made him want to fight the dog, but pain told him he should follow the cows.

Dog snarled and held his ground while giving the bull a chance to run. He didn't. Dog attacked, took a nip at a front leg, backed up, and circled. The bull charged. Dog dodged, and repeated his actions.

All the cows were running down the hill at a loping gallop, leaving the bull behind. He grew agitated, wanting both to follow the cows and to continue the fight while his anger was raging hot and furious. Dog backed up, gave him distance and the chance to end the fight. He took it, leaving behind drops of blood from his still torn and bleeding ear.

Raven climbed down, called Dog to her, and ran her hands over his body to approve of his bravery and check for injuries. . He was wet with sweat, his muscles taunt and quivering as he glared in the direction the bull had gone.

"Good Dog," she said. "Good Dog, Good Dog."

Her voice and hands seemed to have a calming effect on him, but there was that look in his eyes, the look of an animal with a longing to kill.

Chapter 2

The cattle belonged to George J. Ball. He owned over a thousand acres of land, which included the bald and went all the way to the rich valley where the river ran cool and clean. He had one hundred and two head of Hereford beef cattle, a sixty milk-herd of Jerseys, and twice that amount of sheep. Sheep weren't his favorite animal because they grazed the grass into the earth, but wool was bringing good money, and money was the big number one. Without money a man might as well have both arms and legs tied together. He would never accomplish much.

He grew enough corn to winter the animals and sell a few hundred bushels at the market, along with any vegetables that would grow in the mountains, which were mainly cabbage and other cool-weather crops. He was a big-time farmer who knew how to make money, and kept what he made. He was always ready to challenge weather, man, or animal if his assets were concerned, and his bull was one of his prized assets. He had paid a high price for that fine-blooded, registered brute. After all, a bull was half of a man's herd. That bull had produced three breeding sons, gets almost as good as him, running with cows in different sections of his grazing land. But neither young bull was as good as their father.

When the bull showed up with his sides heaving, half his nose missing, and gashes over his body, George Ball suspected wolves had migrated from the upper mountains onto his land. There weren't many wolves in the area, but occasionally a pack would wander down from way up north for some odd reason.

He didn't think it could be a dog, or even a pack of dogs, for a dog couldn't possibly take out such a large chunk of nose or leave bite marks so high up on the bull's flanks. A pack of dogs would have killed his calves instead of attacking the bull, as would a pack of wolves if they were hungry. More than likely, it was a big he-wolf and his mate. Probably ones that had been run off from some place and were traveling to safer hunting grounds.

The bull most likely protected his herd by fighting them away from the cows and calves. However, if there was another attack on his herd, or the herd of another nearby farmer, he would arrange a wolf hunt. Farmers couldn't afford to lose what they had grubbed their fingers to the bone to obtain.

George Ball was in town buying supplies at the feed and seed store and decided to check around with the other men to see if any other farmers had troubles with their cattle. If they did, perhaps they could join together in a hunt. That way Ball wouldn't have to foot the bill of hiring someone to kill the wolf by himself.

"Anybody had problems with their cattle?" George asked as he sat down on the bench in front of the store.

The three men, already sitting in chairs and jawing about the weather, shook their heads. "What kinda trouble are you having?" one of them asked.

"Something tore my Hereford bull up right bad."

"How's that?"

"Had the biggest part of his nose torn off and bites all over his body," George Ball exaggerated slightly.

"You think a dog done it?"

"It would have taken a mighty big and tough dog."

Mitch Kenilworth came out the door with his sack of supplies and stopped to listen.

"I've seen some mean dogs," another man said.

"Too much damage for a dog. Figured it had to be a pair of wolves."

"Just that one bull?"

"Yeah, so far. Had my prize Hereford herd grazing the bald. Figured that bull was mean enough to protect his cows from most any animal. I've never seen nothing like him. He'll fight man or beast. Reckon that's why I didn't lose any of my cows and calves. He did protect 'em, but he paid for it with his pound of flesh."

"Did you have to put him down?"

"Naw, like I said, that bull is one tough hunk of bovine fury. Worth every high-priced dollar I paid for him."

Mitch knew there were a few wolves, coyotes, bears, mountain lions, and other large creatures seeking solitude in the high mountains, but he had never made contact with any during his surveying. Wild animals were afraid of man. Man represented danger, and danger represented death.

Once Mitch got back to his tent, he took out his map found Ruffian Mountain and the bald where the bull had been attacked. A big grin split his face. If the girl was no longer on the Ruffian, then he had an idea where she would go. She was headed straight toward Big Hump Mountain, the tallest, most inaccessible mountain in the Black Mountain range. Then his big grin faded as he remembered his geography. From September until May its peak, or its big hump, was almost always capped in white, either hoar frost, ice, snow or a combination of all three. The girl couldn't possibly survive a winter there. Ruffian was tropical compared to the Big Hump.

He had better find a way back to the cave in a hurry. If she had left, then he had to find her within the next two months. Even he wouldn't be able to travel into Humpback Mountain during winter.

By the time the sun was setting, Raven was feeling the stress and strain of her traveling. The mountain that had looked so close to the Ruffian had become many miles away, much further than she could ever have imagined. She had gone over hills and along ridges, and then climbed smaller mountains in her attempt to stay away from houses. She wanted no one to see her or even know she existed. Still, she had seen many houses in the distance. They were built near ribbons of roads that twisted like snakes along the valleys and over hills. The mountains themselves were pristine, no roads and no people.

The thought of snakes made her extra cautious where she placed her feet. The possibility of being snake-bitten again was vivid and an all too real possibility. The pain and sickness she had suffered was something she did not want repeated, not to mention coming into contact with the awful man who had captured her. Having him wash and dress her was almost worse than the snakebite.

A renewed streak of anger flared. Confound his mangy hide. If he had not found Aggie's cave, she would not be traveling right now, not without knowing where a cave was located beforehand and if the cave would be safe for her and Dog.

She rubbed her hand over his clothing. She had to admit that she liked wearing clothes in the coolness of the mountain air. The pants and long sleeved shirt also helped when she went through briars. Her skin was tough, plus she was used to scratches and scrapes, but they were still painful. As for her feet, she wished she had taken a pair of his shoes instead of the sleeping bag she had taken and then returned. When she went back to the cave for the rest of her supplies, she would find shoes somewhere, from someone.

Most of the driving force to continue-on had left her, and she had only reached the foot of the high mountain. The climb that had looked so easy from her viewpoint on Ruffian Mountain was not easy at all. Actually, the climb she was attempting was as rugged as climbing the rockslide she had caused.

But she was confident she could do it come morning's light. It would be too dangerous for her to climb during the darkness of night even though she could see in the dark almost as good as any nocturnal animal.

Right now, she needed to find a safe place for her and the big black to sleep, for the sky had filled with swirling gray clouds, and the wind was picking up. A smell was in the air that made her restless, almost frightened her. It was the smell of coming winter, but that could not be possible, not in July.

The rocks on this mountain were piled high, much as if a gigantic rockslide had happened here, also. Somewhere nearby there would be rocks that created a three-sided shelter from the chill of the night as well as the storm that was threatening to blow in.

She hunted from rock pile to rock pile, hoping she would not roust wild animals or snakes. Probably no snakes, she assured herself. The weather was too cold and Aggie always said snakes stayed in the lowland unless the weather got mighty hot. In weather this cold, snakes would head for the valley where they could bask in the sun. Still, after her painful experience, she was leery. She realized all too well there was no longer Aggie or her mother to look after her when she had an accident, nor did she want to encounter another human like she had encountered that man.

Oh, but she didn't want to think about Aggie and her mother. If she did, she might cry now she was exhausted. She needed strength not to mourn the people and things that were lost to her forever. It was better to savor the good memories, memories of her walking between Aggie and her mother, each holding her hand; or the times she would sit on the big flat rock on Ruffian Mountain, with Aggie basking her crooked back in the sun, as they watched the Valley below. Her mother, Lu, seldom looked down in the valley, she was far too afraid of seeing a man. Lu hated men, feared them beyond all reason, but not so with Aggie. Aggie had been raised by people until she was thirteen years old. Aggie said that was her age when she ran away to the cave on Ruffian Mountain.

The big black lifted his nose and winded the air. He whined as though something was disturbing him, but it wasn't a warning sound. There were no threats of wild animals or man, just a long, disturbing whine emitted from his throat. She figured he was missing their previous home as much as she did.

"Come," she said needlessly, as she went down on her knees and crawled into a crevice, maneuvering her travois until it was also sheltered by the crevice. If there was a storm, she didn't want to get her precious bags of dog food wet. It might be a long time before she found men like Pete Jenkins and Evert Wilson who kept hunting dogs and food to feed them.

During the night Raven kept somewhat warm with the big black curled up beside her, but the July chill was enough to warn her of what would come in January. She arose with the faint morning light, remembering the reason she had chosen this mountain. It stood tall and majestic as the early morning sun hit its peak until it gave off a haunting glow of pale mist. She was certain the morning sun would heat the mountain.

"When we reach the peak of that mountain," she said to Dog, "we'll surely have climbed all the way to Heaven, or a place almost as pleasant."

She was wrong. The peak, or the hump of the mountain, was nothing like the Ruffian. It was barren of trees and only had a few straggling bushes clinging to the cracks in the rocks. How they held on in the continuous wind was a mystery to her. The wind was blowing everywhere without one sheltered spot, not even low down on the ground beneath the rocks did the wind stop blowing. The mountain was entirely different than the Ruffian, alien, cold, uninviting in every way.

"I don't like this place," she said to Dog as she stopped pulling her travois over the huge rock formations. Part of the time she had to lift each end of the travois to get it over rocks because there wasn't enough space between rocks to pull it. "We'd better find a nice cave or we're leaving here."

It was the big black who found the cave. Its entrance was narrow and hidden by the straggling bushes that managed to grow along the rock outcroppings. He stood in the opening and wagged his stub of a tail as though he knew what she was looking for and was proud he had found it.

Raven left her travois and crawled over the outcroppings to where Dog was waiting. She stuck her head into the entrance and took long deep breaths of the air, checking for scents that would warn her away. There was an old, unused, mustiness emerging, but nothing that frightened her or Dog.

"What do you think?" she asked Dog. "It might do for now. Don't guess we'll know for certain until we go in and look about."

She went back to her travois and searched among her things until she found the pine limb with a sap-knot on the end. She had searched the Ruffian for a limb that would make a good torch, one just for the purpose she had in mind.

Aggie had always warned her not to go into a strange cave without a lit torch to guide her steps. Many caves had floors that opened up into pits and made death traps that couldn't be seen in the dark. Plus fire was good protection from animals, bats, and snakes that happened to be in the caves. Nothing scared animals like fire, Aggie told her, nothing. Not even the presence of man brought the kind of fear fire brought.

"That's why folks say hell is a fiery furnace. Fire is the most horrible death there is," Aggie always said.

She thought of the gun and shells Aggie had once stolen from a hunter. Unthinking, she had left them in the cave on Ruffian. She was certain she knew how to use the gun, but animals had no natural fear of a gun. To them, it was nothing but a stick. A hot, blazing fire was something entirely different. It warranted instant respect.

Yet, the gun might come in handy, especially if she needed to kill something like a deer to have meat during the winter. She needed to make a quick trip back for the rest of her supplies before that man found a way back to the cave and stole her things. She went into the narrow opening of the cave before she took out the precious matches Aggie had kept stored in a moisture-proof container. There weren't many matches left and she couldn't chance the wind blowing one out.

She wadded up a piece of paper from the dog food sack, struck the match, and lit the paper. She held the sap-knot end of the stick in the flame. It sizzled and caught fire, but Raven continued to hold it in the flame until the paper burned out just to make sure the knot had caught fire enough to continue burning. It had.

She had gone into the cave about eight feet before it opened up enough for her to get up off her knees and stand up. She knew right off this cave wasn't anything like the cave on Ruffian. This cave was narrow without the branching off from other prongs, and it was only about a hundred feet in length, where Aggie's cave went on and on. However, there was enough of an updraft that the smoke from the pine knot lifted upward in a natural chimney. That meant she could keep a fire without filling the cave with smoke.

She lifted her torch and studied the walls. They appeared to consist of pure rock, which was good. Rock didn't cave in like dirt, but the rocks had big gaps where they did not fit together and let air in which was cold during the winter. A dirt cave made for good insulation.

Her feet crunched on something. She moved the torch down, casting light on the floor. There were small animal bones. She picked up one and looked closer at it. Gnaw marks from small teeth. Probably a fox had caught a rabbit, nothing for her to be concerned about. Dog would make a quick-fix out of a fox if this happened to be its den, which she didn't think it was, at least not a permanent one, for there was no fresh scat about.

She held the torch higher so she could inspect the ceiling. Again there was rock, and most important, no bats. Aggie always said to pick a cave without bats. Bats and even bat manure could contain the rabies virus. Aggie was always telling her the sign to watch out for in animals, except for bats. Bats showed no signs. This wasn't the cave she wanted to find, but it would do until she and Dog could find a better one.

She made her way to the entrance and looked around for deadfall to build a fire. Again, this section of the mountain differed from the Ruffian. There was no deadfall where there were no trees. Yet, she had seen many trees on the mountain when she looked from a distance. She had been viewing the other side and would have to cross over the hump to get to the other side.

She picked up a sharp rock, went back inside the cave for about ten feet and hacked out a hole in the floor of the rocky cave deep enough to bury the end of her torch and leave the burning end standing upright. She didn't want to waste another match by letting her torch go out. Also, the fire would keep animals from entering the cave in case something came along while she was away.

To ease the hunger rumbling in her stomach, she opened the sack on her travois. Dog ate the dog food she gave him and she ate a few grains of corn as she poured water from one of Aggie's jars into a cup for Dog. She took a few swallows from the jar and wished she had thought to drink and refill the jar when she had been closer to water.

After easing their hunger and thirst, she climbed to the top of the hump to get a better idea of what to expect from their new home. The top was a huge, almost level expanse of rocks, worn smooth by continuous winds. What a view she had of the surrounding area. She turned in a complete circle as she took in the hazy, blue distance. A few small dots were houses along with thread-thin ribbons of road, rivers, and creeks, but they were too far away to ever be a bother to her.

"Let's hope there's a water supply closer than that," she said to the big black sitting by her side, "but as rocky as this mountain is, I won't count on it."

She talked out loud which she seldom did, again a sign of how much she missed Aggie and Lu. Aggie always talked, telling her things Aggie thought she needed to know. *"Survival depends on how well an animal teaches its young,"* Aggie would say. *"I'm all you've got to teach you, so you best learn fast and plenty."*

She remembered Aggie going through trash dumps, and sometimes houses, to find books, paper, and pencil so she could teach Raven how to read and write. Aggie insisted that Raven read every book Aggie got her hands on. Raven learned of things she was sure would never be needed, things that weren't a part of survival. Right now, she was wishing Aggie had taught her how to find water and food in a mountain of solid rocks.

On the North side of the mountain were the trees, bent, twisted, and dwarfed, but a thick forest of stunted trees, nonetheless. It would not be impossible for her to find a supply of firewood before winter set in.

She decided to gather deadfall and get a fire going in the cave before she investigated her surroundings further. After all, her fire could very well be a life-saving element.

Chapter 3

Raven was tired. Her legs were stiff and her feet sore and throbbing from where she had pushed herself the last two days. Her shoulders were red and raw from pulling the travois and carrying bundles of deadfall up and over the rocky hump of mountain. She built her fire close to the cave opening because the narrow opening could be filled with fire. She knew, as the night wore on, the fire would die down and the chill would come, but she was used to the cold, just not in July.

She took the ragged bedding from the travois and made a bed near the fire for her and the big black. Before winter set in, she knew better bedding would be a necessity. Unless her instincts were wrong, this mountain would be a frozen place and she had no winter supplies.

Tired, weary, and bewildered she settled down for the night the best way she knew how in the strange, drafty cave. At least her big black was curled up with her.

Along in the silent hours of night, she was awakened. She opened her eyes to total black silence, but didn't move. She lay still and listened, trying to figure out what had caused her to wake up. At first, she thought it was the big black because he had raised his head and was sniffing the air. She reached out and touched him. The bristles on his back were standing straight, but he was silent even though his massive muscles were tense.

The fire had burned down, leaving only a glowing red body of coals. Chill from the night had crept into the dark and silent cave. Raven got up, gathered wood to pile on the coals, when she heard what had awakened her. At first she thought it was a woman screaming, much like the way she had screamed when Aggie had died. She listened, and her heart began to pound.

It came again, closer to the cave entrance. She shuddered all over as the high pitch of the scream shattered the silence of the night as it neared the entrance. Raven knew what it was and piled the small pieces of wood on the coals so they would flame up faster, wishing she had not allowed the fire to die down

It came again, the piercing scream, vibrating into the cave from nearer the entrance. Raven's blood froze in her veins. She was terrified for she knew what it was even though she had never heard its scream before, a mountain lion, the devil cat of the mountains that Aggie had told her frightening stories about.

The big black was on his feet, his bristles standing straight up, a warning growl rumbling from deep in his chest, his body stiff and rigid.

"Stay," Raven ordered, not wanting him to rush outside to meet the big cat, but he had been blessed with survival intelligence and was not leaving Raven or the fire she now had blazing.

Now, the devil cat was at the mouth of the cave, hardly ten feet away, as he screamed his angry challenge for a fight. The scream rang through the cave, echoed off the rock walls, and vibrated through Raven. The big black paced, growling fiercely, ready to meet the challenge of the cat with bared teeth glowing in the light from the fire. There was no question about it, his instincts were telling him to fight, but his intelligence was keeping him beside Raven.

"Stay," she ordered again and her voice shook as she placed her hand on the big black's head. His muscles were taut and quivering with readiness. He was wanting to fight, but she knew it would be a fight to his death, and perhaps so did he.

The devil cat had winded her and the dog's scents and was stalking for a fight that would end both girl and dog. It was the fire that was keeping him back, the fire she had placed windfall on until it filled the narrow space of the entrance. She was glad of the narrowness and the amount of wood she had gathered. She just hoped she had gathered enough to last throughout the night.

She remembered one of the things Aggie had warned her about. Aggie said animals, especially wild animals such as mountain lions and bobcats, were a far greater danger to women than to men. When a woman was having her monthlies, she was to stay away from places where animals would cross her path because the blood-scent would drive them into a killing frenzy. That must be the reason the devil cat was so determined to reach her.

Raven tore herself a fresh rag, taken from families trash dumps she and Aggie raided, and tossed the used one into the fire, hoping the scent would no longer be as strong, but it didn't seem to help for the sounds from the cat were still getting closer.

She went down on her knees and locked her arms around the big black's neck as the devil cat came inside the cave. Raven could see it clearly. Its eyes were burning almost as bright as the fire in its huge, broad head. Its tan body was tall and long, even in a crouch, it was much bigger than the big black. It snarled and raked at the rocks forming the walls of the cave with its powerful claws as it came close enough to feel the heat from the fire. It wanted to make the opening large enough until it could get around the fire without being burned, but the rocks held.

She thought Dog was going to leap through the flames to meet the cat's challenge despite her struggle to hold him, but before that happened, the cat felt the burning singe of the flames and backed out of the cave. The big black settled down once the cat was outside and Raven snuggled up against him, getting what comfort she could from her dog and his willingness to fight opponents much larger and deadlier than himself.

The cat prowled around the cave alternately screaming and growling, but it didn't enter again. Raven heard it on top of the rocks trying to find an entrance that didn't contain the burning heat from the fire. Then it tried to the right and the left and even down below the cave. Finally, in the wee hours of morning, it gave up and left to stalk other parts of the mountain in search of an easier meal.

The devil cat was huge. It measured nearly ten feet from nose to tip of tail and would weigh over two hundred and sixty pounds, a whopping giant considering most males never got over one hundred eighty pounds. Females were considerably smaller. He had grown that large from being intelligent enough to live a long life, but his huge size was not a blessing. He was no longer sleek and lithe. His kills could not be made with phantom-lightning speed, and his bulk allowed him to be seen easier when stalking deer, which were his main food source. Deer were getting more difficult for him to kill with each year that passed. That's why he was turning to easier prey. At least his tremendous strength plus his years of cumulative intelligence kept him surviving well.

The devil cat was hungry and the smell coming from the girl was powerful. He had been traveling for days to escape the dogs and men that were on his trail. At first, they had pushed him hard and fast.

His easiest prey had come in the form of calves, as they were easily caught and easier killed. Angry farmers had gathered dogs and their guns and rode on horseback into the hills where the mountain lion had his den. He was wise enough to know when it was time to clear out.

The dogs and men had chased him for days until he was a good many miles ahead and the dogs lost scent of his trail in the rocky terrain of the high mountains. Both men and dogs had given up and gone back home to rest-up and see if the cat returned to their area to kill more calves.

The cat was a good hundred miles away from the men and dogs as the crow flies. He had crossed several mountain ranges until he was no longer fearful of the men or their dogs. For him to go up against one dog offered no threat when there was something tempting him greatly, and the girl was tempting him beyond all reason.

Burned by the newly encountered fire, and bewildered from not finding another entrance, the cat left while the night was still dark enough to find other food. Daylight was not the best time for stalking and the smart old cat knew it. Still, the smell of the girl had made an impression, and he could not resist her scent. His nose latched onto her barefooted trail and he started backtracking her until he reached the bald.

Some basic instinct returned to the mountain lion warning him of men and dogs, but the smell of calves was too great to resist. The strong scent of cattle reached him on an updraft of air and he headed off the bald into the river valley. He crouched low on his belly and his eyes narrowed as he observed each and every animal. They were grazing peacefully or lying down in the shade. Over near the woods in a shady spot laid a cow and her young calf. He slunk soundless and upwind until he was within fifteen feet of the mother and calf. He gave one mighty lunge and made fast work of the week-old calf. He locked his teeth into the back of its neck and carried his prey into the woods to eat the first kill he had made in days.

After the terrifying night, the morning light was a welcome reprieve. Raven had slept none, afraid if she closed her eyes the mountain lion would find a way into the cave, or the big black would meet his challenge and rush through the fire to get at the devil cat. Thankfully, neither disaster occurred.

Raven gave the big black his ration of food and water and she ate a precious raw potato and a few more grains of corn. Somewhere, in her new surroundings, she would have to find a food supply and a source of water closer than the river she had seen. But that would have to wait. More important was to make sure her cave was secure from the devil cat. She feared that once it had scent of her, of Dog, and of the supplies on the travois, it would not leave the mountain.

She must haul rocks and lay up a thick rock wall that the devil cat could not tear down, much like the rock wall Aggie had made surrounding their living space. Trouble was she had to figure out how to make a door that would keep the cat out and let her and the big black enter and leave the cave. That meant rolling big rocks when she entered or left the cave, and had the time and strength to do it. If she needed to get in or out of the cave fast, there would be a problem.

Raven piled wood on her fire and banked it with dirt and rocks to keep the fire from burning out while she searched for more rocks the size and shape she needed. The task of finding those rocks was much more difficult than she thought, being the mountain was made of almost solid rock. The rocks needed to be big enough to make them strong and not easily moved, and square enough to mesh on top of each other. Those rocks also needed to be lain until they overlapped in an interwoven pattern so something strong like a mountain lion or a bear could not tear it down, which she knew would be no easy task for a hundred pound girl to do.

Raven only had a vague idea how strong these animals were from books she had read and the stories Aggie had told her. There was no doubt in her mind they were vicious, dangerous animals with a keen knowledge of how to stalk and kill. She knew a lone girl and a dog were almost helpless against the devil cat. Only the fire had saved them.

The sun was high when she had enough rocks gathered to start the wall. She chose to leave the narrow entrance and build her wall further inside the cave where the rocks opened up enough for her to stand, which was behind her fire. She built another fire further back and let the one in the narrow tunnel burn low, but not out.

She began to realize why Aggie always wanted to keep a fire burning, even in summer. It was an extra bit of security that helped to ease a worried mind. Trouble was the amount of wood it required and the time it took to gather it. She had hoped to wait another month, or even longer, before she started gathering deadfall. What she wanted to do now was to find a better cave and a source of water, but that would have to wait now the devil cat was after them.

Raven scraped the cave floor clean of loose dirt and crammed it between the layers of rock. She longed to have mud, like Aggie had, to mortar the rocks solid, but that would have to wait for a time when she had found the closer water supply - not to mention when she had time to do a better job of her rock laying. She feared the mountain lion would come back once it got dark and she had better be ready for it.

Suddenly the big black bristled and let out a challenging growl as he lunged past Raven and out the cave entrance. Raven grabbed the torch and shoved it into the fire coals barely waiting long enough for it to ignite before she ran after her dog. She could hear the vicious roars and squalls of a fight in progress as she ran beyond the entrance and climbed up over the top of several large rocks. She knew her torch, even if it was in full flame, would not make a mountain lion hesitate, but she could not allow her dog to fight the cat alone.

When she reached Dog, she sank down on the rocks; her torch almost dropped from her shaking hands. The big black had his teeth clamped in the back of a big coon. The coon let out one last blood-curdling squall as Dog shook the life out of him.

Raven felt like beating the dead coon with the torch for scaring her so badly. She wasn't real happy with the big black either.

Dog was happy. He trotted to her with the coon still in his mouth and gave it one last shake before he dropped it at her feet. Raven put her arm around Dog, breathing deep and long with her relief. Suddenly she realized what she had lying at her feet—an aspect of survival. She would skin the coon and they could eat mighty good tonight.

Not only that, she would use the coon's brains to tan its hide, just as she had read in one of Aggie's books. If she was successful, she would make herself a pair of moccasins to protect her feet from the sharp rocks. She picked the dead coon up by its hind legs, surprised by its great weight, and carried it back to the cave. Dog followed, his big body wiggling with happiness.

Mitch Kenilworth had studied the map from all angles as he tried to decide what would be the best way to climb the backside of the mountain. There didn't seem to be any way that would be quick or easy. It would take several days at best.

"Had to see it for myself," said a voice near Mitch. He looked up to see the scarred face of Cade Williams.

"You're able to be out and about?" Mitch asked him.

"Barely. I've been inside too long." He nodded toward the slide. "What do you make of that?"

"Slides happen," Mitch said.

Mitch knew all about Cade, his monsters, and the moonshine fire that had exploded and burned his face. Cade talked about the angel-faced girl who saved his life by pulling him on a travois after he had been burned unconscious by the fire. Most folks laughed about his monsters and especially about him claiming to have gotten saved by such a beautiful girl.

Mitch knew Cade was telling the truth. Raven had saved Cade, and she was the prettiest girl he had ever seen. It wasn't just her face. It was a vibrant, wild kind of beauty that made her almost shimmer. If he hadn't held her in his arms, washed her, dressed her, he might have thought he had imagined her. Even when he was looking at her face through his survey scope, her face, showing both anger and fear, had been strangely beautiful. In her was the same allure men went crazy over in the gold rush or the fight for free land grants.

"It has something to do with them," Cade said with confidence.

"Them?"

"The monster and the pretty girl that has my dog."

Mitch folded his map and stuck it in his hind pocket.

"What you looking at your map for?"

"Checking where I'm supposed to survey next," Mitch lied. The less Cade Williams knew, the better for everyone.

That explanation satisfied Cade. "You finished here?"

"Almost. I had another line to run on top of the mountain, but the rockslide has made it difficult. Might have to move on without that line."

"Care if I sit down?" Cade indicated a folding chair. "I've not got all my strength back."

"Help yourself."

"You can go around that rockslide, you know."

"I can?"

"Oh, yeah, but it hain't easy." Cade looked pleased with his forthcoming information.

"So I've heard."

"I don't mean by driving all the way to Tennessee and coming up that long, rough mountain. You can go over that mountain there and onto the Ivy Ridge and work your way onto Ruffian Mountain."

"Have you done it before?"

"When I was young," Cade licked his scarred lips as though he wanted to say something but hesitated.

"Do you suppose I could manage?"

Cade cocked his head at an odd angle. "Strange things are on that mountain," he finally said.

"Such as?"

"Some kind of demon holes up in that place."

Mitch thought of the lovely girl. Not exactly his idea of a demon.

"I've seen it," Cade said.

Mitch lifted his brows.

"Chased me all the way home one night. It was short and squatty like some kind of animal. It cast a shadow like one of them gorillas I've seen on television, like that King Kong thing."

Mitch recalled the stories Iva Dean Grearity told about her half sister, Aggie, the name the girl kept calling when she was snake-bitten. Most likely that's who Cade saw and thought it was a monster, especially if he'd been drinking his own famous brew.

"Think you could show me the path leading into the mountain?"

"No, not with me messed up like I am. I can't hardly walk on flat ground much less climb a mountain."

"Suppose Pete Jenkins or Evert Wilson could show me the way? Men that hunt always know the secrets a mountain holds."

"Doubt it, but Don Donavan could. He knows these hills almost as good as I know 'em." Cade let a long, drawn out sigh escape his lips. "You know, just walking here wore me out more than I expected. Reckon you'd be kind enough to drive me back to the house in your truck?"

"Yeah, I can do that."

"Be mighty obliged."

Mitch drove to Cade William's home, dropped him off, and then headed to Don Donavan's place. When he got there, the old man sat on the porch not looking pleased to see him.

"You know why I've come, don't you?" Mitch said as he sat down on the edge of the porch.

"Its because you're wanting something, as usual. Suppose you go ahead and tell me anyhow."

Mitch didn't hesitate in coming to the point of his visit. Don was right; he wanted something. "You have to show me how to get onto the mountain."

"Why's that?"

"I've got to find her."

"Why's that?" Don repeated.

"If she has left that mountain, she might not be able to survive come winter, not if she's going where I think she's going."

Mitch waited for Don to comment, but he didn't.

"When I was in town, George Ball was telling about his bull getting his nose tore up. Sounded to me like the work of a Rottweiler dog. I believe she's heading toward Humpback Mountain"

"Why would she do that?" Don asked in a seemingly uninterested tone of voice.

"For the same reason she caused the rock slide."

"Could be," Don finally said. "Most wild things run away from aggravation."

"She won't be able to survive the winter on the Humpback. You know that as well as I do."

" I've heard stories about that mountain. Some say it's the North Pole and hell mixed together. Exactly what do you have in mind?"

"Finding her." Mitch said, more than a little bewildered with Don. If he cared about the girl, he should be helping him.

Betsy came out onto the porch with a determined step. "He's right," she said. "A girl ought not to be left on her own. Don, if you know how to get on the mountain, show him."

Don gave his wife a long, searching look.

"I've been thinking about that child. Somebody has to help her, even if she don't want help. Besides, there's no reason to pretend she don't exist. Mitch knows she does. He's seen her."

"It's against my best judgment to climb onto that mountain when she don't want us up there," Don said.

"Don," Betsy drawled his name out in the tone she used when she was determined to have her own way.

"But I'll do it. Just keep in mind that I don't want to."

Mitch stood up. "Let's go."

Don didn't move out of his chair. "Not now. It will be dark before we could get to the top. We'd kill ourselves getting back down. There's a tricky rock ledge we have to walk over and we don't want to fall off. We'll start at six o'clock in the morning."

Mitch didn't like the idea of waiting a moment longer in finding the girl, but he didn't know an alternative. "I'll be here," he said.

Mitch wanted to find the girl, wanted it with a passion that even he couldn't understand fully. He told himself that it wasn't a sexual need drove him, for he was far beyond that little-boy emotional, unreasonable drive that ruled his youth. He told himself there simply was something about the girl made him want to protect her, and he longed to have her with him. His driving-force was a deep-seated anxiety that would not let his mind settle. There was a fear in him, an urgency as though something bad was about to happen and he was the only one could stop it.

He could hardly sleep and was up before five o'clock. He carefully filled his backpack with things he thought might be needed, not only by him, but by the girl. Two of the things he included were large boxes of matches along with flint and steel. He wasn't sure if the girl would know how to use either one, but the flint and steel had written directions along with diagrams. This girl could probably figure it out even if she couldn't read.

He was at Don Donavan's door at twenty 'til six because he couldn't stand to wait a moment longer.

"Come on in," Don hollered at his knock.

Mitch opened the door and stepped inside. "I'm a little early," he said apologetically.

"Thought you might be. Come on in the dining room and pull up a seat. Have a plateful of Betsy's sausage gravy and biscuits. We'll use up a good breakfast by the time we climb all the way to the top of Ole Ruffian. It's a good day's work for a man my age. 'Course you might not fare as bad, being you survey all over creation."

Mitch had never heard Don string together so many words. He knew the man was nervous about the trip. He sat beside Don as Betsy put biscuits covered in sausage gravy, plus two fried eggs in front of him and went back into the kitchen. She returned with a mug of strong, black coffee.

"You know, if you ask me, you ought to leave that girl alone. She don't want to be messed with."

Don gave Betsy a confused and aggravated look for changing her tune from yesterday, but Betsy glared right back.

"We all know there's a girl up there, and there's no need in pretending there's not," Betsy said. "And that girl has Cade's Rottweiler dog with her. Besides that, she knows she can come to us anytime she wants. You two men just can't get it through your thick skulls that she don't want to." Betsy reached for the gravy bowl to refill.

Mitch was feeling somewhere between delight and bewilderment. Delight in knowing Betsy agreed that there was a girl, and bewilderment that she said to leave the girl alone after telling Don to help find her.

"She can't survive on her own," Mitch told her.

Betsy pointed the gravy bowl at Mitch. "She's survived in that mountain for years, and you know it. You've just come in contact with a pretty girl and you can't let her be." She set the gravy bowl back down on the table with a pop. "So don't you go telling me you're doing this for her sake. You're hot on her tail because you want to be."

Mitch was speechless. There were no words coming to him he could use as an argument. If there had been, he wouldn't have said them to Betsy.

Don chuckled. "Kinda changed you tune since last night haven't you old woman?"

"I have. I thought about her most of the night, and I don't think you should go on that mountain chasing after her, regardless of what I said before."

"You're right," Don agreed. "We ought to leave her alone, let her live or die the best way she can."

"Then why aren't you?" Betsy asked.

Don lifted his coffee cup and drank before he spoke. "I promised Aggie I'd look after her, and I aim to do my best. I just don't know what's best as of yet."

"Humph," Betsy gave him a disgusted look.

Don ignored it. "And," he continued. "The girl closed off the mountain with that rock slide because Mitch found her cave. In my mind, that means the girl is leaving the mountain and going somewhere else."

"That's what I think," Mitch added. "She's headed toward Humpback Mountain."

"So?" Betsy demanded.

Don answered before Mitch could. "So, she won't be able to find food and shelter on that mountain like she did here. I'm taking a couple of your old quilts, if you don't mind. Also, this frisky young man is going to carry a bushel of shelled corn to leave in the cave. That way she'll stay warm, plus she'll be able to eat until she finds places to get food."

"No!" Mitch burst out before he caught himself.

"No?" questioned Don.

"We don't want to help her stay in either mountain. We want her to . . ." he hesitated.

"To run into your arms?" Betsy added.

Mitch squirmed as he sought for words to state what he wanted to say.

"If that's what you're after, I'll wish you luck, because luck is all you'll be left with. You don't seem to understand that girl is wild. Like wild animals are wild. She was raised away from people, and that's how she wants to stay," Betsy told Mitch. "If you did capture her, she'd end up turning on you."

Mitch pushed his empty plate away from him to indicate he was finished eating and finished arguing with Betsy. "I'm taking her some matches and flint and steel just in case she should need them."

Raven did not stop building her rock wall until it was pitch-dark outside. She rolled several big rocks inside the narrow mouth of the tunnel opening, and built a fire on her side as close to the rocks as she could get it. She wanted the rocks hot in case the cat tried to move them.

Once she had the fire going, she got one of the knives Aggie had taken from the rich people's cabin, gutted and skinned the coon, cutting off every strip of fat for rendering lard. She spitted the carcass on a long stick and held it over the fire. Liquid sizzled and dropped into the fire giving off an aroma that Raven feared would draw the devil cat. But the cat didn't come.

The big black was ready to eat the coon meat raw, but Raven wouldn't allow him. Aggie had warned her time and again that all meat should be cooked thoroughly before eating. Raven knew there were all kinds of things in meat that could make her sick, such as worms and diseases, not to mention fleas and ticks. Only the heat from cooking would kill the parasites.

As for fleas and ticks, she heated rocks and raked them on the fur side of the hide. Aggie used to soak hides in water for a day's time to kill the pests, but water was precious to Raven. She couldn't waste a drop until she found a nearby source.

Once she and the big black had eaten a portion of the roasted raccoon, she curled up near the fire with the big black beside her. She hadn't slept much last night because of the devil cat, and needed to sleep now, but she was afraid to close her eyes. The unusual meal of meat lay heavy in her stomach and forced a lethargic feeling to take over. Her eyes closed and she started dreaming about the mountain lion breaking through her wall of rocks. She woke up with a jerk, listening for the cat, but heard nothing.

The big black lifted his head and watched her stoke wood on the fire for a moment before he settled back down and fell right back to sleep. His actions eased Raven's fears and she curled up beside him.

Still, she could not rest. Aggie arose from her grave and filled Raven's twilight sleep with warnings. *"Get the gun,"* Aggie kept telling her. *"Kill it with the gun before it kills you. You have to go back to the cave and get the gun!"*

Raven was awake before morning's light had diluted the darkness. She spitted the coon and heated it again, ate a portion and gave all but a leg bone to dog. She wanted to chew on the bone and suck the marrow out. When she had finished that, she let the big black have that bone, too.

She wrapped the kitchen knife in a rag so the point would not stick through the material of her britches pocket, pulled the empty travois from the cave and over the rocks. She rolled rocks in the mouth of the cave opening until no animal could enter and destroy her precious supplies, got the travois and started down the mountain as morning was finally lighting the sky enough for her to climb over the rocks. She knew Aggie's warning was something she could not ignore. If she did, the devil cat was certain to kill both Dog and her, for she did not believe the cat had given up. She suspected the cat had made a kill, eaten his fill, and was now sleeping somewhere. At least, she hoped that was what the cat had done. The trip she was about to make would be long and hard, but she could make it fast now that she knew the way and the travois was empty.

Still yet, it would be pitch dark by the time she reached the cave on Ruffian, and she knew mountain lions preferred stalking prey at dawn and dusk. She was in danger traveling this early, but she would be in more danger if she had to spend the night out in the open.

The cattle were huddled together stomping and snorting when he went to make his second kill. This time they had caught the fearful scent of the devil cat. Never before had they winded such a smell, but they knew danger when they smelled it. They bellowed and rolled their eyes while the big bull pawed up chunks of sod with his front feet and shook his huge curly head. He worked himself into a sweat-lather as he bellowed his challenge for the owner of the dangerous smell to attack, but no attack came.

The mountain lion was suffering from hunger, not daring for a fight. The young calf he had consumed earlier had not been enough for two meals. This time, he picked a larger calf clinging close to a frightened mother. He crouched with his belly on the ground, stalked through the grass in steely silence until he was within a few yards of the calf, and made one pounce. The mother cow bawled and butted in a useless attempt to save her calf. The other cattle quivered while watching with frightened eyes. The bull tried to determine where the thing was he was supposed to fight, but he was too late.

The mountain lion disappeared like a phantom in the mist as he dragged the calf against the base of a large Red Oak tree and buried his long fangs into the calf's belly. The skin ripped like paper, making easy access to the heart, liver, and lungs. The vital organs were the most nutritious and the most succulent to the cat.

When the big male had eaten his fill, he curled up in the warmth that had penetrated the river valley and drifted contentedly asleep. He would wake up at dusk and eat again. Afterwards, he would go to the river while it was dark and drink his fill, return to the remains of the calf, and sleep again. He normally needed the equivalent of one large deer a week, but he had been run long and hard without food. He needed a lot of food to regain his normal vigor. He was much like a nursing female, which needed three times the amount of food normal males needed.

The second day of the kill, the cat finished the head, backbone, and legs and then drifted back to sleep. The dogs had run him hard and he needed rest as well as food. By dusk, he would awake and be on the prowl again, even though his hunger would not be as great.

✣

Fortunately, for Raven, the devil cat was sleeping in the wooded area near the river when she crossed over the bald.

Raven made sure she didn't go near the place where the bull had attacked her. One encounter with a bull was enough for her, but seemingly not for the big black. He winded the air, raised his hackles, but kept beside Raven, as though he was determined to stand between her and danger.

She feared the bull but it was nothing compared to her fear of a mountain lion. Occasionally Aggie told her stories about mountain lions that were black. *"When they're that rare black color, folks call them panthers or pan'ters. For some reason, those black devils like to stay in trees more than the tan ones do."* At least the one after her had been tan and not black.

The devil cat had her scared and she longed for the gun. A gun was the only thing would make an even fight between her and the mountain cat. Just thinking about it and remembering some of the stories that Aggie used to tell her about the size and the cunning of such cats had her blood pumping faster than normal.

Because of her fear, and having traveled this way once, Raven gave in to her need for speed. Her strong, young legs stretched out in a distance-eating gait as her callused feet hit the ground in rhythm. She wished she could run as fast as the big black. She pretended to be an animal making herself run faster and faster until her legs could pump no harder. The travois bumped and bounced behind.

Raven wished she could have left it behind. If she had, she would need to build another, which meant she would need an ax and rope. The man whose clothes she wore had both ax and rope.

She could not call her feelings toward him hate, because she knew that emotion. She hated Cade Williams even though she had saved his life when his moonshine still exploded. What she felt toward the man went far deeper than hate. It was what she felt toward the mountain lion.

Pete Jenkins and Evert Wilson, she despised instead of hated. They had run dogs as they hunted on her mountain, causing her mother's death. That was something she could not forgive or forget. Yet, they had drawn her curiosity and bought bags of dog food she took during the night, because they owed her.

As for Don Donavan, Raven's dislike for him was only because Aggie wanted her to live with him. How could Aggie have wanted that? Aggie never lived with him, or anyone else. Aggie had never asked him for help before. Yet, when Aggie knew she was dying, she ran straight to Don Donavan and pleaded with him to take her and raise her as his own.

Aggie's explanation for her behavior was she was too ugly and deformed to be exposed to human eyes. It didn't hold as truth to Raven. Nor did Aggie's insistence that Raven would be accepted by other humans because she was whole and pretty. She wasn't like other humans. She would not know their ways and they wouldn't understand hers.

To Raven, she was born wild and free and she'd rather be in her grave, like Lu and Aggie, than give up her freedom.

The color was leaving the sky as Raven neared the narrow ledge of rimrock that allowed entry on that side of Ruffian Mountain. The big black's hackles rose on his back and a low rumble sounded deep in his chest. Raven moved her hand indicating for him to be silent while she listened. She heard voices. Rapidly, she backtracked until she found a grouping of large rocks where she and Dog could hide.

She clasped her arms around Dog's neck and hissed for his silence. The big black's powerful body tensed. His hackles remained erect, but he was silent as they waited in hiding.

"I knew she left the mountain. That girl, Raven," Mitch said her name as though saying it would make her appear. "Raven," he repeated. "She must have been named for the color of her hair and eyes. I've never seen hair and eyes that black."

"God rest Aggie's soul," Don spoke as though he hadn't heard Mitch. "She was my childhood friend. I was fond of her. I promised her I'd look after the girl and I didn't keep that promise. I just don't know of a way to keep it. If I could only let the girl know I want to help her in whatever kind of life she wants to live. I don't want to change her, or make her stay inside a house if she doesn't want to. I just want to see she's safe and she has what she needs."

"We could set a trap, capture her," Mitch said wistfully.

"You don't set traps and capture people. What's got into you? You're not thinking right."

"We have to do something. As I've been telling you, she'll never survive a winter on Humpback Mountain. It's not like the Ruffian. It's the most hostile and rugged section of the National Forest. I'd say not one person climbs over that mountain in a five-year span, and there's a reason for it. They would have to be an experienced hiker. I can't do a thing knowing she's out there all alone without anybody to help her when she's hurt, not to mention dangerous animals."

"I think she can survive," Don told Mitch. "Aggie was crippled-up so bad she could hardly walk and she survived. Raven is whole and strong. Besides, it don't take much for one person to live, and Aggie will have trained her well."

Mitch slowed his steps and looked down the sheer rock face where the rock ledge dropped off. The ledge was barely wide enough for his feet. "They had a rather good set-up in that cave. I never realized there were so many sections to it."

"Keep moving. We don't want to slow down here, not when we could slip and fall."

Raven saw her chance to get rid of two people that threatened her way of life. All she had to do was roll a few rocks from the top of the cliff, or even throw rocks and hit them in the head and they would tumble to their deaths. Her arms loosened around the big black's neck. She rose, and then sank back down. She couldn't kill two people. Not when it was the only man Aggie trusted, or the man whose clothes she wore. Neither of them had done her wrong, except for finding her cave. That was wrong.

Mitch moved on and the ledge widened.

"No telling how far those caves go back into that mountain," Don continued once their footing was secure. "A man could get lost in there and never find his way out."

"Maybe she just moved into a different section," Mitch said hopefully.

"Maybe."

"You think she left, don't you?"

"Yeah. She's gone and we both know it." Don said.

"Do you think she'll return?"

"Yeah, I think she'll come back in an attempt to feel close to Aggie and her mother, or maybe to gather winter supplies, but she won't stay. You see, Mitch, once humans have defiled a wild animal's den, they're afraid to stay there ever again."

"You see her as a wild animal?"

"No, I see her as a young girl, but she was raised with the instincts of a wild animal, and some animals refuse to be domesticated no matter how hard we try."

"If only she knew how good she'd have it in the civilized world."

"She might not think it was a better way of life."

"Of course she would," Mitch said, and then was silent as he became absorbed in his thoughts. "What about the things we left for her?" he finally asked Don.

"She'll get 'em, sooner or later. If she don't, it won't matter."

"I hope so, because she'll need them on the Big Hump now that she's all alone."

The strangest feeling came over Raven as she listened. These two men were actually talking about her, seemingly caring about her welfare, concerned over her survival. They were not Aggie or Lu so why would they do anything for her? She was nothing to them. For some strange reason, she felt like crying. She lowered her face into Dog's fur and felt his warmth, his comfort. She assured herself she wasn't alone. She had Dog.

Once they were down the mountain and had reached the wooded area, she moved from behind the rocks and crossed over the narrow ledge where one runner of her travois was over the rock's edge, but it scooted along nevertheless.

She felt safe once again. They would not come back to her cave, and they hadn't found her stash of supplies. She had been wise in hiding them further back in a different section of the cave.

"What about the things we left her?" resounded in her mind. What could they have left her? Was it something she should fear? Could it be part of the trap the younger man mentioned? What did he mean by she'd need them on the Big Hump?

She stopped at the mouth of the cave and watched for Dog's reaction. He was wiggling all over, showing delight at being home again. He raced inside the cave, was gone for several minutes before he ran back to her.

Raven knew the cave was safe as she dragged the empty travois inside. She dropped the ropes from her shoulders and moved in the darkness until she reached Aggie's grave. It had not been disturbed. She kneeled beside it and all the built-up emotions came to a head. Tears streamed down her face until her body jerked with sobs. Her past life played through her mind, Aggie, Lu, the hunters. Why was it the hunters were still alive when Aggie and Lu were not?

The devil cat woke up, stood, and stretched his long muscular body until his tawny skin rippled. He was rested and no longer afraid of men with dogs. His lips curled back from two-inch teeth as he winded the air. Nothing but the smell of cattle reached him. He flexed his knife-like front claws until they extended from his footpads, long and sharp. He drew his claws back in and moved on in silence.

Hunger was rumbling his guts again, even after eating two calves. The tender meat of the calf had been nourishing but not plentiful. He needed to make another kill and carry it to a den beneath a rock overhang. He didn't like caves unless there was a rain storm or a freezing blizzard. Caves were confining, hampered the vision, kept scents from reaching his nostrils.

It was just before dark, a time when everything took on deep blue shadows in the gray light. His preferred time to kill – a time when he would have the cover of darkness while filling his gut and then sleep off his contentment.

Sounds from the herd of cattle were hushed as they settled for the night in a sheltered draw, mothers bedding down with their calves lying by their sides.

His eyes scanned the herd, seeking his perfect prey. He could be choosy now that his hunger wasn't as great. He picked a calf larger than the first two he had killed and yet small enough for him to drag easily.

He hunkered until his belly was touching the ground. His instinct positioned him upwind from the cattle as he stalked forward a few inches at a time. His eyes never left his chosen prey as it slept against its mother. The mother's presence, along with that of the herd, had given it a false sense of security, and it had no fear, no warning of death coming in the next few minutes

The devil cat drew out his stalk just for the pleasure it brought him. He liked playing with the weak and helpless. Providing torture to a victim was always fun for the devil cat. He was within twenty feet when he sprang. His teeth sank into the calf's neck, but he did not kill it instantly. He loosened his grip and let it leap up, followed by its mother.

The calf let out a pitiful moan as it tried to run while blood ran down its gashed neck. The mother bellowed and turned to fight the cat. The cat lunged and raked the mother across her face, leaving inch-deep cuts with edges that spread apart. She stopped her charge and watched as the cat playfully leaped for the calf. This time he sunk his teeth in its neck in a killing hold. He ignored the injured mother as he trotted off, dragging the calf regardless of its weight.

He was over confident and careless as the force hit him in the side without him seeing it coming. It rolled him over causing him to drop the already dead calf. He sprang to his feet and faced the angry bull as it charged again. The cat sprang upward in to the air and landed on the bull's back. His front claws sank deep in the flesh in order for him to hold on tight, while his hind legs jerked, ripping the bull's tough hide. His teeth buried deep in the muscles of the bull's neck as he tried to provide a paralyzing bite to the bull.

The big bull raised his head and bellowed his rage and pain as he flipped over backward and came down hard slamming the cat on the ground underneath his heavy body. The bull rolled and twisted, trying to crush the attached cat into the earth.

Never had the cat been beneath a ton of crushing, smothering flesh. His instinct turned to escape instead of kill. His claws loosened from the bull and dug into the dirt as he freed himself from beneath the smothering weight. He disappeared before the bull had regained his feet and all but stampeded his herd toward the home pasture.

It was several hours later when the cat slunk back to drag his kill away.

🕊

Raven had planned on staying only one night in the cave, but she could not force herself to leave the next morning. Memories of Aggie and her mother were holding her tight, stirring the ache inside her until she was consumed with longing. It didn't seem possible her life had changed so drastically in such a short time.

She spent one more night in the cave wrapped up in the quilts that Don Donavan had left behind. She had used the matches the man had left to build a fire where Aggie always kept one. She relived being a little girl, knowing she was loved and never alone back then, as she sat in the cave watching the fire burn in slow, orange flickers. It was strange and so unfair how life could change. One moment she had people and the next moment there was no one but her – and Dog.

She also found the flint and steel the man had left for her. It made her mad for that man to leave things for her, but she wasn't foolish enough to leave them behind. It hurt her pride to think people, especially a man, gave her things. She wanted to provide for herself – take nothing from anyone unless they owed her. Then it was up to her to choose what and how much they owed.

What really got to her were the other things left in a little backpack. It contained soap, shampoo, toothpaste, toothbrush, hairbrush, a roll-on bottle of deodorant, and worst or best of all, a pair of britches, shirt, socks and shoes. She hated the man for thinking she needed such stuff, and yet, a part of her wanted them because she had read about them in one of Aggie's books.

This time, she packed everything she owned, including Aggie's books and the glass jars she wrapped in the remaining rags, on the travois and secured her load with ropes. She pulled the heavy load from the cave into the dim light of morning. A strange type of heaviness came over her as though she was carrying too heavy a load for her body to support.

She dropped the rope to the travois, went to the rock outcropping where she had stood so many times with Aggie, and looked down on the valley for what she was sure would be her last time ever. Mist was lifting from the winding creek, lifting upward to vanish before it reached the Ruffian. Cattle were lowing in the pasture as they awaited the morning milking, roosters were crowing, a hunting dog barked from its lot. Smoke was struggling from chimneys in thin, blue lines as fires were first lit. There was something about watching the valley come awake that touched her deeply. It felt almost like watching a part of herself, a part of Aggie and Lu; a part that would soon be gone forever never to be captured again.

The path to Tetters Pond was blocked as well as the path where the rich folk's cabin once stood. Another cabin was being built near by, and the man was running around packing up his tent to leave.

How dare he? He was leaving now he had destroyed the sanctity of their cave. He had been the one who caused her to leave, and he was now leaving too. It wasn't right. She considered taking his backpack from her load and stomping it into the rocks, but she wasn't that foolish. She wouldn't destroy something she could use because she was angry at the man it came from. Yet there was something inside her that was disquieting, something she couldn't ignore.

Her eyes came to rest on the pile of rocks covering her mother's grave. Hurt swelled. She ran back inside the cave and kneeled beside Aggie's grave. She didn't want them to be dead. She wanted them back, if just for a few moments. Long enough to tell them how much she loved and missed them. Oh, if only she could do all the things she wished she had done when they were alive.

Tears eased from her eyes and her shoulders shuttered for one fitful moment. The big black came to her, nudged her with his nose, and whined.

"I know," she whispered to him. "We have to go." She rubbed her fingers over the grave. "I won't be back, Aggie. Never again."

Dawn had arrived with full light. She had lingered away precious time and would have to run the whole way now or she'd be caught in the dark. Dark meant the devil cat could slip up on her, but she had the gun lying on top of her belongings. She'd loaded and unloaded it several times just to get the feel of it, but she hadn't shot it because of the noise. A shot fired on top of the Ruffian would echo throughout the valley below. She'd use the gun if the need came. Plus, she had Dog to warn her if the cat was near. She wasn't afraid, she told herself, she wasn't.

Once she had eased her loaded travois over the narrow ledge, she broke into a trot instead of a run. She wanted to cover distance but not suffer from exhaustion early on. She had sixteen or eighteen hours of hard-running travel before she reached the far mountain.

Her shoulders were aching and her feet felt bruised by the time she ran the ridges and reached the bald. She knew where the houses were she was to avoid, knew the trails she needed to take in order to travel the fastest. What she didn't know was where the cattle would be. She didn't want to slow down long enough to fight the bull again, so she didn't go near the wooded area, and crossed the bald instead.

Chapter 4

George J. Ball was furious. Three of his young calves were missing from his prized beef herd and presumed dead. A heifer, that was now without her first calf, had been clawed in the face, while his expensive bull was ripped like a torn feed sack.

"It was a mountain lion, no doubt about it," the veterinarian said as he stitched up the cow. "I heard some of the farmers saying that one has been in cattle a couple of counties from here. Appears the mountain lion went from their herd right to yours."

"He's a big 'un. Saw his tracks in the mud near the river where he drank. Had no trouble finding where he attacked my bull. According to the tore-up ground, my bull put up a good fight."

"If the bull's still alive, it was a good fight. Say it was a big mountain lion?"

"My bull's still alive, and it was a mighty big mountain lion. Most likely the biggest one that's ever been around these parts. I've never seen cat tracks that size, not that I've seen more than a couple, mind you."

The vet strung out another piece of cat-gut and threaded it through the eye of the curved needle.

"You realize you'll have to kill it or it'll keep killing your cattle. Once a mountain lion starts killing cattle, it doesn't stop. It is most likely a cat that's grown old and too big and has to kill easy prey to stay alive. They're the most dangerous kind. They get smart and mean when age hits them."

Ball spit out the side of his mouth. "How the hell am I going to kill it? I'm a farmer not some big game hunter."

"I know of a man that is a big game hunter. He's half Indian and half white. Takes after the Indian side. I've heard all kinds of stories about him. Seems he is the best there is. He wiped out wolves in the area while he was still a boy. Bears haven't fared too well with him around, either."

Ball grunted. "What's his name and how do I get in touch with him?"

"His name is Reuben Rivers. He lives in a cabin on White Top Mountain."

Ball knew of White Top Mountain. It was another peak in the Appalachian range, once known as Iron Mountain. White Top Mountain cornered in three states: North Carolina, Tennessee, and Virginia. It rose to a tall and majestic 6000 feet above sea level. It was similar in height to Grandfather Mountain, but not as high as Humpback Mountain which was almost 6700 feet and could drop to a bone chilling −34 degrees below zero during winter.

"Send word that I want to hire him."

"You'll have to do that on your own. I don't know the man, and from what I've heard, he's pretty much of a recluse. Does what he wants to do when he wants to do it."

"Recluse?"

"Hermit. Doesn't like living with people. Rather strange, I've heard, but people say he can track down an ant crawling over solid rock and can kill anything that ever took a breath of air if he takes a notion."

George felt irritation stir. "How am I supposed to get in touch with a wacko recluse?"

The vet finished stitching up the clawed face of the cow, patted her on the head before he released her from the staunch.

"You'll probably have to drive to White Top and find his cabin. He doesn't make a point of hiding from people. He just likes his own company, so I've heard. Now, lets see if we can round up that bull of yours and put in a few stitches without him killing us both."

Chapter 5

Reuben Rivers could not remember the day of his birth, although at times, it seemed he did that very thing. Inside him was the knowledge of a strange darkness along with a continuous tightening of pain, as though in reverse of being swallowed by a snake, before he was projected into bright, blinding light. His lungs burned as they struggled for oxygen, the life-giving substance that would keep him in this uncomfortable existence instead of in his previous contented state. He heard his own lusty screams for he was not happy with his change of residence.

"It's a boy. Huge!"

He heard the words and was angry at the speaker for reasons he did not understand.

"Another boy. John will be pleased," said a soft voice, one that sounded of exhaustion instead of conviction. "Huge?"

"Much larger than the other three boys and of course your daughters."

"Much?"

"That's why he took so long arriving. That plus the fact you are no longer young. "

"John's a big man," said the soft voice, obviously ignoring the comment about no longer being young.

"In size," returned the voice in a derogatory manner to which the soft voice did not respond. "I don't recommend you get with child again. Six births have taken their toll, especially on a woman of your age."

There was a moment of silence. "Bring him to me," the soft voice now sounded weary as well.

The cold, hard arms lifted and moved him to similar warmth and security from which he had been so rudely ejected.

"Hold him then while I massage your womb. You're bleeding heavily."

"Bleeding is a new mother's curse," muttered the soft voice. "He has taken back after my people. I see my ancestors in his face."

"Your people are white as well as Cherokee."

"Not the whites, but the Cherokee, *my people*," she added in her tender voice as she continued to look at her crying baby's face.

"Humph," came a dissatisfied snort. "Let him suck. See if that will stop his infernal squalling."

"What day is it? I seem to have lost track."

"This is the second day of your labor. It is the 10th day of December. I shall write the date of birth in your Bible, just as I did the other five. Have you chosen his name yet?"

"Reuben, my fourth son shall be called Reuben Rivers," replied the soft voice as he felt something warm press against his lips.

Once his mouth had secured itself to the warm flesh, there came contentment at last.

🕊

His entire existence centered on the person he recognized as his mother, or Momma. His eyes could not take in enough of her face. There was something transfixing about her lovely black eyes and wide smile that was reserved for only him. Equally, his fascination focused on her hair. There was an extreme amount, more than any other person obtained. It was black with reflected blue lights. When she sat, it fanned out from her head and enticed his hands to grab and clutch. When she stood, the shroud almost reached the floor. He worshiped that long hair and more so the woman it belonged to, his Momma.

His father, Johnny Rivers, was another matter entirely. Fear along with resentment stirred within his body and mind when his father was present. He did not want him touching Momma; did not want his father touching him, which did not occur often.

Johnny Rivers was a harsh, hateful white man who had only harsh words and no smile on his face. He cared only for one person, and that one person was Johnny Rivers.

His mother's love was divided among four others that were at home. His oldest sister, Rachel, married before he was born, and he wished the others were married as well, regardless of their age. His brother, Bill, did not require as much of his mother's attention. Julia Zelphia, two years Bill's junior, tried to alternately boss and mother Reuben. James and Thomas spent a great part of their day picking at him. They wanted to make him cry so they could call him sissy-britches and momma's-boy. Early on he came to distrust others, even those related to him.

"Pay them no mind," Momma said after she pulled Reuben from the mud hole Thomas shoved him in. "Stop your blubbering, for you are special. Yours is the spirit of my people. Great warriors never cry."

Reuben wanted to be a great warrior, Momma's pride. Therefore, he refused to shed tears even during humiliation and pain.

"I'll take you to the water where you can wash yourself. My people . . . your people considered mud a great healer. Mud has the strength of mother earth within it. Many take mud baths in order for its strength to enter their flesh." Momma told him in that special tone of voice reserved only for him.

Reuben did not want mud baths forced upon him by his brothers, but he did want strength regardless of where it came from. He did not like being two years old and unable to take care of himself. He longed to be a grown man. One that was big and strong; one that could whip all adversaries.

Momma waded into the water with him. "See the little fishes," she said. "See how they swim? You too must learn how to swim much as the little fishes do. There is safety in water only if you can swim. Even a fish would die if it could not swim."

Reuben could not conceive of a fish drowning as he stretched his arms out in the water.

"Lift your legs," Momma said, and Reuben did. Her hands were firm under his stomach as she allowed his head to submerge then lifted him up with a chuckle. "Now, you see that you cannot breathe while under water. Learn to hold your breath until your head is out of the water and the time is right to breathe."

Reuben pretended he was a fish as Momma allowed him to play, but their fun was all too short for his Momma had work to get done and could not spend time playing with her baby son.

Reuben almost smiled as he thought of his mother. She had been the only person he had ever loved. He was four years old when she died giving birth to a still-born son, but his memory of her was unfailing. It seemed to him that she still walked with him, talked with him, and guided him each day in the ways of her people. He couldn't claim to actually hear her voice talking; he could claim to feel her mental presence and sense things she wanted him to know about.

That's how he knew a man would be coming today. The man was to offer him a job and he was to take it, even when he didn't want the job.

He already had his animals turned out to pasture and his game chickens would be able to fend for themselves while he was gone. He had a small knapsack he carried a few supplies in. The knapsack, a gun, and a knife were all he ever needed. Mother Nature would take care of the rest if a man would let her.

He sat on a stump in the edge of the woods outside his log cabin and waited, although he should be working and there was a lot of work to get done before winter set in. Among other things, he wanted to make a stout door to replace the one a bear ripped off. Seemed he was getting a bit careless. Back during the winter, when a really bad freezing spell came, he had shot a bear and drug it into his cabin to skin by the warmth of the fire only to discover that the bear was only addled instead of dead. It ripped the door clean off before he was able to finish the job of killing it.

Most folks thought bears hibernated all winter long, but that was not true unless it was a pregnant female bear. The boar bears slept lightly and would leave their dens. He had killed many a bear in the dead-cold of winter.

He now used the bear's skin as a door, but it would be warmer inside, if more confining, once he rebuilt the door. He didn't know why he suddenly had the urge to make his cabin more comfortable when it had never mattered in the past, but the urge was strong within him.

Strange thing was, he just didn't like the feeling of being confined inside a building, even during winter. That's why he hadn't replaced the door. He remembered the years he had spent in a tent, remembered snows so deep he had to

dig his way out of the snow-buried tent, but that was years
ago when he was young. Now, that he was older, comforts
were exactly that and nothing more. He could take them or
he could leave them. Yet there was that confounded urge to
make his cabin bigger and warmer. *A man is always a man,*
his Momma seemed to be telling him. *Man must go into the
world and multiply.* Reuben heard her thoughts but he
thought them silly woman talk. All a man had to do was
live until he died.

Irritation filled him as he heard the sound of a truck
engine trying to growl its way up the mountain. He didn't
hold with roads through his land, had none on it, but the
truck could get closer than he liked.

Someday, when he earned enough money, he intended
to buy that track of land so he could close off what served
as a road, but that would be a time in the future. Money
was a hard thing to get hold of when a man didn't put much
store on it. But then, others held a great longing for it,
therefore it was a good bartering tool.

He heard the truck reach the end of its travel and the
engine shut off. He could save the man some time and a
steep climb if he met him, but he wasn't so inclined. Just
because he knew the man was coming, didn't mean he had
to welcome him.

A good while later, the man showed up, looked the
rough-hewed one-room cabin over, including the bearskin
used for a door.

"Hey, Reuben Rivers! You around?"

Reuben took his time in sizing the man up. The
arrogant fellow was overweight with a round belly that
hung over his belt. His britches hung so low they wouldn't
stay above his hips, and he had a pair of squatty legs that
were too short for his body. He wore a hat but Reuben
suspected he had a perfectly round baldhead. His face was

strawberry ruddy. Reuben could tell his disposition was bad by the miserable look on his face.

Reuben let him wander around a while before he stood up from his stump, left his knapsack, but carried his gun in his hand. His knife was in a leather case fastened to his belt.

The man started and then became stock-still once he saw Reuben.

"You called." Reuben stated.

"You Reuben Rivers?" The man managed to get out.

"Rightly so."

"Then I called. I'm George J. Ball "

Reuben looked him in the eyes and said nothing.

"I was told you're a big game hunter."

"I'm not that big," he said in all sincerity.

Again, Ball looked surprised, and then said, "You're about the biggest cuss I've ever set eyes on. The ugliest too."

Reuben nodded his agreement. "Had similar thoughts concerning you."

Ball almost grinned, but Reuben's face remained firm.

"I need your help."

Reuben was silent for he had figured as much, just hadn't expected the man to admit it.

"Mountain lion has been in my cattle. Killed three, tore two more up."

Reuben didn't comment.

"Can you kill it?"

"It's likely that I can."

"I'll pay you two hundred dollars for its hide."

Reuben thought of the land he wanted to buy. Two hundred would be a help, but that wasn't why he was going to take the job. It was the spirit of his mother and her people telling him to do it.

"Throw in a box of shells for my gun and fifty pounds of nails and I'll do it."

"Done," said Ball . "When can you come to my place?"

"Now."

"Now? This minute?"

"When do you want the cat killed?"

"Now, this minute."

Reuben went back to the stump, got his knapsack, and headed off the mountain to the truck. Ball couldn't keep up. Reuben was sitting in the truck bed when Ball arrived.

"Get up front," Ball told him.

"Nope."

"Why not?"

"Don't like enclosed places."

"That why you got a bearskin for a door?"

"Nope."

"Suit yourself." Ball suspected that he usually did.

Mitch was waiting at George Ball's farm when Ball and Reuben drove up. He got out of the truck and met them as Ball's truck came to a stop. His gaze went to the big man that got out of the truck bed and it was all he could do not to drop his mouth open in astonishment. Mitch had read about men who looked like this, but he had not believed any existed, at least not in today's time. The man was actually wearing well-worn buckskin pants and vest over a hairy body that was about the width of a workhorse's. The strange man had a full beard and a head of hair that had never seen a barber's shears. Who could this man be and where did such a man come from?

Ball looked Mitch over and grinned in amusement, suspecting his thoughts about Reuben Rivers. "What can I do for you?"

"I'm Mitch Kenilworth and I'm a surveyor for the Forest Service. I'll be doing some work on Humpback Mountain and wondered if it would be all right with you for me to occasionally park my truck on your land?" He wasn't about to tell him about the girl he was seeking. He didn't know if he would be laughed at or if Ball and others would believe him and hunt for the girl themselves.

"Don't like folks trespassing on my land," Ball told him.

"I won't be trespassing or bothering a thing. Just need a safe place to park my truck for a day or two while I do my job."

The expression on Ball's face showed he was ready to say no, when suddenly his expression changed to thoughtfulness.

"Got a gun?" Ball asked.

"Do I need one?"

"You might."

"Why?"

"Mountain lion. Been killing my cattle. Figure it has holed-up on or around the Big Hump. It's nothing but a rocky crag on that mountain, perfect place for mountain lions to hole-up in."

A touch of icy fear spread over Mitch. The girl wouldn't have a chance if a mountain lion was in the area. It would get her a lot quicker than cold weather could.

"I'll get a gun," Mitch told him. "And I'll make a point of hunting it down."

Ball thought a surveyor used to roaming the land just might be able to run up on the mountain lion. He looked around. "Where did Reuben Rivers go?"

"Who?"

"The man that was with me."

"That strange looking man?"

"Who else was with me?"

"Last I saw of him, he was headed toward the barn."

Ball nodded. "I'll give you twenty-five dollars for the cat's hide if you'll kill it," Ball said in a lowered tone.

"It's a deal if I have permission to park my truck."

"Don't you pilfer a thing."

"Never have." Mitch stuck out his hand and Ball shook it.

Reuben wasn't impressed by the scrawny little fellow that got out of the truck when he and Ball drove up. Actually, he was rather amused for the little fellow was too restless and sure of himself. Obviously, the little fellow wanted something right bad by the way he was acting. That's why he made a point of listening.

Having exceptionally good hearing, Reuben heard Ball offer him twenty-five dollars for the cat's hide, but he didn't mind. Scrawny would not be able to kill a panther if somebody held it for him.

What he did mind was having Scrawny running over the mountain getting in his way, and most likely getting himself into trouble. He didn't have time to waste keeping the little fellow from getting lost or hurt. Then again, Scrawny wasn't his responsibility. He was there to kill the cat, collect the two hundred dollars, and nothing more.

Reuben went behind the barn to the small lot where the injured bull and cow were. Yeap, mountain lion all right. Nothing else could slice 'em up like that, nice even claw marks, far apart and deep. Big cat. It had to be an old one that was losing his hunting ability and had to rely on farm stock for food. Cattle offered no challenge for the young and aggressive mountain lions. They tended to take pleasure in running down or stalking difficult prey before the kill. It was a different story when the cat got old.

He went into the lot to get a close-up look at the bull's neck. The bull pawed, snorted, and shook his head in a threatening attempt to scare Reuben away, but he didn't attack. Poor devil. Still had bluff in him but the cat had taken the want-to for a fight out of him – at least for a while.

By the deep puncture wounds in the bull's neck, Reuben knew the cat still had a fine set of teeth still tight in his jaws. All cats had a gutting instinct in them. They held onto prey with their teeth and forefeet while their powerful, sharp-clawed hind feet gutted. That's why it was never wise to be on top of a belly-up cat. Straddle of their back was a much better position if a man was given a choice.

Reuben backtracked the bull straight to the river bottom where the fight had taken place. He read the ground as though he was seeing the fight as it happened. Had to admire the bull and understand the cat, but as Ball had said, a farmer couldn't have a cattle-killing mountain lion on the loose. When an animal stepped out of its natural place in the wild and moved in with mankind, it was time for killing.

Reuben picked up the cat's tracks along with the drag-marks of the calf. He was on the trail with one purpose in mind. Sell the cat skin to pay on his wanted land and go back home where he belonged. He would do it fast and get it over with.

He knew the habits of the big cats well, even if there weren't as many roaming the region as there were when he was a boy. Most everybody and every location had a name for the big cats. The mountain lion, panther, puma, cougar, had over thirty-six different names, depending on what part of the world it inhabited. Reuben knew they spent most of their time on the ground instead of in trees as some people thought. Like most cats, they could bound to the top of trees in the wink of an eye, or leap on their prey without a sound.

They preferred rocky areas although they seldom chose a cave as their den as it was too enclosed and confining. They tended to avoid dense brush and heavily timbered areas for they loved to stretch out their lanky bodies on a hot rock in full sun. Always on the alert, they liked a clear view of their surroundings, even while at rest.

Reuben found several scrapes, which were small piles of grass, leaves, and twigs that male mountain lions scraped up and pissed on. It was their signpost, their territorial marker that warned other males off and intrigued females enough to give consideration to mating. The more territory the scrapes encompassed, the more interested the female became. Therefore, he knew this cat was a big male, marking his domain, longing for a female to breed come the cold nights of February.

Cat-squall month was February. Everything from house cats to the mountain lions came in heat during that month. Their mating squalls could raise the hair on a grown man's head. A lot of times the cats themselves lost a good deal of hair, for their mating rituals were not tender loving moments. Their foreplay was savage fights in order to cull the weak from reproducing, a procedure Reuben thought was both wise and necessary if the fittest was to survive and reproduce as Mother Nature had planned.

The wild world did not make allowances for the incapable and useless as man did. Pity that man had to be so foolish. Before long it would keep all the able-bodied humans busy just taking care of the incompetent humans. Survival of the fittest would be a lost cause, for mankind would destroy themselves by contributing to what they referred to as humane treatment, but then, what could be expected from such foolish people?

Reuben came upon the spot where the cat had stopped to eat his fill of the calf, but he had not scratched sticks and leaves to cover his kill until he was hungry again. The cat had moved on, carrying the half eaten carcass with him.

It meant the cat was already familiar with cattle killing and knew that soon he would be hunted for his killing ways and wanted to hide his kill on safer ground. Reuben had an idea where the cat was headed—the incredible rocky slopes of Humpback Mountain.

Reuben wanted a better view of the surrounding area. The nearby bald would serve that purpose well. Once he had reached the bald, he found what he never expected to find. Tracks that told him a very interesting story.

He knew that a small footed, lightweight person had crossed the bald several days before pulling something made from two crude poles hauling weight. Perhaps it had been a crude attempt at a travois. A large, heavy bodied dog was with the person. The tracks led off the trail into the woods and he found the spot where the dog and the bull fought. He also found small footprints leading to a tree the small person had climbed.

He found the same fresher tracks going in the opposite direction. According to the bend of the grass and the dew that had fallen, these tracks were made two days before. The small bare-footed person was running and pulling an empty travois behind them.

He put his heavy foot beside a track and took a step in order to measure how deep a track his weight would make in the ground. According to the running distance between tracks and the depth of the prints, he judged the person to be about five feet two or three inches tall and weighing one hundred to one hundred-ten pounds. A female, he concluded, a young female with a dog that weighed more than she did. If it had been a young boy, the foot placement would have been different. The toes would have been much longer and the foot broader.

Reuben ran his fingers through his straight black hair and grunted – a sign that he was deep in thought as he bent closer to the ground. The older tracks led toward the wilderness, no houses or people were in that direction. So, that was the direction he tracked her, wanting to see where the girl had gone and what she did with her load.

What he found chilled his flesh. The mountain lion had been following her trail. It had backtracked her until it came across the cattle. The cattle's presence had most likely saved the girl's life for he didn't doubt the cat would have tracked her down. Not even the big dog could have saved her.

Reuben had had enough experience with mountain lions to know they were delighted with small things, such as children, just as house cats liked to play with mice before they killed them. Cats were intimidated by large. A person needed to appear as big as possible when confronted by cats. The girl wasn't large, and she was female, another irresistible attraction, for women, as in all mammals, had a different odor than men.

He was near a laurel hell when he heard a scraping noise some distance away. He cocked his head until he could catch the sound carried on the wind. He had an idea what the sound was as he vanished into the tangle of twisted limbs and leaves. He lay flat on his belly, covered himself in leaves so that his smell would not carry, and waited. It didn't take long.

The girl came up over the rise, running with a long, distance-eating gait and drawing deep breaths of air into her lungs. Reuben found her strangely attractive although something about her appearance was odd, much different than any girl he had ever seen before. Her hair was just as black as his and reached below her slender hips. It caught the wind and flowed back from her face as she ran. Her ragged clothes were not clean and once belonged to a man. There wasn't one ounce of fat on her wiry body, but none of this did he find odd. What was odd was her overall demeanor. There was an energy force radiating from her, a life force such as he expected to see surrounding the mountain lion or one of the bears he loved to hunt, a savage appearance that warned to keep a safe distance away.

Holy shit, he thought. *She's wild!*

Never in his entire lifetime had he ever met a person that was animal wild, not even among his mother's people, nor had he ever heard a story of one. Actually, he was the closest thing to being a wild human he knew about, and he was refined compared to this girl. This girl . . . he just didn't know what this girl was, or where she could possibly have come from, but she had his full attention.

A Rottweiler dog was protectively trotting less than a foot from her side, as though he was fearful of getting further away from her. To Reuben, the dog appeared tense. Even the scruff of his back was raised in apprehension. Reuben knew the dog could smell the lingering trace of the mountain lion.

A rope was looped around the girl's chest and she was holding onto it with both hands. She pulled a packed, shabbily constructed, travois that had to take strength and determination for the runners dug into the ground instead of gliding on top of it. She certainly was leaving a trail that a blind man could follow.

When they were within a few feet of the laurel hell, the dog sniffed the ground where he had stood. Hackles came up on his back as he lifted his blocky head and sniffed the air, but he didn't appear to pick up Reuben's odor or feel a threat toward his mistress for he continued to run by her side.

The wild girl wasn't paying attention to her surroundings, nor even glancing in his direction or noticing the dog's interest, for she had reached a decline in the terrain, and picked up speed. Obviously, she wanted to get somewhere in a hurry. Thing was, the mountain lion's tracks were going in the same direction. Foolish girl, it appeared she hadn't had a reliable person to teach her the ways of the wild. Actually, it was more than that, he thought as he studied her closer.

Something wasn't adding up with her, not in her behavior or her looks, and that something made him more curious and puzzled than he wanted to be.

Reuben let her get far enough ahead so the dog wouldn't hear his movement or pick up his scent, before he raked the leaves off and left the laurel hell. Wherever she was going, he would have no problem following the well-marked trail she left behind.

Reuben picked up speed until he was lightly trotting. The wild girl didn't slow down although she was obviously winded. Her tracks were showing that she was becoming more nervous, more concerned as darkness deepened the shadows in the wooded area. He had a very good inclination that she knew of the cat's presence and knew twilight was the time a mountain lion went on serious prowl.

He hadn't expected her to go all the way to the base of Humpback Mountain, but she did. Fool girl. She headed straight in the direction the big cat had gone. It was holed-up somewhere on that mountain for cats liked to be in high clear spaces where they could watch their surroundings. It would most likely have taken shelter underneath an overhanging rock, never in a cave unless it was a female with kittens.

Her actions made him question his former conclusion. Perhaps she didn't know about the mountain lion after all. It couldn't have been in the area long or there would have been more cattle killed. Which reminded him, he was following a girl instead of the cat, but it made little difference. The cat wasn't far away, most likely was watching them from top of the Big Hump at this very moment.

Fortunately, for the girl, its belly was full and it likely had part of its kill to keep down his urge to hunt, but that was no guarantee the girl was safe.

He stopped, hidden by laurel hells and greenberry briars, near the base of the mountain and watched. Crazy girl! She was pulling that rickety travois straight up the steep, rocky mountainside, bumping and banging over the rocks as though the devil himself was right behind her. The dog was following, paying little attention to her frantic movements for he had his nose lifted, winding the air.

Exhaustion was threatening Raven. She knew if she stopped to rest, she might not be able to continue. She had to climb to the top of the mountain, had to reach the safety of the cave. If she took shelter under a rock and the devil cat showed up, she wouldn't be able to keep Dog from fighting it. The cat would kill her only living companion and she couldn't bear life without her dog.

She had seen the huge paw prints in patches of soft dirt as she ran. She knew the cat had been tracking her and expected it to attack at any moment. She considered getting the gun from the travois but she couldn't pull the travois as fast if she carried the gun. She would have to rely on the big black to warn her when the cat got near. She never once considered the possibility that a mountain lion was able to stay up-wind of its prey and stalk within a few feet without detection.

Still, some sixth sense told her it was watching and biding its time.

Over the rocks she climbed, worming the travois along in what seemed slow motion. She couldn't go fast enough, couldn't breathe deep enough. Sweat soaked her clothes and stuck her hair to her face. She longed to tear a rag and tie her hair back, but she couldn't spare a moment's time.

She could feel eyes on her, knew her every movement was observed. What she couldn't understand was why the devil cat hadn't attacked – unless it was afraid of Dog and the noisy travois.

🕊

The devil cat was watching from the top of the mountain, on the flat peak of a rock outcropping across from her cave. A deep gorge separated the cat's ledge from the cave, a distance of nearly four hundred feet in mid-air. The distance was far enough for the cat to feel safe and yet close enough for him to attack the girl when he was ready.

Under the rock ledge were the half-eaten remains of the calf. The cat was feeling the drowsy fullness in his stuffed stomach, after all he had eaten almost three calves before his ravenous hunger had subsided. He was in no hurry to go after the girl for he knew he could do that whenever he was hungry again or felt the playful urge to toy with his prey.

But that wasn't the only thing keeping the mountain lion on his ledge instead of crossing to the girl. The updraft of wind was bringing him the scent of man, and that made him cautious and slightly afraid. Had there been more than one man, his fear would have increased for several men meant a hunting party had formed, while one man was one man. His beady eyes narrowed, focused on the distance, and caught the movement of the man following the girl.

The memory of being recently hunted by men and dogs stirred inside his brain, and he didn't dare move, wouldn't until the threat from man and dog no longer bothered him.

It wasn't difficult for Reuben to hide in the rocks while he kept watch on the girl. She wasn't moving fast, but she was continuously climbing even when the heavy travois would slide backward, or flip sideways. He admired her determination and endurance as she righted the load and inched onward, almost straight up the mountain of rocks.

Shadows had already turned the valleys dark and the top of the mountain was gray by the time the girl reached the Big Hump. She stopped, took the rope from around her, and disappeared from his vision. Just as he was becoming concerned, she returned, half-lifted and half-dragged the travois over more rocks. She didn't appear again.

Reuben followed behind her, right to the top of the mountain where she had disappeared. He suspected she had found a fissure cave, a place where the rocks has spewed up forming a rock cave, and gone inside.

He smelled smoke and had no trouble finding the opening of the cave. The smart little thing had rolled rocks into the cave's mouth and then built a fire further back in the cave. The rocks would slow the mountain lion down if it tried to enter, and the smell of the smoke would put the fear of fire in him. Reuben realized the girl had known all along about the mountain lion. That was why she was pushing herself so hard. She was after the safety of the fissure cave.

Reuben moved away from the cave and sat down on a
rock. What was he to do now? Stay nearby and protect the
girl, backtrack and find out where she came from, or hunt
the mountain lion? Easy choice for he could backtrack her
better when it was light, and the mountain lion was sure to
come for the girl, in a day or two. All he had to do was be
patient, and he was very good at that.

He found shelter in a rock crevice not far from the cave,
put his gun in easy reach just in case the cat showed up, and
then he slept.

Once Raven got her fire built, she sank to the cave floor
in relief and exhaustion. She not only had pushed herself by
running as fast as she could, emotion had taken its toll on
her. It wasn't just fear of the mountain lion, it was leaving
her home-cave behind knowing she was starting anew with
almost nothing. Aggie had done it many years before and
so could she. As the old man said, Aggie had survived as a
cripple. Surely, she could survive when she was strong and
whole with a set of good legs and a good, straight back.

Raven took some corn, Aggie's wooden bowl, two
rocks, and pounded the corn into a coarse meal. She mixed
a small amount of her precious water into the meal and
poured it in the pan she had heating over the fire. She had
tried to render lard from the coon's fat and had obtained a
couple spoonfuls of grease. She needed grease to fry things
and she was out of the hog lard that Aggie had taken from
springhouses. It was going to be much more difficult living
in the wilderness than it was on the Ruffian where the
valley's plunder was to raid, but she would manage. She
had no choice.

When her cornpone fried enough, she ate half and gave
the big black half. She shared water with him. Tomorrow

morning she would take Dog and the gun and hunt for a water supply. Shelter, fire, food, and water were all she and Dog needed to live.

She now had two bushels of shelled corn, counting what the man left in Aggie's cave. No apples, no dried berries, no potatoes, and no dried beans. She needed to start gathering things immediately, but how would she manage if the devil cat was still stalking her? She would have to kill the big cat with Aggie's gun, or scare it off. She wondered if it was possible to scare off a mountain lion. Aggie had never told her any stories where they were scared off, but surely it was possible.

She wanted to come up with a logical plan but was simply too tired to think about anything. She wrapped herself in the quilt Don had left and was instantly asleep.

Chapter 6

It was a sunny, dry day with no storm clouds in sight as Mitch drove his truck as far as he could go through Ball's property. He parked it next to a heavily wooded area, a place where it would be safe from rubbing, kicking cattle, and hard to see by human eyes. He didn't think his truck would be bothered, even by cattle butting dents in the metal or licking at the paint, but there was no use in tempting fate. His divorce had left him with few possessions and he believed in taking good care of what he had. Strange, how his ex-wife used to accuse him of not caring about what he owned, including her. Now that he had little to nothing, things seemed extremely important and even harder to come by. Even having somebody to call your own took on an entirely different meaning.

Perhaps that was the reason he was so obsessed with the wild girl. She had no one, not one living soul, even the clothes she wore were his. He wondered if she had dressed in the new clothes he had left for her? He hoped she had.

He knew the girl would choose a remote, hard to reach area where only the hardiest, most determined hikers might venture. There were some things about the girl that puzzled him. He couldn't believe she would willingly run from her own kind. Once she realized how much better her life would be in the civilized world, she would condemn her own stupidity in running away from him after he had found her snake-bitten and then taken such good care of her.

84

But that wasn't his major concern right now. Finding her before the mountain lion did, was. The nearer Humpback Mountain he could get, the faster he would find the girl. Her being snake-bitten was nothing compared to being attacked by the mountain lion. Knowing she didn't have a chance against the big cat caused a feeling of dread to surge through his body. After seeing what the cat did to the huge, tough bull, he feared he might already be too late.

If only he hadn't wasted time driving to town and buying a high powered rifle, but he had no choice. If he couldn't find the girl soon, he hoped the mountain lion would find him. That was why he bought ten pounds of hamburger meat – a little incentive to attract a wild, carnivorous animal.

Mitch got out of the truck and strapped the loaded pack on his back. He made sure his rifle was loaded and he had a good supply of bullets. He locked and left his truck behind as he tried to find a trail that would lead him toward Humpback Mountain. Finally, he found what appeared to be some sort of animal path that led in the direction he wanted to go. It was probably an old buffalo trail, or even going many hundreds of years back, a wooly mammoth trail that led through the Carolina mountains to the salt slicks in Virginia. Such were the trails Indians and hunters traveled on when they came to the mountains in search of game. He thought the girl, Raven, would do the same as him, find a path to travel on, but he saw no tracks on the ground that would indicate she traveled on the path. He had no way of knowing exactly when the girl had left the Ruffian. It could have been almost a week since she left, and tracks of a small, barefoot girl and her dog could easily have been wiped out by wind and rain. He could also be overlooking the obvious, especially in the gloaming of a summer evening when a man was in the deep woods.

As Mitch moved through the thick growth of forest, gray squirrels quarreled angrily at him for disturbing their rummaging on the ground in search for food. They ran up tree trunks, stopped on high limbs to chatter and jerk their bushy tails in anger. How dare a human disturb their evening feeding? How dare he come into their territory? He counted four squirrels near him and heard many more in the distance before he lost interest in them.

He hadn't gone far into the woods until he was blinded by the forest. He could no longer see any portion of Humpback Mountain and had to rely on his compass for directions. Again, he was irritated because of lost time in going back to town for a gun, but again he assured himself that he had no choice in the matter. He didn't want to be killed by the mountain lion any more than he wanted the girl to be killed. He should be grateful to Ball for forewarning him about the maundering cat.

By the time he came to a small stream trickling down the mountain side, it was too dark for him to continue. He found a large rock formation with dry dirt underneath its overhang and decided it was as good a place as any for him to pitch his tent, and yet he hesitated to get it from his pack. It would take time to set up and even more time in the morning when he had to take it down, fold it, and repack it. He would be wise to build a large fire and bed-down in his sleeping bag. Besides, being inside a tent would keep him from seeing a mountain lion if it approached.

Mitch gathered deadfall and got a hot fire going. He took out his camping kit of utensils, folded out the handle of the frying pan, and broke off a chunk of his hamburger meat to fry. He was hoping the mountain lion would be drawn to the smell so he could kill it right off, without having to waste time in hunting for it.

The cat lay stretched-out on his rocky vantage point as he watched the mountain, the wooded area, and the valley below him. He knew the girl and dog were in the fissure cave. Plus, the hated smell of smoke was reaching his nostrils. He feared the smell of smoke as much as he feared the crackling orange flames that reached out to hurt him.

Several times during his life, he had seen those flames grow big and consume great patches of his hunting ground, charring everything else that was not fast enough to escape. Men would always gather in clusters and fight with the flames. All the animals would scream with fright as they tried to outrun the flames. Those that failed left a momentary stench of burning flesh before the flames moved on in continuation of their greedy existence.

Once the roaring flames stopped, and the humans were gone, only black remains were left behind where a forest once thrived. Nothing was left of life, no animals, no birds, and few, if, any insects. Even the waters that oozed from hot rocks were no longer fit to drink. It would take years before it was a fit place for his return.

He grew more nervous. Had the man come to fight the little fire that was burning a short distance away instead of joining with the dog to chase him? If so, why was the man bedded down in the rocks instead of beating at the fire with sticks and dirt, and why was he not in the cave with the other human?

The lifting winds brought a different sound to his twitching ears. He knew the sound. It was one of the hard metal things. They bellowed out stinking smoke and ran over roads or turned up dirt in fields. They were many and often differed in appearances, but were all similar. He hated the sound and the smell those things left behind, but he had found no way to fight them and no life in them to kill. Some often sat in total silence and refused to move when he came near.

The thing came close to the mountain and stopped near the woods. Still, it left its stink on the wind. Along with the thing's stink, came the familiar smell of another man. The cat twitched his tail with sharp jerking movements. There were two men, a dog, and fire, and he wasn't liking it at all. Not only did they bring danger, they scared off his food supply.

The cat glided off his rock in one fluid movement, eased under the rock where the remains of the calf awaited him and consumed the small amount of flesh clinging to the bones. When all was gone, his appetite had only been heightened.

He turned his nose toward the cave and sniffed. The girl was not giving off the great tempting smell she had emitted a few days before, but he was still attracted to her smell. He licked his mouth, his feet, legs, and chest, careful to consume every remaining morsel of the calf. He wanted more, needed more as his amber eyes narrowed on the cave entrance. A meal was in there, waiting for him. All he had to do was go get it.

Suddenly, his attention was distracted from the girl. An irresistible aroma reached him, one he had only experienced whiffs of before, whiffs that oozed from human houses. This time the smell was coming from the woods. It was too powerful for him to resist. The smell lifted up the mountain and the big cat licked his frothy mouth. Determination filled him. He instantly forgot about the girl, lowered himself to a crouch, and then sprang into great distance eating leaps that took him down the mountainside.

Once he reached the heavily wooded area, he winded the smoke of fire, but it didn't faze him. His fear was small compared to the greasy smell of flesh that heightened his hunger. The smell enticed him until there was no caution.

His huge paws padded silently on the moss-covered ground as he drew near the smell that beaconed him. Anger flared when he saw the orange flames. Beside the flames sat the man he had winded earlier.

He dropped to his belly, his ears lying flat against his head, his eyes narrowed, his upper lips twitched, drawing his nose upward forming wrinkles above huge, exposed canine teeth. An unwilling hiss of savage anger escaped as he watched the man, something he had never done before when he crouched for the kill.

The forest creatures became silent. Not even one night bird called.

Mitch had eaten over half the fried meat when a shiver of icy-cold crept up his spine. He took it as an omen of warning, set the tin plate of meat on the ground, got a long stick, and pushed the meat as far away from him as the stick would reach. Slowly, without jerky movements, he got the rifle, cocked the hammer, and gently scooted over the ground until his back was against the rock with the fire in front of him. Suddenly, the rock at his back seemed like a poor means of protection from the things he feared lurked near by. He began to be violently afraid.

He waited, listened, tried to make his eyes adjust until they could see into the darkness beyond him, but the brightness of the fire was hurting his night-vision. All he saw was black tree trunks outlined against the darkness of the woods. The fire flickered, made shadows within a few feet of him. His nerves were on edge.

"Shit," he mumbled. "I've let the fire die down too far."

He eased forward, still holding the rifle in his right hand, picked up pieces of the deadfall he had gathered and placed them into the fire as fast as he could with his left hand, afraid to let go of the gun even for a moment.

A feeling of inadequacy gripped him. What was he doing sitting here in the wilderness of a national forest, in the dark of night, with the odor of meat surrounding him? Not only could the smell draw a mountain lion, it could draw every bear and wild animal within miles. He was alone, not sitting back to back with a hunting partner, one who had knowledge of hunting along with how to shoot a gun and hit what he aimed at. An animal would have to be on top of him before he could see it. A bear might crack a few limbs of deadfall as it approached, but a mountain lion would never make a sound. It could draw in its claws into footpads and creep over eggshells without crushing them. It could spring from a crouch and be on him before he blinked.

It was then that something made a sound, or so he thought. Not much of a sound, more like a movement of air hissing, perhaps an amplified sound coming from a snake.

His next conscious acknowledgement was the woods had become exceedingly quiet. The screech owls that sat in the trees, where the firelight reached and drew moths, were no longer visible. Not one of the night birds was making a sound. The forest and everything in it was waiting for something to happen.

And it happened.

The tiniest trickle of dirt fell on his arms from the shelf of rock over his head. He looked at his arms and then looked up to see the underbelly of the mountain lion glowing from the firelight an instant before it landed on the tin plate of fried hamburger.

It was the ting of the tin plate that brought him out of his stupor. He swung the gun around and fired into the shadows. He cocked the gun and fired again, but the huge mountain lion had disappeared with the tin plate in its mouth.

He tried to swallow the lump that had constricted his throat. The mountain lion had been right there, on the rock ledge above his head. It landed not ten feet in front of him. The mountain lion and the tin plate were gone.

He swallowed hard again, tried to breathe normally, tried to make his hands stop shaking, but all he managed to do was shake worse. Suddenly, he was cold, freezing to death cold, but couldn't move an inch toward the blazing fire, couldn't even pick up another stick of deadfall to toss on the flames.

All he could manage was to jerk the trigger and shoot the gun again – just in case. How many bullets did the clip hold? How many would it take to kill something as big and fast as what he had seen going over his head before it landed on top of him? The thing looked to be as big as a car. How could he have thought it would be easy to kill?

And, even more important, would it come back? The smell of fried meat was still in the air. A small bite of meat and a tin plate wouldn't be enough to satisfy that huge beast. Furthermore, what if he had actually hit the mountain lion? A wounded animal was the most dangerous kind. He had heard many stories about a wounded animal being shot through the heart and still being able to kill the hunter. At least that thought gave him incentive to toss more limbs on the fire.

Reuben Rivers smelled the campfire long before he smelled the meat cooking. One thing was fact, that scrawny fellow didn't have a lick of sense. The smell of cooking meat would draw every meat-eating animal within miles. He knew there were several bears, wild cats, a couple of wolves, plus the mountain lion were in smelling distance of Humpback Mountain.

The scent of cooking meat would have permeated Scrawny's clothing, hair, and even settled on his skin. The idiot had a death wish for it couldn't be the twenty-five dollar hide he was after.

At first, Reuben thought a man that foolish deserved what he got. Then his basic do-gooder instinct got hold of him. He couldn't allow an idiot to be ripped to pieces just because he was an idiot.

He checked the cave entrance to make sure it was still closed off, the fire was still burning, and the girl would be safe if he left her. He decided the cat would be focused on the smell of meat. Something about the smell of meat cooking had a strong appeal, even to him.

He headed down the mountain hoping he would get to Scrawny in time, but his going was slowed slightly by the darkness and the placement of rocks. At least he knew exactly where Scrawny was camped because of the wind draft.

Reuben was less than five minutes away when he heard the first shot. By hearing the second and then third shot, he figured Scrawny was still alive, and hopefully he was killing a wounded mountain lion not the other way around.

He silently eased up to the site while keeping the thick trunks of trees between him and Scrawny. Once Reuben could see him, he had compassion for the little man huddled against the rock, clutching the gun, and looking as though he had already wet his britches. Cautiously, he eased around behind Scrawny and got on top of the rock to be out of gun range.

"If you'll lay that gun down, I'll come to you," Reuben said.

Mitch jumped and let out a squall.

"It's all right, nothing's up here but me. Don't see anything dead. What did you shoot at?"

Mitch made a great effort to calm himself. "Mountain lion, you scared me half to death," he added. "I thought it must have come back. Who are you anyhow?"

"Reuben Rivers. Saw you at Ball's place. Take your finger off the trigger and I'll ease down beside you."

Mitch moved his hand and let the end of the gun drop slightly. Reuben eased over the rock ledge in exactly the same spot where he had seen the underside of the cat's belly. He almost fired the gun again, but Reuben Rivers moved almost as fast as the cat had moved.

"Did you hit it?" Reuben asked, seeing right off that Scrawny hadn't killed it.

"Don't know, but I'm mighty glad to see you instead of that cat," he admitted.

"You shot three times."

"I scared it off."

"That depends."

"On what?"

"If you hit it. A wounded animal might not run far. Where was it when you shot at it?"

Mitch pointed. "Right there."

"Lay your gun down beside you."

"Why?"

"So it won't accidentally go off and hit me."

Once the gun was on the ground, Reuben went in the direction Mitch had pointed. He saw tracks where the cat had landed and then leaped again. It had landed further into the woods where he couldn't pick up its tracks in the dark.

Finally, he found scuffed leaves near a rhododendron thicket, but no drops of blood on the ground or the leaves.

"I'm coming back," Reuben called from a distance. "Don't pick the gun up."

🕊

His words irritated Mitch. He wasn't a total idiot and he had shot a gun before. There was no need for the hairy reincarnation of a cave-dwelling Neanderthal to insult him.

It was then that a twig snapped on the opposite side from where Reuben's voice came, but it didn't alarm Mitch. He suspected how fast and quiet the man could move through the woods.

His next thought was of the girl's Rottweiler dog as the black shape came out into the open, but it was larger than the dog. It wasn't until it reared up on its hind legs that he realized a bear stood before him. He grabbed the gun and fired without taking aim at any vital area. The bear let out a grunt, dropped to the ground, and bounded off into the darkness before Mitch got the second shot off. Again, he fired into the darkness in hopes it might prove a lucky shot.

The gun was jerked from his hands. "Idiot," Reuben's voice rang with anger, even though his tone was almost normal. "There's no doubt I now have a wounded bear on the loose that I'll have to kill. The blazing fire must have deterred him, or I'd be pulling chunks of your flesh from his claws."

"I got him between the eyes," Mitch said in his own self-defense, and hoped that his words were truth.

"Don't see him lying on the ground, do you?"

"He staggered into the woods. I heard the brush snapping when he fell over."

Reuben didn't comment further as he moved beyond the fire toward the spot where he had seen the bear disappear. Scrawny obviously had never hunted big game or he would know the importance of staying calm and taking precise aim at a vital spot like the heart or brain. Getting the bear between the eyes would be a perfect brain shot, but Reuben was skeptical, but then Scrawny could have gotten lucky.

In the blink of an eye, the night was filled with what sounded like the entire laurel hell was being torn up by their roots.

A shadow charged straight toward Reuben. He was acquainted with the disposition of a wounded bear as well as their deadly attack speed. He didn't have time to take aim or fire the gun as he leaped toward a small sapling between the fire and the bear, hoping the firelight would momentarily blind the bear's already poor eyesight.

It worked, for the swipe of powerful claws missed him and tore bark from a small sapling, but his glaring eyes fixed on Reuben. He whirled and raged at him. Reuben shot for the heart, but the bear didn't slow its attack. Reuben leaped from the small sapling, hit the ground, and rolled as the bear's leg fur brushed his face.

The sound of Scrawny firing the rifle scared him more than the bear. He put everything he had into his next roll hoping it would take him to the trunk of a large tree. It did.

"Don't shoot," Reuben yelled as he leaped for a low hanging tree limb and swung himself up just as the bear passed below him. The bear stopped with such sudden force its claws tore up chunks of dirt and flung them upward. Scrawny was shoving limbs into the fire, making flames flare up until the bear could spot him hanging from the limb.

Reuben balanced on the limb, took exacting aim, and fired his rifle as swiftly as he could manage. A tuff of hair on top of the bears head moved, the bear raised upward on his hind feet. The bear's huge, heavy body reared backward, his front paws reaching for Reuben balancing within easy reach of the razor-sharp claws. The bear's body didn't stop rearing. It toppled over backward and lay on the ground.

"Don't shoot! Stay where you are!" Reuben yelled without looking toward Scrawny or his fire. He needed his vision to be clear as he took careful aim at he bear's eye socket and pulled the trigger.

The bear made one last attempt to rise, rolled sideways, and clawed at the earth with all four feet kicking up dirt and small rooted plants.

Reuben waited on the tree limb until all the bear's movements stopped. He had learned the hard way how deceptive a wounded bear could be. He had to build a door because of that deceptiveness. Bears had a natural habit of not moving a muscle until their enemy was upon them, and then they exploded like a volcano.

Finally, he dropped to the ground, took his knife from the sheath, approached the bear from its backside, and kicked it with the toe of his boot. The bear didn't move. Still alert, he moved to its head, grabbed it by an ear and slit its throat in hopes its heart would beat long enough to bleed the animal. It made for better eating if the animal was bled, and he believed in eating what he killed.

When Reuben looked up, Mitch was still standing by the blazing fire cramming in wood as fast as he could manage. Reuben looked around just to make sure there wasn't wood or piles of dried vegetation near enough the fire to set flame to the entire forest.

"Don't just stand there feeding the fire. Come on over here and help me drag this thing into the light so we can see to skin it properly."

Mitch came to him.

"Grab his hind paws and I'll get his front ones."

Mitch reached down and grasped its leg behind baseball-glove sized paws. Its claws were well over two inches long and were as strong and sharply pointed as building nails. He imagined what one swipe of such deadly weapons could do to a man.

"You're really going to skin him?" Mitch asked as they inched the heavy bulk forward.

"Yeap. Not much that's warmer than a good bear hide during winter, and not even a fat coon has better tasting meat. Of course, it'll take us a couple of days to slice him up thin enough to dry into jerky over the fire. We'll have to work fast though, and as soon as its light, you'll have to go back to town and bring a fifty pound bag of salt."

"What? Why?"

"Have to soak the thin slices of meat in salt before we hang them over the fire. Like I said, we'll have to be fast for meat rots quick in July, not to mention blow-fly maggots. There will be swarms of blowflies by morning. Won't hurt the hide much, being we're working it, but I do hate to get maggots on my meat. Piles of little white worms crawling on what you're eating sort of turns a man's stomach."

Thoughts of blowflies and maggots crawling over meat did not appeal to Mitch. Nor did he want to waste time with a bear or buying salt when he needed to be finding the girl. Yet, he didn't want to tell this strange man about her.

"I don't have time to go into town," he said.

"If you don't have time to buy fifty pounds of salt, I won't have time to keep the mountain lion and bears off you. Do you realize what would have happened if I hadn't been here? You would have unloaded your clip into that bear and he'd still have killed you. You can't kill a wounded bear once you've got it mad."

"You killed it, didn't you?"

"Look how many shots it took, plus he came close to getting me. What if you had been in my place?"

Realization dawned on Mitch. He wasn't foolish enough to think he could have moved as quickly and accurately as Reuben Rivers. After all, the man had to be half Indian and the other half animal.

"I'll get the salt," he said grudgingly. "But you need to hunt the mountain lion down fast."

"Nope," Reuben said. "I don't have to hunt him down. He's smelling fresh blood right now and is watching us. Question is how hungry is he?"

Mitch grabbed up the rifle lying at his feet.

"Put that thing down before you accidentally shoot your foot off. And, for both our sakes, leave the shooting to me. Having to kill a wounded animal maddened by pain isn't much fun when you're my age. When I was younger, I didn't mind."

Mitch did lay his rifle down but his eyes kept riveting back to it.

"Does a government surveyor carry a sharp knife?"

"Of course I do, and how do you know I'm a surveyor?"

"I heard you tell Ball."

"I see."

"I don't."

"What?"

"Most surveyors I've ever come across carried a transit and chain with them. You're a long ways from your truck to be without your equipment. Might as well tell me what you're really up to."

Mitch couldn't make himself tell about the girl. She was private. "I always take a day or two for inspection of the area in hopes of finding a few blazed lines before I set up my equipment. Saves time."

"Humph," Reuben grunted without conviction. "See if you're strong enough to split the hide down the bear's stomach – only the hide. We don't want to jab a gut and contaminate the meat with fecal."

Mitch was surprised at the words the rugged, dirty man in buckskin used. He took out his knife and carefully tried to make a cut. It was like cutting through metal. "The hide is tougher than I thought."

"Most things are."

The mountain lion had not gone far considering the frightening noise that exploded near the man. He had seen such sticks before, heard the noise they made, seen the puffs of smoke that came from them along with the horrible smell they emitted.

He knew the smoking sticks could kill. Saw it just happen to the bear for he had not run all the way up the mountain before he took cover and stopped to watch his enemy.

The good smell was still rising from the man and he wanted more of the wonderful tasting meat, but the stick and the fire made him run away. All that remained for him was the hard tin plate that he alternately licked and sank his teeth into.

Yet, he was hesitant to return and attack because of the danger two men offered. If there had only been one man, he would have circled back on the rock and pounced. One man, even with fire and stick, wasn't unreasonably frightening, but two men were, especially when the big man gave off a foreboding odor that screamed out the need for caution. His instinctive warning hit and made the big cat slink into a sheltered spot where he could watch and wait for his chance.

Rising from the big man was also the smell of the bear's blood. It both attracted and repelled the mountain lion. He had been able to scent the pungent odor of the bear's anger and the scent excited him, made him restless with a need to fight, but the odor of death was equally as strong. It demanded respect.

It was nearing midnight by the time the bear was without skin and guts. The fire had burned low and the night sounds were becoming less noticeable. Soon the morning hours would come into their own and most all things would sleep, but not just yet.

"Put more wood on the fire," Reuben said.

"I used all I gathered."

"Then gather more."

Mitch hesitated to go into the shadows for more deadfall and yet he didn't want the fire to go out. "Why don't you go?" Mitch said rather sheepishly.

Reuben's grin made Mitch feel even more cowardly, but he was extremely tired and his mind and body longed for rest. Still, he dared not fall asleep without a roaring fire for protection.

Reuben Rivers made no comment as he sheathed his knife and lumbered into the woods without his gun.

Mitch moved to the fire and pretended to be busy picking up a few stray sticks as he listened for an animal to attack the blood-covered man. All he could hear was the snapping of limbs as Reuben broke them up for wood. Minutes later, Reuben returned dragging a tremendous load of deadfall behind him. He dumped it near the fire and turned to Mitch. "Here, work on that a while." His eyes took in Mitch's appearance. "Put your sleeping bag close to that fire, but not close enough for the sparks to land on it."

Mitch didn't comment.

"From here on out, you'll just be in my way so you might as well get some sleep," Reuben said over his shoulder.

Mitch shrugged, put deadfall on the fire, and went for his bedroll. He was up-tight, exhausted. Even though he didn't want to admit it, he was glad the smelly, mountain man had shown up. Without Reuben Rivers, he might be dead or horribly wounded. He certainly wouldn't be curling up in his sleeping bag ready to fall asleep.

Reuben was accustomed to spending nights without sleep. He worked when there was work to be done, and slept when the time was right. He could stay awake for extraordinary long periods of time and then could sleep equally as long. A man that lived alone didn't have use for a watch or a schedule. Nature took care of such things.

He remembered once when he was a boy he stayed awake for over thirty-six hours. His father had sold him when he was ten years old to a man who lived in the flat land. His dad owed Jay Richardson money and was overly willing to trade his son for the debt.

He was a big lad even at ten and Richardson expected him to do the work of two men. Reuben stuck it out for a year before he realized his father's debts were not his. Being inclined to always tell the bold-faced truth, he told Richardson he would not do another minutes work for him and intended leaving immediately. If his father still owed him money, then it was up to his father to pay it.

Richardson yanked off his belt and commenced whipping the hide off the rebellious Reuben. Not only was it painful, but mortifying to Reuben's pride. Reuben had developed a strong sense of what was right and what was not from a very early age, and he had no inclination to alter his judgments.

Unexpectedly to Richardson, the young Reuben grabbed the belt and yanked it out of Richardson's hands. Reuben held onto the end of the belt and swung with all his eleven-year-old force, which was considerable. The over-large buckle struck Richardson on the side of the head with a solid thunk and felled him like a poled oxen. Reuben tossed the belt on top of Richardson and left, wondering why one person thought he had the right to brutalize another.

As he walked away from Richardson, he promised himself he would never be whipped again, nor would he be owned by another. Freedom was a God-given right and he was prepared to accept it.

It seemed Richardson had different ideas once he regained consciousness. He hired several men to go after Reuben with the intent of having him arrested or worse. He wanted him back dead or alive.

They had bloodhounds and were on horseback while Reuben ran on foot, but he had a head start. He also had his mother's Cherokee blood pumping through his veins and a strong sense of vengeance. It took all of three days to outsmart dogs and men, but outsmart them he did.

He never heard hide nor hair from Jay Richardson again. Didn't expect he ever would, but if he did, the now ancient man would regret it. In the old-time, enduring mountain tradition, Reuben Rivers never forgot an injustice or a kindness.

Reuben folded the bear hide to enable him to carry it easier. The rough textured hair felt good to his hands, but he wished the hair was winter-thick instead of thinned by summer's heat. Still, it would help keep the girl warm during winter-cold although it would not be nearly enough. Humpback Mountain was known as a savage deep freeze with winds that destroyed what little vegetation the warmer months had managed to bestow along with any hope of allowing the sun's warmth to penetrate the rocky mountain terrain.

He grunted as he thought about the girl's situation. She had to have a good reason for living the way she did. He'd find out what it was once he was finished here. He hefted the weight of the wet hide and carried it to a large rock and then spread it out to drain blood and fluid from it until morning when he would prepare the brains to work into the hide. The curing process would take a long while if he wanted the hide to remain soft instead of stiff and hard to use. He figured the girl deserved a soft hide. If his instincts toward her were holding true, she hadn't known much that was soft in her young life.

Reuben glanced at Scrawny snuggled near the fire. He was sound asleep but still had a frown on his face. Like most men, Scrawny was softened-up by modern gadgets. He was not used to living with things nature provided. He knew just enough about animals and the land for them to be a danger to him. It reverted back to the old truism that a little knowledge was a dangerous thing, more so than no knowledge.

Yet, ignorance and stupidity could not be cured rapidly. Nor could good advice be given to a man when he did not want it. It would take some time for Scrawny to settle the things that haunted his insides. When that happened, he might turn out to be a decent man.

But right now, something wasn't adding up about Scrawny. He might be a surveyor but he wasn't camping here in that capacity, nor did he fry-up more meat than three men his size could eat without a mighty good reason. Reuben saw the amount of grease in the frying pan before Scrawny dumped it into the fire. He also saw the remainder of meat in the waxed paper. Scrawny planned on baiting the cat, but not for the twenty-five dollars Ball had offered him for the hide. Scrawny had another reason for being where he was.

Reuben's eyes narrowed as he studied Mitch. Could he be after the girl? Was this the man she was running from? He needed to think on this one a while and there was no better thought-inducer than work. He went back to the bear he had hanging upside down on a strong sapling, sat down on a rock where he had piled its innards, and started the process of stripping fat from the guts. Bear fat rendered oily lard that was almost as good as hog fat, and it was even more flavorful. Thing was, he'd need a large container for rendering the lard plus several containers to store the lard in. The bear's bladder could serve as one container, but would hold only a drop in the bucket to what he needed. He'd have to get Scrawny to bring back a rendering canner and containers along with salt.

While he worked, Reuben allowed his mind to drift backward remembering his first encounter with a bear. It was a year or so after he'd left Richardson behind. He had taken up with a farmer who allowed him to sleep in his hayloft in return for work. There was no money involved but Reuben always had a full belly, for the farmer's wife could cook like an angel from heaven.

Reuben had traveled with the farmer to another farmer's house where he was buying a new variety of seed corn for next year's planting. The man had a small, two hundred pound bear chained to a large stake driven into the hard ground.

While the two farmers were discussing their dealings, Reuben was drawn to the bear. He reached in his britches pocket and pulled out a hand full of chinquapins. The bear reacted instantly by grabbing them and eating them hungrily. Reuben gave him another handful and then another.

In grateful appreciation, the bear became overly friendly and placed its paw on Reuben's shoulder. Delighted at the animal's show of affection, Reuben gave it all the chinquapins he had and the bear gratefully placed its other paw on Reuben's other shoulder. When no more chinquapins were presented, the bear clung to Reuben's shoulders and placed both hind feet on Reuben's knees.

It didn't take Reuben long to realize that bear-hugs were not the most gentle form of persuasion. Fearful of any sudden movements, Reuben eased backward with the bear still attached until he and the bear had reached the end of the chain, then he gave a sudden and powerful spring backward, tearing himself loose from the bear.

Reuben considered himself lucky to escape unharmed even if he did lose his clothes to the bear's claws. He had to find himself a long pole to retrieve his torn clothing from the enraged bear who did not like losing his newly found playtoy and chinquapin supplier.

That had been a good number of years in the past, a time when folks didn't think a thing about keeping pet bears around the house. When he was a few years older, and had built himself a not so substantial lean-to but a solid corncrib and barn, he had gotten himself a pet bear.

Now, that was some pet, worth the effort of capturing it. Naturally, he was a bit reckless and totally fearless back then. He considered himself as tough, everlasting, and invincible as the Blue Ridge Mountains themselves. Reuben believed that a man should take on the personality of his surroundings if he was to survive. Reuben became rock-hard and totally independent. Time might erode Reuben Rivers but nothing was going to change him.

It was in the Fall of the year, right after the timber had changed colors but not yet dropped leaves, that he saw bear "sign". The sign beckoned and he followed it to a tall cliff near the summit of one of the highest and most inaccessible peaks in the Blue Ridge range. A place very similar to the hump on top of Humpback Mountain.

Once he had reached the peak, he found himself to be greatly exhausted from working his way up through tangled vines, laurel hells, and over huge rock formations. Plus, the sign he saw appeared to be several days old. It wouldn't matter much if he stretched out under a shelving of rock and rested himself for a minute or two. He hadn't planned on falling asleep, but that was what he did. When he awoke, he heard grunts and the breaking of brush. He rose from his resting place and climbed up over the shelving rock to get a better view of the bear. It had found a late crop of huckleberries and was gorging on them.

Reuben had with him a gun plus a tomahawk, but he didn't have time for a thought to escape him much less time to aim and fire his gun. What he hadn't realized when he climbed on top of the shelving rock was that he had gotten between the mother bear and her cub.

The mother bear was a black blur as she charged him. The rock saved him. He instinctively stepped backward and fell off the rock, his gun gripped in one hand and his tomahawk in the other. He rolled backward taking what shelter he could from beneath the shelving rock where he had napped, but the bear, equally fast, was filled with righteous fury. Her beady eyes were red with rage and her violent roars caused froth to dribble from her mouth in long streams as she tumbled off the rock and her powerful front paws reached for Reuben.

She was too close for him to lift the gun and fire, so he swung with the tomahawk, slicing one of her paws. She drew her paw back for a moment, but then came at him again, this time with an even greater inducement from her pain. She swung two inch, razor sharp claws at his face as he tumbled sideways underneath the confining rock, lifted the gun without taking aim and fired.

It was then he discovered what an injured mother bear could do. Blinded by pain, she ripped off a portion of the shelving rock giving Reuben a precious second of time. He gripped his gun and tomahawk and leaped sideways, dropped, and rolled down a twenty-foot cliff to land in a clump of mountain ivy bushes.

The bear wasn't giving up that easily. She rolled down the cliff right behind him like a tumbling rock ready to smash and kill. Fortunately, for Reuben, her weight took her past the ivy thicket to land below him. He cocked his gun and took careful aim at the back of her head where her skull ended and her massive neck began. The impact jerked her and caused her to tumble another ten feet, which again saved his life.

Her poor eyesight kept him hidden in the ivy thicket as she attacked everything within range, tearing rocks out of the ground as though they were turnips. Whole ivy roots flew into the air as she gouged and ripped with all four paws. Her powerful legs worked like firing pistons. It was her unstoppable rage, in her effort to kill him, which took her all the way down the steep, rocky, one hundred foot drop. She lay at the bottom still fighting with each dying breath.

Reuben climbed back up the cliff, found the baby bear clutching a small sapling it had climbed. He retrieved the baby bear, took it home, and fastened it in the corncrib before he returned to skin and carry the bear meat home on a quickly constructed travois.

He had slept with that bear cub all winter long and stayed toasty warm, but alas, all huge wild animals become dangerous when there no longer remains a fear of humans in them. With time, the bear had grown big and mean. Hating to butcher his pet, he ended up selling him to a man who was working on a circus act. He never heard from bear or man again. He still wondered whatever happened to his pet bear. Most likely it had the man for a snack one dark night.

When Reuben had finished stripping fat, he carried the guts a long ways into the woods in the opposite direction of the girl's cave and dumped them. He didn't want the cat to be hungry when dawn broke and the girl came out of her cave.

🕊

By the time he returned, Mitch was waking up and placing more deadfall on the fire.

"Where've you been?" Mitch asked.

"Dumping guts."

Mitch frowned.

"Figured I might as well take food to the mountain lion rather than have him come after it."

Mitch could not believe what he heard. "You're deliberately feeding it?"

"It's better for me to feed it than have it eat you on your way to the truck. You still smell like fried meat and dried blood."

"You smell the same. Why didn't it attack you?"

"I'm not young and tender."

Somehow, Mitch felt insulted.

"Pull out your frying pan and let's have some of that hamburger you were baiting the mountain lion with."

"You're willing to fry more meat after last night?" Mitch's voice sounded with disbelief.

"I'm hungry." Reuben noted Scrawny did not deny he was baiting the mountain lion.

"But the mountain lion?"

"I just told you I fed it."

Mitch wasn't sure if he was joking or serious, but he got out his frying pan.

"Hate to waste good hamburger meat and you might as well get rid of it while it's getting daylight."

"What about the bears?"

"What about them?"

"Won't the smell draw bears as well as the cat?"

"Isn't that what you want? Another bear or two to salt down?"

Mitch tried to hide his flare of anger.

"One thing's for certain," Reuben continued. "You need to remember when you set a trap for wild animals, make sure you're not in the middle of it."

"But . . . "

"Fry the hamburger meat. You need to get rid of it as fast as possible."

Mitch dumped the rest of the hamburger meat in the pan and put it over the fire, dumped in some salt and pepper, and then took out his coffee pot, filled it with water and coffee, and hung it over the fire on the tripod of metal wiring. He could feel Reuben River's eyes watching him even when Reuben's back was turned.

"Why is she running from you?" Reuben asked suddenly.

"What are you talking about?" Mitch was too quick in replying.

"You know."

"Know what?"

Reuben turned enough to see his face in the firelight. "She doesn't belong to you. She's a wild thing. Wild and free."

"I don't know what you're talking about," Mitch denied while wondering how Reuben might know about the girl.

"I think you do."

"Well, I don't."

"Truth always serves the better purpose. Lie to a man that's trying to help you and most likely you'll end up regretting it." Reuben told him firmly.

Mitch doubted that. Nor was he about to tell this strange man anything about the girl, or even admit there was one.

Reuben allowed several minutes of silence to pass. "Ever do any tracking?" He asked Mitch.

"I'm a surveyor."

"Does that mean no?"

"It means no to tracking, but I can find a cut line or a marked tree in my sleep."

"I'm good at tracking," Reuben continued without bragging. "I can read tracks easier than most men can read a book."

"So?"

"So, I know about nature and about the things that surround me."

Was that how he knew about the girl? He had come upon her tracks while tracking the mountain lion for Ball. Still, Mitch refused to talk about her to this hairy savage.

"I can waste a few hours in backtracking her or I can stay right here and busy myself with bear jerky while waiting on the mountain lion to show up. Until the cat's dead, my time is best spent here instead of finding out where the girl came from and why."

"Then spend your time here."

"She doesn't belong to you," Reuben repeated.

Mitch wanted to tell him the girl didn't belong to him either, but that would be admitting the girl existed. "Why don't you spill out what nature and your track reading told you?" Mitch countered.

"I can do that," Reuben said. "The tracks told me the mountain lion was after the girl. It came across her fresh tracks and was following behind her. Fortunately, for her, Ball's calves got the cat's attention, but Ball has now brought the cows to home pasture where the cat can't get to them as easily. That leaves the mountain lion ready to go for the girl."

Mitch felt himself tense-up at what Reuben told him. It put a cold knot of fear in his gut to know the mountain lion really was stalking the girl. "Ball hired you to kill it. Why don't you do your job?" he demanded.

"I was doing just that until you intervened," Reuben told him in a soft, noncommittal tone.

Mitch stirred the chunks of hamburger around in the pan and moved the coffee pot to a cooler spot. He had to know more. "What else did you read from the tracks?"

Reuben hacked the huge front shoulder and leg from the bear's carcass and carried it to the fire. He expertly sliced knife-blade-thin slices of meat from the shoulder, placing them on the rocks that surrounded the fire.

"Don't you need to cook that meat good and hot to kill the parasites?" Mitch asked.

"Yeah, I intend to do that, sooner or later," he said as he laid another piece down and answered Scrawny's first question. "The girl was scared and running fast, but not from the cat. Although she knew the cat was in the vicinity, she didn't seem to know it was tracking her."

"If there was a girl, how would she know about the mountain lion?"

"She saw its tracks crossing hers. Why was she running from you and why are you after her?" Reuben stopped what he was doing and looked Mitch in the eyes.

"I know what winters are like on Humpback Mountain. A grown man with a house and plenty of firewood would have difficulty surviving a winter up there." Mitch took his remaining tin plate from his pack and placed half the meat in it. He nodded toward the frying pan, indicating for Reuben to take the rest.

Reuben picked up the hot handle without even wincing and stabbed chunks of meat with his knife as Mitch observed the thick calluses on his huge hands. One thing Mitch had to acknowledge was that Reuben Rivers was work-honed to a fine edge and tough as a man ever became.

"Is she your wife?" Reuben asked, although he knew the girl belonged to no man. Such a wild thing could never be owned, especially by someone like Scrawny.

"No, she's not anyone's wife. As for me, I'm no longer a married man," Mitch answered and remembered Helen, the ex-wife who had done everything but castrate him. He hadn't thought about her in a long while, and hoped he never thought about her again. Their marriage had been a mistake, a big mistake on his part. Helen hadn't suffered so badly.

"What was your wife's name?"

"Helen," he said. "She and most everything I once owned are in Virginia."

"What's the girl's name?"

Mitch didn't answer.

"Let's stop playing *I'll never tell* games with each other. I've seen the girl and know that you and the mountain lion both are after her. Fact is, if I don't kill the mountain lion soon, you won't need to worry about the girl surviving winter."

"I intend to kill the mountain lion," Mitch said boldly as he thought of Don Donavan and his refusal to admit there was a girl when they both knew different. It was foolishness.

Reuben didn't comment on the improbability of Mitch killing the big cat, even though he probably should. Instead he asked, "And then what? Will she return to you? Can you make her stay with you or will she run to some other place and hide?"

Mitch observed the man across the fire from him. His appearance was such a foreboding force it would make the bravest woman run for safety. Plus, his smell was worse than his appearance. Reuben Rivers smelled almost as bad as the girl did when he found her snake-bitten. In Mitch's book, such a man could not be trusted.

Mitch feared the girl would not be safe with him around. Reuben Rivers had lived alone too long and had way too much animal instinct about him, while Raven was young and naïve, a child in all reality, even if she didn't look like a child.

"You talk rather educated considering the way you look," Mitch told him not caring if he insulted the dirty mountain man.

Reuben took his knife from its sheath, went to a nearby tree, and cut a slice of the bark. He bent the bark until it formed a shallow dip. He returned to the fire, poured hot coffee into the dip, and sipped the hot liquid gratefully.

"What does education have to do with the way I look?"

"The more educated people are the cleaner they are."

"You're saying all people who live close to the earth, like the girl and I do, are stupid?"

That remark irritated Mitch. "I didn't say that."

Reuben Rivers allowed his gaze to move over Mitch from head to toe before he spoke.

"I went to school a couple of years but mostly I educated myself." He told it as a fact, no bragging, only fact. "I don't and never have considered myself unclean. Everybody, human or otherwise, has an odor and they're not unclean because of it."

"But . . . " Mitch began and then stopped.

"To you, my appearance indicates I'm nothing more than a beggar."

"Yes," Mitch admitted without hesitation or self-consciousness. He wasn't trying to win a friendship.

"I live my life the way I choose to live it, just as that girl does. "

Mitch sensed the man's protective, and yet puzzling, attitude toward the girl and allowed himself to give in, slightly. "I'm not sure of anything where the girl is concerned, except she's young and needs help."

"Why don't you know anything about her?"

"She didn't talk to me."

"What's her story?"

"I found her snake-bit and almost unconscious. I washed her, fed her, and gave her my clothes. The next thing I knew, she was gone."

Reuben turned cold black eyes on him. "I see. Once she was clean you found her attractive," he stated. "Did anything unworthy happen while she was snake-bit and almost unconscious?"

Irritation flooded Mitch. How dare he imply he would take advantage of a sick or an unconscious girl? "I'm an honorable man."

"Honorable men have passions. Take religions and the men who call themselves Holy Men. When they are denied sex, they become fixated with it."

Mitch knew such a man as Reuben Rivers surely had been denied sex all his life. "Are you admitting you are low-down and worthless enough to take advantage in such a position?"

Reuben let the accusation go right over his head. "I've known men that were, clean, sweet-smelling men who would."

"I'm not one of those men," he noted that Reuben hadn't rebuked the accusation.

Reuben rubbed the blade of his knife with his fingers, removing grease along with bits of meat, before he sheathed it.

"Time you headed into town for salt and supplies. Get a bag of salt, a large canner, and all the metal containers this will buy." He handed ten dollars to Mitch.

Mitch had no idea how he produced the money or where he kept it. The buckskin clothes were tight and without pockets. He hadn't touched his boots. He surely had a hidden pocket near his belt or the knife sheath.

"You planning on taking bear meat and oil back to your place?"

"Nope."

"No?"

"As you already know, for a person to survive winter on the Big Hump, it'll take a lot of supplies and more than one bear skin."

Anger flashed through Mitch. "You can't be serious. You can't help her stay on that mountain. It would be suicidal."

"What she chooses to do is her choice, not yours. Even a surveyor should have enough brains to know that. Now, go while the mountain lion is still full of bear guts."

🕊

Reuben watched as Mitch carefully packed up his supplies, along with the coffee pot and brown bag of coffee, and placed everything in his backpack as though he was leaving permanently or that he was sure Reuben would steal anything left behind.

Reuben was well acquainted with such actions although they were foolish and untrue. Didn't folks know that poor men would no longer be poor if they took things that didn't belong to them?

Rich men needed watching. They had an internal malfunctioning way of justifying the taking of every single thing they wanted whether it belonged to them or not.

Men like Jay Richardson and George J. Ball lived by a different set of rules than most good Christian folks. *Do unto others before they do unto you* fit their mind set, or so Reuben had decided years before when he was being sold from man to man. His convictions about rich men hadn't altered much during the years, nor had much of anything else.

Reuben believed in both God and the Devil, plus his beliefs covered a lot more than those two beliefs. He believed in the law of nature as well as in the law of man. Man was fallible when nature was not. Watch nature and you watched life as it was meant to happen. Watch man and most of the time you would get some jolly good amusement along with a demonstration of pure stupidity.

Mitch hefted the heavy backpack on his back and set his jaws hard. Obviously, he was building his determination not to show any fear of the mountain lion as he started off into the dim morning light.

"Remember," Reuben called after him. "Keep your own eyes open while you are shooting it between the eyes, and don't wound an animal before you kill it."

Mitch kept moving forward without giving sign that he heard.

Chapter 7

Raven woke with a feeling of being watched even though she was inside the cave. She opened her eyelids a slit and looked about. The cave was dark for the fire had died down, giving off only a small amount of light from the hot coals. Dog was snuggled beside her. He lifted his head sensing she was awake.

She saw nothing. Not even a rat or a squirrel had entered through a crack in the rocks or a dug hole. She tossed Don Donavan's quilt aside and put more wood on the fire even though it would have to die down before she could get through the entrance. She was desperate to get the strange chill that had penetrated her flesh out of her bones. For some reason, the quilts had not kept her warm enough during the long and lonely night. She kept having strange dreams, dreams that she could not understand but that left her terribly afraid.

This cave certainly was different from the one she had been born in. Aggie's cave had held the fire's warmth while this one let in the wind and was as foreboding as a snakes den. Its darkness was not a comfort but a black prison. Perhaps today she should search for a better cave. She had the gun Aggie stole from the hunter. She would kill the mountain lion if it was foolish enough to attack her and Dog while they were searching for a better cave and a water supply. Yes, that's exactly what she would do today – find what she needed. That was surely the reason for the strange sensations that had taken hold of her body and her mind.

She fed Dog before she pounded more corn into a rough meal, mixed it with water, and fried it in a pan over the fire she had built up. Her body was craving milk and berries. She remembered the cattle she had come across. Maybe she could find a way to get to them and get a little milk without having to fight with the bull. Even better, maybe she could find a springhouse where the farmer stored milk. She could replace what milk she borrowed from the jug with water and no one would know she had taken a drop. The farmer owed her nothing, but just enough milk to keep her alive would be no harm. In return for the milk, she would surely find something to do for the farmer and the cows that no one would ever know about. Just a little compensation between her and God.

Aggie had read the Bible to her and explained about God in the connection of wrong and right. Aggie had explained that God saw all and understood all. *"Revenge is mine," sayeth God.* Raven certainly didn't want to get on the wrong side of a spirit that powerful.

As for berries, raspberries, dewberries, and blackberries they would be ripening soon. She could pick and dry all she needed if she could find briars in this strange world she had traveled into. Perhaps she would have to leave the mountain and search for fallow, overgrown fields. Then, later in the fall, would come the winter apples, plus searching the harvested fields where farmers had left smatterings of their crops. Really, she had nothing to worry about. Her back was straight and her legs strong. Besides, she had only herself and Dog to feed. If necessary, she would go back to Sodom to get more dog food from Pete Jenkins, Cade Williams, or Evert Wilson.

She carefully banked her fire with ashes. Even though the man had left her matches, she could not afford to be wasteful, not even with one match – because she hadn't gotten used to the flint and steel. When she was satisfied with the fire, she crawled through the narrow entry and pushed the large rocks from the cave opening. Much as Aggie always did of a morning, she went to a rock outcropping where she could observe her surroundings, including the wooded area at the base of the mountain and the river that meandered way below her perch.

The hair on the big black's back lifted and a faint growl sounded. Instantly, she whirled and rushed back inside the cave to get the gun. How could she have gone outside and forgotten to take the gun when she had remembered to bank the fire and pushed the rocks away. She shouldn't have forgotten the gun!

She grabbed the gun plus extra shotgun shells and hurried back outside. Dog hadn't followed her back inside the cave and she was near panicking for fear he would go after the mountain lion before she got back to him. But he was standing where she had left him, his hackles still up with his stub of a tail wagging.

When she inspected what had his attention, she saw that an ant-size image of a man was at the base of the mountain near the woods. He had a hot bed of coals that shimmered the air with heat waves. His appearance was strange enough, but his appearance wasn't what had her attention. It was the huge shape of skinned flesh hanging from a tree limb that had her transfixed.

Had the man killed one of the cows? If so, what was he doing with it now, and so many miles away from where the cattle ranged? He had to be mighty strong to carry a carcass that size that far. She tried to bring to mind the beginning of cold weather when the men in Sodom killed hogs. Aggie had explained to her about the hog-killing process. And once Lu had stolen a whole ham from Cade Williams. They had eaten good for a while, even if Aggie had been terrified the aroma of cooking ham would get them caught.

But the problem was that now wasn't cold weather and the meat wouldn't keep, especially that much meat. Yet, the man was busy doing something to the carcass. She eased closer to the edge of the rocks, lay flat on her belly and looked over the rocky edge, squinting her eyes in an effort to see more clearly.

Dog whined and lifted his nose to catch the mouth-watering scents on the wind. His little stub tail was moving faster.

The man had a long thin stick and was spearing small pieces of meat on it. He left the carcass and crossed to his fire where he placed the stick in the prongs of two larger forked sticks driven on each side of his fire. Why, he was cooking the meat without a frying pan. She had seen Aggie roast vegetables in such a manner.

It wasn't long until the wonderful aroma oozed up the mountain and reached her and Dog's nostrils with a powerful and devastating force. It was enough to drive both of them crazy with hunger. Dog whined again, his body twitching in his need to rush down the mountain where he could reach the cooking meat.

"Stay," she ordered the big black, knowing full well how tempting it was for him not to obey. Dog food and corn pone wasn't enough to satisfy either of them, but what could they do? How could they get some of that meat?

She forced her gaze to leave the meat-laden stick and observed the man. He was different in dress and appearance than any man she had seen before. He had a bushy head of long, dark hair, plus an even darker face covered with beard. She wondered about that beard. Why was it so long and thick? She had seen short stubby beard before but never the likes of his. He was also dressed different from the men of Sodom, different from the clothes she was wearing. She also judged him to be bigger than most men, about the size of the carcass hanging in the tree, she estimated. Could man and animal somehow cross breed with each other and produce the man-thing she was observing?

She tried to recall all the books Aggie had insisted she read as well as the stories Aggie told her while sheltered in the cave during long winters. There were stories of half-men and half-animals She recalled seeing a picture of men with horses bodies with the heads and upper bodies of men. There were also pictures of part billy goats and part men, men who could change into wolves or increase in size when angered. Werewolves were what Aggie called the wolf-men, and then there were vampires – men that would sink their large teeth into the throat of humans and animals and suck their blood to the very last drop.

Raven couldn't control the shudder that spread over her body. It left her insides icy cold with a different sort of fear. What kind of place was this, anyway? A place where July felt like October, mountain lions stalked her tracks, and men and animals had crossed with each other. No wonder Aggie refused to leave their mountain. Aggie must have known what existed in the outer world.

She scooted backward toward the cave, her heart pounding. She couldn't hunt for water, food, or even a better cave while such a thing was near by. He was even more fearful and dangerous than the mountain lion. His powers weren't just physical; his were mental as well, neither human nor animal. He couldn't be the reincarnation of God, but could he be the Devil Aggie always talked about? Had she done something terribly wrong that had drawn him to come after her?

She didn't know what to do next. She certainly couldn't leave the mountain while the man-thing was there. Hopefully, once he had cooked and eaten the meat, he would go back where he came from – unless as she feared, he really was after her.

The big black didn't want to return to the cave. He wanted cooked meat no matter what the price he would have to pay for it. Raven clutched the flesh around his neck, dragged him into the cave, and then rolled the rocks in place. She could hide the rest of the day and night. She had that much water left in her jug.

The mountain lion was nervous, his excitement level stretched tight. Anger, puzzlement, and confusion were surging through him, making his natural instincts behave abnormally. Used to being king of his domain, with all other animals scattering when he approached, he was bewildered at having the man and fire near. His only enemies were men and dogs and the occasional dreaded fire sticks. Men were supposed to chase him instead of building little fires and feeding him bear-guts.

Here at this strange place was the hungry temptation of the girl that still stunk of being a human, a big dog that wasn't chasing him, two men that put irresistible smells into the wind, and then one shot at him with his fire stick. Another man dumped bear guts where he could find and eat it. Not something he usually ate, but food nonetheless.

He was lying in the rocks, where he could observe the men while licking guts and heart and liver juice off his fur. He watched one man with a fire stick leave. Instinct urged him to follow and kill, but he was not hungry, nor had he finished cleaning himself. Had his belly been empty, he would not have feared one man even if he did carry a fire stick.

Once he had finished his grooming, he became aware of the remaining man's behavior. He left the bear carcass and fire behind and ran through the woods to the bottom of the mountain. There he built another fire and piled much deadfall on it.

The mountain lion was approaching the carcass, belly close the ground in his natural stalk position, feeling the faintest rumbles of hungry, when the man returned.

Instinct urged him to spring from his stalking crouch, kill his enemy, and claim the carcass, but a different instinct caused him to back off and hunker down in the shadows of the woods where the man could not see him.

His slitted, yellow eyes watched as the man lowered the carcass onto his shoulder, bent under the weight, but still carried it away. It was always a good time to attack when the enemy was occupied, yet an unusual fear stopped him. He followed the man, easing through the woods in a half-crouch, keeping the man and carcass in view.

When the man stopped at the new fire and hung the carcass from a tree limb, he circled into the rocks and found a sheltered place to lie down and remain watching. He heard the girl and dog rolling rocks and coming out of the cave, but his interest in them wasn't great. It was the cooking meat that had him confused and nervous. He wanted to attack, and yet his instinct warned him against showing himself during the bright light of day.

His nose told him the dog and girl were near, his ears pricked around as he listened to their movements, but his interest in them was at low ebb. Instinct warned him that if the dog started chasing him, the man would join in. Right now he felt rather lazy and didn't want to be chased. The past few days had pampered him with more food than he was accustomed to eating and it had made him push some of his basic instincts aside for the time being. Easy access to food had produced a greedy cat; one whose body didn't require the need to be fed, but gave him a wanting for gluttony.

His nose twitched again; his tongue licked the skin around his mouth and sniffed his front paws for signs of bear fluids to lick off, but found none. He flexed his paws, extending and then retracting his claws. Smells of cooking meat made his urge to kill and eat grow stronger with every breath he took.

He heard the girl and dog go back inside the cave and roll rocks at the entrance. He eased to his feet, his tail twitching, and slunk toward the man, the carcass, and the cooking meat. When he was within twenty yards, he dropped to his belly, his beady eyes taking everything in much like a man analyzing the set-up for his next victim.

The man was alert, his eyes searching the wooded area, the rocks, and the brush that surrounded him. His hands were slicing meat, but the fire stick was under his arm. He stopped slicing and looked toward the rocks where the cat was hiding.

The cat's tail stopped its jerking. Not one muscle in his body twitched for he knew that the man was stalking him, and this created caution. A survival type of fear surged through the mountain lion, one that had aided him to reach a ripe old age. He knew there was safer prey to be hunted and killed than the man.

Once the man had gone back to slicing meat, the big cat raised to his feet and slunk from the rocks into the woods. He focused on the images of tender calves that offered him no resistance and caused him no harm during this time of plenty.

The cattle were not in the river bottom, only the fading odor left by their sign remained for the cat to find. Instantly, he was angry at the missing cattle, angry at every single thing that slowed him down from killing his prey, carrying it back to his lair and curling up with his prize.

He scratched sticks, grass, and roots into a pile, hunched his body slightly, set his legs, cocked his tail, and urinated backward on the pile of scratch. Marking his territory so that man and animal alike knew he dominated all.

He bounded off through the grass, hot in pursuit of the cattle. He hadn't gone far, hadn't even reached the woods, when something sprang up almost beneath his feet. It was a young fawn still spotted and wide-eyed with fright. His front legs shot out and his claws grabbed the fawn, flipping it in mid-air. It bleated from pain and terror but there was no saving grace for the helpless baby, even if his mother had been near by. Huge teeth sank to the bone in the back of its neck. The baby deer stopped bleating. Its body quivered in throws of death.

The mountain lion held it clamped tight without movement for a few moments longer, stood up, and disappeared into the woods with the fawn's limp body dangling in its jaws.

Chapter 8

Irritation, if not anger, was building in Mitch much faster than he was walking, and he was close to a run. Nothing was going according to his plan, which was to find the girl – and then what, convince her he only wanted to help her? He really did want to help her but the question was in what way? Could it be he really did want her for himself?

Yes, he finally admitted, in a way, but not as a captured wild animal. He wanted to tame her, domesticate her, much as a wild horse was captured and trained to carry a pack-burden for man. He wanted that, but he wanted more too.

More what? Came the nagging voice of reason. Was he willing to marry her, trust she won't run away when the mood strikes her, or even slit his throat during the night? Hadn't he learned enough with Helen? Marriage wasn't all it was cracked-up to be. Some people simply weren't suited for each other.

"Face the truth, Mitch Kenilworth," he told himself harshly. "The wild girl has your gonads pumping hot juice and you're willing to do anything, absolutely anything, to cool them off."

Just as soon as he had that thought, he tried to deny it. It wasn't sex driving him. It was the girl and her pitiful circumstance. And yes, he wanted to know her life story, not from Iva Dean Grearity Stewart, but from the girl. If, indeed, she was the girl Iva Dean told him about, she might be in luck. If she was the right girl then she would be in financial heaven. She would never have to live in a cave like a wild animal and scavenge for food ever again.

As for Reuben Rivers, he was beginning to form a powerful dislike for the overbearing, ragged, perfect example of a stereotyped throwback of a mountain man. Who was he anyway? A Daniel Boone wanna-be? A legend in his own mind? A man with a cross-wired brain, or possibly a criminal in hiding?

Once Mitch reached town, along with acquiring salt, he might acquire information on this Reuben Rivers fellow. In Mitch's estimation, he didn't appear to be the trustworthy sort and was way too much of a know-it-all for Mitch's liking.

Darkness was fading from the woods as the sky turned from gun-metal gray to morning silver. There wasn't enough light for the trees to cast shadows, but enough for him to make out the tree bark and leaves he was walking through.

He breathed easier. The mountain lion hadn't attacked him and most likely wouldn't in the light of day. Yet, he had heard horror stories of mountain lions doing unexpected and uncharacteristic things, such as attacking men while they rode their bicycles, or killing and dragging off women and children for no apparent reason when there was plenty of game available. Most likely those cats were old, without speed, claws, or good teeth. Was this also the case of the Humpback Mountain cat? He should have asked the know-it-all Reuben Rivers more about the cat's condition. His stomach tightened at the thought of returning back to that man, but he would. It was the only way he knew to save the girl from a sure and painful death. He gritted his teeth as he picked up speed. It would help if he knew where she was right now.

A twig nearby snapped. He whirled around and lifted his gun, held his breath to enable him to hear better. Nothing! Even the morning birds were silent – a bad sign. He looked around trying to find a place to take a stand against an attack. There was a large maple tree near him. He moved until his back was against its trunk before he dared draw breath again. He searched the dim outlines of forest vegetation and then lifted his gaze to the trees. A mountain lion could hide anywhere without him seeing it. It could leap through the air and land on him before he could fire his gun – just as it had done earlier.

What had Reuben Rivers said: keep his own eyes open and shoot the cat between the eyes. Just how in Hades was a man supposed to do that when the animal was known to leap thirty feet in seconds? He recalled a mountain lion's impact when hitting its prey could flatten a man to the ground and render his weapon useless in the blinking of an eye.

He waited in silence for several minutes, straining his ears for the slightest sound. Nothing, not even the scuttle of a ground squirrel running through the leaves. Slowly, he eased downward, his back sliding against bark, picked up small pieces of deadfall and tossed the sticks into the surrounding brush. Still nothing! As the sun turned the silver sky rosy, he drew courage from greater visibility and cautiously left the tree to continue on his way.

Mitch's back felt so very naked as he eased through the woods and he found himself looking over his shoulder as often as he looked forward. He ran the last few yards to his truck knowing the cat was about to pounce, unlocked the door, and hurriedly climbed in. He breathed deep, ignoring the icy feeling in his chest and the rubbery feeling in his legs. Even a tingling kind of sensation was running over his flesh and bringing up goose bumps on his tense body. It was as though the mountain lion had been seconds away from attacking him.

He turned the key, cranked the engine to life, and drove away. What a wonderful feeling to be surrounded by protective metal.

The small town was civilization, lifetimes away from the silent ruggedness of Humpback Mountain, and the men sitting on the porch of the local feed and seed store were centuries away from Reuben Rivers. Although Mitch loved the rugged life, thus the job of surveyor, he had an appreciation for people and the security their unity brought, especially right now.

He parked and got out of the truck, amazed at how different in feeling secure felt than from feeling helpless. Had Raven ever felt secure? Was she afraid right now? What would she think if she could go into the store and buy a bottle of pop and a moon pie? She would surely be astounded at eating a cup of ice cream on a summer day, or sipping hot chocolate in the freezing cold of winter. Would she love wearing a pair of gloves, boots, even a warm coat and hat? Would she like perfume or scented soap and shampoo instead of always smelling of her own sweat mixed with dirt?

One of the men spat a stream of spit and tobacco juice off the porch, nodded toward Mitch, and said, "Mornin'."

"Good morning." Indeed, the man didn't realize just how good a morning it was to be able to sit and talk to friends without fear for your life.

"Store's not open yet," the man continued. "Seems to be runnin' a little late. You can sit with us a while. Might even take a notion to jaw, but you'll never be able to out-lie little James."

The man that must be little James gave the talker an evil look but didn't say a word.

Mitch sank down in a vacant chair. Jawing a while was a good idea. "Didn't realize I was this early," he said.

"What you in a hurry for?"

"Need salt and some other supplies."

"What for?" The man spat again and worked his chaw to the other jaw with his tongue.

What should he tell these men, if anything? He probably needed to talk to them if he wanted to know about Reuben Rivers. "I'm getting it for a man I met in the woods while surveying," he said. He couldn't get information from these men without getting them talking.

"Oh, yeah. You're the fellow the government sent in here to mark their lines. They pay you a right smart for trompin' through the woods?"

"A little."

"Wish I had my property line surveyed. I know the cornerstones my great granddaddy showed me. Would the government pay you to mark those lines while you're at it?"

"They will only pay me to mark boundaries for the forest service."

"That's the government for you. Willing to waste our tax money on their own stuff. Never willing to help out a taxpayer. Take, take, take that's all the government ever does," the man continued. "Only things sure in life is death and government taxes. Someday folks are liable to wise up to the government, but by then it will be too late. The government will own them down to their raggedity underwear."

"They've already wised up," another man said. "Trouble is the government is like God. You can't never reach out and get a hold on 'em. Government hot-shots hide behind law books. Change the rules whenever they want and then tell us we have to abide by those rules. Ask me, we've all been made into whores and the government is our pimps."

Mitch managed to force a grin but not the other men or little James. He narrowed his eyes and asked: "What does a man in the woods need salt for?"

This was a question Mitch could use for his own benefit. "For salting down bear meat."

"Bear meat? In July?"

"Reuben Rivers shot it when it attacked his camp last night." Mitch figured that was not only true enough, but enough information to divulge. "Said he always ate what he killed and needed salt to cure it with."

"Makes sense. No man can eat a whole bear at one time."

"Not even Reuben Rivers, and I've heard he eats a lot of bear meat."

"You know the man?" Mitch asked.

"Oh, yeah," several of them said at the same time. "Most everybody knows of him."

"Who is he, anyway? He appeared . . ." Mitch hesitated. "Rather strange."

"Hermit type," the spitting man said. "Throwback to his Indian heritage. Likes to live off the land all by himself. Surprised he didn't go all the way to the salt-pits in Saltville Virginia and carry himself a sack home."

"Couldn't," said little James. "Meat would rot before he got there and back."

The men ignored little James as they continued to talk.

"Best bear hunter ever was. Heard tell he once jumped on a bear's back and slit its throat with his knife when his gun jammed."

Mitch gave a disbelieving grin.

"It's the gospel truth," the spitting man added. "Bill Eller's boy saw the bear before Reuben skinned it.

Naturally, it had roughed up Reuben some, but nary much considering. Said he didn't have a choice in the matter. It was kill the bear or be kilt."

"Back a dozen or twenty years ago, Reuben Rivers was hell on wolves. Why there were so many around here a man couldn't have a flock of sheep or hardly a herd of cattle. Only good thing the government ever did was put a bounty on wolf hides."

"And the WPA," another man added with a chuckle.

"Don't pick on the WPA. My daddy worked for them during the depression."

"Is Reuben Rivers dangerous or a criminal?" Mitch asked.

"You're alive hain't you? And he's more of a legend than a criminal. Don't reckon he ever done anything illegal in his life."

"Run away from some man when he was a boy."

"That was Jay Richardson," the spitter said. "Wouldn't have been a crime to of killed that asshole."

The men grinned as though they shared some sort of secret.

"I take it Richardson was a mean man?" Mitch said.

"You might say that." The men nodded in agreement.

"Where were you surveying to meet up with Reuben Rivers?"

"I'm doing several of the national forests in this area. Where does Rivers live?" Mitch hedged. He didn't want to tell them anything about Humpback Mountain because of the girl.

"On White Top Mountain. Heard he built some sort of a cabin up there, right in the coldest and windiest spot. Don't reckon you could freeze that man to death."

"Heard he burrows himself in the snow like a dog. Sleeps that way and never gets cold."

"He sounds like some sort of wild animal," Mitch said the words that were running through his mind.

"You might call him that, wild."

Mitch didn't want to think what he was thinking. A wild man just might fit in with a wild girl. "Is he married? Does he have children?" The girl might be his child. He looked old enough to be her father.

"Never heard of him being married," one of the men said.

"Reckon all us men over fifteen has got children running around somewhere or other," Spitter said with a sly grin.

"Not you," another man said to Spitter. "Never seen a kid that danged ugly."

"If you did, you'd a probably thought they were yourn," Spitter shot back

"Hear about Reuben and that fancy city lawyer?" One of the men asked.

They shook their heads.

"This lawyer went up to White Top Mountain on some kind of sightseeing trip and he ended up at Reuben's cabin. Just like a no account lawyer, he started snoopin' around and spied a fur stretched on a board.

'What kind of fur is that?' the lawyer demanded.

'Mink,' said Reuben.

"Mink was the right kind of word for that city lawyer. 'Give you five dollars for it,' the city lawyer offered.

'Eight," said Reuben.

"The lawyer bought it an headed to town knowin' he could make a good profit off that mink fur. Now, it wasn't but a few day later until here come that city lawyer back.

'Reuben,' he said right mad like. 'You cheated me. The furrier said that was a weasel fur and it was worth only two dollars.'

"Ole Reuben looked him right in the eyes and kinda shook his head sad like. 'Surely a smart lawyer like you didn't let that fellow beat you outta that mink hide."

"Say?" Another man seemed to have a bright inspiration. "I bet George Ball hired Reuben to go after that mountain lion that's been killin' his cattle. Was that what he was doing?"

Mitch saw no way out of admitting that much truth. Ball would tell them anyway. He was just thankful that Ball didn't know about the girl, at least he hoped he didn't know.

"Ball did say he'd hired him when I asked permission to park my truck on his land."

"Ah, you're surveying Humpback Mountain. Best get it done in a hurry. Wouldn't want to be up there during a cold spell."

"Wouldn't want to be up there during any spell. I've seen hoar frost coating that mountain in July."

"Cold won't bother Reuben Rivers. It's might nigh that cold on White Top Mountain."

"No it hain't."

"I'd reckon it is."

"Wind don't blow up there like it does on the Hump."

"Trees grow leaning one-sided on White Top."

"Wind blows so hard trees can't grow a-tall on top of the Hump."

The lock clicked open on the door from the inside of the feed and seed. Mitch was somewhat relieved to stand up without listening to any more of the men's arguing or having to sit there and watch the continuous spitting. He now knew a little about Rivers and a little was enough. He wanted the man away from the girl.

Raven huddled in the cave with her heart pounding so hard the material of her shirt moved. She had never experienced this kind of fear before, not even as a child. This strange, unreasonable kind of fear made the image of her mother, Lu, return to her mind.

Lu was always unreasonably afraid, especially where men were concerned. Lu had rather have a dozen mountain lions surrounding her than to see one man. Even two dozen devil-spirits couldn't scare Lu as much as one harmless man could. It was Lu's unreasonable fear that ended up killing her, and Raven did not want to be possessed with unreasonable fear, or fear of any kind. She wanted to be strong in mind as well as in body. Strong enough to always take care of herself and Dog.

Suddenly, after all these years, Raven understood her mother's fear all too well. Fear when it was not called for was a very bad thing. Was her present fear called for? If that thing below was some kind of powerful devil-spirit, couldn't he come get her any time he chose?

"I'm being silly," she whispered to Dog and looked into his dark brown eyes to see if they contained fear. There was hunger not fear. The big black whined pitifully and licked his blocky mouth with a slobbering tongue. He was pleading for her to get him meat, or at least move the rocks and allow him out so he could go get it.

She reached out and stroked his velvety body. How could she make Dog understand the *wolf-man's* presence when even she didn't understand? She patted his huge, square head, got up from her fearful, huddled position and dipped from the dog food bag three times the amount of food she allowed the big black to eat. He wouldn't be as likely to disobey her and go after the meat if his belly was completely full.

While he ate, she removed one rock, crawled through the opening with her gun in hand, and rolled the rock back, leaving the big black inside. On her belly, she inched toward the rocky ledge where she could observe the *wolf-man* down below. She had to know what he was and what kind of danger he presented to her and Dog.

ॐ

The mountain lion lay in the powdery dirt beneath his projection of rocks. His tawny color blended in perfectly with his surroundings. An inexperienced person would have trouble seeing him even within stepping distance of the big cat. His piercing, see-all eyes watched as the girl came out of the cave and crawled to the rock's edge – and she was without the dog.

Lying on her belly made her appear small and helpless, something mountain lions liked for small offered no more threat to the mountain lion than the tiny fawn had. It would be nothing for him to rise, leap on his rock, circle the chasm that separated him from the girl, come up on the rocks above her, and pounce.

The mountain lion raised up and as he did he saw the man turn from working the meat and look directly at him. He hunkered back down and turned his fiery eyes on the man.

The man picked up his fire stick, lifted it upward.

Instinct made the cat crouch back down and take cover.

ॐ

Reuben had spent most of his life observing the wildlife that surrounded him. His sharp eyes could catch movement from a great distance away, and a movement from the mountain lion was what he had been watching for. He knew there would be no sound made by the cat for him to detect.

He had also heard the scraping of rocks when the girl moved them and left her cave. There were times when the wind came down a mountain bringing sound with it until the sound was clear enough to be only a foot away. Sound was carrying downward on the wind today instead of lifting upward.

He knew she was watching him and the mountain lion was watching her, but the big cat was too far away to be a danger to her. It was when it moved that he became concerned and took a closer look through the scope on his gun.

The cat had moved with steely determination. Reuben knew it wanted the girl, but suddenly it stopped, looked toward him, and went back to hiding. Could the mountain lion possibly realize that it was in his sights? Was it intelligent enough to know what a gun was and the gun was aimed at it? Was that why it took shelter back under the shelving of rock?

Little good the gun would do at this distance. The mountain lion was too far away for the gun to reach, but if it went after the girl, he could shoot. The noise alone might scare it. The firing of the gun was certain to scare the girl and make her go back into the cave where she would be safe.

One thing was for certain, just as soon as he finished with the bear meat, he would have to bring forth his own stalking skills and kill the cat. If he allowed it to live, the girl would soon encounter a painfully horrible death.

Where in the dickens was that scrawny surveyor? It had to be past mid-day according to the sun. He needed the salt if he was to preserve the meat for winter and the girl would need a lot of meat this winter – if he killed the cat before it got her. Otherwise, she didn't have a grasshopper's chance in a whirlwind of living through a long, cold winter. And, if he wasn't badly mistaken, the coming winter was going to be a doozy.

Animal hair was already starting to thicken. Plants were drawing in their energy and hardening off earlier than usual. Hornets had their nests built in the very tops of trees instead of lower to the ground. Fowl had hatched out early and not laid another clutch of eggs. Even the insects had started singing their lonesome songs of mourn. Plants, animals, and insects always knew more than humans did about weather. Nature was always predictable if one took time to read and understand her signs.

Once the mountain lion settled back down, Reuben placed his gun within easy reach and continued to slice the meat until he had a huge pile. He removed the stick from the fire and used his knife to push the sizzling meat off the stick onto a rock. He speared his freshly cut meat on the stick and forked it back over the fire. Scrawny, the girl, the dog, and he could eat three and maybe even four sticks of freshly cooked meat. He had no doubt the girl and dog both would somehow manage to get at the meat if he made it easy for them.

Reuben heard the noise a long ways off and knew exactly what it was. Scrawny was returning with salt and containers. The containers were dinging together as Scrawny walked. Reuben suspected the noise was Scrawny's way of hoping to keep the mountain lion scared away. Reuben just hoped he didn't have another chunk of hamburger meat to fry. The smell of bear meat cooking was bad enough. He would have preferred not to have any kind of meat, but he had no intention of wasting a good bear just because of Scrawny and his stupidity. Besides, the wild animals would settle down in a day or so. At least, all but the mountain lion would settle down. He wouldn't stop until he killed the girl and her dog. Reuben knew there was no other choice than to kill it. It was too old, too smart, and too determined in its stalking of the girl.

Seemed to him that one girl was getting a lot of attention when she obviously didn't want it. Unless he missed his guess, all she wanted was to be left alone. Not an unreasonable want in his opinion. Folks were all right when they knew their place and stayed in. They had no business forcing themselves on a body when they wanted to be left alone.

He was a prime example of that. All he'd ever wanted was to live his life the way he chose, but folks were continually coming to White Top Mountain wanting this or that, or worse, snooping through his meager belongings as though they were some great curiosity instead of the few things he needed to survive.

Yeah, he understood the girl and he'd help what and when he could.

"You moved the camp site," Mitch said accusingly when he finally reached Reuben. He dropped the large tub containing a smaller tub plus salt near Reuben as though it was heavy.

"Yeap."

"Why?"

"This one's in the open."

"What does that have to do with anything?"

Reuben's expression didn't change nor did he slow his slicing of meat. "Can see what's comin' at you."

"Oh," Mitch said as the wisdom of the open campsite dawned on him.

Reuben didn't tell him he wanted the girl to watch what he was doing, nor that she was watching them right now. He had heard the vibrations of rocks as she scooted them against each other while opening up the cave entrance. There were certain sounds a man learned to listen for when he spent his life living with nature. He was surprised the girl hadn't learned such things also. It was highly possible the girl never lived among others, never learned the sneaky, conniving ways of man.

Raven stopped crawling over the rocks and froze. Her breathing caught in her throat and came to a complete stop for several long seconds. She couldn't believe her eyes as she stared at the base of the mountain. Every emotion, every fiber of reasonability was exploding inside her with no opening to release the pressure. She couldn't possibly be seeing what she was seeing, not after all she had gone through. She had caused a rockslide and moved everything she owned in order to rid herself of that man and right there he stood.

Panic beyond all reason gripped her. She longed to aim at his head with Aggie's gun. She even lifted the gun before enough control came until she could stop herself. Besides, the distance was too great for her to kill him. Most likely all she would accomplish was letting him know where she was hiding – and then what would she do?

She forced herself to breathe normally as the second realization hit. He was talking to the wolf-man and he wasn't afraid of the bushy headed thing. They actually seemed to be working together.

She lifted her head for a better view and then jerked it back down in case one of them looked up. The question haunting her mind now was why? Why would he be with the wolf-man? Could they be after her? Surely not. She was of no importance to anyone, yet, both men were here, and this wasn't their normal range. They both lived somewhere else. She was sure of that.

Another idea formed in her mind more from hope than likelihood. Could they be after game? No, logic told her they would not be hunting this time of year. Late fall and early winter were the seasons for hunting, not the late part of summer.

Suddenly, right out of the clear blue, it hit her, the letter that Don Donavan wrote to Aggie. She remembered every single word.

Dear Aggie,

I know you hain't gonna believe this news I have. Your real mother has come back. She's dead old and not in sound mind or health. Her name is Agatha Roten, the one you were named after. The preacher, Dale Elder, was your daddy, but he died years ago. That's why she left you in the church house. She thought he would take care of you.

I've got more news, good and bad, I reckon. Your mother is also the mother of those Grearitys. Those rich folks, Joe and Iva Dean, are your half brother and sister. The girl's daddy is your half nephew. Raven really is kin to you. That's the good news. Just thought you ought to know all this.

Come see me if you want. My woman said I could help you. I hain't gonna sign my name in case somebody finds this paper and you don't get it.

Could that possibly have something to do with why she was being hunted by two men. Were the rich folks after her? Lu did burn their cabin, but that was a long time ago when she was almost a baby.

"The girl's daddy is your half nephew". What did that mean? Was she the girl the letter mentioned? Of course she was. What other girl would have the name Raven? What other girl would have been with Aggie?

She recalled those rich folks. The one called Iva Dean had Pete Jenkins building a cabin for her. She sucked in a breath and held it as though the act could help her think.

Slowly she let her breath ease out. No. It couldn't be true. Aggie could not possibly be that woman's half-sister. As for her daddy, he would have to be Joe or Iva Dean's son. If she remembered correctly, the Iva Dean woman didn't have a son that she knew about. The other rich folks did and Lu always went crazy when she saw him.

Oh, shit! Reality hit her like a rock in the face. It really was true. She remembered that *he* was in the cabin when Lu burned it down. It all came back to her even though she was a child when it happened. The flames burning hot as they leaped into the night sky, the shouting voices of the man and woman inside, the way Aggie dragged Lu away from the burning cabin.

Those two men were following her because of the Grearitys. It was obvious that something was going on here, something she didn't understand or like at all. She told herself that she didn't have to understand it to know she had to disappear fast, but where?

A tiredness came over her, one that went bone-deep. She hadn't even settled in on this mountain when she was being forced to leave again, but where could she go? Back to the Ruffian? Perhaps she was never meant to leave Aggie's cave. Perhaps she was meant to live and die there just as Aggie and Lu had.

The possibility of her staying with Don Donavan, or any other human, was beyond her imagination, beyond her ability. She was wise enough to know she could never do that. So, what could she do?

Leave, was her only answer, and just as soon as it was dark enough for the men not to see her. A warning chill crept over her. What about the mountain lion? It could track her in the dark even if the men couldn't. It could smell her no matter where she went or how fast she ran. Her only answer lay in Aggie's gun, one that hadn't been shot in years, and never by her, but she knew how it was done. What could be so difficult about aiming and shooting a gun? Men did it, so could she.

From where she hid on top of Humpback Mountain, she could see not only the valleys but also the mountains beyond. There were many, so very many mountains to choose from, but which would serve her purpose, which would give her shelter, and privacy and escape from the two hunters? She looked at the rivers, the roads, the thickness of forest. A thin forest meant that people were near by. They cut trees for their houses and to heat their stoves. And those horrible roads! The better the roads the more people that traveled them.

Behind what seemed to be a row of similar, nearby mountain tops was a mountain rising higher than the others. It seemed different, as though it had strength to stand alone. Most likely it would take her several days to reach the mountain, but what did time matter as long as the men weren't following her. If only the mountain lion wasn't stalking her, it would be easy to escape the men.

She took several calming breaths. "Think," she told herself. "Think of all the things Aggie taught you about the way of animals." Like in everything, there were ways around a mountain lion. She had to think like a big cat, and then…what?

She inched backward until she was out of view from the men below, got to her knees and crawled back inside the cave. There was no other choice for her. She had to ready the things it would take for her to survive while on another escape run from that man. What was it kept him tormenting her? Surely, she had done nothing to deserve it.

She looked around her new cave and tried to rationalize her need to leave it behind. This wasn't the best of caves and there was no nearby water. She had been planning to find another cave and the men's presence was just rushing her a little.

"Everything will be all right," she assured herself. *"When animals are threatened the worst thing they can do is take-off running. They hunker down, stay out of sight by not moving, and wait until the time is right to escape."* That's what she would do. She'd prepare to leave by packing only the necessities, stay very silent and out of sight until it was time for her to run.

Chapter 9

Wind started blowing and the sky turned dark. It happened so fast it took Reuben by surprise. One moment he was feeling the heat from the sun and the next moment the sun was gone, covered by near-black clouds swirling low and fast. Usually he knew when a storm was approaching but he hadn't picked up on this one. He must have been thinking too hard on the girl. He always worked hard no matter what he was doing, so it couldn't have been working the bear meat caused him to ignore the weather signs.

"Get the salt in your tent," Reuben told Scrawny as he felt a huge drop of rain fall.

Mitch gritted his teeth together, but he picked up the salt and put it inside the tent he had just set up at the new campsite, which Reuben thought was a stupid thing to do when the entire mountain was covered with better shelter. But then, every man was entitled to his own whims.

A brilliant, jagged streak of lightning flashed through the dark clouds followed immediately by thunder. Reuben gathered the sticks of almost dried meat and shoved them in the tent behind Scrawny as huge drops of rain started to fall.

"Scrape that meat off the sticks into the salt."

Reuben sensed the resentment in Scrawny. Obviously, he didn't like being told what to do, but Scrawny's likes or dislikes didn't phase Reuben.

"My tent's full-up."

Reuben heard him say but Reuben was already a distance from the tent without having any intentions of squeezing himself in it with Scrawny. He rapidly took his waterproof gun cover from his knapsack and covered his gun before many drops of rain hit it. Gunmetal would rust fast in a storm. He then filled his knapsack with the fully dried meat and headed for the mountain of rocks with his gun and meat-filled knapsack in his hands.

He didn't want to be too far away from the girl. If he were, the rapidly building storm would muffle her sound if she decided to leave the cave, plus hinder his sight where the mountain lion was concerned.

Cats didn't like water. It was sure to find a better shelter if a hard rain came for the rock ledge it was under wouldn't provide a dry place for long. If Reuben wasn't badly mistaken, the rapid way the storm-clouds boiled over Humpback Mountain meant a doozy of a storm was just arriving. That would mean the mountain lion wouldn't be hunting during the storm and would take to its den for a long nap being its belly should still be full of bear guts.

Reuben found himself a good dry place underneath an overhang of large rocks. It was a perfect place to be during a rainstorm but not as good as he would like for observing the girl. Had he been paying attention to the weather, he could have picked a better place to take cover and still watch for the girl, but he wasn't over-worried. The girl wouldn't like getting a soaking any more than he or the cat would.

He settled down in the dry place as the rain hammered around him, took a good look over the rocky mountainside before he closed his eyes. There was nothing like a rainstorm to induce a man to makeup for lost sleep.

𝔶

Mitch was angry at everything including Reuben
Rivers, the weather, and himself. He was trapped inside his
tent by a rainstorm, plus he was extra mad at being bullied
by a hairy, stinking mountain man with an arrogance that
far overpowered his intelligence. At least the big hulk
hadn't demanded shelter alongside him in the tent. He had
read a novel once about what dirty, hairy mountain men did
to a man visitor.

Mitch lifted the flap and looked out. It could have been
the beginning of the night according to the light factor. Not
only was the sky black, the cold rain was hitting hot dirt
and rocks, causing a mist to rise making visibility almost
nonexistent.

He let the flap close back, kicked the canner of salt
against the wall of the tent, and rolled out his sleeping bag.
He stretched himself out in hopes of making up for the poor
night's sleep. But sleep didn't come. He kept thinking
about the conversation he and Reuben Rivers had about the
girl earlier. Was Reuben Rivers really wanting to help her
survive or did he want her for reasons of his own?

The best thing for him to do was part company with the
hulking man and find the girl on his own. He was perfectly
capable of killing the mountain lion and then finding the
girl without Reuben Rivers' interference. The only reason
the cat and the bear had shown up was because of the
frying meat. Mitch had to be honest with himself and admit
that he should have handled that situation better. He was in
such a hurry to kill the cat he hadn't taken time to think
straight. He was thinking straight now.

He stripped off his clothes, opened the flap again, and
tossed his clothes out in the rain. He got a small, travel
bottle of shampoo from his supplies, opened the flap wider,

and plunged out in the rain stark naked. No time like the present to wash away what smell of frying meat might have lingered.

The coldness of the July rain surprised him, as well as the force of it hitting his flesh. It felt as though it had bits of hail mixed with the rain, but he couldn't detect any. He poured shampoo in his hand, scrubbed it into his hair until he had a good lather, and then ran the lather over his body.

The rain had picked up speed and velocity. The shampoo washed off almost instantly, but it had taken the smell and the dirt with it. Water was pooling in low places. He poured a glob of shampoo on his clothes and scrubbed them together before he rinsed them in the pooled water. He rung the water from them as good as he could and took them inside the tent where he had a change of clean clothes.

Too bad Reuben Rivers wasn't civilized enough to follow his example.

Raven was huddled in the cave trying to determine what to do next when the powerful clap of thunder trembled the earth. Instantly there was a different smell to the air, even inside the cave. She knew the smell well. Aggie always told her a body could smell when a bad storm was coming. There was something about the air that smelled so fresh and potent that it almost hurt the lungs to breathe. *"Never fails,"* Aggie would say. *"You can always smell those big 'uns a comin'."* If Raven read the smell right, this was a *big 'un.* And it wasn't just coming, it had arrived.

She considered the storm a blessing if not an omen. It would provide her the perfect cover for leaving the cave. Not only would the men be taking shelter, so would the mountain lion. Another advantage the storm gave would be to wash away her tracks and her scent. By the time this storm ended, she could be miles away. The man whose clothes she wore, plus the wolf-man would have no idea which way she went and no way of following her.

She sprang into action, filled one of Aggie's sacks part way with dog food and the other part with corn. She got the gun and wrapped it carefully in hopes of keeping it and the shells dry. She knew the storm might delay the mountain lion, but she wasn't foolish enough to think she could escape it, even when she was hoping she would. The only safe thing would be to kill the cat. She could do that, she assured herself, of course she could.

She considered taking her water jug along, but decided against it. It would only slow her down. She should be able to find enough as she traveled. It wasn't like she was going to settle in any one place. This time she would hunt over every mountain until she found the perfect cave for her and Dog – a place without people or mountain lions. A place where she could simply live and let live.

Her fire was burning bright enough to make shadows dance on the rocks and reflect on what meager supplies she had stored. She longed to take the warm quilt but it would be too bulky to carry. And the pine-knot torch? No, it would only slow her down. Even the ax would slow her too much. She got Aggie's largest knife and stuck it in the waistband of her britches. The matches, oh goodness, she must never forget the matches. Fire was definitely something she couldn't be without. Fire and the gun were her only protection against the mountain lion.

She considered pouring the remainder of her water supply on the fire but decided against it. It would hurt nothing to let it burn itself out. None of her supplies were close enough to catch on fire.

She stuffed the matches in her britches pocket, pushed one rock from the cave entrance, and crawled out with Dog at her heels. Dog whined. She thought she might have whined too. The rain was coming down harder than she expected, and the darkened sky surprised her.

Better to escape in, she assured herself. But she would be escaping in almost total blindness. She couldn't see more than ten feet in front of her if she squinted her eyes and tried very hard, but what did it matter? All that mattered was she was leaving. By the time the storm had worn itself out, she would be far away where she could stop and get her bearings. She hefted her sack and gun and hoped she was heading in the direction of the distant mountain she had seen earlier.

She couldn't go down the mountain in the same place she came up for the men were down there. She had to climb over the hump and go down the backside, which would be more difficult. Once she was off the mountain, she would stay in the wooded area away from the river, the roads, and the valleys.

Dog kept bumping against her legs, whining his displeasure as she maneuvered her way over rain-slick rocks. Strange how a wet rock could be as slick as ice.

Her feet flew out from under her and she fell with a thud. Dog nuzzled her face. "Good Dog," she whispered near his ear.

A jagged streak of lightning flashed over her head seemingly so close she could have lifted her hand and touched it. Thunder roared before the glow of lightning faded. It seemed to her the lightning had sliced the dark clouds open for rain was literally being dumped on the mountain top.

"Don't be afraid," she told Dog and herself.

She wasn't afraid, not really. It was not knowing where she was going, along with the blinding rain, that had a hardknot growing in her chest. It wasn't fear. She couldn't afford to be afraid, not now.

Never on the Ruffian had it rained this hard. It was the first time she had ever seen rivets of water gushing on top of a mountain, but she wasn't going to let a little water and a storm send her back to the cave, not when there were two men after her.

"Come on," she said to Dog as she gained her feet. "A little water won't stop us." She climbed away from the running water to the highest rocks on the mountain.

Reuben was awake instantly. The ear-splitting sound of thunder was right over his head, but that wasn't what brought him to his feet. It was the roaring sound of rushing water. He grabbed for his gun and knapsack as he sprang from his shelter and leaped onto the nearest outcropping of rock. He slipped, gripped his belongings in one hand, and clutched at the rocks with the other hand. His fingers caught in a crevice enabling him to pull himself up as water flooded the space where he had been sleeping.

Damn if it wasn't a cloud-burst! A river of water was pouring down the mountain taking with it small rocks along with what vegetation happened to be growing. For a moment, he stood still, mesmerized by the power of the rushing water as it gushed through the mountain of rocks. He had seen cloudbursts and he had seen flashfloods, but he had never seen either hit this hard and this fast.

Once the shock of seeing such a phenomenon had ebbed, he thought of the girl. Would the flood of water by-pass her cave or would the water run straight into it? He tried to see the cave entrance but he was too far from it to see through the blinding rain. Without hesitation, he headed up the wall of rocks, straight toward the mouth of the cave. It no longer mattered that the girl wanted to be left alone. Only her safety mattered.

He leaped from rock to rock as water gushed around them, churning up foam and building up force before it tore its way downhill. To Reuben, it seemed to take longer to reach the cave than it did to kill a dozen bears, possibly because of what he expected to find – a drowned girl inside a flooded cave.

The cave wasn't flooded. Water hadn't even reached the entrance where the rock was roughly closing the entrance. He hesitated and considered leaving without letting her know he was there, and then changed his mind. Something didn't feel right. He easily moved the rock aside, kneeled down, and stuck his head inside the entrance. Only the dying embers of the fire cast a faint light in the darkened cave.

"Girl," he said in what he hoped was a friendly voice. "Are you in here?"

There was no answer, not even a growl from the dog. He scooted his gun and knapsack in front of him and entered her cave. He saw her pine torch, held it to the embers until it caught, giving off enough light for him to look around. It wasn't much of a cave, not high enough for him to stand straight, or wide enough for him to stretch both arms out without touching the sides of the rocks.

A brisk, chilling air was surrounding him. It wouldn't hold warmth but it was dry. No rain had entered although the place was very damp. How could it help but be with this cloudburst?

Against the cave wall was her travois with her few belongings roped on top. Such a few things, all old and worn like the dented tin pan she used to cook her food in.

He saw a jar with a little water remaining in the bottom, a pile of rags against the rocks where she had slept.

Emotions stirred inside him, emotions that he wasn't sure what name to call them. Perhaps pity, certainly sympathy, and definitely a sadness that any human being lived with such a small amount. The only food he saw were sacks of dog food plus a bag of dried corn. Not even a chicken could live on corn alone.

At least she wasn't entirely stupid. She was smarter than he was, actually, for the storm had caught him napping. She had evidently sensed the fierceness of the storm that was coming and surely headed for higher ground, afraid water might fill her cave. But what higher ground was there? Only the top of the hump. If she was hunkered-down up there, she wouldn't be caught in a gushing flood of water half drowned and freezing, being she was so small of body mass.

He took one last look around the cave and saw the drying skin of a coon. Poor girl, no one ever taught her how to tan a hide, which led him to wondering again where she came from. Someone had to take care of her for the first portion of her life. Where was that person and why was the girl running? He asked himself the same questions that refused to leave his mind.

He had a notion to go back down the mountain, and if nothing else worked, beat the truth out of Scrawny. He suspected Scrawny had the answers to all his questions about the girl.

He rolled the torch in the dirt to put out the fire and placed it back where she had left it. She would be back, he was sure. He resisted the urge to place more wood on the embers so the girl wouldn't have to rebuild her fire if she was long in returning, but didn't. The girl would probably notice wood missing from her meager pile.

It was best for him to leave as though he had never been there.

Once he crawled out of the cave, he realized that it was better protection than he thought. The cave was somewhat dry when nothing else on Humpback Mountain was. If anything, the rain had increased. It pelted his head and stung his eyes. Hail, he first thought and then changed his mind. It was raining straight down with an uncommon force.

A man would need an ark to survive this, he told himself, while his thoughts remained on the girl and her light body mass. He took off over the rocks in the direction he thought she would have gone.

Mitch Kenilworth couldn't believe what was happening when he opened his eyes from a troubled sleep. His tent was filling up with water. He jerked open the tent flap to find it wasn't only his tent that was filled with water. The entire open space Reuben had chosen for a new campsite was covered in at least a foot of water.

He had to move his tent now!

He tossed the heavy container of salt and bear-meat out the opened flap, and rapidly begin to collapse his tent. At least he was able to jerk the metal posts out of the wet ground without needing to pry them out. That few seconds was probably what saved his life. He was that much closer to the rise where the huge pine tree grew when he heard the roar. He saw a foaming river of water heading straight toward him.

"Shit!" he said as he lunged for the tree, forgetting about dragging his tent to safety. A tent could be replaced. He had never been as thankful for a towering tree with plenty of limbs in his life. He climbed it to the very top much like a squirrel scrambling for its life.

He stood on a limb and hugged the trunk with both arms as he looked down. He saw no sign of his tent, but he did see rocks and small trees tumbling over and over in muddy water as everything rushed past the tree.

How in the dickens did such a gully-washer take place on the side of a mountain? It didn't seem possible for such an amount of rain to fall in one location. He had often read about the sudden floods that would rush down the gullies out west, but he had never heard of it happening in the North Carolina mountains.

Surely, he was still inside his tent sleeping and this was a nightmare, but it didn't feel like he was asleep. He banged his forehead against the rough bark of the tree. It hurt, and he wasn't asleep. This was real, but it wasn't happening, it just couldn't be.

Raven was bewildered to put it mildly. She couldn't see where she was going nor could she stay on her feet. Even the moss covering the rocks had turned into something slicker than grease. She knew she was starting down the opposite side of the hump where the wind didn't blow as hard and the scrubby trees grew. Water was halfway to her knees, and there was a strange roaring in the air.

Her feet flew out from under her again. She dropped her gun and her sack but her arms managed to grip around Dog who was touching her side. The water lifted them both and shot them down the mountain of rocks as though they were plummeting down a waterfall. Never had Raven gone downward so fast. It might have been fun if she hadn't been so afraid of what she had no control over.

She held her breath when water covered her face, gulped in breath when it didn't, but she never loosened her grip on Dog. He was the only thing she had left to hold onto.

It seemed to take a lifetime and yet it could only have been minutes until she and Dog landed against a pile of rocks and uprooted trees while the water parted and rushed by on both sides of them. She tightened her arms around Dog and dared not move an inch in case the lodged pile of debris broke loose from its mooring and took them down the mountain again.

The main thing she was thinking right now was how badly she regretted leaving Ruffian Mountain.

George Ball was doing everything in his power to drive his cattle to his barns before the storm hit. The radio was giving warnings of the tremendous storm that was approaching the mountains. He had every man who worked for him busy, every neighbor that wasn't working with his own cattle, even his wife had lent her hand in driving his truck behind herds of cattle.

At least his herds of cattle and sheep were close to home and no longer down by the river. If they had been, he could have lost his entire herds. He almost chuckled. That damned mountain lion had done him a favor.

The storm hit just as he closed the last barn door. He ran for the truck his wife was driving, climbed behind the wheel, pushing her aside.

"Where you going?" Jennifer Ball asked her husband.

"I'm taking the high road home. Don't trust being on the lower road if we have a storm like they're predicting."

"It'll take a whole lot longer," she said.

"Better safe than sorry."

"We don't usually have floods here in the mountains," Jennifer said needlessly.

"Said something about a hurricane off our coast."

"Who said?"

"The weathermen."

"Oh."

"At least the livestock are safe. Guess that mountain lion helped me more than the cost of a vet bill and a few calves."

"Oh, my!" Jennifer said.

"What?"

"That man. The one you told me about."

"Reuben Rivers? Don't worry about him. He can most likely out-swim a water snake. Besides, he knows how to take care of himself in weather worse than what's coming."

"I know and I wasn't thinking about him. What about that poor little surveyor?"

Ball shrugged his beefy shoulders. "Nothing we can do about him. He'll survive or he won't."

"It doesn't seem right."

"This storm hain't right either, but we're stuck with what we've got."

"We ought to do something," she insisted.

"What?" Ball asked rather irritated at her, the storm, and everything else. "Just tell me what a body can do during a time like this?"

She let out a sigh. "Pray," she said.

George J. Ball let out a weary breath. "Yeah."

The mountain lion was perfectly happy. He had smelled the storm when it was miles away, which wasn't much of a feat. Storms always sent out waves of tension in front of them and this one sent out a beaut. The tension tingled and rippled in the air like the coiling of a snake. The cat knew to keep out of striking range.

He had left his shelter-rock before the first drops of rain hit, and while the men were still out in the open. Only the girl had shut herself inside the cave as though she would not be coming out for a long time. Besides, the girl wasn't giving off the irresistible scent she had given off days before, plus, he wasn't much hungry. He had eaten more in the last few days than he usually ate in a month. Thing was, he had grown to like the feeling of being over-full instead of empty.

He had eaten of the bear innards, the heart, liver, and lungs especially. They, along with a baby fawn, had given him the nutrition he needed but it wasn't the kind of food that lasted. He craved firm muscles laced with tender fat even though he wasn't hungry right now. Gluttony had taken over, and he knew hunger would come all too soon, for the storm would make hunting unpleasant if not impossible.

Rain had a way of running game off or making deer hide in close-growing thickets where he had trouble getting at them. Cattle were a different matter. They clustered together while their people hid inside houses.

Such timid creatures, people.

He had yawned, stood up, stretched his long, lean, tawny body, and then disappeared from the rocks into the wooded area before the men down below even knew he was gone. He didn't stop to hunt or kill even when he passed a newly born fawn. He picked up speed, crossed over the bald, and found the place he was searching for.

It was one of George Ball's barns, the one further from the house.

His sleek body fit perfectly under the closed doors, which had been built with a narrow space above the ground to help accommodate the opening and closing of the doors during winter snows. From there, he went straight to the wooden ladder and bounded into the loft where he bedded down in warm, sweet-smelling hay.

He instinctively lay still while Ball drove his cattle inside the barn until they stood together as thick as flies, and closed the doors on them. It didn't matter how long the storm lasted. He had all the food he could want for a long time to come, and he wouldn't even have to get wet.

He slept while the rain pounded on the tin roof of the barn, and woke near morning with a rumble in his stomach. A mountain lion normally ate only several times a week, but he was now lazy and spoiled. Plus, the cattle bedded down below him were too much temptation even if his stomach hadn't been rumbling

He rose from the hay, went into a crouch, and leaped downward onto the back of a young heifer lying in the barn hall along with the other cattle. She let out a bellow of pain and fright as she tried to get to her feet, but the weight of the big cat was keeping her down. Her stable mate sleeping beside her did not have the weight on her back or a problem rising. Once she gained her feet, she kicked out with one hind leg in a powerful, lightning fast blow. It caught the cat in the right eye causing the eyeball to pop out like a pitted cherry.

The mountain lion let go of the heifer and rolled off her back, landing among the stomping hoofs as the cattle tried to stampede with no place to run. Everyplace on his body was kicked and tromped as he made a desperate rush for the door and the narrow slit that would save his life. He made the slit and slithered outside to safety only to find himself surrounded by flood water. Ball had chosen well when he built the barn. It was on a knoll and therefore hadn't flooded.

Pain and the need to escape the cattle made the mountain lion reckless enough to charge into the rushing water. He was carried downstream with only his head lifted above the water.

He hurt, mewed in pain, couldn't see where he was being washed away. All he could do was manage to keep his head from going under the swirling current. Things bumped into him causing him more pain.

His strength was almost gone when his body was slammed into the trunk of a tree that had been uprooted and the limbs and roots were catching on debris making it wash slowly down stream. Bark broke off as his claws tried to get a hold. The cat tried again. This time his paw caught a branch and it held. Inch by painful inch, the cat worked its battered body onto the tree trunk. He clung desperately trying not to tumble back into the churning water, hurting like he had never hurt in his entire life.

Chapter 10

Reuben Rivers had spent the night clinging to the trunk of a tree. To be more specific, he had taken a rope from his knapsack and tied himself, his gun, along with his knapsack to the sturdiest tree he could find on the backside of the mountain. It most likely was the only reason he was now alive for the water had been a force in itself.

Never had he seen anything like the rain that had poured down on him. It was much like standing under a waterfall while the water rose around his legs. He could see nothing and could barely feel, for his fingers were cold and numb as he tied himself and his possessions to the tree. It took every bit of his strength and endurance to keep from washing down the mountain before the rope was secured. Again, he was thankful for his size and weight. Had he not been the size of two men, he could not have held out against the water's force long enough to tie the rope. As it was, it took all the strength that was in him just to stay alive. There was no doubt in his mind water was the strongest force in nature. Nothing could stop it, not even fire, or wind.

Several times water had come to his chin but never did it reach his nose. Strange how a flashflood could actually flood a mountaintop when the ground sloped downhill. He looked down in the still, darkened light of morning and saw that his shirt had been torn off by the rushing water. He felt with his hand for his pants. They were still there. He grinned. A half naked man was far better off than a naked one. He certainly wouldn't want the girl to see him wearing any less.

His grin faded fast as he thought of the girl. Could she have roped herself to a tree? Probably not, for he had seen her frayed rope tying her belongings to the travois. It wasn't likely the girl would have two ropes, nor was it likely she survived the flood. She was such a slight little thing the water would carry her off like a tree-leaf.

A great sadness came over him because he had not been able to save her after all. The fact he was lucky enough to still be alive should be compensation enough, but it wasn't. The girl was too young to die. A wild spirit like hers should never be extinguished before it ran its full life-course.

He felt for his knife, surprised to find it still there and started to cut the rope that held him to the tree, but decided against it. Rope was too hard to come by to shorten it from impatience. Besides, he would most likely be unable to stand in the fast rushing water that had not completely abated. He might as well stay tied to the tree for a little longer while allowing the rain to slack off and the water to go down while the morning grew light enough to see. It shouldn't take long. Water ran downhill fast. The mountain would be dry days before the valleys. He couldn't see the valley yet, but he knew what it would look like in its flooded condition. Everything would be a river with only the high places in sight.

Scrawny came to his mind. Poor little fellow, he was most likely half-way to the Mississippi by now. Yet, Reuben couldn't work up much sympathy for the little fellow. Had it not been for Scrawny, he'd be two hundred dollars richer, and the girl just might still be alive, depending on how he had handled her.

He leaned his weight against the tree trunk, took a steadying breath of the damp air until it reached all the way to the pit of his stomach, and tried to make sense of the situation. He would do what he came to do, collect the two hundred dollars, and then go home, but right now, he had to wait.

🕊

George J. Ball came close to sweating blood all night long. He had never been as thankful for his and his wife's vanity. She had insisted, and he agreed, on building their house on top of a high-rise where they could view their holdings, and where people could gaze upon their home. He knew the high-rise saved them.

"Suppose we're the only ones left alive?" his wife asked as she looked out the upstairs window into the total blackness. Water had to be everywhere for it had flooded their downstairs.

"It's just a little water, Jennifer," he tried to sound positive when he wasn't feeling positive about anything.

"At least we have our house left," she continued. "Others won't."

"Barn's on higher ground. The cattle and sheep in those barns should be safe."

"Won't be nothing left along the river," she said. "Houses, people, or animals. It might have washed all the bottom land away."

"There'll be a lot of damage all right. Some folks won't be lucky but others will be. There's been floods before and there will be floods again." He tried to console his wife and himself, but it didn't work.

"This one's extra bad," Jennifer continued.

"Maybe not. It's too dark outside to see much."

"I can see," she insisted. "It's like Noah and the ark. It'll take forty days and forty nights before this much water goes down."

"It'll take a day, two at the most, and several more for the mud to dry up enough for me to turn the livestock out. Maybe I can run them on the bald. Shouldn't have flooded that high up," he said hopefully. "I'm glad I've already got some hay up. Won't be enough to last all winter and we won't have a lick of corn left. But I can sell the sheep if I have to. Never liked sheep much."

"Do you suppose there will be dead animals floating in the river?"

"Could be," Ball admitted. "Hope none of them are mine."

"I never did see that much water come down at one time. It came down from the sky and rose up from the earth."

"You can't see how much water there is out there. It's still dark," Ball reminded her again.

"Don't need to see much. I can feel it, can't you?"

"Feel what?"

"The water rising downstairs."

"It's not rising. The rain has stopped. You're feeling the water going down."

"So you do feel it."

Ball turned from the dark window. He didn't want to think of all the destruction, all the work he had done through the years would be gone, and he was nearly too old to do such a great amount of work all over again. "Come on, let's lay back down until daylight comes. Can't do nothing else."

Jennifer Ball didn't move from the window where she stared into the blackness. "The Lord giveth and the Lord taketh away. Do you suppose he's taken away all we've worked for?"

Ball shook his head even when his wife couldn't see him doing so. "Don't be silly. We'll have a lot of cleaning up to do, but we won't have lost much," he said, but he was far from being as positive as he tried to sound. He suspected he had a worse feeling in his gut than his wife had. He had been a farmer too long not to know life hung by an extremely sensitive balance. One catastrophe and all was lost.

"What about that man you hired to kill the mountain lion? Do you suppose he's all right?"

"Like I told you before, you couldn't drown Reuben Rivers if you tried. He probably knew a flood was going to hit before the weathermen did."

"That young surveyor and his truck? I bet it washed him away."

"Probably got his truck washed away, being I never saw it go out." He figured the surveyor would take shelter in his truck, maybe even try to drive it to safety, which would be his last mistake as he would have to drive off the bald and go through low ground.

"I saw it go out early yesterday morning, but it came back."

"Too bad."

"We may not have a single neighbor left alive."

"Come on Jennifer, lay down a while and try to rest. There'll be enough to worry about when daylight comes."

"I can't rest. I'm too upset. How can you lay there all calm?"

Ball almost laughed at being called calm. He couldn't remember ever feeling this frustrated and at a loss of what to do next.

᪥

There was something special about morning air after a rainstorm. The pureness of each indrawn breath was beyond description. To Reuben it was like breathing in a little bit of God Himself. That's how he felt as he watched the light slowly squeeze out of the darkness. The faintest of pastel colors lit the morning. Palest pink touched the gray sky over the far mountains to the east. The sky became light blue in patches, while a slight breeze chased clouds that were losing their density with each minute that passed. It was going to be a beautiful day.

Reuben untied the knot that held him to the tree. It was time to find out what Mother Nature had done. He carefully wound up his rope and placed it in his knapsack. He wasn't about to forget what had saved his life. He gave the rope the proper respect it deserved. He climbed the rest of the way on top of the Big Hump where he had a better vision of the surrounding areas.

He was stunned. Down below must be what the ocean looked like. It was a world of muddy-brown water swirling and rushing to get somewhere when there appeared no place to go. Whole trees were moving in the water with their roots sticking up. Others trees and debris were twirling around and around to be sucked underwater only to pop up again somewhere else.

He saw bodies of cattle floating rapidly until they lodged against something or were sucked under by a forceful current. What appeared to be portions of sheds bobbed about, bumping things and then continuing on their way down one huge, never-ending river.

He had seen floods before, but never anything like this. The only way he could tell where the hills were was by the tops of trees sticking up above the water. At least the bald was holding its head above water, a bare spot showing wet but green in the never-ending ocean of brown.

From where he stood, he determined where Scrawny's tent had been. Nothing. Like everything else, it was covered in floodwater. The huge rock formations on Humpback Mountain were still visible, but he could tell what small amount of loose soil that had once settled in their crevices was no longer there. Thin, life giving soil had been washed somewhere down below to be carried away in the muddy water.

He wondered what damage his home on White Top Mountain had suffered. Had the flood reached that far? He hoped not. Admittedly, he didn't own much, but it was his and he valued all the worldly goods he could lay claim to. The thought of losing his home caused a chill to creep inside his guts. He suspected there were many people feeling the same way this morning – those that were still alive.

And then his sharp eyesight spotted something. It was a small dark spot in the top of a pine tree. A bear, he thought. At least there was something still living besides him. He was thankful. It helped him stop feeling as though he was the only living thing in existence.

He had the oddest need to get a closer look at the bear and slowly started working his way over the slick rocks along the top of the mountain. It would take him hours to get above the spot of pine trees with their tops sticking up above water, but what else could he do? The floodwaters had him marooned.

He laboriously worked his way around the side of Humpback Mountain, climbing over rocks and down washed-out ravines. Progress was much like projecting himself through the eye of a needle, except his needle was made of rocks and the eye was deep gullies that had been washed out by the flood.

He figured, by the position of the sun, that it was near mid-day when he was close the pine trees. He climbed to the top of a rock outcropping where he could observe his surroundings better. The rocks were thoroughly dry from the heat of the sun, yet washed clean of everything, even moss. Interesting how hot the sun could shine and how calm a day could be after a disastrous Mother Nature struck, but women were noted for being like that. It was one of the reasons he had never sought a woman of his own – one of many reasons, he mentally added.

Reuben had good vision of the treetops down below. Through the pine needles, he could make out the dark form of a small bear huddled almost in a round ball. It was clinging near the very top of the tree even though the water had gone down at least fifteen or twenty feet. Poor thing, it would be safer if it climbed down to sturdier branches, but it was afraid to move, afraid to get even a few feet closer to the floodwater.

There was nothing Reuben could do for the bear and precious little he could do for himself. He could continue climbing the rocky side of the Humpback or he could go back the way he had come. He saw no purpose in doing either one, as it would get him nowhere. He might as well sit down on the warm rock, watch the little bear, and wait for the earth to absorb.

After a long, sleepless night, the heat from the sun made Reuben feel drowsy. He yawned loudly, flung out his arms, and stretched his big body. The sound must have carried on the wind for the bear became extra still before the pine needles started shaking with a sudden vigor.

A desperate sound reached Reuben. The poor bear must be scared out of its wits and wanting to escape its precarious confinement, but there was nothing he or the bear could do about their circumstances. They both had to be patient as the water went down. At least he would be able to stretch out on the dry, warm rock and take a little nap.

Just as Reuben was about to lie down, the wind changed and brought sound toward him. Danged if the bear didn't seemed to be making sounds similar to a human. It sounded as though it was hollering for help.

Reuben cocked his head sideways and listened carefully. Be danged, if it wasn't yelling *help* in a high-pitched screech. He tried to reach a better vantage point on the rocks where he could see beyond the pine needles, but could not.

He cupped his hands to his mouth and yelled. "Ho, there!"

"Help!" returned the high-pitched screech.

"Who are you?" For a moment, he dared think of the girl.

"Me, Mitch."

Disappointment hit. It wasn't the girl.

"Can't help you," Reuben called back

"Get me down!" Reuben thought he heard him holler.

"Can't. Water has to go down first."

"Get a boat!"

Reuben almost laughed. Poor little fellow was scared out of his senses. It had to be traumatic clinging to a tree when muddy water was swirling everywhere, crashing tree limbs and parts of buildings into the trunk of the tree he was in, never knowing if the water had washed enough dirt from the tree's roots to allow it to topple over.

"Hang on," Reuben shouted. "You'll be able to get down tomorrow or next day."

"Get me down now!"

Reuben ignored him and stretched out on the warm rock. He could work up sympathy for a scared-to-death bear, but Scrawny was another thing entirely. Pure stupidity was an intolerable fault in his opinion, and Scrawny had an excess of it.

It was mighty hard to sleep when a man kept squalling his head off for help that couldn't be given. It got right disturbing. Reuben rolled over without getting up and slid off the backside of the rock so Scrawny couldn't see him leave. He might as well circle the highest, driest part of the mountain. He just might find some evidence of the girl, and if not her, maybe find sign of the mountain lion. Which he doubted. The mountain lion would have found shelter, probably on higher ground miles from Humpback Mountain.

Reuben frowned, just where was higher ground than Humpback Mountain? It certainly wouldn't be hard to find. It would be sticking up above the floodwater. He had an idea the storm had dumped water on several counties if not states, but he doubted all of them had floodwaters like what surrounded the area he was in.

Maybe if he climbed back onto the Big Hump, the fog and mist had cleared enough for him to see in the distance. He might be able to tell where it had and hadn't flooded.

Chapter 11

Don Donavan listened to the rain pounding on the roof as he lay in bed. No matter how hard he tried, he couldn't fall asleep. He usually slept like a baby when it rained, but this was different. It had rained way too hard the last two days for his comfort.

"If you can't sleep, get up and go sit on the porch," Betsy told him. "No need for you to toss and turn all night long. All you're doing is keeping me awake."

"Some said a flood hit the Humpback Mountain area hard," he told her what was on his mind.

"But not here," Betsy told him. "All that rain was way over in a different county from us. They say we'll only get a lot of rain from the tail-end of the storm."

"I know."

Betsy let out a long, suffering sigh. "It's not the rain you're worried about, is it? You've still got that girl on your mind."

Don didn't bother to answer for there wasn't any need. The girl was always on his mind just as Aggie had been.

"You beat all, you know that? You spent most all your life worrying about that Aggie woman and now you're going to spend the rest of it worrying about a girl you've never set eyes on and don't know for certain exists."

"She exists," Don said in a low voice. He would have been wiser not to speak at all and pretend he was going back to sleep.

"How do you know?" demanded Betsy, showing her irritability.

"Mitch Kenilworth took care of her when she was snake-bit, besides, I was in her cave, remember?"

"And she was long gone."

"Yeah, that's what's worrying me so much."

Betsy sat up, her back as stiff as an ironing board. "You wanted her, didn't you? You wanted to take her in and raise her as your own." Betsy's voice held a tremor. "You can't forgive me can you?"

"Forgive you? For what?"

"Being barren."

"Ah, Betsy," he said softly.

"Well, you can't. You wanted children and I couldn't give 'em to you."

"Yeah, that's true. I wanted children but I wanted you more and I still do. Betsy," he said in a whisper, as though he was ashamed of saying what he was about to say. "You're my life, always have been." He was silent again for a few moments. "If I'd a known you was barren way back when, I'd a married you anyhow. I rather have you and no children than have somebody else and children."

Betsy sniffed, caught herself, and snuggled back down in bed, ashamed of showing her emotions like a teenage girl with her first boyfriend.

"You'd say that anyhow," she mumbled.

Don reached over and patted her arm.

Time passed and the rain continued beating on the roof.

"You think she went to Humpback Mountain, don't you?" Betsy finally said after a long period of silent wakefulness for them both.

"Yeah."

"How come?"

"I've been on the Ruffian when the sun rises. That mountain is beautiful when you're looking out over the distance. Makes you feel like you're looking at paradise. A young girl might be foolish enough to think Humpback Mountain is paradise."

"There's no such thing as paradise, not while you're still on this earth."

Don didn't want to disagree with her, but he had to say it. "Our mountains come right close. They sure-enough do, except for Humpback Mountain. Some say it's the upper end of Hell."

"Ah, Don, don't talk such."

Don grunted. "Hurts me to think a child is on that mountain."

"Nothing we can do about it."

"No, reckon there's not a thing."

Reuben Rivers couldn't help himself. He was drawn back to the girl's cave without questioning why. He was in no hurry and took a slightly different route as he made his way over rocks that were larger and more craterous than before the storm.

The girl was really the only person he was personally concerned about, even though he suspected many lives would be lost when folks were able to do a headcount. As for the land itself, Mother Nature continuously changed things and always would. A man had to realize that and accept it.

His mother's people would say the flood happened because the gods were mad, but he didn't share their beliefs. He believed it was nothing more than Mother Nature's way of rearranging her space. He grinned.

Naturally, Father Time would try to put things back the way *he* wanted them.

Always was and always would be a battle going on between male and female. Both wanted their own way – in humans and in nature. That was another reason why he never wanted a wife – and still didn't.

It took little imagination to know what having a wife would entail. First thing she'd want to do was change his way of living. Next would come money, a house, fancy furnishings, a vehicle, fancy clothes, children, and probably even visitors. To add to all that she'd insist he bathe daily, shave his beard each morning, cut his hair, wear prissy cloth clothes, go to church, stop swearing, and wash all the tobacco from his mouth before he kissed her goodnight.

And what would he get in return?

Such thoughts were enough to scare the daylights out of a grown man, and enough to take his mind off the flood damage for a while.

A lone man was a free man, he continued to tell himself as he climbed up the mountain. Even Scrawny was a free man, once he got down from the pine tree, and he would get down before long. He's see to it after he checked the girl's cave. By that time, the floodwater would have gone down enough for him to reach the tree. He figured mud would be a problem in the flatter areas, maybe even worse than the water. A man could manage in mud up to his knees. Once mud got to his straddle, he was trapped.

The girl hadn't returned. The cave was unchanged except it felt colder, damper, and more uninviting than before. Actually, it felt deserted in a way that told him the girl would never return.

The girl would not light the sap-torch from a fire she had built to keep the mountain lion out of her cave, nor would she need the fire to chase the night-chill from her slender body. Her crudely constructed little travois would never move again. It would rest by the rock wall until it dry-rotted and fell apart.

Worst of all was he would never again hide in a laurel hell and secretly watch a young, wild thing run.

Finally, he left her cave and sat on a rock near the opening for a long time. He needed the warmth of the sun to take away the bone-chill he had gotten from the empty cave.

The July sun had burned away the morning fog except for mist that was rising from the flooded valleys. From where he sat, he had a good view of the valleys and surrounding areas. If he climbed on top of the Big Hump again, he would have an even better view, but he didn't need it. He could tell how much the water had gone down and it was considerable. Mountains were naturally fast in shedding floodwaters – along with rich topsoil. What a mountain lost the flatland would gain. Talk about taking from the poor man! Without good dirt a man couldn't even muster-up hope.

Ah, well, enough of those thoughts. He'd best be heading back down the mountain and rescue Scrawny. The little fellow was probably still screaming his head-off because no one had brought him a boat.

Mitch Kenilworth wasn't up the pine tree. He was ten feet from it with mud reaching his waist and water reaching his chest. The water was slowly receding but the mud wasn't.

Mitch decided it was safe for him to climb down and swim to safety after seeing Reuben Rivers leaving him behind, and clinging to the tree for several more hours. He never expected to find mud instead of water.

At least his arms and chest were not in mud so he could still breathe. Trouble was he couldn't move his legs. Mud held him like a suction cup, and no matter how hard he paddled at the water with his arms, he couldn't free himself from the horrible stuff.

How would he ever be able to get himself out? Reuben Rivers had deserted him and there was no one else around and most likely wouldn't be, unless it was the mountain lion. He could imagine how hungry the cat would be when it came upon him stuck in a mud-pit. He would be like all those prehistoric animals stuck in the tar pits.

He shivered, and started struggling anew but only sank a little deeper for his effort.

"Calm down," he told himself. "Don't think about a mountain lion that's nowhere near when you have enough problems with mud. How does a man get out of mud? The same way he gets out of quicksand? Nope," he continued talking out loud. "Quicksand takes you under faster when you struggle, mud takes you a little deeper but you don't go under."

What he should do was let the water go down and the mud harden just a little on top, enough so his hands wouldn't bury up when he placed his weight on them. Surely, he could lift himself out of the mud. If not, he would dig himself out one handful of mud at a time.

He felt better now he had a plan with two options.

It didn't take long until the hot sun reflecting on the water made him close his eyes. He was exhausted and wanted to sleep, but sleep wouldn't come. All he could do was close his eyes and wait. Even that didn't give him relief for he was afraid to keep them closed. Small pieces of debris were washing toward him, even in the shallow water. He used his hands to keep them from ramming into him.

A piece of tin roofing came at him. He hit it with his hand and regretted it. The tin cut and blood oozed from his hand. At least it wasn't a serious cut when it could have been. He didn't feel lucky, especially when the carcass of some animal hit him in the back of his head. He raked at it with his uncut hand, steering it around him to float on down stream.

It was a calf.

Ball was a least one animal less.

Perhaps Ball was already trudging along the high ground in an effort to save his herds. Perhaps, if he yelled loud enough, Ball would hear him and come to his rescue. "Help! Help!" he yelled until his throat was sore, but George Ball didn't show up. A dry throat did. He longed for water and was tempted to dip up the muddy water in his uncut hand, but couldn't stomach the thought. He wasn't that thirsty – yet.

He looked around him and determined he wasn't that far from the rocks, twenty, no more than thirty feet at the most. He raked away a floating limb.

"Shit!" What was he thinking? Limbs could help him get free. If he had long enough limbs to place around him, he might be able to use them as buoyant force to dissipate the weight of his mass and pry himself out.

He grabbed a limb that was too short but he couldn't let it float away. He jabbed its end in the mud and reached for another limb as it floated by. He almost panicked when limbs were not within his reach, totally the opposite to what he felt before he had developed his new plan for escape.

He wished he had never seen the girl in the first place and doubly wished he had never aided her with the copperhead bite on her leg. It was nothing but a cursed day for him when he found that girl. If he ever got out of this mud, he would never go after another woman if he lived to be a hundred.

"I was a fool," he said to the receding water. "I should never have chased after her like a dog after a bitch in heat." Knowledge of his own stupidity hit him. What could he have been thinking? That the girl would fall in his arms and worship him forever after he saved her from the only life she had ever known?

"If I get out of this," he promised the world and himself. "I'll leave these North Carolina mountains and never return."

He was looking like a man in the middle of a beaver dam when Reuben Rivers returned. Actually, Reuben saw the pile of limbs before he ever spotted the head and shoulders sticking out of the muddy water. It so amused Reuben that he had to sit down and watch as Scrawny worked at catching limbs with a passion. He had to give the little fellow credit for never giving up.

After about an hour, Reuben gave up on Scrawny's success. "Need a little help?" he called out over the distance.

"Hell no!" Mitch hollered back. "I'm having the time of my life."

"I believe that," Reuben returned. "I'll go on then."

"Get me out of here!" Mitch yelled.

"Say you want help after all?"

"Hell yes!"

Reuben took his rope from the knapsack but knew it wasn't long enough to reach Scrawny unless he waded into the water. Considering the circumstance Scrawny was in, that was out of the question. They would both be out of luck if they both were stuck in the mud.

"It's too short," Reuben called. "I'll have to cut a tree limb."

"Hurry," Mitch yelled back.

"There's no hurry. You're safe."

It was then Reuben saw it. Mitch didn't. It was clinging to the trunk of a floating tree, braced safely by the leafless stubs of broken branches. It was the mountain lion looking for the world like a giant almost drowned-rat. The strong, lean muscling of the mountain lion's body was even more visible because the water had plastered its hair to its body.

Reuben reached for his gun and then realized that it would do him no good even if the gun and shells had dried out enough to fire. The cat was in direct line with Scrawny. Still, he thought he could hit the cat without hitting Scrawny. If the cat was dead, then the girl would be safe if she had survived the storm, which he doubted. He lifted his gun, had the cat plus Scrawny in his sights, and then lowered it. As much as he wanted the big cat dead, it was too risky.

From where Reuben stood, he could see that one side of its face was swollen until an eye wasn't visible, but the other side was uninjured. Out of that side shown the angriest eye Reuben had ever seen in an animal.

It saw Reuben, lifted his upper lip and snarled, showing long white teeth. The floating tree was rapidly headed straight for Scrawny. The cat was sure to leap off the tree trunk once it hit the piled up limbs, and then the mountain lion would be able to vent its anger and pain on the helpless man.

"Don't say a word! Don't move!" Reuben called out very plainly.

It was then the cat let out a paralyzing scream and Scrawny turned his head. He froze, unable to say a word if he had wanted to.

"Sink down into the water!" Reuben yelled, but Scrawny didn't move, didn't seem to hear. "Sink down," he yelled again."

Reuben put down his gun, yelled even louder, grabbed rocks, and threw them at the cat. They splashed in the water many feet from the cat. Reuben didn't stop throwing rocks. He had to keep the cat's attention away from Scrawny and hope, pray that the tree didn't lodge on the dam of limbs.

The water wasn't deep enough to float the tree. Its branches hit the mud and stopped, allowing the current to suck the tree back into the flow and take the cat away from the pile of limbs that Scrawny clung to.

Scrawny's upper body looked as though it crumbled and almost disappeared into the water as the cat floated away.

"Little late for that you lucky devil," Reuben mumbled as he ambled off toward the nearest pine tree. It would take a little while to cut a sturdy branch from a tree with his knife.

The shock of seeing the huge mountain lion coming right at him had almost been more than Mitch could take. He thought his heart stopped beating; he became light headed and everything was a blur. Even after surviving the flood, becoming stuck in mud, and finally knowing he would be rescued, he was going to die.

It was all because of that girl. He hated her, hated everything about her. Cursed the day he had decided to chase after her.

The cat had been hurt. A red glob hung from its eye socket and the entire side of its face was puffed up. The injured side looked horrible but not nearly as horrible as the uninjured side. The one eye was fixed on him with a killing rage.

And then rocks hit the water causing loud splashes. The eye looked away.

"Sink down," he heard. "Sink!" but Mitch thought the yelling was directed at the tree the big cat was perched on. It wasn't until the tree had floated away that reality hit him. Reuben was telling him to sink into the water.

It didn't matter who or what Reuben was yelling at, for Mitch couldn't have moved an inch, still couldn't.

It wasn't until Reuben returned dragging a long pine branch with all the small limbs cut off that Mitch started to recover from his shock. He tried not to think about that one eye as he watched Reuben tie the rope to the large end of the branch. Reuben tossed the pole into the water, but it floated away from Mitch. Reuben shook his head as he pulled the pole back to him. He climbed over rocks and muddy patches of earth as he went up stream.

What was he doing? Surely, he knew the rope and branch would never reach him if Reuben got further away.

Reuben was a small speck in the distance when he finally threw the branch into the floodwater again. The branch floated out and away from Mitch, but Reuben held on to the rope as he made his way back over the rocks toward Mitch.

Mitch wanted to shout with joy as the water brought the branch straight toward him. It came on rapidly until it hit the dam and stopped ten feet from his outstretched fingers. Mitch knew he cried.

"Pull up the limbs and throw them away," Reuben called. "Move all the limbs out of the way."

It took a minute or two for him to realize what Reuben intended. When he did realize the branch could reach him if his dam was gone, he worked with every ounce of strength left in him. He was about to give up hope when the tied branch started to move closer.

With every limb tossed away, the branch inched closer. He lunged forward and grabbed the branch, his face going into the water, but he didn't care for he could not draw a breath, dared not breathe until he felt the tug on the branch.

He lifted his head up and saw that Reuben had his feet braced against a rock and was pulling with every bit of his strength, but it wasn't enough to pull him free of the sticky mud.

Reuben stopped pulling. "Hang on. Don't turn the branch loose."

There was no way Mitch was going to turn loose of the branch, even if Reuben was leaving.

It seemed like hours before Reuben came back with another pine branch. He tied his rope to the large end of the branch before he dragged as big a rock as he could carry on top of another rock. Reuben placed the branch over the rock in a seesaw fashion. He straddled the branch and sank his weight down.

Mitch felt himself being stretched almost in two. "Wait!" he screeched, but Reuben didn't wait. He stood up and dropped down hard on the branch. Pain shot through Mitch's arms, but he didn't turn loose of the branch. He was determined not to turn loose of his lifeline even if his arms were yanked from their sockets.

They weren't. He felt and heard a sucking before he came loose from the mud. The next thing he knew was the feeling of being pulled over mud at a rapid speed. When he looked up, he saw Reuben jerking lengths of rope backward.

"You can stand up now," Reuben said when Mitch was only five feet away from him.

Mitch sat up but couldn't stand.

"Feelin' a bit weak, are you?"

Mitch nodded.

Reuben stood in the edge of the water as he untied the branch and looped his rope into a small circle. That rope had saved two men from the flood. Reuben wished it could have also saved the girl.

He tried to push her from his mind as he reached for Mitch and helped him to his feet. "Sit on the warm rocks for a while. It'll warm what's left of you while you get your strength back."

Mitch was wearing a tattered shirt, no shoes, no pants, and no underwear.

The water had gone down enough for George Ball to reach the barn near his house. His cattle in that barn were on the soggy side, but all were alive and wanting turned out into the sunshine, but it was still far too muddy.

"Mornin'," said a cheery voice. "Bit wet and muddy today it seems."

Ball jumped and whirled to see Reuben Rivers supporting the surveyor.

"What in the name of . . ." Ball began.

"It seems our friend has lost his britches," Reuben said. "Got an extra feed sack or something?"

"You're both alive." Ball's voice rung of his disbelief that they could have survived such a flood.

"Yeap," Reuben said. Mitch didn't comment.

"I'll get a feed sack and then take you both to the house. He looks peaked."

"Spent the night in a tree," Mitch managed in explanation of his weakened condition.

"And you?" Ball directed toward Reuben.

"Spent the night on top of the Big Hump. How did things fair with you?"

"All's alive so far, but I've only inspected this barn. Chances are mighty good that I've lost a lot of expensive cattle."

Reuben didn't comment. Most likely Ball wouldn't be as lucky in other places.

When Ball returned with the feed sack, Mitch was alone and sitting on the ground.

"Where's Rivers?"

"He must have left right after you did."

"Where did he go?"

"He didn't say."

"Will he be back?"

"I don't know. He has a habit of disappearing."

"Can you walk?"

"Some."

"Stand up then and I'll help wrap this around you. Don't want the old woman to get all tore up. She don't like seeing naked in any shape or form."

Jennifer Ball cried when she saw Mitch standing in the muddy yard with nothing but a feed sack around his muddy body. "I'm glad someone is alive." She glanced at the feed sack with trepidation. "Oh, my. Don't move an inch until I find something for you to wear."

She was back almost instantly with a pair of her husband's pants and shirt.

"Here. You can change behind the house."

A rain barrel was at the corner of the house; stuck in mud, but still standing even after the flood. He washed himself with the sack as best he could before he donned the clothes. They were way too big, but he was glad to get them for he had lost everything. His truck, survey equipment, tent, everything was long gone, water under the bridge, so to speak. He didn't even have money to buy a loaf of bread.

His spirit sagged even worse than when Helen had left him high and dry. He leaned against the house, more dejected than he had ever been in his life. The thought that he'd have been better off drowned in the flood came rushing at him making him want to do nothing more than sit down and cry.

Before he could give in to the feeling, Ball came around the corner. "Old woman says to come into the kitchen once you're decent."

"I'm as decent as I can get."

"You'll do."

Mitch followed Ball inside. Jennifer had managed to get a fire built earlier and had hot coffee on the stove. She handed him a cup. Nothing had ever tasted as good as that coffee.

"Do you know anything about the other man?" she asked.

"Reuben Rivers?"

"The one hunting the mountain lion."

"He survived."

"Good. I was afraid everyone was drowned. I thought George and I would be the only people left alive." She shivered from the image her imagination wrought up.

Ball rolled his eyes. "I have things to see about." He went back outside.

Mitch spent two days with the Ball's before the roads dried out enough to travel. It was Allen Granger, from another county, who came to check on the Balls. Jennifer Ball cried when she saw the man. Mitch nearly did.

After writing in his book that George and Jennifer Ball, Mitch Kenilworth, and Reuben Rivers were still alive, he said he had to get back to town and report that he had found three other people that day who were still missing and assumed drowned in the flood.

Mitch considered telling him that the wild girl would make four, but he didn't. Reuben Rivers had told him he could stop searching for the girl. He had found some of her things after the flood, but not her. He was certain the girl and her dog had perished. He said the only thing that saved him was tying himself to a tree. Reuben told about the girl with such remorse on his face that Mitch believed him.

Mitch also knew by his own instinct that the girl was dead, and at the moment, he didn't care. If not for her, he'd still have his belongings.

What he wanted right now was to get back to civilization. George Ball was trying to work him to death while his wife was crying him to death. He had wondered a dozen times or more during the past two days why a man like Ball would marry a woman like Jennifer. One was made of nails and the other was made of silly putty.

"Can I hitch a ride into town?" Mitch asked Granger.

"Sure can."

"Stay here," Ball said quickly. "I need help and there's nobody else available."

"Folks will be worrying about me," Mitch lied as he climbed into the passenger seat.

"I'll pay good money for your help," Ball added.

He hadn't offered to pay him so far. "Maybe Mr. Granger can send you some help."

"I'll put the word out," Granger said as he got in the truck.

"You're wearing my clothes," Ball said in a last-ditch effort to keep him there.

"They were in the rag pile," Jennifer added. "You outgrew them years ago."

"I'll send them back when I get something else," Mitch said.

"No you won't," Jennifer said firmly. "Burn them."

Ball looked like a whipped man, one that was also angry because he was unable to command his world in the direction he wanted it to go.

"We'll manage," Jennifer whispered to her husband. "Everybody is trying to get themselves together just like we are."

Ball said nothing more. He stood there and watched the truck drive away.

"Did every place flood?" Mitch asked after riding in silence for a while.

"Like I told Mrs. Ball, this was the worse hit area. Most other places got hard rains."

"What about the Ruffian Mountain area?"

"No flooding."

Relief hit Mitch. "How far do you live from a place called Sodom? It's near Ruffian Mountain."

"A good ways, but I'll be glad to drop you off in town. You'll be able to hitch a ride from there."

Mitch wanted to beg him for the ride. He knew Don Donavan would give him room and board until he got in touch with the Forest Service and the insurance company. Just maybe he'd be able to scrape together enough money to buy another truck. He even considered calling his ex-wife and asking her for a loan. Knowing Helen, she would probably tell him he was getting what he deserved and then hang up.

Mitch couldn't believe his streak of good luck. Iva Dean Steward was coming out of the feed and seed store when Granger dropped him off. Her eyes grew big as she took in his appearance.

"Mitch?"

"It's me."

"What in the name of heaven happened to you?"

"I got caught in the flood. Lost everything."

"At least you're all right."

"Say, you wouldn't be heading toward Sodom would you?"

"I am."

"Could I get a ride to Donavan's place."

"Sure."

Once Mitch had confided that he hoped Don would let him stay there a few days, Iva Dean's eyes brightened.

"Why don't you stay at my cabin? It's not finished, but it stayed dry during the storm. You can help Pete Jenkins finish it."

"I don't know."

"Of course you will. Now, don't argue."

Mitch wasn't about to argue.

"What about the wild girl? Did you find her?"

Mitch's jaws clinched then relaxed. "The flood got her."

"Are you sure?"

"Positive."

"How can you be positive? Were you with her?"

He didn't want to go into any kind of explanation with Iva Dean but he had to tell her something. "She and the dog were caught in the flood. Only a few of her belongings were found. She didn't have a chance. It was the closest thing to an ocean I've ever seen."

Iva Dean's homely face took on a sad look. "I hate for anybody to drown, but it was probably for the best. I know Rhonda and Jordan Grearity will be delighted."

"They won't have to split the inheritance with her," Mitch said.

"Would never have had to, legally," Iva Dean admitted. "As executor of Mother's estate, I checked into things. There was never proof Mother had another daughter regardless of what Mother's will stated. I simply wanted to carry out Mother's wishes." She grinned. "I never miss an opportunity to berate the queenly Rhonda. One of these days I'm bound to cause her to have a heart attack." Iva Dean gave her loud horselaugh. "Do me a favor, Mitch, will you?"

"What?"

"Don't tell Joe, Rhonda or Jordan the girl is dead."

"I won't see them."

"Don't tell if they should ever happen to show up." Her grin had faded but her eyes still held a sparkle.

"What happened to the girl?" were almost the first words Don uttered when he saw Mitch Kenilworth.

"Didn't make it," Mitch told him frankly. He showed little sympathy for he no longer cared about the girl. It was her fault he had lost everything he owned and it would be a long time until he could forgive her for causing that to happen.

"No," Don said.

"A man found some of her things after the flood went down, but no sign of her."

"No," Don said again. "She's alive. She was smart enough to survive a flood."

Mitch shook his head firmly. "Smart had nothing to do with it. Besides, you wouldn't be saying that if you'd seen the flood that hit Humpback Mountain. It looked like the ocean during a hurricane. Cattle, buildings, uprooted trees, everything imaginable was washed away."

"You survived," Don said in defense of the girl still being alive.

"Only by pure luck. If it hadn't been for that pine tree and Reuben Rivers I wouldn't be alive." He didn't want to even mention the mud and the mountain lion.

"She's alive," Don's voice was pleading.

"Believe what you want, but Reuben Rivers said the flood got her, and I believe him."

"How would he know?" Don persisted.

"He said he was watching her and the dog. He tried to rescue her, but he couldn't. He had to tie himself to a tree in order not to be washed away."

"You're telling me the gospel truth?"

"Of course I'm telling you the gospel truth. Why wouldn't I tell the truth about something like that?"

"I was just hoping," Don admitted. "Just hoping."

After Mitch left, Don walked around in a daze, blaming himself for things he didn't do that might have saved the girl.

"Stop it," Betsy finally told him. "You did all you could."

"I did nothing."

"For goodness sakes. Can't you get it through you thick head Aggie lived the way she wanted to live? She's the one who ran away from people, and she's the one who could have come to you any day during all those years she spent in that cave."

"Aggie didn't care what happened to herself. She cared about Raven and she did come to me to get help for the girl."

"She could have brought the child to you the day she was born, but she didn't. When she asked for your help, you tried to give it. The girl wouldn't let you."

"I should have tried harder," Don stubbornly insisted.

"If you don't stop blubbering around because of that girl, I'm gonna conk you on the head with my fist."

Don stopped pacing and sank down in his chair, reached down, picked up a stick of pinewood, leaned the back of his chair against the wall of the house, and started whittling.

Chapter 12

Raven was huddled on a giant pile of debris, cold, stiff, and shivering, but she still clung to Dog who was lying as close to her as he could get, his heart beating at high speed against her arms.

It was still raining, but not nearly as hard as it had been. The night had been a long, dark torture she thought would never end, but it was ending. She could see the sky beginning to lighten slightly on top of the mountain.

"It's morning," her lips formed the word just to prove that she was still capable of speech. Dog lifted his head and licked at her face. She wasn't sure if she laughed or cried as she lay her cheek against his huge square head. She had been so afraid the flood would rip her arms from her precious friend and they would be separated. It hadn't happened, thank the good Lord, it hadn't happened, although it still could.

She could hear the water swirling around them even though she couldn't see it. She knew she was in a wooded area and on the side of the mountain according to the slope and the speed of the water rushing by. It sounded like a much larger waterfall than was at Tetter's pond.

She wished Aggie was with her, and then changed her mind. An old, crippled woman would never have survived. Besides, she would not have wanted Aggie to be as scared or to suffer as she had during the long night.

193

Oh, how she longed for daylight to come so she could at least see what was happening around her. She closed her eyes and tried to concentrate on breathing in and out – in and out. If Dog could stay still on the uncomfortable pile of debris, then surely she could.

Finally, by creeping smidgens, the world around her lost bits of darkness until she could see outlines through the rain. Then the darkness turned gray and then almost white with rising mist.

She forgot about being cold and uncomfortable with the shock of seeing her surroundings. Trees were lying down with their roots up in the air. Huge boulders were piled on top of each other and dirty water covered everything. Never had she seen such destruction; never could she have imagined it.

The place she and dog had lodged was where rocks and small trees had piled up against larger trees and boulders. Had they not landed on that exact spot, they would undoubtedly have been washed away to drown in the floodwaters that covered most everything.

She looked for the tent and the place where the men had been, but there was nothing but rushing water. Everything was so unfamiliar, so frightening. There were no longer places and things where they had once been; all things were buried beneath an ocean of muddy, debris-strewn floodwater. Worst of all was she could do nothing. She would have to sit there clinging to Dog until the rain stopped and the floodwater went down.

She looked up the mountain in the direction from which she had been washed down. It was a matted, tangled mess of trees, rocks, and running water. Her chin trembled.

"We're alive," she said out loud just to give herself enough courage to draw the next breath. "Still being alive has to be something special."

Dog only whined, but didn't move. He didn't want to fall off the debris and into the water any more than she did.

"*He* had to drown," Raven said to Dog. "Now, I can keep the clothes without owing him anything." She brightened a slight bit. "We can go back home where we belong. I hate this place. I really, really hate it."

Raven was stiff and sore and hungry by the time the water had gone down enough for them to get off the piled up debris, which wasn't an easy task. She and Dog had to crawl over and under an unending supply of uprooted trees and brush that had been covered up with water only hours before. She figured the entire mountain of trees and plants had come down with her and Dog in the flood.

Once she was free of the tangled mess and standing near the bottom of the mountain, she thought of her travois and the supplies tied to it. She had to go back to the cave before she and Dog could return home. Dog needed dog food; he had to be as hungry as she was. She knew it would be difficult climbing back up the mountain after the flood, but she had no choice if she didn't want both of them to starve.

Even her determination couldn't wipe out the fact that she was bone-tired and her ankle hurt. She sank down on a damp rock intending to rest for a few minutes. Her ankle was swollen twice its normal size and there were blue splotches all over her leg. It had been hurt during her tumble down the mountain along with the rocks, water, and trees. She remembered hearing a roaring noise, looking behind her, and seeing a river of water coming at her. She didn't have time or a place to run to. She locked her arms around Dog's neck an instant before the water tumbled her. Water had gone in her mouth and up her nose, but she couldn't cough, couldn't breathe. She knew for certain that she and Dog both were done for, but they weren't. After what seemed hours, they stopped tumbling while the water rushed over the top of them. She now suspected that her leg had lodged between rocks and trees. How she had managed to hold onto her precious Dog, she didn't know.

She looked at Dog now huddled next to her. Every one of his ribs were showing and there were places where the hair had been scraped off, but he wasn't limping. Still, she ran her hands over his body searching for injuries.

He licked her face and whined, not the whine caused by injury, but the sound of impatience. He wanted her to get moving, do something other than sit at the bottom of the mountain where floodwater was still gushing near.

He whined again when she started up the mountain. She knew he wanted to go back home to the Ruffian as badly as she did, but the travois came first, now that the men were washed away.

The sun was going down by the time she climbed over the rocks and destruction the flood had left on the mountain. With each step she took upward, her hopes fell. She knew the cave would have gotten flooded and her precious things destroyed.

She couldn't believe the rock was in front of the entrance exactly as she had left it. It was even harder for her to believe the cave had remained relatively dry.

She had no matches left to light her fire, so she left the rock rolled away from the opening in order to let a little light enter the cave. Dog had already found the travois and sack of dog food. She grabbed a handful and ate too. It was just as good as dried corn and a lot easier to chew up and swallow. She and dog went outside and searched for puddles of water caught in dips in rocks. They drank all they could find.

Once they drank enough to ease their thirst, she rolled the rock in place, found the driest spot possible in the dark cave, and fell asleep. Dog snuggled against her. Another flood could have come and gone without her knowing it.

The night had passed all too soon. It was mid-day when she woke and rolled the rock from the opening. She stuck her head out and listened to the sound of birds singing. Surely, she was mistaken or still asleep and dreaming. Birds wouldn't sing after such destruction.

She crawled out. The sun was bright and warm, and indeed, there were a few birds singing from piles of debris. She wondered how such small things could have survived? Dog came up behind her and gave her a nudge without sniffing the air. Could that mean the scent of the mountain lion had been washed away? Did it mean the mountain lion was gone? Could a mountain lion swim? Would he drown or be caught on a pile of debris as she and Dog had been?

"Let's go home," she said to Dog, and knew that he readily agreed.

Nothing was easy. She had piled the travois extra high with all her belongings, planning never to return to that cave. She had been wrong in staying there in the first place. The mountain of the rising sun was hostile instead of welcoming. How could she have been so stupid?

Getting the travois down the mountain was extremely difficult, especially with her aching, injured leg and ankle. Traversing along the mountainside was impossible. It was getting dark by the time she was in the bottomland where the mud was still soft and deep. She dared not continue on, if she did, it would mean crossing the bald in early darkness. Most likely the cattle would be there. The bald was high enough to stay out of the floodwater. Neither she nor Dog were in condition to put up a fight with a bull or a mountain lion.

She found a rocky crevice that was rather dry, shared a handful of dog food, and fell asleep without any complaints from Dog.

This time she woke with morning's first light. Dog was still beside her, his eyes bright and eager. Raven only allowed herself the necessary time to relieve herself before heading homeward.

They hadn't gone far when they both needed fresh water, but could find none as they were no longer in the rocks where water had lodged. The mud where they walked had started to crack but it was still soft beneath the crust without any water visible. She considered going toward the river where the water was still rushing high and frothy. The acres of soft mud stopped her. Surely, they would come across a stream soon. All the rain should have every hollow and gully filled to the brim with gushing water.

It was late afternoon before they came across water. Raven dropped to her belly and drank with her face in the water. She sat up, saw a clump of mint, chewed a few leaves, and drank again of the chilly liquid.

She rubbed her swollen ankle and longed to stick it and her bruised leg into the coolness until the pain stopped throbbing, but she couldn't take the time. It was a slow and tedious job pulling the travois over muddy, debris-strewn land making progress slow and painful with her injuries. If only she could run over the familiar path she had taken before, they would be home by now, but she couldn't run or take the familiar path. Instinct told her she had to go around the bald.

Raven forced herself to stand up, strap the travois ropes over her shoulders and move on. She hadn't gone far when she saw the dented truck lying upside down in a gully. Both doors were torn off leaving a clear view of the steering

wheel and empty inside. She almost smiled. Not only did
the flood get *him*, it got his truck too.

Instantly, she was ashamed of her satisfaction and a
touch of sadness threatened, but she pushed it away. She
hated he was dead like her mother and Aggie, but his death
allowed her to go home. As for the old man, she tried to
assure herself that a well-placed rock would keep him from
climbing along the narrow ledge to her cave, her wonderful
dry and safe cave. Oh, how she longed to be home again.

Relief hit her once she was able to travel the familiar
ridges again. The bottomland was frightful for it held the
tracks of her travois too well. It wasn't likely to rain again
for a few days; therefore, she could be easily tracked if
anyone was left alive.

A far-off whippoorwill was mourning the loneliness of
things passed by the time they reached the narrow ledge on
Ruffian Mountain, a sound that stirred emotions she wasn't
prepared to acknowledge, not when she was this weak.

She needed all her strength, all her concentration in
getting the heavy loaded travois over the narrowest places,
but she didn't dare leave it behind, and it was out of the
question for her and dog to stay with it. She had become
obsessed at being inside her very own cave, had a need to
be near Aggie even when Aggie was in her grave.

The narrowest section of the ledge had been made even
narrower because the heavy rain had washed dirt and rocks
onto it. She had to stop and shovel the rocky soil over the
ledge with her hands. She could hear it rattling down the
side of the mountain although she couldn't see below her
for the darkness.

Dog, going in front of her, had already made it across.
Occasionally, a pleading whine escaped him, but Raven

dared not rush the job she was doing. One mistake on her part and both she and the travois could tumble down a mountain of rock. After escaping the flood, she didn't want to lose her life now she was finally home again.

Once she had the ledge cleared, she was almost too paranoid to attempt the crossing. It was Dog's whining made her try it, and nothing short of a miracle kept her and the travois from falling.

Tomorrow or perhaps next day, she would have to find a good path the back way to leave the mountain; either that or never leave the mountain with her travois. She didn't want that. She needed to gather food and the travois would make it easier and faster.

If only she could take back the rockslide, now that *he* had drowned.

Chapter 13

Iva Dean Grearity Stewart wasn't satisfied, even if Mitch Kenilworth claimed the girl had died in the flood. Nor was she satisfied Aggie was dead, although logic told her they both probably were. Her dissatisfaction had nothing to do with her mother's wealth or her mother's will. It had to do with her own curiosity and her own blasted need to know every answer to every question that popped into her head. Admittedly, such curiosity was a fault of hers, but a fault she adored and had no intention of remedying.

That's why she stopped at Cade William's place – to see what was going on with them. She dearly loved to torment Cade and enjoyed watching the power struggle between him and Carrie. Cade may have been a dominant force before he was burned in the fire, but Carrie was rapidly gaining ground on him.

Cade was sitting in his favorite chair under the shade of the walnut tree. His scared face had gray beard growing in patches, his unsuccessful attempt at hiding his scars. The hair sticking out beneath his cap was just as gray and ragged in appearance as his beard. His stomach had increased in paunch size, while his shoulders had started to round-off and slump forward.

She almost sniffed in disgust. She hated to see a man who let himself deteriorate with age. Men should spend some time looking in a full-length mirror. The arrogant military posture of a city man was far better than being a hunchbacked, dirty mountain man. But what did she care how Cade Williams looked?

"Resting?" she asked rather cynical.

"Shading," he shot back. "What tom cat dragged you here?"

"Same one that scratches dirt over you."

He continued giving her the evil eye. "Heard you have the *pretty boy* living in your cabin."

"Yep, lost everything he had in the flood."

"He'll be driving your Jeep next thing we know."

"He's trying to collect insurance for his truck so he won't have to drive my Jeep."

"Figures. City folks always want things given to them."

"While mountain men think they were born owning everything."

"Sounds like a little intelligence has penetrated that thick head of yours cause we do own everything a man could want."

"Intelligence is more than I can attribute to you."

Carrie came up the bank carrying a bushel of green beans from her garden. "If you two are determined to waste time quarreling with each other, break these beans while you're at it."

"I've got fifteen minutes to spare," Iva Dean told her.

Carrie sat the hamper of beans at her feet. "I'll get you a chair and the dishpan."

"Fifteen minutes more of hell," Cade grumbled. "No wonder your old man sends you to the mountains while he stays behind. A man needs a little peace once in a while."

"Seems I'm just luckier than Carrie, doesn't it?" She turned toward the open screen door. "Carrie, bring out an apron for Cade to tie around his waist. He doesn't have big enough balls to rest a handful of beans on."

Cade gave her his dirtiest look. "You're a foul mouthed, slick-straddled buzzard," he shot back.

Carrie brought out a chair, two towels, and the dishpan. "Keeps your clothes clean," Carrie explained of the towels, while ignoring both Cade and Iva Dean's harsh words. "I'll get the cans ready while you two break the beans."

"Bring another chair," Iva Dean insisted. "I'd like your company being I can't stay long."

Carrie reluctantly went back for another chair.

"Your garden do well?" Iva Dean asked after Carrie returned with another chair and towel.

"Good enough, at least we won't starve to death this winter. Heard about Mitch Kenilworth. You're being mighty kind letting him stay in your cabin."

Cade snorted. "Kind had nothing to do with it. She's needing a good screwing to settle her so-called nerves."

Both Carrie and Iva Dean ignored his remark, knowing it would hurt him worse if he was ignored.

"Felt sorry for him." Iva Dean waited a couple of minutes before she broached the subject she had dropped by to discuss. "Mitch said the girl that saved Cade's life drowned in the flood."

Cade's head jerked around until he was glaring at Iva Dean with disbelief in his eyes.

"You don't say?" Carrie said. "How would he know?"

Iva Dean strung and snapped a handful of beans and then carefully tossed them into the dishpan before she continued.

"You ever heard of a man named Reuben Rivers? According, to the men at the feed and seed store, he's a legend in the White Top Mountain area."

"No," Carrie said. "Can't say as I've heard of him."

Cade snorted through his nose vibrating what few gray hairs grew on his upper lip. "I've heard of him. Folks don't hold to him living near them, has to hideout in the woods all by himself. Some say folks ought to form a posse, do humanity a favor, and go lynch him."

"Now, isn't that strange? From what I've heard, most men hold him as an icon."

"Yeap, he's some kind of convict all right. Had a price put on his head when he was just a boy."

Iva Dean laughter was loud and derogatory. "If that's true, which I doubt, no one has had the balls to collect it, have they?"

"What about him and the girl?" Carrie interrupted before they went at each other again.

"On with my story," Iva Dean said triumphantly. "According to Mitch, George Ball hired Reuben Rivers to kill a mountain lion that had been killing his cattle. While hunting for the mountain lion, Rivers came across the girl. When the storm hit, Rivers tried to save the girl but she was washed away, as had Mitch been. Rivers managed to save Mitch, but not the girl. He found only a few of her belongings ravaged by the flood water."

"Such a pity." Carrie tossed beans into the pan. "But things do happen."

Cade's scarred face sagged and his entire body slumped even further. Evidence the news had hit him hard.

Iva Dean almost smiled with satisfaction at being the first one to deliver Cade such news. It was good enough for the old goat. He had no business slobbering after such a young girl.

"My dog," Cade moaned. "She had my dog."

"Gone," Iva Dean added. "They went down together."

"I paid good money for that dog."

"Down the drain."

Regardless of what she told Cade, she had to have proof that both Aggie and the girl were dead, along with proof they existed in the first place. She was a *show-me* woman and she wanted Mitch to do exactly that – show her.

Cade watched Iva Dean drive away in her Jeep. He had the greatest urge to take his high-powered rifle and put a bullet in her head because of what she had told him. If the act could have brought the girl back to life, he'd have done it in an instant. Being there was nothing he could do about bringing the girl back, he could at least get relief from killing the messenger. Too bad the law was against him even when it was Iva Dean Grearity.

Cade sorely hated to lose both his dog and his money, but he hated to lose the girl far worse. She had not only saved his life, she was what kept him living, kept his groin tingling with a life-giving need. Not only that, her face had replaced the hideous face of the monster that once haunted him.

He shuddered and tried to wipe the monster from his mind, thankful he hadn't seen the ugly thing lately, hadn't felt it looking in the windows at him while he slept. It was most likely because he had been bedfast and couldn't go hunting alone, or even go with Pete Jenkins and Evert Wilson like he normally did.

Seemed when a man got old and disabled all his pleasures were denied him.

Iva Dean didn't bother to go by Don Donavan's place. Mitch had already told Don about the girl's death and she knew he genuinely took it hard. Don was probably the only man she had even known that truly had an unselfishly kind heart. Thing was, kind hearted men never amounted to much, not to mention their wives and children most always went ragged and hungry. When a man gave to others, he had to take from somebody.

"Shit," she muttered. "I've turned into a danged philosopher. Best remedy that before I reach my dotage. Can't stand pussy-footed wimps spouting platitudes."

She found Mitch at her cabin sweeping up wood scraps while Pete Jenkins sawed. He hurriedly put down the broom and went to meet her.

"You don't seem too busy," she greeted him.

"Pete thinks I'm in his way," Mitch admitted. "I'm not much of a carpenter.

"That's all right because I have another job for you."

Mitch cringed. He didn't like the look in her eyes when she got out of the Jeep. Now, he didn't like what she was saying.

"We're going to climb Ruffian Mountain today," she stated firmly. "I want to see the cave where the girl lived."

"You're joking?"

"I assure you that I'm not joking."

"Why?"

"She doesn't feel real to me and I want reality."

"Take my word for it, she was real. If you want proof, take another look at that rock slide she caused."

"I want to see where she lived; and I want to see where Aggie lived. After all, Aggie was my only sister and I deserve to know her just a little."

Mitch shook his head. "We can't climb that mountain."

"Why not? You've climbed it before with Don."

"Once was enough."

Her chin lifted and she looked him in the eyes. "Once will probably be enough for me and I do expect you to go with me."

"No way, I'm not getting us both killed."

"You and Don weren't killed."

"We easily could have been."

"But you weren't."

"Look, you're a woman and you don't understand how treacherous the climb was. There's a rocky ledge up there that's nothing but a death trap. Once Don and I were on solid ground again, I promised myself I'd never set foot on that ledge again."

"Fine. I'll go by myself and you can move out of my cabin."

"Consider me out."

"Get your things."

"I have no things to get." He turned his back to her and walked off.

She watched him until he reached the woods. "Wait," she called. "You just wait a confounded minute."

With reluctance he stopped.

She caught up with him. "You're going with me whether you like it or not."

"You're a bossy broad."

"Yes, I am. I'm persistent also. As I just explained to you, Aggie was my sister and the girl was most likely my great niece. You should understand my need to visit their cave. You had a need when you forced Don to take you there. It's time you did the same for me."

"Get Don to take you. I don't want to be responsible for your death."

"Don's an old man. You're not."

"He took me."

"You're returning the favor."

"The girl was alive when I went. She's dead now and there's nothing you can accomplish by climbing that mountain."

She wanted to tell him the only thing he had accomplished was making the girl run away in the first place, which caused her to be caught in the flood and ultimately caused her death, but she didn't. "Her death has nothing to do with it. Let's get going," she said firmly.

"You can't go now."

"We most definitely can."

"Leaving now would mean spending the night in the cave. It would be suicide to cross that ledge in the dark."

"Then we'll stay the night."

Iva Dean saw that Mitch was giving in. Truth be told, she suspected he wanted to visit her cave one more time. She knew that Don hadn't allowed him to explore the area as thoroughly as he wanted.

"We'll leave at daybreak in the morning. Wear good hiking shoes and bring enough food and water for us both."

Iva Dean smiled. Her plan had worked much easier than she expected. Mitch Kenilworth was such an unworthy opponent.

Raven had no matches to build a fire, but it didn't matter. What mattered was that she and Dog were home again, and they were safe at last. The man was dead and the mountain lion was gone. Finally, she and Dog could live in peace, just as Aggie had lived in peace. She would ask for no more than that. She no longer wanted to see what other places were like, nor did she believe there was a better cave for her to live in. From now on, she would only leave the Ruffian to gather food and firewood. Unfortunately, she would have to visit the valley in order to get dog food from Cade Williams or the other two men, but that would be several months down the road. Fortunately, she had left the dog food on the travois in the cave and it had stayed dry.

She put her arm around Dog and they both snuggled up in the soft dirt next to Aggie's grave. It was almost like being a little girl again and having Aggie there to protect her.

Raven expected to sleep late enough to allow her exhausted and injured body to heal, but Dog woke her up growling. When she didn't get up, he nuzzled her with his nose and raked at her with his front feet.

Groggily, she opened her eyes and lifted her head. She was still exhausted, sore, and hurting. Once night's sleep hadn't been enough to revive her.

"Hush," she ordered Dog, but he refused to quiet down. Instead, he went to the opening of that section of the cave and gave a fierce growl.

Raven recognized his warning growl. The mountain lion had followed them. She was on her feet, rushing for Aggie's gun regardless of how much her injured leg and ankle hurt. Realization hit. She had lost the gun in the flood. She tried to find a club, even a long pole to fight the mountain lion with. She couldn't allow Dog to fight it alone, but Dog wasn't snarling a challenge. He was whining now in a quiet sort of way, acting as though he wanted her to follow him.

She followed him out of the cave to the rock outcropping Aggie used to view the valley from. The sun was just rising, drawing white mist from the valley below, just as it had always done. She sighed. This was what Dog wanted her to see, the same July morning she was accustomed to seeing.

Hackles raised on his back and his upper lip quivered until his fangs were showing, but he no longer growled. His stance was rigid as he glared down the rockslide. Raven followed his gaze and froze. She couldn't believe what she saw. Surely, her eyes were playing tricks on her. This was a nightmare and she was still inside the cave dreaming. *He* couldn't be for real. He was dead! His tent had been washed away. His truck had been destroyed. She saw the flood water covering the place where his tent had been. She saw the wrecked truck with her own eyes.

"No," she whispered to Dog. "No, no, no." But there was no use denying what she saw. *He* was climbing the mountain and that big woman was with him. How could they possibly know she was back? How did they know she had come back? Why were they after her?

Raven wanted to cry, to give up, to toss herself down the rockslide she had caused. She was tired, and hungry, and her leg was swollen and aching. She didn't have enough strength to fight them, but she couldn't let them find her, not now, not after all that had happened.

"I'll kill them," she whispered to Dog. "I'll knock them off the ledge."

She hunkered down on the rocky outcropping to watch their progress as she ran scenarios through her mind of how she could kill them. She would hit them in the head with rocks. They would tumble down the mountain, bouncing off rocks until their bodies were broken and busted.

Then what?

People would come searching for them. They would come to her cave, find her tracks, her belongings, know she had returned. They would know she had killed him and the woman and she would never be able to live in peace.

Tears slid down her cheeks. She had been wrong all along. She could never return home. She had no home now that the man was alive.

All she knew to do was run again. And she had to run fast while they were just starting the climb up the mountain. If she waited any longer, they would be able to see her crossing the ledge.

She rubbed her hand over her bruised leg and swollen ankle. It was worse this morning. It would be more difficult for her crossing the ledge than it had been last night, but she had no choice unless she hid in the rocks and hoped they wouldn't find her.

She dared to hope that she could hide while they searched. Once they left, she and Dog could return to her cave. What if they found her? Could she brush away all signs that she and the big black were there? Did she dare chance it?

Her answer was no, she couldn't chance it. She had to run just as she had run before. Her mistake had been going to the far mountain where the sun rose. Her expectations had been far too great and her knowledge far too little. This time she would go in the opposite direction. From the big hump, she had seen land with no roads running through it. That meant no people lived there.

She could live in valley land. She didn't have to live on top of a mountain, nor did she have to live in a cave. She could build a shelter out of limbs and brush.

She jumped up and ran back to the cave as fast as her injury would allow. Dog was at her heels, encouraging her, hurrying her with his whines.

Fortunately, she hadn't unloaded a thing. All she had to do was loop the ropes over her shoulders and pull. Once she reached the ledge, she dropped the ropes, commanded the big black to stay, and ran back to the cave. She took off his shirt, bunched it in her hands, and hurriedly brushed inside the cave with it. She took precious time to backtrack to the rock outcropping brushing tracks as she went.

Each minute she took was a minute they were closer, but she dared not leave a track behind, dared to hope she had brushed away signs where she and Dog had relieved themselves.

What a terrible thing to encounter, finally reaching home only to discover they could never stay there because of the man whose clothes she wore. The first thing she intended to do was find other clothes and burn his – just as soon as she and Dog were safe again.

She made Dog cross the ledge first while she inched the overloaded travois along the rocks. "Let the ropes hold," she prayed. "Don't let them come apart now."

How the wooden poles scooted across the ledge was nothing short of a miracle. The too heavy load had loosened the ropes and allowed the poles to spread apart. The pole on the outside of the ledge often hung in the air.

If the travois tumbled over the ledge, Raven knew she would not be able to get the ropes off her shoulders in time to save herself. But she couldn't stop and tighten the ropes. She had to continue onward. Any moment now, those two would reach a point where the ledge would be visible.

She dared not draw breath as she eased over the narrowest spot, but the travois continued inching forward.

Dog was waiting on solid ground. He wagged his stub of a tail when she reached him.

"Hurry," she whispered. "We have to get out of here fast."

Once they reached the safety of the woods, she dropped the ropes from her shoulders, ordered Dog to stay, and took off the shirt for the second time. Again, she had to cross the ledge to wipe away tracks.

She took time to pry a rock from the almost sheer rock wall and beat the narrowest spot, which she had worked so diligently to widen last night, until the thinnest portion of ledge broke off, making it even trickier to cross. Perhaps the narrowness would frighten the woman as she looked straight down the sheer drop, making her insist on turning back. It was Raven's last attempt at protecting the sanctity of what was once her home.

Raven didn't want to take time to wipe out their tracks as they went through the wooded area, but she dared not do it. The man had followed her all the way to the far mountain; he had followed her back to the Ruffian; he would most likely follow her trail into the woods. He was a plague, one she didn't know how to get free from.

"I regret the day I saved that girl's life," Mitch told Iva Dean as they struggled up the side of the mountain in the hot sun.

"You didn't save her life."

"I did save her life."

"She wouldn't have died from the snake-bite."

"How do you know she wouldn't. You weren't there."

"She wasn't dead when you found her, was she? If she was going to die from the poison, her heart would have already stopped."

Disgust showed on Mitch's face. "You'd argue with a fence post, wouldn't you?"

"I'm not arguing. I'm stating a fact."

"All right then, I regret finding the girl in the first place. I regret even worse that I was foolish enough to follow her all the way to Humpback Mountain."

"Why did you?" Iva Dean asked.

"Most likely it was for the same reason you're insisting on going to her cave. Pure, hardheaded stupidity."

Iva Dean grinned. "On my part, yes. As for you, I think it was more lust than anything else. You probably hadn't had a good lay in a while. Although, I agree that you were stupid."

Mitch ignored her comment about not being laid in a while. He was getting somewhat used to her vulgar form of truth. "Just as I'm stupid for taking you up this mountain. Most likely we'll both be killed."

She smiled and increased her walking speed, forcing him to keep up. "Tell me more about Reuben Rivers."

"I don't know more about him."

"Sure you do. What was he actually like? Was he intelligent? Did he talk normal?"

Mitch had to admit he was intelligent. "He was somewhat educated, better than I had expected from his appearance. He smelled."

"Smelled?"

"He needed soap and a lot of water. Deodorant and a razor would have been helpful."

"Was he good looking?"

"How would I know?"

"You looked at him, didn't you?"

"I thought he was crude and ugly."

"Was he big and strong?" she asked with a sly grin.

"Yes, I suppose you could say he was big and strong."

"And he saved your life?"

"It was the pine tree saved my life."

"Didn't you say he saved you?"

Mitch stopped climbing. He was winded and needed a rest. It was hard to climb and breathe at the same time, much less talk.

"Why are you stopping? You said we had to hurry."

Mitch gave her a bewildered look. "Listen, either I talk, or I climb. Which do you want me to do?"

"Complain, complain. That's all you ever do. You know what, you'd make a man a good prissy wife if you could find one that would have you."

Mitch chose to ignore her.

The heat of the sun had lifted the fog from the valley until clouds had started gathering on top of the Ruffian. Mitch looked up and frowned.

"Surely we're not going to be caught in another flood," he said.

"It does look like rain. I feel moisture in the air. How much longer will it take to reach the cave?"

"Two, three hours."

"That long?"

"I warned you it was an all-day trip."

"I've been wet before," she said.

"I never want to get caught in the rain again. Believe me, one flood in a lifetime is more than enough."

"Was it horrible?"

"Horrible doesn't describe it. Pure terror doesn't come close."

"Poor girl."

"Poor me," Mitch admitted. "You'd have to be there to believe the horror and destruction water can cause. Once the water went down, there was mud everywhere."

"Where did he go?" Iva Dean asked.

"What are you talking about?"

"Reuben Rivers. Where did he go after he took you to George Ball's place?"

"I don't know where he went, most likely back to White Top Mountain."

"What happened to the mountain lion?"

"How should I know?" Mitch started climbing again.

"Do you think it drowned in the flood?"

"I doubt it."

"Then I doubt the girl drowned," Iva Dean stated firmly. "She's as wild and capable as that mountain lion. Wild things have an instinct that domesticated things don't have."

Mitch laughed. "You're foolish for saying such as that. She was just a young girl, one that's now dead."

Mitch was wishing he could have wired Iva Dean's mouth shut by the time they reached the path leading to the rock ledge. She had talked his ears sore even when he was trying not to listen to her continuous prattle.

"It's starting to rain," she stated needlessly. "Do you believe in fate?" She didn't give him time to answer. "You were intended to drown in that flood and fate has returned, determined to get you this time."

"It'll drown you, too," he said rather wishfully.

"I can swim like a fish."

"Good. If this rain gets harder, you'll need to swim across that rock ledge."

"What rock ledge?"

"The one we'll have to cross in about ten minutes."

"I've crossed ledges before."

Mitch grinned, almost pleased to say, "Not one like this."

It was raining hard when they reached it. Mitch reached out and took hold of her arm as she stepped onto the ledge. "We'll have to wait until it stops raining. We can't attempt it when it's wet."

"Sure we can."

"Not if we want to live."

"Coward."

"A live coward." He noted one black cloud had covered the sun. "We'll take shelter over there in the woods. It won't rain long. The sun is almost shining."

"We don't need to take shelter. As you say, this is only a fresh-it."

"Do as I say and don't argue. I'm exhausted and so are you."

She allowed him to lead her to the woods where they sat down under a stunted oak tree. Little did they know Raven had passed that same spot only a short time before. If she hadn't taken time to wipe away tracks, they would have seen them plainly for it had not yet rained hard enough to erase them.

"The cave would give us better shelter," Iva Dean said.

Mitch agreed. He remembered being in her cave during a rainstorm. He could still feel how the hair raised on the back of his neck as though his very life was in danger. At least he wasn't suffering from that feeling right now.

"Tell me something," Mitch said. "Before the rockslide you could have climbed up this mountain anytime you wanted and you didn't, why are you doing it now?"

Iva Dean didn't hesitate. "Two reasons, maybe three. First, when they were alive, I had no right to trespass on their territory. Two, I didn't know as much about them as I now do, and three, I want closure."

"And four," Mitch added for her. "You didn't give a rat's ass and probably still don't. You're just determined to be the center of attention."

Iva Dean chuckled. "Think you know me rather well, don't you?"

"Well enough."

"Then you know that I'm tired of sitting here in the rain. I'm ready to tackle that ledge."

"Not yet. I'm not about to fall to my death because of your impatience."

Pulling the travois along the familiar path wasn't difficult in the early morning light, even with her throbbing ankle. It became more difficult when she changed directions and headed into more open space. The brush, herbs, and grasses tangled the pole runners of her travois, making progress slow. Yet, that was the direction she knew she should travel – away from the Ruffian, away from Humpback Mountain, away from people who would not let her live in peace.

The sun grew unreasonably hot as it glowed down on her head. At first it felt good, but as the fiery ball rose higher in the sky, its burning rays took their toll on her. She remembered she was thirsty and hungry. She had eaten nothing but a few bites of dog food for several days, and her throat was scaly-dry from thirst. She stopped, stuck her hand into an opened sack of feed, and gave Dog the food. He ate it readily, but she couldn't stomach more dog food. She craved something fresh, something that could put renewed life back into her.

When Dog had finished eating, Raven lifted her head and winded the air. She could smell water on the wind. She moved forward, heading deeper into the bottomland knowing that was where the river ran.

She longed for fish roasted over a hot bed of fire coals. She remembered the blindfish that once swam in pooled water that ran through the cave. Aggie told her how Lu had slipped and caught them all out. She now understood her mother's craving for fish and wished she had at least one fish, even if it was blind and the very last one in existence.

She didn't find fish for she hadn't reached the river. What she found was a patch of briars covered in half-ripe blackberries. She ate until every one was gone but her hunger had not abated.

She remembered the aroma of meat roasting on long branches over the hairy man's fire. If he was roasting that meat again, she'd be willing to fight him for it, but that meat was washed away in the flood. At first she thought the strange, hairy man had gone with the flood, but now she wondered if that was the case. If *he* had survived to return to the valley of Sodom, and then have enough audacity to climb the mountain after her, the strange, hairy wolf-man could have survived also. Would the hairy man still be hunting for her, too?

She left the briar patch pretending her belly was full, but the rumbling in her guts would not be silent.

"Soon," she said to the big black. "Soon we'll come across people and a spring house. We'll drink milk and perhaps find a ham," she said wistfully.

The sun was growing hotter. She looked over her shoulder, back toward the Ruffian. Dark rain clouds surrounded its crest and it appeared as though it could be raining. She shuddered at the thought of rain and flooding water. Still, she was drawn toward the river.

She came to dried, cracked mud the flood had left behind long before she found the river. Carefully, she stepped onto the mud to make sure it was dry enough to hold her weight. It was. She pulled her travois onto it and checked to see if it left slide marks. It did, but not as clearly as she feared. There were only two very thin drag marks, and no prints of her and Dog's feet were visible. If someone saw the drag marks, they wouldn't know what caused them.

She continued onward toward the smell of the river, drawn for the need of fish. She reached soft mud long before she came to water. She stopped, daring not to continue. She lifted her hand and shaded her eyes, gazing over acres of mud. She would have to forget about fish, stay on the hard mud until she found some other type of food and water. Perhaps she could find a fresh stream of water with crawfish hiding under rocks. There wasn't much meat on them, but it might be enough to ease her craving.

She pulled her travois over miles of mud before the mud began to thin out and give way to rocky ground. She had left the muddy bottomland behind and was now traveling along the toe of hills that would eventually turn into mountains. She was in land where she felt more secure, more at ease. Finally, she came to the clear, fast running stream of a creek. She flung the ropes from her burning shoulders, and dropped to the ground, stretching out flat on her stomach, and gulped greedy mouthfuls of cold water. It helped ease her parched throat. When her thirst was finally slacked, she stood with the intent of traveling on and called to Dog who had already drunk his fill.

Chapter 14

Reuben felt as though he had done his duty as a good Samaritan and delivered Scrawny to safety. He didn't care to linger and chew-the-fat with Ball or anyone else. Now that the girl was gone, he only had her body to find, a mountain lion to kill, plus two hundred dollars to collect. He prided himself on doing exactly what he intended and he intended to earn that money to help pay for land.

Finding the cat ought to be easy. The cat would float down the rapidly deflating river of floodwater until the tree lodged against a bank and the cat jumped off. Discovery of the girl's body would prove more difficult. She would likely lodge somewhere and then get covered up by acres of mud and trash.

His plan was simple. He would go back where Scrawny had pitched his tent and follow the flow of water. The girl's body and the cat had to float downhill from there.

He hadn't gone far, less than a mile from where Scrawny was stuck in the mud, when he found one of Ball's cows in mud up to her belly. He longed to walk on past her as he was in a hurry to get on with his intent, but he couldn't leave the poor thing to such a slow death.

He looked upward at the buzzards already circling in the pure blue, cloudless sky. For the next few days, the buzzards would have the time of their lives. They would find everything they wanted to eat stuck fast and rotting for them. Once their bellies were overfull, they'd puke and eat it again.

He took another look at the cow. Most likely they would gouge the cows eyes out long before she took her last breath – a horrible thing in Reuben's opinion.

He knew the cow would be a lot tougher to get unstuck than Scrawny had been, being she couldn't grab hold of the rope. He'd have to get close enough to lasso the head and then rig up a pulley. Danged if he wasn't tempted to go back after Ball. The temptation didn't last. He most likely could do the job better and faster without Ball's and Scrawny's help. He remembered the old saying: One man is help; two men are help and a half; three men are no help at all.

On the other hand, if the mud had dried out enough, it might be easier to get a shovel from Ball and dig a big enough hole for the cow to walk out herself. Popping a cow out of dried mud would not be easy, not that popping her out of soupy, clinging mud would be either.

Reuben took time to find himself a long limb to take with him before he walked out to check the mud, knowing he had to be careful not to get stuck himself. If he did, he could lay the limb long-ways on the mud and it would act as a lever to pull himself up.

The mud was drying and held Reuben's weight until he was within twenty feet of the cow. When his feet sunk to his ankles, he quickly stepped back on more solid mud.

The exhausted cow rolled mournful, pleading eyes toward him. She no longer attempted to struggle. She had already given up hope and was willing to take whatever came without any more fighting of the killing mud.

"Hang on," Reuben said soothingly. "You're not done for yet."

Reuben knew what he had to do. He had to gather enough limbs to construct something similar to a ladder to keep him from sinking into the mud. For that, he would need to find enough wild grapevines to secure the cross pieces to the long poles. He couldn't use any of his rope as he would be needing that to pull the cow out.

By the time he had scoured the mountain for supplies and had his ladder constructed and in place, the sun had gone past mid-day and was blistering hot as it beamed down on him, the cow, and the continuously cracking mud. Reuben worked as fast as he could, not wanting the mud to dry hard around the cow. If it did, he'd have to take time to get a shovel from Ball and dig her out.

He managed to get close enough to lasso her head. The rope tightened on her neck as he pulled. She was stuck tight for she didn't budge. He looped the rope over his shoulders, turned his back to the cow, braced his feet on the ladder, and pulled harder. She still didn't budge.

He dropped the rope, went back to solid ground and picked up the largest rock he could carry over the ladder, dropped it at the ladder's end where it sank lightly in the mud. He tried the see-saw lever that had worked on Scrawny. It didn't work on the cow. Despite his own massive weight, he couldn't pop the cow up. The cow was much heavier than his two hundred plus pounds and the mud was too dry.

He untied the rope from long pole and tied the end to the ladder so it wouldn't get lost in the mud, shoved the pole's tip into the ground near the cow and used the large rock as a pivot to flip a chunk of mud away from the cow's front feet. If this worked, it would be faster than walking back to Ball's place to borrow, and then return his shovel.

It took hours for him to get the hole dug deep enough for her front legs to move, but her hind legs were still stuck solid. He had no choice other than to dig out around her hind legs too. The pole wasn't as fast as a shovel, but he would have to build a longer ladder if he went for Ball's shovel, plus he was out of grapevines and far too impatient to scour the backside of Humpback Mountain for more. Once it was dark, vision would be limited and make it easy for him to overlook the girl's body and the cat.

Once he had given the cow's hind legs some room, she humped her back and relieved herself with a couple of gallons of water dumped on the fast-drying mud that surrounded her hind legs.

"Yeah," Reuben said. "Soften it up all you can, ole girl. We both could use a little help right about now."

The sun had sunk beyond the distant mountains, leaving a patchwork of darkening sky overhead, by the time Reuben had inched the cow out of the mud and onto solid ground. She stood on shaky legs and took her first unencumbered steps toward freedom.

Reuben was pleased although it hadn't been an easy job. It had been a much too lengthy one. He wouldn't be able to travel far in search of the girl's body or the mountain lion before total darkness claimed the land and made it impossible for him to read signs. The need to hurry was within him

The mountain lion was in unaccustomed pain and it made him angry, made him want to kill to avenge such a hurting as had hold of him and would not let go. Part of him remembered being kicked and stomped by the cattle, but mostly he blamed the floodwater for his torture because it was all around him, taking him where he didn't want to go. He didn't like the feeling of being trapped. It made him want to fight everything in his path and frustrated him because there was nothing to fight except the swirling water or the very tree that was saving his life.

His claws were clamped continuously into the bark of the tree as it tumbled in the rapids, and bumped into other trees, floating parts of buildings, and unrecognizable other things that were being swept along at dizzying speeds. He was afraid of falling into the water if he relaxed his hold even for a moment, which aided in keeping his pain throbbing sharp.

A day passed and then two as the water carried him onward. Sometimes he would zoom along and sometimes the tree bogged against something and seemed to hang in suspension, not going anywhere. Never did it come close enough to a bank for him to jump off. When the tree did bump into building parts, or other floating debris, he was afraid to loosen his hold among the branches of the large tree. It was at least giving him some degree of safety.

Finally, in a matter of hours, the floodwaters began to sink into the earth and the swollen tributaries stopped feeding the flow. Mother Nature was through with her destructive spree and Father Time was settling things back into place.

Dead animals stopped moving long enough for the mud to bury them. Trees, limbs, whole bushes, and scraps of lumber that had once been buildings, pilled together and stopped anything that washed against the pile.

The tree lodged, but the cat still clung fast. He trusted nothing. Besides, he had floated for such a long time his mind still thought his body was floating. That misguided instinct was what probably saved his life. If he had left the tree and the pile of debris when it first stopped moving, he would have undoubtedly been stuck in the mud with his first leap. As it was, he clung where he was for several hours as the hot sun baked the mud hard enough to hold his weight.

Not only was his hunger increasing to desperation, the sun was drawing fluids from his body until he was dehydrating. No longer could he reach water from the tree trunk and the surrounding debris was on drying ground.

It was time for him to move, and he did. One tremendous leap took him twenty feet onto the mud. His feet barely touched ground when he sprang again. In the blink of an eye, he disappeared into the brush.

Raven had traveled a long distance from Ruffian Mountain, back toward the lowlands where the aftermath of the flood was still in evidence. She didn't know where she was or where she was going, but she knew she was starving and had to find food. She hadn't eaten anything life-sustaining since she had roasted the coon that the big black had killed. Her energy had left her and her leg and ankle hurt worse than she had ever hurt. She no longer felt young and filled with vigor. All she wanted to do was eat and then sleep for a very long time. Dog seemed to understand her need for he was willing to stay near her and stop to rest often without running ahead.

Finally, they came to a creek where the water ran fast over rocks. At least, they had found another creek where they could drink their fill of cold, clear water.

She longed to stop beside the water and sleep, but she couldn't because the creek had no food source, no crawfish, not even a frog or lizard. Some instinct told her to stay near the water and to travel upstream, but she couldn't. She had to go into the woods in hopes of finding something to eat, eggs in a birds nest or a rabbit Dog might kill.

Aggie had warned her about eating rabbits during the heat of summer. That was the time when their fur was filled with fleas and ticks. Catching a disease would be possible even if the rabbit was skinned and cooked thoroughly. She was hungry enough to eat the rabbit raw and toss disease to the wind.

She continued on, getting her aching leg over the next obstacle, crossing the next gully, climbing the next hill, getting over trees that had fallen because the rain had soaked into the ground enough to loosen their roots and allow them to fall over. Many of the trees had not fallen completely, but lodged in the branches of their neighbors. She had never before seen such destruction caused by a storm and it made her feel as though the world as she had once known it had ended. She had no idea where she was going. All she knew was to go upward, away from the floodwaters, hoping to find a place where she and her dog would be safe.

After a time, the emptiness in her stomach became a numb ache that equaled the pain in her leg and ankle. Somehow, all the pain seemed to deaden her mind until she couldn't think right. When she did think, it was about food, any food except dog food and dry corn. The thought of eating more of those made her stomach revolt and cramp into a hard knot.

By the time the evening sun was setting, she was getting lightheaded enough to be willing to sink to the ground and lie there forever. It was then that Dog became alert. She dropped the ropes from her shoulders and walked a few feet over a rise to see what had gained the big black's attention. Through the woods in a distant clearing were buildings. A house had a curl of blue smoke rising from its chimney indicating a cook-fire had just been built. There were other outbuildings, many of them, but they were all too near the house for her to feel safe, but she was almost beyond caring. She had to find at least a springhouse where she could get milk.

It was then she heard a hen cackling not too far from where she stood. On rare and wonderful occasions, she had eaten a chicken egg. Aggie used to bring one to her. Usually Aggie boiled the egg in water because frying an egg could waste a precious bite if the egg happened to stick to the pan. Right now, she would be glad to eat the egg raw.

She blinked her eyes a few times in order to clear the haziness that had gathered. Not too far away from her, and yet a great distance from the house, was the remains of a field-barn in need of repairs. Someone had used it for hay storage once, but had evidently abandoned it when it grew leaning and leaky. But those conditions hadn't stopped the hen from laying her eggs in it, and it certainly wouldn't stop her from having an egg for food. She savored the thought of swallowing the first mouth full. Determination returned if not energy. She had to have that egg.

She left the travois behind and headed for the barn as fast as her injured leg could manage. Dog was right by her side, his hackles raised, and his nose twitching in the scent-filled air as though something had disturbed him but he wasn't sure if it was friend or foe.

Once Raven reached the barn, she realized it was in worse condition than she had realized. Not only was it leaning, half the bottom walls were missing. At least the loft part appeared stable enough to hold her weight, and it was in the loft that the hen was still cackling.

She looked around for a way to reach the loft. The shaky remains of a pole ladder were leaning against a wall with the ends sticking through a scuttle hole. She headed for the ladder, not caring how flimsy it appeared. She had to find that egg, couldn't wait one moment longer.

The ladder proved strong enough to hold her weight as she climbed upward. Dog lifted his nose and growled. He put his front paws on a rung and whined, but Raven's need for the egg had shut out Dog's warning growl.

A soft moan escaped her from the pain as she hefted her dragging leg through the scuttle hole into old molding hay. Her eyes were slow adjusting to the dim light as she crawled over the hay, searching for the hen's nest.

"Well, now, lookie at that," said a somewhat amused voice.

"I don't believe my sorry eyeballs," said another voice.

"When it decides to rain favors on a man, it pours," said the first voice.

Raven stopped dead still. A man was on each side of the scuttle hole. One held a black colored chicken in his hand while the other man held several brown eggs. Panic filled her.

The man closest her let his lips slash into a wide, open-mouthed grin that showed snaggled teeth with tobacco flecks stuck in them. Tobacco juice mixed with spit was running down both mouth corners and beyond his beardy chin. He stuck out his tongue and wiggled it at her. She glanced over her shoulder at the other man. He was not an improvement.

Both men looked far more frightening than the hairy wolf-man had looked. Their clothes were ragged and filthy, while something about the men themselves didn't seem right. Everything about them oozed of derangement and danger. She had rather have met up with the mountain lion.

She eased backward toward the scuttle hole.

"Grab her," the man with the chicken hollered as he leaped at her, dropping the chicken.

The second man leaped at the same time as the first. He was closer and hit her hard, knocking the breath from her as her head hit the barn wall. The second man landed on top of her only a moment later, pinning her down before she realized what had happened.

"I got her," he squawked and spattered tobacco spit in her face.

"You damned lost the chicken."

"Don't care. I'd rather screw than eat."

"Hell, if I hadn't too."

"We can eat when we've finished with her."

Breath came back to Raven as hands tore at her clothes. Her fist flew out and jabbed a man in the nose.

"Hold her," he yelled. "Help me some. She's gone wild."

"I'm takin' my britches off."

"Won't do no good if'n I lose her. Get holt of her legs. I'll pin her arms"

Raven had never been attacked by men, but she remembered her mother's fear and she panicked. All she could think about was getting away from them, back down the scuttle hole where Dog could help her with the fight.

One man was sitting on her head and holding her arms while the other man was tussling with her kicking legs. She heard him puff when her toes got him in his spongy paunch, but it had no affect in stopping him. He grabbed both her legs and twisted. Pain from her injured ankle was like liquid fire running through her. She moaned as she twisted her body in an attempt to ease the pain.

"Damn, if she hain't a tough 'un."

"I like 'em best when they're putting up a fight. Does a man good to quiet 'em down."

Raven couldn't draw a single breath. The pressure of the man sitting on her nose was making streaks flash in her head.

"I've got her britches off."

"Get at it while I've got her choked down. Hurry, I want my turn while she's still alive. Don't want to fuck a corpse."

She felt the man's bony knees pin her legs to the floor as his hand poked at her private part.

The other man leaned forward to obtain a better viewpoint of what was happening to the girl.

Wild rage shot through Raven as she twisted her head until she drew air through her opened mouth. She pushed upward with her chin and felt the give of his crotch. Her mouth widened and strong teeth closed, capturing over half of his hanging-down part. She gritted her teeth together much like a dog intent on crushing bone.

The man raised himself from her face, squalling louder than the mountain lion could have squalled.

The man straddling her raised himself to see what had happened to his friend that brought on such a commotion. It was then that she saw the ugliest sight she had ever seen in her young life. Bull, horse, nor dog had ever possessed as ugly a male-part as what she was seeing.

The bit man was still squalling but she hadn't loosened her jaws. Something hit her on the side of her head. She realized the man straddling her had yanked up a plank and slammed it against her skull. Still she held on with her teeth and kicked at the repulsively ugly thing with her good leg. She made contact and the man grunted and doubled over. The plank dropped in mid-swing, losing force before it struck her again in a glancing blow. The two hits were strong enough to cause her mouth to open and allow the stinking man to leap free and grab his straddle with both hands.

Something went over the top of her, scratching her bare flesh with its toenails. Dog had managed to climb the ladder and had the ball-bitten man by the shoulder. Dog's weight took him over backward, and the savage rumbling from his throat warned of his killing intent.

"Kill it! Kill it!" the ball-bitten man squalled out in painful desperation as his hands now clutched at Dog's head in an attempt to escape from his teeth.

Raven was on her knees when the man she had kicked grabbed the plank and swung at Dog. The plank made loud contact with Dog's hind leg, but Dog held on to the ball-bitten man. Strength that must have been hiding in reserve surged through Raven as the man drew the board back for another swing. She shot upward with both index fingers locked. Each ragged fingernail drove into his eyeball as the man's weight came forward. He blindly swung at her, grazing her shoulder.

She instinctively dropped to the hay. He lost the board as both hands grabbed for his eyes. Raven seized the board and rammed its jagged end at the naked, hanging-down part. The man doubled up.

Rage equal to Dog's was running through Raven. She was as much an animal as her big black. No way could she hit the man's head hard enough or fast enough with the board. She saw blood squirt, and hit even harder. How dare him strip her naked! How dare him jab at her private parts! How dare him hit her dog. Kill was not a word that entered her mind, but kill was what she intended.

He was no longer moving when she turned the board on the ball-bitten man, but he wasn't moving either. Blood covered his face and head. Dog was lying quietly beside him, whining. He was hurt.

She was no longer shaking from fear but from rage as she dropped the board and ran her hands over her dog. His hind leg was broken from where the man had hit him. She kicked at the man, kicked at them both, but they didn't move. She wished they would move, wished she could rip them into small pieces with her teeth as Dog had done.

She sank down beside Dog and let tears slide down her cheeks, but her tears didn't last long. Survival was back and she needed to think what to do next. She remembered the eggs, scrambled in the hay until she found where the man had dropped them. They were cracked, but the goody was still contained. She ate one and offered one to her dog. The big black whined as he refused the egg. She gulped down every last one. She needed strength and clarity of mind to care for Dog and knew food was one of the keys.

She found small pieces of boards that had rotted away from the barn and broke them to the right size for splints. Neither man wore a belt, so she ripped their shirts from their bodies and tore them into strips. She bound the splints to the big black's broken leg. Dog whined but he never once offered to snap at her although he was in great pain.

"Good Dog," she whispered. "I'll take care of you, I promise. They'll never hurt you again. No, they won't."

After she had done all she could for the big black, she fished through the hay for her clothes. They were torn and dirty, but not nearly as bad as the men's clothes were. Her britches no longer had a snap on them, nor did her shirt have any buttons. She took the boot strings from the men's boots, tossed boots and pants down the scuttle hole, and then fastened her clothes back together with boot strings.

She was ready to leave the barn loft if only she could figure out how to get Dog down the ladder. He weighed as much as she did; therefore, she was afraid she wouldn't be able to hold his weight in one arm while she climbed with the other. Yet, she had to get him down so they could leave. With all that squalling the man did, someone might have heard and come to investigate at any moment.

She looked around for a solution. Of course, if she could tear long enough planks loose from the barn walls, she could form a ramp from the scuttle hole to the floor and slide dog down.

She picked up the loose board she had beaten the men with, went to the side of the barn, and started prying. The boards had been seasoned by sun and winds until the nails had vibrated large holes in the planks, making them easy to pop off. She got three boards she thought would be long enough. They reached from the scuttle hole to the ground.

She gathered her arms full of moldy hay and placed it on the edge of the boards. She knew what kind of long splinters would be waiting in dried-out boards. Carefully, she scooted Dog toward the pile of hay, trying not to cause pain to his crudely splinted leg. Once they reached the hay, she sat on it and maneuvered the big black's body onto her lap. She clasped her arms around him and kicked with her feet.

It worked. They scooted down the planks as though it was a real slide. It was the sudden stop at the bottom that jarred her teeth and her injured leg and ankle, plus brought a yelp from Dog.

She stood, shook her head to clear away the dullness the hits from the board had brought on. "Stay," she commanded dog and hurried back toward her travois.

Everything had to be rearranged so dog could ride on top of their supplies.

Reuben chewed on dried bear meat for breakfast as he traveled over the rapidly cracking mud. He had searched for the girl last night until darkness forced him to lie down and sleep. Fortunately, he had learned years before to grab sleep when his eyes closed and to become alert once his eyes opened.

This morning he opened his eyes knowing the dread of what he would surely find today, but at the same time he longed to get it done and over with. If a man rushed the unsavory, he'd have more time to linger with the pleasurable.

He left the mountain range behind and entered the flat bottomland where the floodwater had spread out wide. No longer was it so wide. He could see from mud bank to mud bank. Still, an over-full muddy river moved swiftly.

It was high-noon when he made a decision. He would travel along the river for another mile or so, until the river ran parallel with the highway, and then he would give up his hunt for the body and the cat. If the girl's body had washed further down, people would find her. If the mountain lion's tree docked itself further down, it would make a bee-line toward the nearest mountain. He would find it or he wouldn't. Either way, he couldn't waste any more time. He had things to do on White Top Mountain, and he was getting closer to the trail that led to his mountain with each step he took.

He was surprised at the need that arose in him. He wanted to be back home, to leave the hot, flat land behind and breathe of the sweet mountain air, but first he would continue on with his plan. He wasn't one to go backward once he had made a decision.

He found the tree not more than a half-mile away. The cat had left very clear skid-marks in the mud. He was still in good condition by the distance he had jumped. Plus, the tracks were fresh. It had to be that morning when the cat departed his tree.

He'd go the rest of his designated mile looking for the girl's body and then he'd return after the mountain lion. He didn't want to allow the cat to get far ahead of him. It would be hungry and ready to make an easy kill, especially when it had such a head injury as he saw when it floated toward Scrawny. Reuben figured folks had lost enough in the flood. They didn't need to give up a cow or calf if they were lucky enough to have one left.

Luck was with him, he supposed, when not three hundred feet down the river he spotted what appeared to be white flesh protruding through brown muddy water at the edge of the river. Carefully, he made his way to it.

He saw a portion of a hip and back almost covered by twigs, leaves, and silt. The last smidgen of hope drained from him and a strange depression set in. He'd seen the dead before, but nothing affected him quite like this. The beautiful, wild thing was gone. No longer would the slender legs run. Never again would the wind catch in her long black hair, blowing it backward from her face. And, no longer could he hide and watch her while his breath quickened inside his chest.

What he would find when he reached down and pulled her out of the mud would be a swollen body that was already putrid with rot.

He stilled himself to seeing her dead face as he leaned down, got a firm grip on the slimy body with both hands and pulled upward. The body came out of the water and he dropped it on the muddy bank.

Tarnation, if it wasn't a man. His spirit soared while he tried to realized the sadness in anyone's death. At least this man was old and gray headed. He had obviously lived a long life and was not being cut down when he had the best years ahead of him.

Reuben frowned. He had no intention of carrying a rotting body to civilization, but he couldn't leave him there for scavengers to eat. He made his decision and took off at a ground-eating trot. It took only a few minutes for him to reach the road. It took longer for a vehicle to drive by.

He thought the driver was going to run him down as he stood in the middle of the road waving his arms. He could realize what the driver was seeing. A huge, shirtless, hairy-chested, long-haired, beardy man wearing deerskin britches that had shrunk during drying. And all this was covered in a splotchy coat of mud.

Finally, the driver did stop the vehicle only a few feet from him. He might have known there was a wide-eyed woman behind the wheel. Her hands shook as she cracked the window with the utmost hesitancy.

"Sorry to bother you, madam," he used his most refined tone of voice in hopes it would relieve her apprehension. "There is an emergency you need to report to the proper authorities. Tell them that beside the riverbank, in a direct straight line from this spot, is the body of a drowned man. Please, give his family my truest apology for not being able to carry him to their doorstep." He nodded his head toward the speechless woman and disappeared into the woods. He was a good distance away before he heard the woman start her vehicle.

He took the fastest, most direct route he thought would intersect the direction the mountain lion's tracks were heading. He wanted to kill it quick. Finding a body that did not belong to the girl gave him a renewed surge of hope. The girl might still be alive, and if she were, the wounded cat might find her before he did.

The rain on Ruffian Mountain stopped just as suddenly as it had started. The sun came back out to draw the earth's moisture into a hazy mist as it lifted from the valley and fogged the mountain.

"Let's get on with it," Iva Dean said. She was cold, wet and impatient.

"Not yet."

"And why not?" She demanded.

"The ledge has to be dry," Mitch told her firmly. "It's tricky enough without the rocks being slick. I'm not interested in dying today just because you're impatient."

She seemed to accept his decision. "What was it like in her cave?"

"Like all caves. It was dark, dank, and chilly, but the fine dirt that covered the floor was dry."

"Was it a fissure cave?"

"Probably, but there was a lot of soil as well. There were several sections that branched off. The section the girl lived in had sides laid up of dry stone and part of the opening was enclosed with laid stone as well. There was also a rocked-in corner where a fire had burned in what appeared to be the updraft of a natural chimney."

"I always wanted to live in a cave," Iva Dean's voice sounded wistful.

Mitch burst out laughing.

"I'm serious."

"Sure you are."

"Well, I am. In case you haven't noticed, I'm a very earthy woman."

Mitch held back the words he longed to say. Instead, he said: "No one is keeping you from moving in."

Her chin lifted slightly and her eyes hardened. "You never know, I just might."

"If you do, can I have your cabin?"

"No. Besides, you're already living in it."

"It's not finished."

"Yeah, that's why your rent is free."

"What will rent be when it is finished?"

"You plan on staying here?"

"Nope."

"Didn't think so. If you do, you can stay in the cave if I decide not to."

"A tent is more my speed."

"You'll get another one. You do still have a job with the Forest Service, don't you?"

"I do if I can get another truck and more equipment."

"Didn't you say you had insurance?"

"If they'll pay up. You know how insurance companies are. They do everything in their power not to pay a claim. When they finally have to pay one, they take months."

"I'll talk to Joe and get him to contact the insurance company."

Mitch smiled rather mockingly. "That's right. Your brother is a big-wig in the political circle."

"It's all in whom you know," she told him and she was serious. "Is it dry enough now?"

"Maybe. Let's check and see." Mitch got up and went to the edge of the rock ledge that was a natural bridge, if a very questionable one at best.

It was dry enough.

"I'll go in front. Stay several steps behind me in case I step on a bad spot and the rock ledge breaks off. No need in both of us falling to our death," Mitch told her.

"What a wonderful pep-talk to give a woman."

"It's the truth."

Iva Dean didn't seem to believe him. She acted as though they were going on a jolly adventure and Mitch was trying to spoil the fun in it for her.

"It's wide enough where we're standing, but just around that corner it starts to grow narrow. About half-way across you'll be lucky not to wet your pants. Try not to look down, and concentrate on carefully placing one foot in front of the other. ”

“Did you wet your pants when you crossed it?”

“Not quite.”

“Oh goodie. You’re getting a second chance.”

“One I do not want,” Mitch told her empathically as he went around the corner.

“Holy shit!” Iva Dean said and stopped dead still.

“I warned you it was dangerous. Like I said, try not to look down.”

“Dangerous? It’s beautiful. Look at that sheer drop down to that pile of rocks; and to think, it was my kin that caused part of that rockslide.”

Mitch rolled his eyes. “You’re a fruitcake,” he said without rancor. “You don’t have the brains of a cricket.”

Iva Dean smiled as though he had given her a treasure. “Thank you. I take that as a compliment. The way I see things, I can only die once, but I’ve got many chances of living if I am willing to take them.”

“Are you ready to chance going over the ledge?”

She looked him in the eyes. “I want in front of you. I should have the right to cross first.”

“No.”

“What do you mean, no. I can go first if I want.”

“Not unless we turn around and go back to the beginning. The ledge is too narrow to change places.”

“Nonsense, I’ll show you how.” She moved toward him.

Mitch moved faster without spending another moment glaring down the steep drop-off. His feet covered the treacherous distance causing only a small amount of rocks and silt to tumble downward.

“Worked,” she mumbled to herself as she looked at Mitch standing safely on the other side of danger, took a deep, steadying breath, and then carefully crossed the ledge herself.

Mitch had been thoughtful enough to bring along a flashlight Iva Dean had in the cabin and had it in a crudely constructed knapsack along with matches, food, and water. He had no trouble finding the entrance to the cave for this would make his third time visiting the place. He switched on the light and held out his hand in a grand display of escorting her through the entrance.

She jerked the flashlight out of his hand and entered in front of him while Mitch told her which section of the cave to take.

"Shouldn't we be dropping bread crumbs?" she asked.

"We can smell which direction the fresh air is coming from."

"What fresh air?"

"The stuff you're still breathing easily. Go far enough back and your lungs will constrict and cause a tightness in your chest."

"Do I hear water running?"

"Surprisingly enough, Don and I found a small stream of water. I suspect it is only viable after heavy rains. I can't imagine there's much water in a cave this high on a mountain. Take a right and you'll enter their living quarters."

The cave was not what she expected. It looked like a cave – dark, dank, and depressing. She had expected some sort of comfort after all the years her half sister had lived in that place, but there was nothing. Even the crudity of the rock walls gave off a pitiful aura of the meager existence her half-sister and the girl had to endure. For a moment, she wanted to refute that any female could live in such condition. Even she would have a rough time living in this.

Iva Dean shined the flashlight over every inch of the place, trying to satisfy her continuously seeking mind. "Look," she whispered.

"At what?"

"That place right there in front of the fireplace."

"What about it?"

"The rocks, look at the rocks."

"So?"

"They have been carefully placed. Here, hold the flashlight on that spot." She squatted down and started flinging rocks aside, paying no attention as they hit the wall.

"What are you doing?"

"What does it look like?"

"If I knew, I wouldn't have asked."

"I'm digging up a grave."

Mitch almost dropped the flashlight. "Stop!"

"Nope. If I can't see my sister, I'll see her bones."

The light quivered. "You're not serious."

"I certainly am."

"But she's dead."

"Duh-h."

"Digging someone up from their final resting place is sacra-religious," Mitch insisted. "Don't do it."

"I'm not being disrespectful and I mean no harm. I have to see what's in there."

Mitch said no more as she grabbed up different rocks to dig in the rocky soil with, hoping for one that did the job best.

"I should have brought a shovel," she huffed after she was about two feet down. "At least this dirt has been made soft by previous digging. I'd hate to think of how difficult it was for the one that dug it first. Here, give me the light and you take a turn."

"No!" Mitch could not hide his repulsion. "I'll have nothing to do with disturbing the dead."

"Believe in ghosts do you?"

"I believe the dead should rest in peace."

"Do you believe in God?" She continued digging.

"Yes," he stated.

"Me too, but I don't believe in organized religion. You know why I don't?" She gave him time to comment, but he didn't. "Because people use it as a cop-out. They blame everything that happens on God, especially if it's bad."

Mitch still didn't comment, and his arm was getting tired from holding the light.

"You've heard people say: *'It wasn't my fault. It was an act of God.'* That's bullshit plain and simple. It's not an act of God; it's an act of nature. Or if someone is killed or dies at a young age, they say, *'It was God's will.'* I'm telling you right here and now, I don't believe it. God is a merciful, loving God. He doesn't want anyone killed or for them to be cut down in their prime. He wants people to have a long and happy life while they come to love and understand him. Trouble is, he gave everybody beneath the heavens freedom of will. They make bad choices; or are at the wrong place at the wrong time."

She hushed for a minute in order to give Mitch a chance to talk. He wouldn't.

"Then there are those who use religion to make themselves feel superior to others. The *'I'm more godly than thee, complex.'* False prophets, in particular, like that one. Not to mention the people who use religion as a crutch because they don't have the gumption to stand on their own two feet."

"Hurry," Mitch groaned. "And stop flapping your lips."

"I'll flap you," she said lightly as her words trailed off to a whisper. "Oh, my! Oh, my goodness, look at that. Someone's bones really are in there."

Iva Dean continued the excavation ignoring the smell of death. She dusted away dirt from the remains of rotted flesh more gently than any anthropologist would have done on a well-publicized scientific dig.

She uncovered legs that were bowed and crooked beneath their partial covering of rags. Next were hipbones and a back as twisted as a corkscrew. The last was the face and head, or what remained of a face. It was misshapen with a gaping, toothless hole for a mouth. The skull was small and knobby. After all that, it was the pitiful, dirt filled tuffs of white hair her fingers were touching that brought her tears.

🕊

The mountain lion found a dry spot, where the sun beat down hot to stop and groom himself. He licked all the bruises and scrapes except for his eye. That side of his face was even too painful for him to touch with the soft pads of his paw. When he had finished with his grooming, he stretched his huge, over-tensed body and fell asleep.

He woke up hungry and with renewed strength, ready to hunt, and eager to kill. The land he traveled through was barren of game. Instinctively he knew the storm had driven everything to higher ground. He headed for the higher hills in hopes of finding a baby deer, or better yet, a nice tender calf.

After several hours of being on the move, he hadn't even found a rabbit and he was thirsty. He scented water and headed toward it. Suddenly he stopped. His nose twitched. The closer to the water he came the stronger the scent. It was the girl that he was winding. The ordeal he had gone through during the previous days left him and he was again on the trail of his chosen prey. This time she would not escape him.

Deep shadows of evening were taking over the heat of the sun by the time Reuben came across tracks, but it wasn't of the mountain lion. It was of a travois. Instantly, he was no longer weary and his spirits soared. She's alive; she's alive, sang through his head. Those tracks belonged to her for no one else would ever construct a travois as crude as hers.

Carefully, he followed the parallel scrapes until he came to a soft spot of ground. There was a small footprint, dainty and light. He looked further ahead and frowned. Something was wrong. The second print was not small and dainty. It was the print of a foot that had not been fully placed down, nor had it fully lifted, as it should have. That foot was dragging. The girl had been hurt.

Concern filled him. At least dog tracks were with hers, and the dog seemed not to be injured according to weight placement and his movement. How old were her tracks? He studied the unfolding of the bent weed her foot had mashed and how the dirt had slid from the sides of the travois track. Dew had not fallen since the tracks were made, which meant she had left the tracks sometime from early morning to a few hours before he found them. As slowly as she was traveling with an injury, plus pulling the travois, he could soon overtake her. He took off at a trot.

He heard the gurgle of water running in a creek bed and picked up speed. She would stop to drink and hopefully to wash her injury in the water. Panic filled him before he ever reached the water. Tracks of the mountain lion were dead-center of the travois scrapes. The cat was after her and it was a good distance in front of him. His trot became a flat-out run.

He saw the farm in the distance and came to the place where the girl had left the travois. He stopped and studied the jumble of tracks, reading what had taken place. Yes, she had indeed left the travois sitting while she and the dog went toward the ramshackle barn. Then the girl came back alone and got the travois. What did that mean? Why had the dog stayed behind? Only one way to find out.

The answer was clearly left behind in the tracks. The girl had rearranged the travois to haul the dog. The dog had been hurt and she was pulling him, but why the boards and hay?

He heard a grunt. It came from the loft. He didn't bother using the ladder but walked up the boards as easily as a squirrel. A man was humped up holding his bloody head in his hands.

"What happened?" Reuben demanded.

The man didn't speak.

Reuben grabbed his shoulder and gave him a hard shake. "What happened?" he repeated.

The man dropped his hand and glared at Reuben.

"Don't hurt me," he pleaded.

"You don't know the meaning of hurt unless you tell me what happened this instant."

"We were attacked by three, four men," the man mumbled. "Me and my buddy." His eyes shot a look at his buddy still lying in the hay. "I think he's dead."

Reuben went to him. He wasn't dead, but a deep gash had been ripped from his throat barely missing the jugular. Reuben knew instantly what had happened. The girl had come to the barn and climbed into the loft not knowing the men were hiding there. They had attacked her and the dog had climbed the ladder to save his mistress.

He saw the bloody board and picked it up. Dog hair was mixed with human hair and blood. He carried the board back to the man and held it in front of his face.

"She didn't do a good enough job. If I wasn't in such a hurry to find her, you can't imagine how much slow-suffering you would endure. Consider yourself lucky until I return."

With those words said, Reuben swung the board. A sharp crack sounded as the wood connected with the man's hard head. He toppled over. Reuben knew he would be out for hours. If and when he returned, the men would be easily found. Right now, their punishment wasn't as important as finding the girl. The mountain lion was still on her trail

.

🕊

The three eggs she had eaten had not given her the strength she had needed. Exhaustion was threatening to the point where objects were blurring before her eyes. She wanted to drop right where she was standing and sleep on the ground for just a little while. What would it matter if she rested now?

Dog whined and started to raise up. "Stay," she ordered as she realized she had been standing still for a very long time.

The big black lay back down, but his eyes were still watching her.

That was why she couldn't rest. She had to find a safe place for her and Dog to spend the night, a place that would give them shelter and protection. The men had done a mighty-fine job of scaring her. She now felt as leery of men as her mother had.

With an effort, she took a step and then another. Ropes cut into her shoulders as the travois moved. Don't think about the pain, she told herself. What you are feeling in your shoulders and your leg doesn't matter. What matters is Dog. He was hurt saving you and you have to save him. He needs a mud-plaster for his broken leg and a place to rest without much movement for a week or two. Aggie had told her once about a fox with a broken leg. It had lain down next to a creek-bed and dug mud over its broken leg. The sun had hardened the mud on the leg while the fox lay there for days without food and only rainwater to drink, even though the creek was nearby. Aggie would slip and check on the fox each day until finally, the fox gnawed the mud-cast off and limped away.

Instead of thinking about the pain, she thought about Aggie and her mother. Aggie had once told her that the Bible said that sons would suffer for their father's sins, and that perhaps Lu was suffering for her mother's sin.

It had taken years before she had gleaned together enough of Aggie and Lu's comments to know what her grandmother's sins were. Men had done to her grandmother what those two men tried to do to her. The difference had been Dog. Her grandmother had no dog to protect her, and so, she had no choice other than to give up and let those men do what they wanted with her. The same thing held true for her mother. Both women were left with a baby growing in their bellies.

An image of a baby came to her mind, and her anger eased. Was a baby worth it? Her mother had loved her beyond all things, but she had never been willing to let another man get close to her.

Did that horrible man put a baby inside her? Raven was almost positive he didn't. It was only his hand that groped her. His ugly man-thing had not entered her, and she was sure it had to enter before a baby could be made. She had often watched the animals mate and asked Aggie questions about the process. She now wished she had asked more questions and Aggie had given her more answers.

Aggie had explained that never once in Aggie's entire life had she ever mated with a man.

"Did you want to?" Raven had asked.

Aggie had shook her head and told her, not really. She said she would be too ashamed for a man to see her deformed body to ever mate.

"Couldn't you leave your clothes on?" Raven had persisted.

Most likely, Aggie had told her. But it would not be the same as being naked. Men and women cling to each other's flesh when they are truly mates.

Raven couldn't possibly imagine clinging to the flesh of either man that had tried to mate with her. All she had wanted to do was rip their flesh to pieces.

An image of her mother came clearly in her mind. That man in the burning cabin had done to her mother what the awful men tried to do to her. That was why her mother had set fire to the cabin all those years ago. Raven now understood her mother's actions perfectly.

She hoped she and Dog had killed those two men. She wanted them dead for what they tried to do to her. She certainly wanted them dead for breaking Dog's leg. The only thing that puzzled her, really puzzled her, was that somewhere deep inside herself was an aching need to hold a tiny baby to her very own breasts.

Another image came to Raven's tired mind. She remembered hiding underneath Pete and Oma Jenkins' window while they mated. They had grunted and groaned, yet they had made happy sounds together.

Again, she thought of Aggie and the way she talked about Don Donavan. She was almost positive Aggie would have liked to have made those happy sounds with that man back when they were both young. That was probably why Aggie had insisted that she go live with Don if Aggie should die. Aggie had dreamed of Don putting a baby inside her. Perhaps, when Aggie's mind went bad, she imagined Raven truly was her and Don's baby.

A great sadness overtook Raven's exhaustion. She found she was wanting Aggie more than she had ever wanted her. Her only consolation was Aggie and Lu's bodies were safely buried in their graves where no one could ever harm them again.

Chapter 15

Don sat in his chair on the porch, pale faced and almost speechless as he listened to Mitch Kenilworth.

"You can't be serious?" he managed to get out of trembling lips.

"I am serious. Iva Dean plans on moving the crippled woman's remains from the cave and burying them beside their mother's grave in Raleigh."

"Why would she do a thing like that?" demanded Betsy.

"Iva Dean said her mother and her first born had been separated long enough."

"Shit!" Don said. "That dead woman gave birth to Aggie and then gave her up the day she was born. She left the little crying thing naked and shivering in front of the pulpit. I hope the devil is tormenting that woman in hell for what she did."

"Iva Dean said her mother thought the baby would have a better life if she was left with her father," Mitch told Don.

"Well, let me tell you something, Aggie didn't. But that's not the reason she deserves hell. She tried to kill Aggie before she was born. It was the herbs she took that left Aggie so deformed that she was tormented all her live-long life. That's what she should suffer eternal damnation for."

"Iva Dean Stewart really dug up her bones?" Betsy questioned Mitch with disbelief ringing in her voice.

Mitch swallowed hard. "I couldn't stop her."

"Ask me, you didn't try hard enough," Don accused.

"Could you have stopped her?" Mitch asked in self-defense of his actions.

"With a big enough rock," Betsy answered for Don.

"I don't know if there is a big enough rock," Mitch added.

"How does she plan on accomplishing it?" Betsy wanted to know. "You said she left the bones in the cave."

"When I left her, she was hiring some men from out of town to go back to the cave and bring the remains off. She'll have a funeral hearse waiting for the body to come off the mountain."

"They can't carry a body over the ledge," Don insisted.

"She thinks they can. She said they could arrange some kind of a pulley. She said once the bones were wrapped in a cadaver bag and tied to ropes, there would be no trouble in getting the body across."

Don's jaws twitched and his clutched hands twitched. "Go back to her right now," he insisted of Mitch. "Tell her I'll see that she is the one that uses the fresh-dug grave if she ever attempts to move Aggie from her resting place."

"She's already dug the body up."

"Go and tell her what I said."

"She'll cut my throat when she finds out I told you. She forbid me to say one word to you."

"Leave," Don demanded. "Get out of my sight and never set foot in the valley of Sodom again. If you do, I will personally see that you never leave, if you get my meaning."

Mitch and Betsy saw the look in Don's eyes. Both knew what he meant and neither doubted he would deliver.

Mitch jumped to his feet and left.

Don went inside the house, got his shotgun and all the shells he owned.

"What are you doing? demanded Betsy.

"No one will ever bother Aggie again."

"You can't kill Iva Dean. You'd be sent to prison."

"Stay here. I'll be back sometime tonight or tomorrow."

Betsy grabbed at his arm, but he pushed her back into her seat. "I said for you to stay here and I expect you to do exactly that."

It was almost dark by the time Don reached the narrow place in the ledge. He didn't care if it had been pitch-black. He was determined to cross that narrow spot at least one more time and hopefully twice.

He wasn't sure if it was his determination or pure luck that took him and his heavy sack of supplies across safely. He was just glad to get across.

He found Aggie's bones exactly as Mitch had described. He sat beside them in the shadowed light from his lantern in reverenced silence as he paid his last respects to the woman he had known as a child.

He convinced himself that the hermitic life she had led had not been so bad. At least, she had not suffered from continuous teasing and humiliation. If only Agatha Roten hadn't deformed the baby, things could have been different. Aggie could have possibly ended up his wife instead of Betsy. Then he could have had children.

The thought left his mind almost instantly. What he had told Betsy was true. She was the only wife he wanted. Aggie was . . . the past and he was going to see things stayed the way they were.

Carefully, he gathered the soft dirt in his hands and placed it on Aggie's bones. It was almost morning, and the lantern oil was running low, by the time he had her covered up and the rocks were back in place. He hoped he had replaced everything in the exact place Raven had left them. Not that it would matter to the girl. She would never be back inside the cave – no one would. Luckily, he was one of the old time farmers that kept a stick of dynamite handy.

Now for the tricky part. He had to rig the explosion to be strong enough to close off the cave entrance without doing more damage to the mountain than Raven had already done with the rockslide. No one wanted the entire top of the mountain to scatter, especially him. Some things deserved their rightful respect.

Once the dynamite was in place, he opened every gun shell he had and poured a thin line of power toward the rock ledge. It didn't go far, not nearly far enough for him to reach safety before the dynamite went off. He used the remainder of lamp oil to extend the length. Still, he wasn't sure if the lamp oil would work, or even if the gun powder would ignite the dynamite fuse but he would try it and hope.

If it didn't ignite, he would walk up to the dynamite and light the fuse by hand. He didn't want to do that, because he wouldn't be able to run far, and he didn't want to leave Betsy as a widow, not yet, anyway. She would think he chose to be with a dead Aggie over being with a live her.

That wasn't the case. He was simply driven to stop an outsider such as Iva Dean Grearity Stewart from exhuming bones that belonged to his friend and Ruffian Mountain.

He struck the match with his thumbnail and held it to the lamp oil. Fire ran the ground like a burning snake. Don couldn't run nearly as fast, but he was on the ledge when he felt the wind from the explosion take him off his feet.

Iva Dean had discovered money could get you just about anything you wanted. If by chance money failed, blackmail wouldn't. She was glad she didn't have to use blackmail on anyone. She knew men who would climb

Mount Everest and bring back a snowball if paid enough, and she had paid them enough.

They arrived before dawn, just as she had instructed. The four men followed her Jeep in the funeral hearse as far as they could go. From there, she led them up the mountain along the same path she and Mitch had taken.

After several hours of climbing by flashlight, the men started thinking they weren't being so well paid. By the time it was light enough to see where they had to climb to, they were sure of it.

"Sorry, Mrs. Stewart," one brave man said. "You didn't tell us we had to climb a mountain."

"I paid you enough to climb two mountains," she told him firmly.

"I disagree," he continued.

"Then go back."

There were a few moments of silence. "Pay us for what we have done so far."

"Pay you nothing. Our agreement was I paid you after the body was delivered to Raleigh, remember?"

The man remembered, but remembering didn't stop his anger. "A woman could have an accident and fall off a mountain."

Iva Dean chuckled, not the least threatened. "Naturally, a woman could easily do that. That's why I would suggest all four of you men take really good care of me. My husband as well as my brother would be greatly upset if something happened to me. I dare say all four of you men and your families would die from starvation, if any of you lived that long."

"Are you threatening us?" the brave man demanded.

"No more than you were threatening me," Iva Dean told him as she happily continued on climbing the mountain.

It was then the explosion sounded – a slight boom that was all noise but no tremor. Iva Dean suspected instantly what had happened.

"Hurry! I hope he hasn't blown up the ledge."

The men followed because they were curious, didn't know what else to do, and they wanted their money.

When they reached the beginning of the ledge, Iva Dean let out a stream of curse words that set all four men back on their heels.

"He blew the ledge off," was the only inoffensive words she uttered. "We can't get across it."

"What's happened?" asked one of the men.

"He stopped me from getting my sister's body. He closed off the only way to the cave."

"And the cave," Don managed to say. "I dynamited the cave closed."

Iva Dean whirled around to see where the words had come from. Lying against a rock was Don Donavan. Blood was dripping from his head. His nose was obviously broken and a foot was pointed in the wrong direction – but he was grinning.

Betsy was pacing back and forth across the porch when two men came carrying a stretcher. She didn't need to ask questions. She knew they were bringing Don's body back to her.

She closed her eyes and said a prayer asking God to give her the strength she would need to endure this.

"Mrs. Donavan?" said a man, but she wasn't ready to open her eyes. "We've brought your husband home."

She heard the stretcher come to rest on the porch, stopped praying, and opened her eyes and saw the battered condition of her husband.

His eyes were sparkling. "These men can bare witness to hearing me saying that I love only you," Don said without the embarrassment he would normally feel.

🕊

Raven had reached a place where the land started to get steep and rocky. She had reached the foot of a huge mountain. The uphill pull of the ropes on her shoulders was more than she could stand. Her mind had grown even more fuzzy and she stumbled and fell down every few steps.

To her right was a small gathering of rocks that formed a narrow crevice in the dirt below them. It wasn't very big, or very deep, only a crack between ground and rock, but it might give her and Dog protection from the elements while they stopped to rest for the night. She knew it would take at least the night before she would be able to wake up once she fell asleep.

She used all her strength to pull the travois as close to the crevice as possible. She didn't want Dog to walk and he weighed as much as she did, so carrying him far would be difficult.

She had him in her arms and was scooting him into the crevice when some instinct made her look over her shoulder. Her breath caught in her throat. For a moment, she thought she was hallucinating. A golden tan blur was coming straight at her.

Dog emitted something between a growl and a sharp yelp of pain as she lunged at the crevice. Her weight rammed Dog against the very back of the crevice as her body pressed against him, blocking his exit as he tried to gain his feet to fight the mountain lion.

The cat leaped with fluid ease, confident of his ability to catch the small girl and not the least threatened by the dog. He actually was pleased to have the dog as a bonus.

The girl would be consumed fast. The tough meat of the dog would last a while. He had never been fond of dog meat, but had eaten it on desperate occasions.

Raven turned until she was pressing her back against the big black and drew her knees up to her chest in an effort to protect her stomach from the oncoming attack. The mountain lion was too confident in himself. Seeing from only one eye distorted his judgment a fraction and he plummeted his huge body against the rocks and fell to the ground.

Raven was unhurt and trembling in every fiber of her body. The big black was clawing at the dirt with three good legs and spitting froth in his rage to get at the mountain lion. His forward strength was pushing Raven out of the crevice while she was doing everything in her power to keep her and Dog inside.

The mountain lion roared and screamed again and again as he came to his feet and paced in front of the crevice, trying to regain his bearings from the collision.

His nose found the girl and his good eye focused. Raven saw it staring right in her eyes and knew what was about to happen. His paw shot into the crevice; his claws sank into the fleshy part of her shoulder and ripped flesh as it pulled her out of the narrow opening. Searing pain shot through her arm, side, and leg an instant before her head hit the top of rock. There was a flash of light before darkness came.

Darkness began to fade to light, and she thought she heard Dog fighting, but the pain was too much for her to bear. She had rather go back into the dark place than feel the suffering as the mountain lion tore her body to shreds.

Reuben heard the screams of the mountain lion and increased his running speed to maximum. He heard the dog attack an instant before he came into view of the rock. He hadn't realized he was taking aim with the gun even before he spotted the big cat. He heard the sound of the gun firing as he realized the dog was shielding the girl's body with his own. He cursed himself for not taking a moment longer. If he had, he would have taken aim higher to make sure the shot didn't go through the cat, dog, and girl, but it was too late now.

In its spasm of death, the mountain lion had rolled off the dog and was digging up rock and dirt with jerking legs. It reminded him of the bear that had almost killed him. This time he took careful aim and blew a hole in the big cat's head. He had rather taken a heart-shot but he couldn't chance hitting the girl and dog again. Once its death spasms slowed, he bent and jerked the dog off the girl. She was a bloody mess. He saw the gashes in her shoulder, her side, and her leg. No vital organs had been ripped out, but she was bleeding freely, too freely. He knew if she was to live, he had to stop the flow of blood, but all he had to work with was what he carried in his knapsack and he couldn't very well sew up such wounds with rope.

He grabbed his rope and tied it around her leg and arm in a tourniquet. He took the pants that had been ripped off her and packed them into her side wound. Then he built a fire as fast as possible.

He held his knife in the flames until it was red hot and moved a section of the pants as he touched the knife to her side wound. The flesh sizzled and the blood flow slowed as he continued to cauterize the wounds.

The girl didn't move a muscle. She was as limp as a dead squirrel. At least he should be thankful that she wasn't feeling the burning of her own flesh.

Once he had slowed the flow of blood in all her wounds, he cut thin rawhide strips from his pants to use as string to close up her gashes. If it hadn't been for the time it would have taken to clean the feces from the cat's guts, he'd of used that. He was using one of the whittled down claws he'd disinfected in the fire to serve as a sewing needle. It was faster than using his knife to poke a hole and then thread the rawhide through.

When he tied off the last stitch, she was still breathing, but he didn't know for how long. He made her as comfortable as he could on the hard ground, not that it would matter to the girl. It was then he heard the dog whine. He turned his head to see pain-filled eyes pleading with him.

He went to the dog and shook his head in pity at what he saw. The mountain lion had ripped his stomach open and a small section of his guts was coming out.

Reuben stood up, hefted a huge rock with both hands, and raised it above his head. He knew what to try to save and what to put out of its misery.

Chapter 16

Days passed as the girl lay in his cabin on his bed of bearskins. She didn't get any better, but she didn't get any worse. Her heart kept beating steadily, and her breathing continued slow and easy. He used the healing medicines that nature provided, medicines handed down from his mother's people, bathing her wounds in his own concoction of herbs, and spooned a similar concoction into her mouth. Sometimes she swallowed and sometimes her throat closed until the fluid ran out the corners of her mouth.

After the second week passed, he used his small pocketknife to cut out her rawhide stitches. Her flesh had healed slowly, but it had healed. She would carry bad scars for the rest of her life, but it did not mar the beauty of her young body. Beside, her scars would fade some with time, if she continued to live.

From the moment he laid her on the bed, pitiful, hurtful moans eased from her both day and night. It tortured Reuben to know he was keeping this precious wild thing alive only so she could suffer the way she was suffering, but he could not contemplate allowing her to pass on into another world where he would not be able to watch her. Even though there were many times he suspected he was only keeping her alive long enough to suffer more than she should, he continued. There were also times he thought about stopping the concoctions and letting her die, but he couldn't give up on her, wouldn't give up.

As long as he could keep breath coming in and out of the girl's lungs, he would do it even if he had to breathe for her. Admittedly, he was a stubborn man, hard of head and strong of will. He had yet to give up on anything he wanted, and he wanted this girl to live.

Every time he passed the hide nailed to the barn wall, he cursed the mountain lion and himself. He could have let the cow die; he could have left the dead man in the water; he could have followed the girl's tracks leading away from the ramshackle barn instead of wasting a few minutes with the two men. Any one of those things would have given him enough time to have saved the girl from the mountain lion's attack. But nothing could be undone once it was done.

He had to live with now.

And he did so, diligently.

Never once did he leave sight of the house. He cared for his cow and new calf with one eye on the bearskin door. When the nights grew chilly, as they did early in the season on White Top Mountain, he built a wooden door in the front yard and replaced the bearskin with it.

When the girl developed a fever, he repeatedly washed her body in cool water and fanned her face with a piece of birch bark.

When she chilled, he fashioned the equivalent of hot water bottles and placed them around her body. If that didn't stop her chilling, he lay with her cradled in his arms and willed his warmth and his life to enter her body.

On the fifteenth day, her fingers on her right hand moved.

On the eighteenth day, she started hallucinating. Sometimes she would cry out and other times her body would grow rigid with what appeared to be fright.

It was when she started mumbling things that he made out the sound of Aggie, men, and Momma. He realized this little wild thing had not lived alone. He wished he could take her back to her people. Maybe if she could hear their voices, she would fight harder to live. As it was, he watched her slowly melt away.

When he became desperate, he started talking to her.

"Sweet thing, you have to swallow. Milk is good for you. It'll put life back into your belly." Or, "Sweet thing, don't be afraid of me. Don't stiffen up so when I hold you. I'm only trying to keep you warm." Or, "You don't want to leave this world yet. You have unfinished business to take care of." What that business was, he wasn't sure, but there had to be a reason for a wild thing running the mountains as though she was an animal instead of human – a mighty good reason. His mother's people would consider her sacred.

Sometimes he would even croon her lullabies he remembered his mother singing to him when he was a small baby. He prayed to the Christian God and he prayed to his mother's Indian gods to bring this girl back to life. He promised to do anything for them, everything, if they would just let her live.

On the twentieth day, she opened her eyes, looked up at him, screamed, and went back into her coma.

That was when he started to give up on all the hopes that dared to enter his mind. Even if the girl lived, he could never tame her. Perhaps that was why the gods were not listening to his prayers. He wanted to own the little wild thing just as he had wanted to own a pet bear.

"Let her live, and I'll set her free," he promised all the gods. "I'll even run her off," he finally added to his bargain.

It was then she started calling out "Dog, Dog". She opened her eyes, said "Dog" and didn't scream at him or blank out.

He sat on the bearskin beside her and snapped his fingers. The big black managed to put his front paws on the skins and licked her face for the very first time. The big black dog had been almost as slow in healing as the girl had been.

Reuben's heart warmed all over again as he watched the girl and dog together. He was thankful he hadn't put the animal out of its misery even when he was certain it couldn't survive. When guts were ripped out of a stomach, it took more than medical care to keep down infections. It took Devine Spirits working over time.

He recalled lifting the rock from the ground with fatal intent in mind. When his hands had been ready to pound the big rock into the dog's head, the dog looked toward the girl with such a mournful expression that Reuben tossed the rock aside. He realized this dog had rather suffer all the pain in hell than to die and leave the girl behind.

He stuffed the dog's guts back inside and sewed him up just as he had sewn up the girl. He placed the dog beside the girl while he skinned the mountain lion and used his hide to wrap both girl and dog in as he fitted them on top of the travois. If it had been the girl alone, he would have forgotten about the hide, and carried the girl in his arms. As it was, he still had not collected his two hundred dollars and didn't know when he would get back to Ball.

He was thankful for all the dog food the girl had so diligently pulled on the travois for that big black dog could eat more than his horse.

"Dog," the girl said her first lucid word and the dog licked her in the face again.

Reuben got up from the bed of skins and looked out the door at the colors touching leaves on the timber. Soon acorns would fall and the bears would grow a thick skin of hair. He always became restless when leaves started to die, and the birds started to migrate. Something inside him ached until he also wanted to run away with the wild animals to a world that held warmth and reproduction. Maybe that was why he went on his long hunting trips.

He turned and looked at the girl. He'd waited a long time for this sweet wild thing to allow life to reenter her body. He wondered how long he would wait until he found her gone.

Betsy called Don all sorts of names before she broke down and cried. How could he have been stupid enough to risk his life just to shut down the entrance to a cave? Didn't the next of kin have the right to determine where their relatives' remains were buried? Did Don care more about an old woman's bones than he did in spending his remaining years with her? Did he not care if he made her a lonely widow woman?

After he was well enough to hobble around on his broken foot, Iva Dean appeared on his porch and started calling him names, also, but Iva Dean didn't cry.

Betsy grabbed her broom. "Say one more word to my husband and I'll crack your head with this broom handle."

"You try and I'll wring your neck like you were a bony chicken."

"Shut up! Both of you," Don told them firmly. When they were both silent, Don asked: "What do you want now, Iva Dean?"

"The same thing I always wanted. A decent funeral for my sister."

"Then have a decent funeral."

"I can't. You dynamited her body inside a mountain of solid rock."

Don looked pleased with himself. "That doesn't stop you from giving her the best funeral service the capital of Raleigh ever saw."

Thought began to flicker over Iva Dean's face. "Why didn't I think of that?" she finally uttered.

"Because you were too hell-bent on condemning my husband."

"Stop it," Don said gently. "I want no more loud mouthing." He turned to Iva Dean. "You never loved your sister because you never met her. I grew up with her, and I cared deeply for her then and I care for her now. She had more courage than any person I've ever met, far more than you and me put together. I know what she wanted and that was to have her bones remain in the cave where she spent all the years of her adult life."

"It's so . . . so primitive."

"That's how she wanted to live."

"I don't believe that. No woman wants to live in discomfort and to continually be hungering for food and such. We like security."

"Then I'll change my wording to that's how she *did* live."

Iva Dean couldn't argue. "How did you know I was going after her bones? Did that creep Mitch tell you? Don't you tell me a lie, either. I know lying is against your religion and that God will punish you if you commit such a sin."

Don did grin. "Mitch did not tell me," he lied. "When Aggie asked me to help her, I swore I would. She came in the dark of night pleading with me from her scavenged grave to run you back to Raleigh without her sacred bones."

Iva Dean gave him a hateful look. "You're lying."

"Do you see God punishing me?"

"He will," she said as she stood up. "And if he don't, I'll do it for him." She might have grinned as she stalked off the porch.

"That is one hateful city hussy," Betsy said.

"Hard as balls on a brass mule," Don added and rubbed his hand over his face, trying not to let Betsy see his own humor in the situation.

"She ran that Mitch off, didn't she?" Betsy said with confidence.

"Not yet, he's still at her cabin. Pete said that city hussy delivered him his insurance check yesterday."

"He'll be gone now for certain," Betsy said with relief. "Maybe we can get back to living in peace and quiet. I'm almost thankful Aggie is in her grave and the girl is dead. It'll be nice to have my husband back."

"You've always had me, Betsy, you know that."

"The word *had* covers a lot of empty territory."

Don ignored her.

Raven remembered when things started penetrating through her blackness. She knew someone was caring for her and it wasn't Aggie or her mother. When she realized it was a man, she willed the blackness to come and take her into a safe place.

She would desperately fight the light in order to stay in her darkness, refusing to open her eyes, refusing to swallow. She fought consciousness so hard she would raise a sweat. When this happened, the man would wash her in cold water until she stopped fighting and sweating.

Other times she would remember her mother's fear of men, and the two men who tried to rape her in the barn loft and she would start to shake. That's when the man would hold her, which brought greater fear and caused her to shake that much harder.

Other times she would remember the mountain lion's attack and wonder if Dog was dead. She had moved her hand to feel him, but he was never there. A deep despondency filled her. If Dog was dead, she wanted to die along with him. That's when it became easy to slip into the dark world.

Somehow, the hairy wolf-man kept forcing the light to come to her. He made the darkness fade regardless of how hard she fought him. Now that her hands were touching Dog, she decided she might be glad to still be alive. There was no questioning her gladness when Dog licked her in the face.

Her eyes sneaked a peak at the man standing in the doorway. He was nothing but a dark outline, one that didn't look so very scary, not scary enough for her to leave Dog and go back into her safe dark place.

The man turned around, and looked at her. Slowly, he returned to the bed, but did not get close enough to sit down on the skins.

"Can you understand what I'm saying? If so, nod your head."

She nodded.

"I heard you say words while you were in a coma. Can you talk?"

She nodded again.

"Is there anything you would like to say or ask me?"

She nodded again.

"Then ask it."

"Did you put a baby in me?"

Pure shock showed on his face. " No. Never. Of course not."

"Oh," she mumbled and almost seemed disappointed.

"Are you afraid of me?" he managed to control his astonishment at her blatant question enough to ask a question of his own.

"Yes."

"I won't hurt you."

"Dog protects me."

"He did protect you. But you and the dog both came in a hair's breath of dying. I can't tell you how many times I thought you and him both were goners."

"The mountain lion?"

"He ripped you both like a piece of shredded cloth."

"You killed it?"

"I wanted to kill it many times over for what it did."

"You killed it?" she repeated

"Yes," he told her. "I killed it and tore the hide from its body with my hands."

She appeared relieved.

He could not contain his curiosity any longer. "Where did you come from?"

She was silent.

"Do you have people?"

Still, she was silent.

"How can I help you return to your people when I don't know where you belong?"

She closed her eyes as though she had slipped back into her own special darkness, but she was listening. She heard his footsteps go out the door, and was glad because she felt weak, much too weak to escape from him right now. Besides, she decided there was a degree of safety being inside his house now that Dog was still alive and the man hadn't put a baby inside her. She would rest a while longer and grow strong. Then she would escape the man and find a cave for her and Dog, one that was big and warm and safe; a place where no men and mountain lions existed.

༒

Reuben did the outside work, split enough firewood to keep the crude cabin warm during the chilly night. He was planning ways to keep the cabin warmer during winter when he realized his promise made to all the gods. He would keep that promise, but not until winter was over. He wouldn't run the girl off knowing she would starve or freeze to death. None of the gods would want that. He would run her off in the spring, he decided and went inside to fix supper.

The big dog had climbed on the bed with her and they were both sleeping. At least he thought the girl was asleep instead of being in a coma. He made a noise but the girl didn't stir. This concerned him. He went to the bed and placed his hand on her forehead. She almost jumped off the bed.

"It's okay," he said softly. "I won't hurt you."

Her eyes were wide. She didn't believe him.

"I was checking for fever. If I was going to hurt you, I'd have hurt you before now."

"I remember hurting." Her hand ran over her wounds, feeling the welts in her flesh.

"The mountain lion clawed you and your dog. I sewed your skin back together, and then I sewed his."

"You didn't hurt me?"

"No, I never hurt you." He hoped he was telling her the truth because every stitch he put in looked extremely painful.

"I'm tired."

"You'll regain your strength soon once you start eating healing foods."

She reached out a hand and touched her dog. "I'll leave soon, after I have rested."

His chest tightened. "There is no hurry. You and your dog are both safe and welcome here. What could you eat for supper?"

"Fish," she said.

It was the one thing he didn't have. "I'll catch you one later on tonight and you can eat it for breakfast. In the meantime, could you eat meat and gravy and pone bread?" He had killed a squirrel that morning and had the meat cooling in the springhouse in a pan of saltwater for most of the day.

She nodded and he got busy. He could feel her eyes watching his back as he stood at the stove.

"Why are you afraid of me?" he finally asked without turning to look at her.

"You're a man," she answered.

"Are you afraid of all men?"

"Yes."

"Why?"

"They hurt you," she hesitated and then added. "And put babies in you."

"I have never done either to a woman."

"They lie," she added.

He couldn't argue with that.

"You are hairy faced," she added.

"You don't like the beard?" He considered telling her that his Indian ancestors seldom grew beards. It was his white father's genes that granted him masses of body and facial hair, but what was the use.

She shook her head. "Wolf-man." She was thinking of the werewolves in one of the books Aggie had for her, but she was too tired to explain that to him.

She did manage to eat a little of the food without him shoving it in her mouth, but she didn't eat much. She fell asleep with her arms clutching the big black dog.

He was frying her fish when she awoke the next morning. She tried to get out of bed.

"What do you need?" he asked as he turned to face her.

She let out a gasp of fright as she glared at him.

"You didn't like the beard so I shaved it off."

She blinked a few times and damped her lips with her tongue. "Put it back."

"It's not that simple. Are you still afraid of me, even without the beard?"

"Yes."

He was disappointed after all the work it took to first cut the beard and then sharpen the razor until it would cut the stubble. "I've caught you a fish just as I promised. Can you eat it?"

"Yes." She squirmed. "I need to relieve myself."

He stepped outside the door, came back with the pot, and sat it next to the bed. "I'll wait outside until you're finished.

She knew what a pot was for. Aggie allowed her to use one when she was little. Aggie never wanted to smell-up their cave. But she didn't want to use his pot inside of his little cabin. She wondered how she had managed while she was in her special dark place. Memory came of him washing her.

She eased off the bed to find that she could stand only if she held onto something. Her legs did not want to work, nor did the rest of her body. She was wearing one of his long shirts. It reached the tops of her knees.

She managed to use the pot and get back in bed.

"Are you finished," he called through the closed door.

"Yes."

He returned with a wash pan. He poured warm water in it from a kettle on the stove, picked up a cake of lye soap and a towel. "Would you like to wash-up before breakfast?"

She washed her hands and face.

She was able to eat only a few bites of the fish. It didn't taste nearly as good as she remembered of those Aggie had cooked.

"You can't cook," she stated.

He grinned. "I tend to agree."

"Are you always bad?" she asked.

"I manage to stay alive, but you're welcome to cook your own food if you like."

"You cook," she returned quickly. "Are you a bad man?" she continued.

"No, I am not a bad man."

"Good," but her eyes were still wary.

"Can I ask you a question?"

"Yes."

"What is your name?"

"Raven."

"Raven," he repeated. "Do you have a last name?"

She frowned. "It's my name alone. Momma took it from the birds."

"Because of your hair."

"Yes."

"Who was your mother?" he asked gently, hoping she wouldn't go silent on him. "Did she have a name?"

"Lu."

"Lu what?"

She frowned again. "Lu. I don't know what?"

"Do you have a father?"

"A bad man. I don't know him."

"What was his name?"

"I want to rest."

He turned away from her, filled a pan with water, and washed the dishes.

"Do you have a name?" She surprised him by asking.

"Reuben," he said without turning around. "Reuben Rivers."

"You have two names."

"Most people do."

She remembered Aggie talking about Don Donavan, and didn't the other people in the valley have two names?

"I have only one name," she sounded rather sad and then brightened. "Aggie had one name like me and Momma."

"Who is Aggie?"

"She died. Momma did too."

"How long ago?"

"Not long." She moved her hand indicating for Dog to come. She curled up with him and closed her eyes.

Reuben knew she didn't want to talk about the two women that had died. Still, he wanted to know all about her. How could he help her if he didn't know?

🕊

By the next day, Raven felt more like herself when she opened her eyes. The man was not in the small cabin, nor was Dog. She heard a noise outside, got to her feet, and peeked through a crack in the plank walls. He was coming from the barn and Dog was trotting beside him. Dog was trotting easily; his broken leg moving without a limp.

She was angry, very angry. Dog belonged to her and no one else. She flung the door open, "Come," she demanded of the big black and he came to her instantly. Raven had the greatest need to head for the woods and get her Dog away from that man, but her body was too exhausted to make it beyond the open door.

The man looked at her thin, shaking body with compassion. At least she was able to stand by clinging to the door-jam.

"Good morning," he said.

She slammed the door shut.

His brows lifted in puzzlement as he went to the cabin and opened the door. She was sitting on the bed with her arms around the big black. He crossed the room and sat down on a sawed-off stump that served for both a seat and a table.

"What have I done to make you unhappy?" Reuben asked.

"He's mine."

"I see. You think I'm trying to take your dog from you. I'm not. He's your dog."

"You lie."

"I don't lie," he told her firmly.

"You had him outside."

"Raven, do you realize what that mountain lion did to your dog?"

She didn't answer.

"The cat ripped his belly open and let his guts fall out. He needs exercised to make sure his guts don't kink themselves up and cause him to die. He can't get that exercise by sitting here beside you. It's nothing short of a miracle that he is alive right now and I think I deserve just a small amount of appreciation from you for all the care and work I have done for the past month in keeping both of you alive."

He stood up and left the cabin without fixing her breakfast.

She was stunned. Was he telling her the truth about Dog's guts? She pushed Dog into a lying position and examined his belly. Raised scars of four parallel gashes ran down his belly. Cross scars showed where the man had sewn him back together.

She lifted the soft shirt she wore and looked at her own scars. They were similar. By the law of nature, she and Dog should be dead. In her opinion, the wounds were too great for them to have lived.

Perhaps she did owe the man some appreciation. On the other hand, if she and Dog were dead like Aggie and Lu were, she would not have the struggle of survival that lay ahead of her.

She patted Dog lovingly and wondered if her own life was worth the struggle required for her to survive?

☧

Reuben swung the ax with all the power he had in him. He allowed the vibration to run through his arms and shoulders without recoil as the ax struck the tree. Something had to ease his anger at the girl.

He swung again, sinking the blade into the tree without giving it the necessary twist that would bring the chip of wood and ax free of the tree's trunk. Impatient with his actions, he jerked the blade free and struck again.

Normally, he never allowed himself to get angry. Anger filled up a man's brain until he couldn't think right. Anger caused him to make mistakes that he would not otherwise make. This was another problem with having a woman around. She muddled a man's brain, made him do things he wouldn't normally do.

He could think of dozens of problems and no benefit whatsoever in having a woman around. So, why was he keeping her here?

He recalled his encounter with a hired woman in the house of one of the men he had been hired out to in Ashe County. He had been a boy in his early teens and his resentment at being treated unfairly for most of his life was running hot in his veins. He had decided that retaliation and vengeance were his.

He had built himself four traps and set them near the barn where partridges were eating grain. Much to his delight, he had caught a bird in each trap. He had cleaned, roasted, and eaten two of the birds and carefully stored the other two for a later meal. The two stored birds disappeared and a son of the household told the hired woman Reuben had accused her of stealing them.

She was fast to confront Reuben. He had not done any such accusation and told her so, but the woman refused to believe him. In a fury, she told him she would destroy his traps so he could not catch any more partridges.

Reuben went to her bedroom in the very top of the main house's attic where he could look out the small window and watch the hired woman. On her bed was the brand new feather tick she had so proudly constructed and slept on each night.

When Reuben saw the hired woman destroy his first trap, he took out his knife and slashed the feather tick. With each trap she destroyed, Reuben retaliated with another cut. By the time the fourth trap was destroyed, the feather tick was in two pieces and feathers were covering the small room.

Having finished destroying the traps, she returned to the house and confronted Reuben who had reached the kitchen.

"Now, go fix your traps if you can," she told him still in her mad passion.

Reuben, equally as mad, turned to her. "If you want to sleep on your feather tick tonight, go fix it if you can."

With those words Reuben went in search of the family member who had lied about him. After knocking out two of the boy's front teeth and leaving several memorable bruises on his body, Reuben gathered his sparse belongings and headed for the mountains.

Reuben deliberately buried the ax blade in the tree trunk and stalked back to the house. The wild girl was asleep, but she opened her eyes at the sound of him entering the house.

Some of his anger faded at seeing her, but not all.

"Do you have any people that are living?" he demanded.

She frowned, trying to think. "People living?"

"Someone you can stay with while you get well. Obviously, you don't want to stay here."

"You want me to leave?"

He saw the uncertainty in her eyes and most all of his anger faded.

"No, I don't want you to leave, but I do want you to be happy and unafraid. If you have people you could go to, perhaps you will heal faster."

"I have Dog," she said triumphantly. "He's all I need. We will leave tomorrow," she said with determination and a quivery chin.

"Not tomorrow. Your dog would be sure to die if you leave the cabin and you don't want that, do you?" His ploy worked. She shook her head as she looked at Dog with grave concern.

"I was snake-bit and I didn't die."

"Did you cut a chicken open and place its warm insides on the bite? That was the only thing gave me ease when a copperhead bit me on the ankle. It took six weeks for me to get well."

She shook her head. "There was no chicken. I was out of my head when a man found me."

"Tell me about the man who found you?"

The pallor on her face deepened. "I hate him," she said with a vengeance Reuben had not expected.

"Why?"

"He defiled Aggie's cave."

"How?"

Her too big eyes took on a far away look as though she was mixing fear and anger. "If he hadn't climbed the mountain, I wouldn't have caused the rockslide."

"What rockslide?"

She didn't answer his question. Instead, she said: "He didn't drown."

"How do you know he didn't drown?"

"He came after me, again."

Finally, the girl was telling him some of the things he wanted to know. "Why was he after you?"

She looked puzzled for a moment before she answered. "He wants his clothes back."

Reuben realized this was the only explanation the girl could conceive of. "I'll get you different clothes and take his back if you'll tell me where to find him."

Distrust came to her face and then hope. Slowly, it faded. "Then he'll know where I am, and I'm too tired to run away again."

"If he has his clothes back, he won't care where you are," Reuben hoped his logic worked with her.

She thought about that and then realized the men and the mountain lion had attacked her while she was wearing those clothes. "The mountain lion destroyed them."

"I'll buy him new clothes."

She shook her head. "I have no money." Aggie had taught her all about money and how people used it to buy things.

"You can sell the mountain lion's hide. You'll have money then."

"Hides can be sold for money?"

"The mountain lion was killing cattle. The cattle's owner offered me two hundred dollars for its hide."

That was the answer to why he was on the mountain. He wasn't after her as she had first thought, but after the mountain lion that was stalking her.

"You killed it. It's hide belongs to you, not me."

"You're the one it hurt. It owes you its hide."

"Aggie taught me about owing," she said softly. "I should have taken better care of my Aggie. She wouldn't have died if I'd done that."

"People die when their time is up, regardless of the care they get." He told her, but he didn't entirely believe his own words.

A strange expression flickered over her face. "Mine and Dog's time wasn't up." Relief claimed her as she said: "We don't owe you much then."

"You owe me nothing," he assured her, but he knew that wasn't true either. She owed him her and the dog's life along with a lot of time and aggravation, and it hadn't ended yet.

For a moment, Reuben thought he saw an image of his mother's smiling face, all smug and self-righteous. What was it about women kept a man bewildered?

Raven didn't trust the shaved wolf-man for no other reason than he was a man. It was true he had killed the mountain lion, cared for her and Dog, had not hurt her or put a baby in her, but she still couldn't trust him. Yet, she was staying in his house, eating his food, and sleeping on his bed while he slept outside or in the barn with the cow and horse when it rained.

What would Aggie think about that?

She closed her eyes and willed Aggie's spirit to come to her. It didn't work. She knew without doubt Aggie's spirit was back at the cave, and there was most likely where she would always remain.

Still, she missed her with a longing that had become a raw ache. Every day that aching increased and bedded itself deeper inside her where it could not be removed. At times, she wondered why she didn't miss her mother as much as Aggie. The answer was simple. Aggie was the one who cared for her and her mother both. Lu was her mother but she was just as much a child as Raven had been. Lu was her mother and she loved her dearly. Aggie had been her everything.

The strangest feeling wrapped itself around Raven. It was as though nothing in the world existed or mattered. There was nothing to fear as long as she stayed inside the cabin while the man stayed outside. No mountain lion, nor another man, would bother her as long as the wolf-man was outside chopping wood with his ax.

For a moment that feeling could have been happening years before while she and her mother slept by the fire during a long cold night while Aggie gathered firewood and food.

As the days passed, Reuben grew more obsessed with knowing the story behind the wild girl. Everyday he made a point of talking to her as often as possible. What shocked him the most was when he came into the house and found her with his book on wild-crafting in her hands. He spent a lot of time gathering herbs and selling them. That along with trapping had brought him cash-money to buy his land on top of White Top Mountain. Nowadays, it seemed, nobody wanted to trade land for hard work. Their value was placed on the dollar bill. Therefore, a man had to find ways of making money in order to own a piece of the earth.

"Aggie taught me these thing," she told him as she looked up from his book.

"You can read?" he asked.

"I read very well. I read every day."

"Aggie teach you?" he guessed correctly.

"Aggie taught me everything except how to run and climb a tree."

"Was there a school nearby?"

The word nearby puzzled her. "How far is nearby?"

"A mile," he said at random.

"Not nearby. One was over two mountains and beyond two valleys."

"Did you go to school?"

"No."

"Did you want to?"

"No."

"Most children want to be with other children their own age. They like to play games." A flash of memory hit Reuben. He had not had children his own age to play with. Actually, since he was four years old he had been made to work. He remembered sweeping floors, carrying water and wood, pulling weeds and feeding animals.

Raven frowned. "I didn't. Children were mean to Aggie."

Yes, Reuben also knew how mean children could be to another child, especially when they were older and stronger. Reuben had been determined to grow bigger and stronger than them all, and he did.

"Why?" Reuben asked.

"They thought Aggie was ugly."

"Ugly as in mean or ugly as in not pretty?"

"Not pretty. She was born crooked. Her back was twisted and her legs splayed out." She didn't go into the deformities of Aggie's face. To her Aggie would always be beautiful.

It was what she said next that surprised him the most. "Aggie's mother, Agatha Roten, ate herbs in hopes of killing the bastard baby the preacher put inside her. It didn't work."

"But it deformed Aggie," he added gently.

She nodded as her fingers reverently caressed the pages of the book as though Aggie herself might have written them. "Agatha left Aggie with the preacher and his wife to take care of. He was mean to Aggie."

"I see."

"Aggie ran away from them all when she was twelve. She lived alone so nobody could look at her."

"Where did she run to?"

"The cave."

"I ran away to live in the woods when I was a boy?" Reuben admitted.

Interest showed on her face. "Why?"

"I was sold to a man who was mean to me. Actually, I was sold to several different men."

"Sold?"

"My father sold me after my mother died. I was four years old. After that, other men bought me." There was no emotion in his voice. "I repaid the men ten times over before I left them behind so I could live alone." He believed that no human being should be bought and sold.

"Momma never sold me. She loved me." Raven said with conviction. "Your father was a mean man. Did you kill him?" She asked as though she was discussing the weather, but her eyes were looking at him with something he had never seen in them before. It was pity.

"I don't know what happened to him or my brothers and sisters."

"You have people?"

"I have relatives somewhere, but I don't know them or want to. I had rather live alone."

"Me too," she whispered.

"What about your mother?" he asked very gently in hopes she wouldn't clam-up on him.

"Those rich people tried to kill her." She told him simply and then hushed.

He wanted more information, needed the rest of her life story. "What rich people?"

"The Grearity people. Aggie said he was a politician."

Recognition hit Reuben. "Joe Grearity is your father?"

"No. His son is my father, but it was the man Joe and his wife Rhonda that tried to kill my mother before I was born. They hit her on the head and pushed her in Tetter's pond. Aggie saved Momma. She kept Momma and me hid in her cave."

"Why were they trying to drown your mother?" He asked but it wasn't a necessary question.

"To keep down scandal. Aggie said their son raped Momma."

Reuben nodded. He already knew more than he wanted to know about rich people and the unthinkable things they did to keep down scandals.

"Aggie said if the rich people know I'm still alive, they'll not stop until they kill me."

"Can I ask you another question?"

She nodded.

"If you don't want to talk about it, you don't have to."

Again, she nodded.

"Did the two men in the barn loft rape you?"

Her dark eyes hardened and she gritted her teeth before she spoke. "I killed them."

"No, you didn't kill them."

"They broke Dog's leg."

"Did they rape you?" he asked in an even softer voice.

"No. They tried to put a baby in me but Dog and I stopped them." She frowned. "I did not kill them? You are sure?"

"I found them alive in the barn loft."

Her lips set in a firm line and she said no more.

Reuben didn't ask Raven Grearity any more questions. He didn't need to. He realized he had all the information he needed. It just hadn't occurred to him all he had to do was go into town and stop at the feed and seed store. The men there would know all about Scrawny. Once he found Scrawny, he would know where Raven came from.

The leaves were in full color and Raven was showing improvement. She was able to build a fire in the cookstove and fix her own meals.

"I'm going into town for supplies," Reuben told her. "Will you be all right if I leave you alone?"

"You can't take Dog."

"I didn't plan on taking Dog."

"Then I won't be alone."

"Will you and Dog be all right with me gone?" He reformed his question.

"Yes."

"I may be gone overnight."

She didn't care how long he was gone. "Okay."

"No one should come here, but if they do, bar the door and don't make any noise."

She glanced at the tree stump where the butcher knife lay.

How silly of him to worry about a wild girl who had been left alone all of her life, but he did worry. It would take another month before her wounds were healed and longer than that for her strength to return. She wouldn't be her normal self until spring came.

"Raven?"

She looked at him.

"Promise me you will not run away while I'm gone?"

She gave him an odd look.

"You were thinking about it, weren't you?"

"If I was stronger," she said, but didn't finish the sentence.

"Dog needs a lot of rest so he can heal right. You want him strong, don't you?"

"I won't leave yet," she knew what he was trying to do. Using Dog wouldn't work. The fact that it was true would work. "I can milk," she told him.

"No. I don't want you out of the house. Besides, if the cow should kick you, it could reopen your wounds."

"A cow needs milked."

"I'll turn the calf loose with her. The calf will get it all until I get back. Okay?"

"Okay," she said, knowing there was plenty of milk in the springhouse for her and Dog for a couple of days. If he didn't come back, she would shut the calf back up in the barn stall and milk the cow, regardless. She had often milked cows to get milk for Aggie.

🕊

Reuben went straight down the mountain and cut across the bottomland where the flood had left its trail of mud. Grass and weeds were already sprouting up with lush greenness from the rich mud that had washed off the hilly land. That was the problem with the mountains. All the good topsoil got washed downstream and aided in making flatland farmers richer. It didn't take much education to know poor land made poor men, and the mountains were filled with poor men regardless of how hard they worked.

He could recall many faces of men who had worked themselves into their graves, worn and shriveled men, without the money to buy their own coffin.

The women were no different. Their backs would grow humped and their fingers cracked from long hours of endless work. He had heard many a woman say that only their death could bring them a day of rest.

That's why he tried to figure out ways to keep all his topsoil on his own land. Which, admittedly, wasn't easy when a flash flood hit.

It was fifteen miles of straight line traveling to reach the feed and seed store. It was a short distance for Reuben who could run down hill at a speed of eight miles an hour. Carrying the heavy cat-hide slowed him down. Returning up the steep mountain would take three times that long. He hoped to be back sometime during the night, although he didn't know how far away from the store the surveyor lived or where that place would be.

It was in a marshy lick where Reuben caught sight of movement. A lick in the mountains is a place where deer and other animals come to lick at deposits of oozing sulfur or salt. It was a favorite spot for deer, and that is what he thought he saw at first. Not wanting to waste precious time by stopping to watch deer, he looked away before his attention was caught.

It was the strange sound made him stop. It wasn't a growl, or a groan, or a mewl. He changed course as he eased around a clump of ten-foot high creek willows that were half covered in mud.

There before him was the sight of a dog that brought back memories. When he was a young boy, he was roaming the hills when a large, tan colored dog appeared. Thinking what a wonderful pet this big dog would make, he tried to call it to him, but the dog continued looking beyond him with glazed eyes and if anything, picked up its speed. Puzzled at its strange behavior, he made no offer to approach it. Instead, he stood still and watched as the dog crossed into a field and promptly bit a grazing milk cow and then her calf.

It was then several men appeared. They told him they were tracking a rabid dog and asked if he had seen it. He described the dog and told them of the cow and calf the dog had bitten for no apparent reason. The men continued on and shot the cow, calf, and finally the dog.

He never forgot how lucky he was the dog had ignored him.

This dog wasn't ignoring him, although, it had the same glazed look to its eyes. It was coming straight at him in a determined speed while globs of slobber drooled from its mouth.

Reuben dropped the cat-hide, lifted his gun without having time to take proper aim, and fired. The dog dropped within a few feet of him.

Not having a shovel with him, he took time to scour the flatland until he found enough rocks to cover the dog's body in a makeshift grave that could not be dug into by other animals.

It was getting close to high-noon when he reached the feed and seed store. As luck would have it, George J. Ball was there buying staples to rebuild his fences.

"Here's your mountain lion hide," Reuben said as he walked up to him.

"What mountain lion hide?" Ball asked.

Reuben's brow lifted and all the men in the store became silent.

"The one who's hide you promised to pay me two hundred dollars for. I'm here to collect it."

Ball tried not to look Reuben in the eyes, but when he finally did, he pulled his billfold from his back pocket and promptly handed Reuben the cash. Reuben dropped the hide at his feet, but Ball didn't bother to pick it up.

"You can have that hide back," he told Reuben rather sheepishly. "I appreciate you killing it, but it hadn't bothered my cattle lately."

"I killed it over a month ago," Reuben told him. "A couple of day's after the flood."

"Why didn't you collect your money sooner," Ball dared to ask.

"It spends the same no matter what day of the year. By the way, the farmers might have a bigger problem brewing than the mountain lion. I killed a rabid dog on my way here," Reuben told him and then walked away from Ball and the catskin.

He sat down on the front porch with the other men and listened to their prattle for a while. When the talk slowed, he said, "I met a surveyor during that flood. Anybody know where he's staying?"

"At Sodom. He's surveying for the Forest Service on Ruffian Mountain."

"He wouldn't survey my line, regardless of all that big money the government is paying him," one man complained.

"Greed," another man said. "That's what's wrong with the world today. Folks won't give a body the time of day unless they're paid for doing it."

Reuben lingered for a reasonable amount of time before he got up and left.

Chapter 17

The man standing in front of Betsy's door was a sight
to behold. He was broader and taller than the door opening.
He had a strong face with eyes that were alive with
intelligence. She wouldn't call him handsome for she didn't
like handsome men, and he certainly wasn't one. She
would call him breathtaking in a very manly way, a way
that was as rugged and tough as the mountains themselves.
At the same time, there was something about him made her
cautious. He had a rawness in him warned to step
diligently.

"Howdy Ma'am," he said in a voice that was courteous
and carried just enough mountain twang to make her feel
comfortable in hearing it. "I'm lookin' for somebody and
figured you'd know where I can find him."

"Who?"

"Mitch Kenilworth."

"Oh, him. He's at that city woman's cabin being she
hain't run him off yet."

"City woman?"

"Iva Dean Grearity Stewart," she said the full name
with a slight smirk, letting him know that the city woman
wasn't, and most likely never would be, accepted by the
locals. "What you want with him?" She pushed the screen
door open wider and stepped out onto the porch. Her gray
twist of hair that was piled on top of her head came to his
shoulders.

"I saved his life in the flood."

"Don't expect him to pay you for it. He's tighter than a preacher's hatband on a Friday night."

"I don't expect pay. Just making sure he's doing okay."

"Men like him always do okay. They come back like a well-sprung door."

A bedspring squeaked and the sound of a foot dragging sounded. A moment later Don Donavan appeared at the door.

"Pull up a chair," Don said. "Ole woman, fetch the man a cold glass of spring water. He's probably parched."

That's what Reuben was wanting to hear. "I'd be mighty obliged."

Don limped his way to a chair and leaned the back against the wall. Reuben did the same.

"You're Reuben Rivers." Don said.

"How do you know?"

"You saved the surveyor."

"It was a bad flood."

"We only got rain."

"So I heard.

Don was silent for only a moment, long enough to stuff his lower lip with a little snuff. "What is it you really want?"

"As I told your wife, I want to check on Mitch Kenilworth."

Don ran his tongue over his snuff-dusty lips. "I blew up a cave entrance and busted up my leg," he said matter of fact.

The mention of a cave caught Reuben's attention but he tried not to show it. "Why did you close up a cave?"

"So an old woman's bones could rest in peace."

"Because he's a danged idiot," Betsy told Reuben as she returned with a glass of water and handed it to Reuben.

She wasn't one to mince words or try to be tactful. "Is that girl really dead as you claimed she was?"

"Girl?"

"The one Mitch chased all the way to Humpback Mountain. Seems he got all fired up after he washed the dirt off her and found out how pretty she was." Betsy said as she watched Reuben Rivers drink the glass of water and then hand her the glass back.

"Thank you, Ma'am. It hit the spot. Are you talking about the wild girl?" Reuben was still pretending to be slow. He wanted them to think she was of no importance to him.

"Yeap," Don said. "The one you came here to find out about."

Reuben grinned in appreciation of straight talk. "I admit that my curiosity did get aroused."

"Long as that's all," Betsy said under her breath.

Reuben and Don both ignored her.

"I found I couldn't rest without knowing that poor little girl's story," Reuben confessed. "For some strange reason, she haunts me. I keep thinking I should have done more for her."

Don knew that feeling all too well. "Did you find her body?" Don asked.

"No, I never did."

"What about the dog? Did it drown too?"

"If the storm got her, I'd say it got the dog. The few times I saw the girl, the dog was always by her side."

"Are you saying she's not dead?" Don became hopeful.

"I didn't find her body, although I followed the wash of the flood down to the river and then to the main road. Beyond that other people would spot it."

Again, Don appeared hopeful.

"I heard there were acres on top of acres of mud. A girl could get buried by mud in a hurry." Betsy was fast to cut down what hope Don might have mustered up. Aggie and the girl were dead, and she wished Don would accept it so they could get on with what was left of their lives. Old folks deserved to spend their last years rocking on the porch as they recalled their happy times. She was sick and tired of having a husband who regretted what he hadn't done.

"At the feed and seed store, they said eight bodies had been found with more missing." Reuben gave them that much information without telling them of the body he had found.

"What do you want to know from us?" Betsy demanded. "And don't say to find out how that Mitch Kenilworth is doing."

"The girl was trying to make her home in a cave on top of Humpback Mountain. After the flood, I checked the cave out just to make sure she wasn't there. She wasn't. I figured she was running away from somebody or some thing. I just wondered where she lived and if she had relatives. You know how it is when a child touches your heartstrings."

Don knew. "She had nobody but Aggie and she's dead."

"Not one single relative that will miss her?" Reuben persisted.

"None." Betsy said.

"Poor little thing," Don added. "She never had a chance."

"Did she really live in a cave?"

"The one Don blew up," Betsy told him. She went on to tell about Iva Dean Grearity Stewart and Aggie's bones. She didn't stop until she had told everything she knew, except her pain over Don and their lack of children, and how she had realized how much Don had wanted that wild girl. She reckoned such as that was a personal matter.

"What about her mother and father?" Reuben dared to ask.

"We think her mother is dead and we never knew who her father was."

Reuben knew that Don wasn't telling him the truth, but he chose not to contradict the old man.

"I was just making sure her people knew what happened to her, if she had any," Reuben told them.

Don frowned and then spat tobacco juice off the porch. Once his mouth was empty, he asked: "Don't reckon you could tell me what the girl looked like, could you? I'd kinda like to know."

Raven couldn't stay inside the man's house one moment longer. She had to get outside, had to feel the wind in her hair and the sun on her face. It seemed she had been shut up forever.

She didn't consider any promise made to a man as a binding promise. Men were not worth anything, not even the wolf-man who had killed and skinned the mountain lion. She looked toward the barn, expecting to feel the same shiver of hatred flow over her when she saw the mountain lion's hide, but the hide was gone.

The wolf-man had taken it to sell. She didn't expect he would buy clothes for her to give to that other man either. He'd probably buy a jug of Cade William's liquor and lay around drunk. She hoped he would do just that so she could hate him. For some strange reason, she needed to feel that hate.

"I want to leave here," she told Dog. "I want to find a place of our own. I don't trust the wolf-man. He'll turn on us, you know. Men always do."

Dog climbed over a patch of rough ground, limped on his broken leg and whined. She found a shaded place in the edge of the woods to sit down and check his leg. That was what saved her from being seen. The two men she thought she had killed, were looking right over the top of her and Dog as they sneaked through the woods, making sure a man named Reuben Rivers wasn't around.

They had seen Reuben carrying the heavy hide and knew he was heading to the feed and seed store to sell it. Yet, it paid to be extra careful. A man could always double back. If he was gone to the store for certain, it meant they would have a chance to get even with him for whacking Hensel's head with the board when he was already half dead.

Dog raised his hackles and started to growl. Raven quickly signaled for his silence. She nor Dog was in condition to fight, but they couldn't stay in the edge of the woods. The two men would surely find them there when they came to rummage through the barn, and she was sure they were there for stealing.

Luckily, their eyes were on the house as they crept toward it in a squatting run. When they went inside and the door slammed shut, Raven dove on her belly and snake-crawled through the woods, trying not to make a sound or leave a trail. Once she and Dog were out of sight of the house, she jumped up and headed deeper into the woods despite the throbbing pain in her side where the mountain lion's claws had cut deep.

She had no idea where she was going, she just knew she had to get to a safe spot before the men picked up her foot prints.

"Look'it this place," Hensel said as a grin spread his lips until his gums showed. "We'll teach him to mess with us."

Manson wasn't as willing to raid Reuben River's place as his brother was. He'd heard enough talk about the Indian man to cause him to shake in his string-less boots at what they were doing. "What if he knows it was us?"

"How's he to know we done it? It could be anybody in this world."

"Heard say he can track better'n ary dog. Heard say he can smell a snake's trail a'ter it swims a river."

"Hain't no man what can do that, you idjet. Let's spread that bear skin out and dump his cookin' things in hit. We'll tie all his stuff in the skin and load it on his hoss. Then we'll drive his cow off. That calf'll make us some mighty fine eatin' tonight and we'll get good money from selling the cow and hoss."

"I got me a better idée," Manson said. "Let's hide out here until he comes back, jump him by surprise and kill him. That away he won't know it was us and we'll have this place for our own."

"Land's registered in his name, dummy."

"We'll tie him up and make him sign it over afore we kill him. We'll tell he sold it to us and then lit out if'n anybody asks."

Hensel grabbed the knife off the tree-stump table and grinned. "Now you're thinkin'. Let's wait here and kill him. I wanna do that myself. Pay him for bashin' my head when I was down and out."

"What do ya reckon happened to that girl and dog?

"Don't rightly know," Hensel said with a pout. What that girl and dog did to them had left a mighty big sore-spot. If he ever set eyes on either one of them, they would pay dearly.

"That couldn't a been his woman, could it?"

"Naw," Hensel was quick to answer. "Everybody knows Rivers don't have no woman."

"He could get him one," Manson insisted.

"Idjet."

"Let's start a fire and cook us some grub. My belly has already met my backbone."

"Do you have to always be such a idjet. He'll smell a fire and know we're here. Let's see what he has in the springhouse."

"Does that mean we can't eat calf tonight?"

"You rather eat calf or own this place?"

Manson grinned. He reckoned they could do both given a little more time.

A crock of raw eggs and a couple gallons of creamy milk inched their bellies away from their backbones – at least for the remainder of the night. By the time they had finished eating their meal, darkness had claimed White Top Mountain. Both men felt completely safe knowing Reuben Rivers would not return until morning. Even they would not chance traveling by night and there were two of them. They curled up on the bearskin bed and fell right to sleep.

🕊

Reuben wouldn't allow himself to lie down and take a nap although he was feeling the strain of running in the dark. It required all his attention not to trip over roots or protruding rocks that were camouflaged by the darkness. Although he had run many miles since morning, he could still travel faster than riding a horse or driving in a vehicle. He could take shortcuts, go over rock cliffs and swampy areas where neither could travel. Plus, he had the Indian-sense for direction. He could set a straight line in his mind and travel it straighter than a crow could fly.

He was in a hurry to get back to Raven. He had an uneasy feeling about her even when she had promised to stay inside the cabin. He almost wished he had left her his gun instead of the butcher knife. But then, what was there to harm her? The mountain lion was dead. Bears weren't likely to be marauding this time of year when there was plenty of mast to eat in the woods. Besides, he had a strong door built. And there wasn't a person with any sense who would bother her while she was in his cabin or on his land. They would know a man, especially him, would protect his woman with his own life.

He almost grinned at his thoughts. She wasn't a woman, and she wasn't his, but others didn't need to know that. While she was staying with him, she was under his care.

The closer he got to White Top Mountain, the faster he ran, and he acknowledged his long legs could cover some ground when they were pumping hard and fast. After a while, his second wind came and he started feeling good. The moon rose in the sky giving him the light he needed to see what might trip him. He hit his stride and contentment filled him as he climbed upward. He even allowed his imagination to roam a bit. Who knew what five years down the road might bring. The little wild thing would be a grown woman by that time. She might even come to like a hairy man that was half wild himself.

He thought of his mother's people. They had been scattered and their blood let and diluted by the white man. No longer could they live off the land as they had once thought was their right. Only he could live off the land if he owned a piece of it by the white-man's-law.

His insides still burned with anger when he thought of his mother's people being herded together and driven out west as though they were a gaggle of turkeys being driven to the slaughter-house.

He forced such thoughts out of his mind. He couldn't change the past; he could only live in the present. And the present was each running step he was taking as he got closer to home and the girl who was tormenting him. Something had to be wrong, for even his mother's spirit was riding on the night winds, telling him to hurry and to use caution.

As he crested the peak where he had built his cabin, a kind of peace filled him. The moon had risen high and full in the night sky and its silvery ghost light shown on the natural bald of White Top Mountain making it appear almost as light as during the day. The difference was during the daylight the land was in color while during the moonlight everything was in black, white, and grays.

He stopped and observed the sight of his cabin nestled in the edge of the woods. He hadn't chosen the bald to build his cabin on because of the harsh winds that blew both winter and summer. Even the grasses grew at an angle on the bald.

His cabin was quiet and at peace. No smoke rose from a fire the girl might have built to keep warm, which, to him, was strange. The girl tended to chill due to her weakened state and liked to have the warmth of the fire during the cold of night. Before she regained consciousness, he had lain on the floor beside her where he could monitor her condition and needs. Afterwards, he had slept outside so as to give her some privacy in the one room cabin.

Silently, he went to the cabin and considered lying down against it so as not to waken her. It was then his ears caught the strange sound. It was loud snoring coming from inside the cabin. He listened closer knowing the girl did not snore, but the short-nosed dog often snored during sleep. This wasn't the snoring of the dog. It was the snoring of a man, two men actually.

They were sleeping in the bearskin bed. Where was the girl? His propensity for a sudden burst of sudden rage filled him, but experience, along with his Indian blood, brought out his caution and the knowledge there was the right time for everything.

There was no need for rushing, if the men were snoring and the girl wasn't screaming. If they had hurt her, their suffering would last a long time regardless when it started.

He went to the barn to find that everything was in order and took his oil lantern down from a shelf. When he reached the cabin again, he lit the lantern, opened the door, and stepped inside.

Reuben recognized the two men who were sleeping in opposite directions with their feet sticking next to each others' heads. Raven and he had failed to kill them which was now proving to be a grave mistake. They would never see morning's light again, but first he needed to find out where the girl was.

They didn't wake up as Reuben sat the lantern on the stump table. Reuben cocked the gun and pointed it a one of the men's head.

"Where is she?" he demanded in a loud angry voice.

The sound penetrated the man's addled brain. He snorted twice before he continued his snoring.

Reuben kicked him hard enough to slam him against the side of the cabin. Both men were now awake.

"What da hell?" one yelled.

"You kicked me," the other one said.

"I kicked you," Reuben said in an unnaturally calm voice.

Both men turned their heads toward Reuben.

"Don't get up, either of you. No need, for you'll both be dead soon."

Neither man moved.

"Where is she?" Reuben demanded in the same calm voice.

"Who?" Hensel squeaked.

"I don't play games," Reuben continued. "Tell me where she is and you both can die fast. If not, you have no idea how much pain you're going to suffer."

Manson swallowed hard as Hensel glowered at him. "This was your idea," Hensel reminded him.

"You were standing first watch," Manson whined.

"It was your turn. I woke you up," Hensel whined right back.

"What have you done with her?" Reuben repeated in deadly calm although he wasn't feeling anything close to calm.

"Who?" Hensel repeated.

"The girl you two tried to rape in the barn loft," Reuben said through clenched teeth. His patience was fast coming to an end.

Neither man said a word.

🕊

Raven was moving onward regardless of how much she was hurting. She was more afraid of the two men than she had been of the mountain lion. In her feverish mind, she was convinced Reuben Rivers had deserted her in the cabin knowing the two men would come back for her. Such thoughts increased her hatred and fear of every human being living. Only Dog could be trusted and he was limping beside her.

She recalled what that horrible wolf-man had said about Dog's guts. She had to stop so he could rest. She wouldn't kill her dog because of her own need to escape.

She crawled toward the dark outline of a thick stand of Lashorn trees that grew tall and thick in places on the mountain and dug a place out of the needled ground and then curled up with Dog against her. She was vaguely aware of his meager warmth because she was so terribly cold. She shivered and shook until her teeth chattered.

Her greatest concern was not the cold. She was wondering what would happen to Dog after she died. She didn't want that wolf-man to have him.

🕊

Reuben was able to pick up her footprints outside the cabin door even though the night was dark and the moon was sinking low. He held the oil lantern until the light shown on the ground enough for him to find the dog's tracks. The big black's toenails sunk into the ground and were much easier to track than the girl's softly placed feet.

He followed them behind the barn and into the edge of the woods where she and the dog had huddled together. Somehow, she must have known the two men were coming and took cover in the woods. Most likely, the big black had gotten wind of them and given her enough warning to escape before they arrived.

He found where she had crawled on her belly until she gained the cover of thick woods before she got to her feet and started to run.

The night sky was silvering when he found the spot where she had fallen down. He realized that it had taken her a long time to get back up, much too long.

He wouldn't have needed the lantern light to track her even if it had been the dead of night, for she had scuffed up moss and leaves where her feet were dragging. And then, he saw the spot where she had fallen again, but she had not given up. Her crawl-path lead straight toward the Lashorn trees.

Reuben found her lying in a ball with Dog curled on top of her as though the dog knew she needed his warmth. Dog wagged his tail when he saw Reuben.

Reuben reached down and lifted the girl from under the dog. She was alive, but barely. Her breathing was slow and she was shivering as though with cold although she was clammy with sweat and her flesh was burning hot. It didn't take long for him to realize the girl had the fever.

He prayed more prayers than he had ever prayed in his life as he carried the wild girl back to his cabin. He felt the helplessness of not knowing what to do for her as he placed her on the bearskin bed. He knew how to treat wounds and certain other ailments but the fever was something entirely different. He had never once treated the fever or heard of how it was done. He knew if he cooled her off too fast, it would be her death. On the other hand, if her fever grew too high it would burn her brain up and make an idiot out of her.

For two days and two nights, he did everything for her he knew to do and she didn't get any better. On the third day, he bundled her up in a bearskin, and headed off the mountain. There was nothing under the heavens that he wouldn't do for this girl. If that meant taking her to the doctor, he would take her.

Reuben's progress off the mountain was slow because he didn't want to push the big black dog beyond his limit. He was still concerned about the dog's guts and knew infection was still a threat from where dirt had entered the wound. Even a gut could rupture from where the cat's claws had scratched the linings. All he had known to do for the dog was stuff his guts back inside his belly and sew the skin back together. There had been no way out there on the side of the mountain that he did a sterile job.

It was getting on in the evening by the time he reached the doctor's house. He'd had to stop several times to ask directions because he had never been there before.

"I've come to see Doc Robinson," Reuben said to the woman who answered the door.

She only nodded and stepped back. Most all the folks who knocked on the door had come to see her husband, especially those who carried a wrapped bundle in their arms. What was unusual was the big black dog that refused to get a foot away from the man's legs.

"It's her dog," Reuben told the woman.

Doctor Robinson had served the mountain community for over fifty years. His face was wrinkled and his bushy hair was snowy white, but his eyes were bright despite of all the suffering he had witnessed.

"Lay her down on the table," he told Reuben as he indicated a wooden table that smelled of pine tar disinfectant. "What's her problem?"

"She's suffering from fever."

"I see."

"She was attacked by a mountain lion about a month ago. She's not entirely healed and the dog is not either. The dog fought with the big cat before I shot him."

"You killed it?" Doctor Robinson asked as he moved the skin away from the girl.

"Lucky shot. I could have gotten her or the dog, but I didn't."

"Was it the mountain lion that was killing George Ball's cattle? Folks were talking about that until the big flood overrode it."

"That's the one."

"What's your name?" He shook a thermometer down and tried to place it under her tongue, but her teeth were clenched tight. He lifted the girl's shirttail for a rectal. Reuben looked away.

"Reuben Rivers," he answered as his eyes took in all the diagrams of human bodies that hung on the walls.

"Who's the girl?"

Reuben didn't hesitate. "She's my woman."

"Heard of you," Doctor Robinson added. "Word is you've never had a woman."

"I do now."

"So I see." He examined the scars on her shoulder, side, and leg. "That was a nasty wound, near fatal if you ask me. Why didn't you bring her to me when it happened?"

"She was hurt too bad. I had to close the wound up on the spot to keep her from bleeding to death. Then I was afraid to move her in case the stitches broke loose and she started bleeding all over again. She was almost well until a couple of days ago." He decided not to mention the two men. Their story made no difference.

Doctor Robinson removed the thermometer, checked the temperature, and raised his brows. "It's high," he said. "She's developed pneumonia fever. How long has she been this way?"

"This is the third day."

"She doesn't look good, I can tell you that much."

Reuben's face drooped. "She'll be all right, won't she?"

"I'll try to help her, but I ought to tell you right now that she's in God's hands."

Reuben refused to leave her side no matter how much Doctor Robinson insisted that he leave. The big black dog proved to be just as stubborn as Reuben.

It took another three days before Raven's temperature went back down to normal, but she hadn't regained consciousness.

"What's taking her so long?" Reuben asked Doctor Robinson.

"I don't know. Perhaps we were too late in cooling her down. She might just stay in a coma. It happens sometimes. The brain is a strange, powerful thing that doctor's haven't been able to master. Don't know if they ever will."

"For how long can she stay in a coma?"

"Forever."

Reuben didn't know what to say or what to do and it showed on his troubled face.

"Son," Doctor Robinson felt compassion for the man who had sat by the young woman's side and asked for nothing, not even food for himself. "I know you care about your woman, but she needs the care of a woman. Men make good doctors but they're almost useless as a nurse. Women simply have that mothering touch."

"She's getting your care and the care of your wife."

"That she is, but she can't stay in my house forever. My wife is getting a bit antsy to say the least. We don't run a hospital here."

"I'll take her home."

"That's what I'm trying to get at. I've heard you live in a drafty cabin on top of White Top Mountain. I'm afraid if you take her back up there she'll develop pneumonia again and she hasn't enough strength left to fight it. The weather has to be cold on that mountain and it's going to get colder. Doesn't she have parents with normal living quarters where she can stay a while?"

Reuben didn't answer.

"I'm only telling you this for her own good."

"If she needs better care than I can give her, I'll see that she gets it."

"Not in a drafty cabin?"

"No, not in a drafty cabin."

"She needs to be spoon fed a lot of chicken soup several times a day, and just keeping her washed and cleaned is a job in itself. Cleanliness has become an important issue in medicine, nowadays."

Reuben didn't bother to tell him that he'd done all those things for her for almost a month and he would do it for her until he was as old and worn down as the doctor if necessary.

꙳

Betsy Donavan was taken speechless to say the very least. Surely, her eyes were playing bad tricks on her. Reuben Rivers wasn't standing on her porch again with a girl wrapped in a bearskin clutched against his chest.

"Beg your pardon, Mrs. Donavan, but I've come up with a problem I need your help on."

Betsy must have said something, but she didn't know what.

"My woman has taken ill," Reuben continued. "The doctor said if she was to live, she needs a woman's care and I want her to live. I'll pay you whatever you want if you'll put her in a bed and care for her until she's better."

It was then Betsy looked down. It was the big black Rottweiler dog that answered most all of her questions. "Oh, no," escaped her lips. "I thought she had drowned, but I was wrong. We'll never live a normal life now."

"It'll only be for a few days," Reuben insisted. "She'll get well fast. She's a fighter."

It was then Don reached the door. He placed his hand on Betsy's arm and almost reverently moved her aside. "Bring her in," he said. "Betsy has a spare room."

Don pulled back the bed covers and watched Reuben place her in bed. His eyes never left the girl's face. "Aggie was right," he finally said. "She is beautiful, and her name fits. Just look at all that black hair."

"I don't intend her staying here for long," Reuben pulled the covers up. "I'll stay right by her side all the time she's here. I wanted to take her back home, but Doc. Robinson said my cabin would be too cold on her. He wouldn't listen when I told him I'd keep a hot fire burning."

"Aggie is finally getting her wish," Betsy said from the doorway. "She's giving Don her child."

"This is my woman," Reuben told her firmly.

"Son," Don said as he continued to stare at the girl's face. "I reckon you'd better tell us the whole story."

When Reuben had finished, both Don and Betsy were almost speechless.

"You should have told us about her a few days ago," Don said.

"There was no need then. Besides, she didn't want the surveyor to know where she was. She's afraid of him. That's why she caused the rockslide."

"We'll never be able to keep him away from her now," Betsy said.

"I'll take care of that," Reuben assured her.

"And that Rottweiler dog," Don added. "Cade Williams will die if he doesn't get him back."

"He'll die if he touches that dog," Reuben assured them. "That dog is to sleep beside her. I think he's the only thing that's kept her alive. She refuses to die and leave him."

Betsy moistened lips that had gone bone-dry. "Having her here means you and that dog will be here too?"

"It's best if they're here," Don told her. "No telling what that Iva Dean woman will do when she finds out the girl is here."

"Iva Dean?" Reuben questioned.

And that led up to a whole new story – one that he had heard a portion of. Now, there was no question about him leaving her side. If he did, those rich politicians would kill her for certain.

"I made a mistake in bringing her here. I'll have to find a new place."

"No," Don said quickly. "She'll die if you leave now. We'll hide her out and tell folks you're the one that staying for a while."

"What about the dog?" Betsy questioned.

"He'll stay in the room with Raven," Don told her.

"He has to relieve himself."

"Reuben will take him out at night."

"It won't work," Betsy told them both. "We can't hide the girl. That snoopy surveyor will find a way to look in the window. When he does, he'll recognize the girl."

"We can change her looks," Don said.

"How? Even if we cut her hair it would still be black as a crow."

"That's it," Don said. "We'll cut her hair and use some of that peroxide you whiten feed sacks with. We'll claim she's your cousin and Reuben's wife. We'll say they came to visit us for a while."

"You going to peroxide the dog white too?" Betsy shot back at Don.

Don's bright idea crashed and hope drained out of him. "We'll just do the best we can," he concluded.

Doing the best they could worked for a about a week, until Carrie Williams became extra snoopy. Carrie thought mountain folks had the right to know everything that went on with their neighbors. Everybody knew the details of her and Cade's life, even that Iva Dean woman knew.

Every morning and evening Carrie Williams would stand at the back corner of the barn when she went to milk and look toward Don Donavan's place.

Betsy was watching too, and saw Carrie ogling her house. Betsy knew that Carrie was a smart woman who knew when things weren't exactly right.

Betsy kept a quilt over the bedroom window, while Reuben and the dog stayed inside during the light of day. Both man and dog stuck beside the bed and watched every move the girl made, but the girl had gotten no better despite all the care and attention she was getting.

For Raven, it was the same as after the mountain lion attack. She had discovered how to go back into her own special dark place, the cave of her early childhood, a place where Aggie took care of her. Everything was safe and peaceful when she was there. Even Dog was safe. She knew that because she could feel his warmth beside her; hear the sound of his breathing.

At times, she even thought Aggie was with her. It seemed that Aggie was propping her up and spooning liquid into her mouth. When Aggie did that, she could feel herself getting stronger as the darkness faded.

But then there would come the sound of men's voices and all the lightness would go away and the saving darkness would return.

Then the strangest thing happened. Aggie told her that it was time she went to live with Don Donavan. Raven was furious. How could her Aggie say such a thing? She had told her repeatedly that she would never live in that house. She hated houses. She hated people. She had rather be dead than live with people.

So the darkness was to become her solution. She would enter into her dark place, never to return. Why hadn't she thought of that before? Once she was dead, she would be with Aggie and Lu. That was what she wanted, wasn't it?

🕊️

Betsy was nearing her wit's end when Carrie Williams stuck her head in the door and hollered. "You in there, Betsy?"

She handed Reuben the bowl of soup and rushed from the bedroom, making sure she closed the door behind her.

Carrie frowned. She had never seen Betsy come out of that bedroom before. Plus there were sounds like something pecking on the wood floor.

"What you got in that room?"

"Oh, it's Don," Betsy said as she rushed onto the porch and made sure both the screen door and the wooden door had shut Carrie outside. "He's been running a fever and sleeping in the spare room."

"What's wrong with him?"

"Fever," Betsy repeated. "I know it's gotta be catching. You ought not to get close me."

"You do look a bit flustered. You ask me, you've lost weight too."

"I'm fine," Betsy insisted. "Was there something you needed?"

"Hadn't seen you in a while."

"I know, but it's best you don't sit down and linger. Wouldn't want you or Cade to catch the fever. It's not been that long since Cade got his self burned up." She regretted saying that the moment it came out of her mouth. She didn't want any mention of the girl that saved him.

"Fall of the year has always been a bad time for fever. It's already colder than normal. I think it's gonna be a rough winter for us. At least I dug a good crop of potatoes. They'll help out since Cade hasn't been able to do a lick of work"

"Indeed. Now, I don't mean to rush you off, Carrie. I just don't want you to catch Don's fever."

"Looks to me like you're catching it. You don't seem like yourself."

All would have been well off if Don hadn't come around the corner of the porch from where he'd been outback at the toilet. Carrie's eyes widened when she saw him.

"Don," Betsy screeched. "How'd you get out the back door that fast? I didn't hear you make a sound. You know you have to stay in bed when you have the fever."

Don faded right before Carrie's eyes. Sickness overcame him. He placed his hand over his heart and humped over in the shoulders.

Carrie laughed. "What's going on here? Both of you are putting on an act and it's a poor sorry one."

"We just don't want company right now," Don said, still trying his best to act sick. "A considerate neighbor would take that at face value and leave us alone."

"Well, I never," huffed Carrie. "If you want to shun me, then go right ahead." She turned and marched off the porch and down the road.

"I think she got mad," Betsy said.

"Better for her to get mad than for us to have Cade Williams come here demanding his dog back."

"He won't come after that dog," Betsy told him. "If you remember, that dog almost killed him. Cade's just blowing steam by claiming he wants him back. He don't want to give the dog a second chance to finish the job."

"Did you ever think Cade wants the dog back so he can kill it?"

"Lordy, lordy," Betsy moaned. "It's just as I warned you. We can't keep the girl here."

"Then we'll have to find another place for her," Don insisted.

"It's time for Reuben to take her back home with him."

"But the doctor said she needed a woman's care."

"Doctor Robinson has softened in his head. That old man thinks the answer to everything is to have a woman taking care of it."

"You're right," Reuben said as he opened the wooden door. "It's time for me to take her home. You've cared for her diligently and she hasn't improved."

"No!" Don said.

"Yes," Betsy countered. "You're too old to have a child. Besides, she's not a child any longer; she's Reuben River's woman. And if you want me to remain yours, she'll have to go. I can't take this any longer."

Reuben had Raven wrapped in the bearskin and was ready to leave when Betsy opened the back door for him to leave by. Dog was quicker and slipped out before Betsy had made sure all was clear.

"That's my dog!" yelled Cade. "I'll have my dog back, by God. Carrie said something strange had been going on here. Now I know what it is." It was then he looked away from the dog and saw the big man carrying the girl. "That's my girl, too. By damned, I lay claim to her as well."

Reuben carefully lay Raven down on the floor and stepped outside. Before Cade knew what was happening, Reuben had lifted him off the ground by the front of his shirt. Cade grabbed hold of Reuben's arms, but it had no effect on the big man. They were eye to eye and Reuben's eyes were glowing wickedly.

"You're talking about my wife," Reuben lied. "And that's her dog. If a man should claim my wife or her dog, it would be my duty and my right to kill him on the spot. Did I really hear you claim either of them?" Reuben shook him slightly.

"Noo," Cade squawked.

"What did you say?" Reuben asked him again.

"I made a mistake. I didn't get a good look at them."

Reuben shook him again. "If you should ever make such a claim to another person, I'd have to come back and kill you, do you understand me?"

"Yeah," Cade managed to get out.

Reuben lowered Cade's feet to the ground and them patted him on the head. "You'd best continue to be a good boy."

With that Reuben picked Raven up, clicked to Dog, who was standing at attention with his hackles raised, and the three of them disappeared around the back of the house.

Don was the first to speak.

"You best sit down a spell, Cade. You're not looking right. Betsy, could you bring a glass of water out here? I think Cade's been imagining things again."

Reuben called himself a fool all the time he was carrying Raven through the woods back to White Top Mountain. What made him think Doctor Robinson knew what he was talking about? What could a woman do for Raven that he couldn't?

As for his cabin, he could keep it warm enough if he had to cut every tree down that grew on White Top Mountain.

He looked at the girl's pale face and held her limp body closer to his. Was he fighting for a lost cause? Was she going to die no matter what he, the doctor, or Betsy did?

Most likely, was his answer.

He knew better than most that some wild things refused to be tamed. If you caged them up, they were sure to lie down and die rather than be held captive. Was that the way of this wild girl?

Reuben Rivers said more prayers to more gods than could possibly have existed by the time he had walked all the way to White Top Mountain. He knew his little wild girl was lost to him forever. He prayed for strength be given him so he could accept what he wasn't going to be able to change. Reuben knew some things just weren't meant to be and all the prayers said to all the gods real or imagined wouldn't change that.

He carried the girl until the evening had turned into night and the night had turned into morning. The sun was warm as his feet shuffled through the fallen leaves. Even his arms had gone numb by the time he reached his cabin door.

This time when he opened the door, no men were sleeping in his bed and everything was just as he had left it. He lay Raven down and got Dog some food from one of Raven's dog food sacks. He went to the springhouse and brought back fresh water to spoon in her mouth. He would do everything he could do for her while she was alive.

🕊

Just as Don Donavan expected, Iva Dean Grearity Stewart came knocking on his door while he was eating his supper. Dad-blast that Cade Williams. Cade never was able to keep his mouth shut. Most likely, if Reuben Rivers found out he'd told about the girl, he'd at the least come back and cut Cade's tongue out.

"Don, are you in there somewheres?" Iva Dean yelled at the top of her lungs, and that was some powerful yell.

Don made an unpleasant face and motioned for Betsy to sit still, as he pushed his chair away from the table and got up. "I'm done anyhow."

Betsy didn't object, but she did roll her eyes in disgust. After the tension and the work of the past week, Don knew she was in need of rest and with Iva Dean around there was no rest to be found for anybody.

"Come in and have a bit of supper," Don invited once he had reached the door.

"What are you having?

"Beans, tators, hog meat, hominy, cornbread, and onions."

"I smell the onions on your breath," she said.

"Things tasted mighty good and there's plenty," he continued his invitation although he wasn't feeling very sociable. His momma had trained him well in the custom of mountain folks, even with women like Iva Dean.

"No thanks, I already ate before I came."

"Then why did you ask what we had?"

"I was curious, not hungry. Come sit on the porch with me. I've been talking to the people of this valley and I have something of grave importance to discuss with you."

Don went through the screen door onto the porch and took his customary chair. He dreaded what was to come for he and Iva Dean already had bad feelings over Aggie's final resting place. She had made no attempt to talk to him since he blew up the cave and her showing up came as quite a surprise.

"You're not limping much anymore," she told him as she ignored the chair and sat on the end of the porch.

"Not much," he agreed.

"Betsy still mad at you?"

"She wishes she'd married that other fellow."

"What other fellow?"

"The one that took her to all those church meetings before I showed up."

"Phooey. I don't hold with churches or preachers. Look what happened to my mother because of them."

Don didn't comment.

Iva Dean didn't seem to notice his silence, or care. Her mind was already on to the next subject.

"You are a devious man," she stated.

Don took out his snuff tin and fingered his lower lip full. Nothing like a good dip to top off a good meal. It didn't hurt in helping settle a man's nerves either. He held the tin out toward Iva Dean, but she ignored it.

"I'm not saying you were right in doing what you did, mind you, but at least you had the balls to do it. That's more'n I can say about most men."

"Is that what you came to tell me?"

"Part of it."

"Might as well spit the other part out," Don dreaded hearing it.

"It's the name. I simply can't stand it and I intend doing something about it."

Don's brows furrowed. "What in tarnation are you talking about?"

"Sodom. It's a shame and disgrace to live in a place called Sodom although it fits some folks perfectly."

Don was stunned silent.

"I'm starting a petition to have the name changed and I'm talking to everybody in the valley."

Don cleared his throat. "What do you want to change it to?" He asked for lack of anything more intelligent to say.

She had thrown him a curve ball when he had least expected it, or perhaps it was a reprieve.

"Oh, hell, I don't know. Anything besides Sodom. Soup Bean Creek, Sweet Water Branch, or even Donavan's Hollow."

Don considered what to say next and gathered up his courage. "Have you talked to Carrie and Cade about it?"

"Oh, yes. She wants to call it Davis Valley after her late husband. Cade wants to have something with his name in it. You know how those two are. Can't keep their mouths shut about anything. Fortunately, folks stopped listening to them years ago."

Don suspected her words had a far deeper meaning but he wasn't about to elaborate.

"You're right," she said suddenly without him having said a word. "I hate to admit it, but you are right. Some things ought to be allowed to rest in peace." She folded her hands in her lap. "However, the name Sodom isn't one of them."

Don just looked at her rangy profile as she sat there on the porch. He was a man left speechless.

"Did you know Mitch Kenilworth is getting ready to leave out?"

"Didn't know that," Don was thankful to find words again.

"He has finished surveying the Ruffian."

"I see." Don figured she had wound herself up and was about to let loose on the girl, her blood kin, staying in his house and him not letting her know.

"I think it's best all around that she drowned in that flood," Iva Dead added. "I don't believe in stirring up a hornet's nest where there is no need."

That surprised Don. "You don't?"

"No I don't. If she was alive, Mitch would still be trying to hunt her down, and I would be trying to do what was right by her. If she was alive, she would have a claim to a portion of my mother's wealth. My brother and his family wouldn't like that in the least. Just think what it would do to a politician's reputation for the public to know their son raped a woman and begat them a bastard granddaughter.

"They might even try to harm her, regardless of what I tried to do. If she's dead, my brother and I can simply inherit without my justful mind bothering me."

"Makes sense," Don told her.

"Yes," she agreed. "It makes better sense to let that little black haired girl and her dog remain dead than to stir up a boiling pot of troubles."

Chapter 18

The moon was high overhead with clouds occasionally drifting over it. At times, the moon lit her path almost as light as day. Raven knew she would have no problem seeing if the night had been pitch-black, but the moonlight was good. It kept her from stubbing her toe or ramming a thorn under her toenail.

She berated herself for wasting a day on Cade Williams. Why had she bothered to take him home after he was burned? It was his own moonshine still that had blown up and burned him.

She hadn't gathered food or even gathered a stick of firewood. Aggie was sure to be upset with her, and she couldn't blame Aggie. She and Aggie both knew Cade Williams was a rotten, no account man. He was always chasing after Aggie, claiming she was some kind animal that needed killing.

Raven saw images of Aggie lying dead on the dirt floor of their cave. Insects were crawling over her body, getting in her eyes and mouth because she wasn't there to keep them away.

Suddenly, she saw Aggie alive and suffering. Her backbone was twisted and her legs were going in the wrong directions. Only a few tuffs of white hair remained on her otherwise baldhead. Her face was hideous, but it was Aggie's face. The face Raven loved.

"It's about time you got home," Aggie told her as she stirred potato soup in her black pot in front of the fire.

Raven stared at her in amazement. "You're not dead?"

"Dead? Why are you asking such a thing as that? You know I'll never die and leave you. Look, I've made you good soup just like I've always done. Come, eat a little."

"But you did die," Raven insisted.

"Child," Aggie said in her loving voice. "You're mistaken."

Raven moved toward the fire and the soup Aggie was stirring. It smelled good and she was hungry, but when Aggie gave it to her, it wasn't soup at all. It was cold water.

Raven looked at Aggie reflected in the firelight. Aggie's legs were trembling from the effort it took to stand. Her hands were trembling also, and her lips.

"Sit down," Raven said to her. "Please, sit down."

Aggie didn't sit, she fell in front of the fire and her black cooking pot. A little puff of dust rose and Aggie died with the spoon still in her hand.

"No!" Raven grabbed Aggie's arms and shook her as the last sign of life twitched away. "Don't die!"

Her pleading came too late. Aggie was gone.

Raven left the cave and started to run. She had to run from her sorrow, run from death.

The air was gentle on her face. A screech owl sounded from somewhere in the trees. A whippoorwill called loud and clear, a sound of loss and loneliness. To the top of the mountain she ran where the rocks turned to huge boulders and the stunted trees were leaning away from the wind. She changed directions, ran to Teeter's pond, and then back to the cave. She couldn't go through the dark, gaping entrance, back to her happy life as a child with her mother and Aggie. There was death inside there now, death waiting for her to come face to face with, and she couldn't do it, not now.

She turned away from death and went to the rock outcropping that Aggie had stood on so many times in the past. It overlooked the valley of Sodom. She hated Sodom, hated the valley, hated the people that lived there, hated everything in the world that was beyond her understanding.

Anger built in her, built like a raging inferno, like the pressure that blew up the still, like the fires of hell. She opened her mouth and screamed, screamed again for everything that had been and could never be again, for her loss, for her pain, for her helplessness.

Reuben Rivers dropped the cup of water he was trying to get Raven to drink. He jumped straight up from where he sat beside her. He hadn't expected Raven to grunt much less scream. And then, she screamed again, a sound filled with all the torture that poor little wild thing contained.

It shook Reuben to the core.

Dog rushed from his food, crawled on the bed with Raven, nuzzled her trembling body, and licked her in the face. Her hand lifted and touched his square, blocky head.

Reuben sank down on the stump table. His body had to be trembling more than Raven's. What had happened? Was that a death scream? Was she finally dying on him?

He couldn't get up from the stump and go to her as he wanted to do. He just sat there and watched her hand touching the big black. Her fingers moved, caressed. Her chest lifted with breath. It lifted and sank again and again. She was breathing; she was still alive.

Her tired eyes eased open, her head moved until she was looking him in the face. "You finally came back," she whispered.

Reuben Rivers cried.

Mitch Kenilworth was grateful to get his insurance check without undue lingering, and he was doubly grateful Iva Dean took him to a car dealer who owed her a favor. Seemed rich folks were always owing other rich folks favors. He wondered what he would owe Iva Dean.

It didn't take long for her to tell him.

"Now that you have wheels again, I think it's best you leave Sodom. You have finished surveying Ruffian Mountain, haven't you?"

"I'm finished," he admitted.

"You were just hanging around because of my wild and pretty relative?"

Mitch wasn't about to admit to that.

"The flood changed a lot of things, didn't it?" Iva Dean persisted. "It got you a better truck, money for your lost equipment, and last but not least, it cut you loose from a girl you could never have had." Iva Dean looked at him and grinned. "You might say that flood washed your slate clean."

"You're telling me I'm not welcome to stay in your cabin any longer, aren't you?"

"Exactly."

"Care to tell me why I'm not welcome?"

"You don't belong in Sodom."

"And you do?"

A frown came to Iva Dean. That question required some thought. "Being I never found the exact place where I did belong, Sodom just might do it for me. Sodom," she rolled the name out of her mouth as though it was a bad taste. "If I stay, I'm bound and determined to see that the name is changed. You can count on that much."

Mitch grinned and so did Iva Dean. He got his few possessions out of her Jeep and stowed them in his newer used truck. He started it up and pulled out of the dealer's lot without even looking back.

There was one thing for certain about a surveyor, he could and would go in any direction his compass pointed.

𓅓

All Raven could remember after she woke up was running away from the two men who had tried to rape her, and wishing the wolf-man would show up before they caught her. He had gone back to the far mountain in order to collect his two hundred dollars for the cat hide. She knew it would take days before he would return. But the wolf-man was there, leaning over her, looking at her.

"You finally came back," she managed to say.

He started crying. She couldn't understand why he would do that.

"Are you hurt?" she asked him through her haze of exhaustion.

He didn't answer, just reached out, grabbed her in a hug, lifted her from the bed, and held her against his chest. She could feel his big body tremble, feel the jerks in his chest as he forced his sobs to stay inside.

"What's wrong?" she tried again.

He took a deep, steadying breath. "Nothing," he whispered into her hair. "Nothing at all."

"You're crying? Why?"

His powerful hug gentled. His hand rubbed her back. "I'm happy," he managed to say.

"You got the money." She concluded it to be enough reason to make him happy, but who cried when they were happy? She laughed, at least a little, when she was happy.

"I got the money."

"Did they hurt you?" she persisted.

He eased her away from him enough to look into her face. "Who?"

"Those two men I tried to kill in the barn loft. They came here after you had gone away."

"No, they didn't hurt me. When you weren't here, I thought they had hurt you," he admitted.

"I ran away," she told him simply, without showing any of the emotions she had felt when she saw those two awful men.

"I know. I found your tracks." He eased her back down onto the bed of bearskins. "I want you to rest, now. You've been a very sick girl."

She lifted her hand and let her fingers touch his cheeks where tears had wet them. She supposed there were some things she just didn't understand about being happy.

🕊

All the pretty leaves had fallen from the timber before she felt strong enough to go outside and walk to the summit of the mountain, which contained many acres without a tree or shrub, and was covered in a thick growth of grass where Reuben grazed his cows and work horse. She stood there watching the wind blow the grass in waves and felt contentment fill her. This place was nothing like Ruffian Mountain and the house that Reuben called a cabin was nothing like Aggie's cave, but there was peace here she had found no place else.

Reuben told her the mountain was isolated and only an occasional hunter strayed near his land, but not often. He said from the summit on which she stood, cornered three states, North Carolina, Virginia, and Tennessee. She tried to figure out what land belonged to which state but couldn't. She'd have to ask Reuben.

A strong puff of wind came and twirled the leaves from the ground. She shivered although she wore a deerskin shirt and britches that Reuben had made for her. It was cold on the summit of White Top Mountain and the wind was bitter. Reuben had chosen a sheltered place for the cabin.

She left the summit to find Reuben. He was chopping firewood near the edge of the woods. He saw her, buried his ax in a log, and came to her.

"What are you doing out of bed?"

"I'm tired of being in bed," she told him.

"Is it not comfortable?"

"Oh, yes. It's comfortable. I used to sleep on rags," she admitted. "On hard ground." She didn't tell him the bed was too soft or that bear skins had an odor she was not accustomed to. Nor did she tell him she wanted to see him, watch him work in preparation for winter. He did about ten times more work than Aggie could have done, and realizing that caused her to ache inside for all that Aggie had managed to do in order to keep them alive.

"You'll never sleep on rags again," he told her softly.

"I wouldn't mind the rags if Aggie was with me," she admitted. "But only my mind can go back there. I can sleep in the barn and let you have the bearskin bed," she offered and hoped he would agree. She wouldn't feel nearly as enclosed in the barn.

"Nothing doing."

"It's your house, not mine. You should sleep in it."

"You don't like sleeping in my house?"

"I never lived in a house before."

"I'll haul rocks and build you a cave onto it if that's what you want."

She looked upward as a flock of birds gathered in an oak tree. Their excited chirping filled the air as they gathered to migrate. It made her restless, ill at ease somehow.

Trouble was she didn't know what she wanted. All she knew was the need to run wild and free. The sound of honking made her and Reuben both look skyward. A flock of geese were flying high-up in V-formation.

"You feel it, don't you?" Reuben said. "Never a fall comes when I don't want to join in with all the things that migrate. I believe all wild things have the urge to run away from changing weather. Change scares them."

She looked from the geese to the man before her. He was big and strong and gentle. He could cry and he could laugh and he could be silent. He was so many things she had never known a man could be. She no longer feared him and his beard was growing back. Perhaps, just perhaps, this was a good man.

"Why are you allowing me to stay here?" she asked. "You owe me nothing."

His black eyes sparkled as he looked at her. "It's not a matter of owing. It's a matter of wanting."

"You want me here?" She could hardly believe he would still want her here after all the work and trouble she had been to him.

"I want you here," he assured her, and the look on his face made her feel funny.

She looked away quickly, back at the sky where the geese no longer were. She had to ask what was on her mind for she knew nothing about being coy or silent. "Are you wanting to mate with me?"

A flicker of surprise touched him. "Yes," he finally answered with the slightest grin. "I believe that's exactly what I want."

"Geese mate for life?" she added. "Would you and I do that?"

"I plan on mating for life," he told her.

"How do people go about mating?"

"First of all, I'll court you all winter long by taking care of you and keeping you safe. After the snows melt and the sun brings the earth back to life, you will be strong again. That's when we'll mate, if you are willing."

"You'll put a baby in me then?"

"If you are willing."

"Does mating hurt?"

"I've heard say people find it very pleasurable."

"Women too?"

"Women too."

She remembered hiding beneath the window and listening to Pete and Oma Jenkins mating. Their moans sounded like they were hurting and yet they sounded very happy about it.

"Spring?" she asked.

"Spring," he repeated.

Years seem to come and go in the blinking of an eye. Time rolls on and everything is destined to change. At the same time, all stays the same. This was and always would be the way between Mother Nature and Father Time.

The best way to immortalize those we love is to live life to its fullest, and that is what a wild girl and Reuben Rivers did where three states corner.

The sun still rises and sets on White Top Mountain, just as it has always done, but the cabin that once stood in the edge of the woods has returned to the earth. It would be impossible for human eyes to find the place where a wild woman lived and loved and bore nine children by the toughest mountain man who ever drew pure mountain air into his lungs.

Even more impossible to find would be the single grave where two men's bones disintegrated with time. They should have known, as others came to know, you never messed with Ruben Rivers' woman.

If you enjoyed this book, visit www.peggypoestern.com to check on the status of Peggy's latest books or leave feedback.

Books are available at regionally selected stores in northwestern North Carolina, southwestern Virginia, and eastern Tennessee. Use the contact information below for locations.

To purchase books online, visit Amazon's website. For autographed books, visit Peggy's website or contact her at

Peggy Poe Stern
475 Church Hollow Road
Boone, NC 28607
828-963-5331 Tel
828-963-4101 Fax
E-mail: moodyvalley@skybest.com
Web site: www.peggypoestern.com

1. ISBN 1-59513-055-1 $16.95

A mountain girl in the early 1900's copes with a marriage arranged by her dad. Her story is titled from an old saying: "I own my land, heaven-high and hell-deep."

"Your pa gave his consent for us to marry." He said the words as though it was a simple matter. It wasn't a romantic proposal of love and devotion. It wasn't a proposal at all. I opened my mouth, but nothing came out. I tried again.

"I don't know your name," I managed to say ...

Tamarack

The Beekeeper's Daughter
Peggy Poe Stern

2. ISBN 1-59513-054-3 $14.95

"What's his name?"

"Jay Press."

"You're Mary Press Tate?"

Her head nodded slightly. She'd never looked at any of them. Her eyes remained on the face of her pa.

"Who shot him?" Big Red asked with a gentle voice.

"Me."

"You shot your father?" Big Red lifted his brows and watched her closely.

Her head nodded again.

"Why?"

"He aimed to kill me."

"Why did he want to kill you?"

When Robins Weep

The Christmas Tree Lady
Peggy Poe Stern

3. ISBN 1-59513-053-5 $17.95

He fitted the jack under the axle. She remained beside him. He smelled her perfume. It was delicate and reminded him of soap. Another whiff and he realized it wasn't perfume at all. *It was soap.* His eyes went to her left hand. She was wearing a plain, cheap looking ring, but he wasn't sure if it was a wedding band. It could have come from a Cracker Jack box.

"You married?" He tried to sound off-handed in his question.

She looked at his left hand and shrugged her shoulders. "Kinda."

"How can you be kinda married?"

"I had a husband for twenty-four hours."

"Divorced?"

"Nope."

The Hills of Home

The Farmer's Daughter
Peggy Poe Stern

4. ISBN 1-59513-052-7 $16.95

He looked confused. I watched the frown pucker the skin between his hazel colored eyes—nice eyes, gentle and warm.

"You are telling me you work seven nights a week and go to high school during the day?"

"Yes."

"Why?"

"I need the money."

"What for? A car?"

I shook my head. "Rent, electricity, food."

"You have to pay for that? Your parents don't?"

"I'm married," I said, got up and took my dishes to the kitchen.

Stud from Horney Hollow

The Collier Mistress
Peggy Poe Stern

5. ISBN 1-59513-051-9 $16.95

"I've searched for her for over two and a half damned years."
He clinched his fists as his eyes glared at the newspaper.

"Why?" asked Effie.

"Why do you think?" said Albert.

"Son, is she the one Nub told me about? The one you've been
mooning over all this time?"

Burl took a deep breath and said nothing.

"It says her name is Willi Smith. Nub said her name was
Anna Jones," Effie said gently.

"She lied," Burl hit the swing with his fist. "She hauled off
and flat out lied to me."

"Why would she do that?" Albert wanted to know.

"Hell if I'm not going to find out in a mighty big hurry."

6. ISBN 1-59513-050-0 $16.95

Mountain Splendor

Long Hope Mountain Gal

Peggy Poe Stern

Needing to make the farm payment, Ramona pretends to be a man and takes on her recently departed husband's next job assignment: guiding a group of Yankees through the mountains.

He watched me from the corner of his eye as I dismounted and walked up to him.

"You Barlow?" I had a naturally deep voice for a woman. Husky some called it, but I tried to make it sound more manly.

He nodded, looked at my horse and then at my clothes, all a trademark of Jake Triplet.

"Where's Jake?"

"Dead," I answered and saw a faint flicker of surprise pass over his face. I took it to mean he was calculating the loss of money as well as the desperation of finding a new guide before morning.

"Who are you?"

"His kin. I come to take his place."

"Take Jake Triplet's place?" he said the words like he was trying to understand them.

"Yeah," I said. "Take his place."

"You any good?"

"Half as good as Jake, thrice as dependable."

He frowned. "You know the land?"

"Wouldn't be here if I didn't."

"You can shoot?"

I nodded.

"Fight?"

"Some. Never had the need, often."

"You're young. Not even peach fuzz on your chin, but then Jake didn't have much either. Reckon Indians aren't hairy."

Blood Moon Rising

Restless Revenge

Peggy Poe Stern

7. EAN # 978-1-59513-049-5 $16.95

The fires of hell would burn me in time for what I was about to do, but right now, that didn't matter. I was on my way to kill him. Someone should have killed Buck Walsh a long time ago for the things he did, but people were scared of him. I'm scared of him, but that no longer mattered either. He had raped me.

Wild Thing

Aggie's Legacy

Peggy Poe Stern

8. EAN #978-1-59513-048-8 $17.95

Cadence Williams settled beneath the quilt willing to go into a deep sleep. He hadn't slept much for the past two nights. Fear mixed with self-anger kept him awake. He hated fear. It was a sign of weakness, especially when it was his own. It angered him to fear when he wasn't sure if the cause of it was real or imagined. Yet, his gut told him *that thing* was near his house, moving in the woods like a dark shadow, stalking him when he went outside to do up the work, and even coming to his window during the night to watch him.

Above-all
a sequel to
Heaven-high and Hell-deep

Laine's Beech Mountain Story, Book 2
Peggy Poe Stern

9. EAN #978-1-59513-047-1 $17.00

His hat was pulled low over his black hair and his shirt sleeves were rolled up almost to his elbows. His hands appeared strong and in control as he held the reins of his high-stepping horse. He looked a little thinner than he used to be and a lot more tired.

"What's wrong?" he asked me fast.

"You've got to go back to Banners Elk," I told him, forgetting about supper.

His eyes widened with concern. "Should you ride? I can deliver the baby here."

10. EAN #978-1-59513-046-4 $17.00

"Leona," he sipped his hot coffee. "I know I'm going to regret asking this, but tell me the story of Joppa and Harry Barnard from the beginning to the end.

"It's a seventeen year stretch of time," I warned.

"This place isn't overrun with customers."

"If I tell you, will you use it against me? Claim I'm crazy? refuse to help me?"

"Attorney-client information is privileged. I don't tell anything you say not to tell."

"You'll think I'm a fruitcake."

"You're not?"

Thunder Hole

The Blackberry Summer
Peggy Poe Stern

11. EAN 978-1-59513-045-7 $17.00

He started to say more, then hesitated before he added, "Do you know what I want, Billie, really want?"

"Besides me being five years older?"

He ignored that. "I want you to go to college."

She laughed.

"I'm serious."

Her laughter stopped too suddenly and she looked at Malone with eyes beyond those of childhood. "It won't happen."

"Why not?"

An Honorable Man

Surviving Daniel
Peggy Poe Stern

12. EAN 978-1-59513-044-0 $17.00

After twenty-four years of marriage to Daniel, Carrie Jane can take it no longer. Leaving everything behind, she slips off one evening to start anew.

"Tell me, Dad, why does this woman interest you?"

He scratched at his gray hair again before he spoke. "Something wasn't exactly right about her. A teenage girl might run away for any number of reasons, but a woman her age doesn't. She was . . . well, I kinda pitied her. There has to be a mighty powerful reason when a woman hides in a moving van."

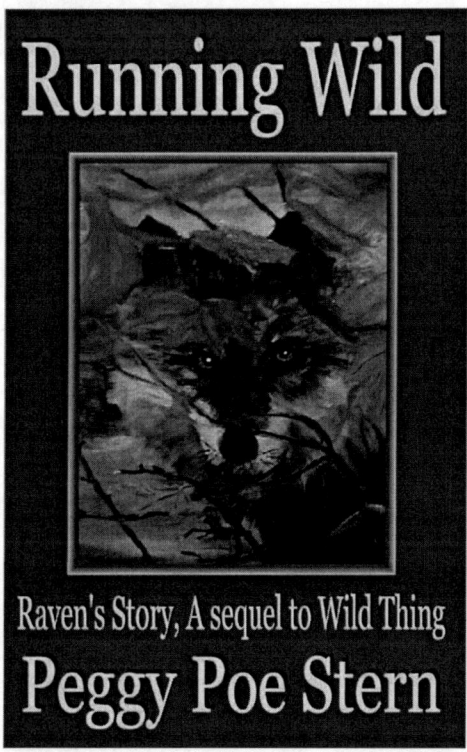

Running Wild

Raven's Story, A sequel to Wild Thing

Peggy Poe Stern

13. EAN 978-1-59513-043-3 $17.00

The girl came up over the rise, running with a long, distance-eating gait and drawing deep breaths of air into her lungs. Reuben found her strangely attractive although something about her appearance was odd, much different from any girl he'd ever seen before. Her hair was just as black as his and reached below her slender hips. It caught the wind and flowed back from her face as she ran. Her ragged clothes were not clean and once belonged to a man. There wasn't one ounce of fat on her wiry body, but none of this did he find odd. What was odd was her overall demeanor. There was an energy force radiating from her, a life force such as he expected to see surrounding the mountain lion or one of the bears he loved to hunt, a savage appearance that warned to keep a safe distance away.

Holy shit, he thought. *She's wild!*

Dream Lover

My Time as Chessy Spade
Peggy Poe Stern

14. EAN 978-1-59513-042-6 $18.00

"What?" I managed to say about my confusion.

Her hand tightened on mine. "Emmilee can't live in this world. This time around the life you are experiencing is meant for Chessy." Her wrinkled face shown with the strangest kindness directed solely at me. "Micah McCall has to accept that fact the same as you."

She had mentioned him before, but I'd never heard of a McCall living around here. "Tell me, who is Micah McCall? I have a right to know."

She ignored my question about McCall. "This life cannot be lived in the past. It can only be lived in this moment. You understand that, don't you?"

It sounded good, but as far as understanding, I wasn't sure.

15. 978-1-59513-41-9

Blood Kin

Deliverance out of Pisgah

Peggy Poe Stern

"Are you hurt?" asked a gentle voice.

I knew I had fallen asleep and the voice was in my dream, but I couldn't make my eyes open. Exhaustion was too strong, as was my ever-present fear.

"Don't be afraid," continued the voice. "You're safe with me."

I wanted to laugh, but my dream world wouldn't allow laughter.

"You're wet and shivering," the voice said. "I'll have to carry you to safety. This cliff is dangerous in the best of times."

He wasn't telling me anything I didn't already know.

Hands touched me, strong hands. Did dreams come with hands? It was then my eyes opened and I saw the face of a man. I let out an earsplitting squeal.

"It's all right," the gentle voice continued. "I need to see if anything is broken before I move you."

The moon was up and shining on the man. I expected to see a hairy monster with only a human face, but I didn't. The face was ruggedly attractive in the pale moonlight. There was no long, shaggy, body hair.

A smattering of relief hit me. This really was a man. With his help, I might be able to survive, but first I had to warn him of what had happened to my team.

"Help me!" My hands grabbed the front of his coat and clung. "There's monsters. They killed my team. All of them."

Blind Faith

Lost Mountain

Peggy Poe Stern

16. 978-1-59513-040-2 17.00

Page 33

Carlee knew she was going to Landreys Fork before she hung up the phone. Business gossip, as well as truth, had her at a homeless shelter in New York City, not a good recommendation, or a good address, when seeking a high paying position with a responsible company. At least she did have a house in North Carolina. She hoped desperately her unemployment check would be enough to buy a bus ticket, with a few dollars remaining for sundry expenses. Goodness knows, it wouldn't cover a plane ticket.

She found herself hating Bernard Madoff all over again, not to mention the despicable circumstance he had put her in.

Page 303

Carlee found herself at Lum's.

It seemed the old woman was sitting on the rock wall watching for her to show up.

"Didn't think you'd get here this quick, but I was waitin'."

"Why didn't you tell me?" she asked.

"I take it you're here about the diary and not about Jason."

"You take it right. Why didn't you tell me?"

Lum cocked her head sideways. "Because it needed to come from your mother, not from me."

"You could have told me about the diary."

"You found it, didn't you?"

"You didn't tell me it was there."

"Thought you needed to adjust to Lost Mountain and your people before you got shocked good and proper. Besides, everybody told you that you were one of us."

Served Cold

Mountain Justice
Peggy Poe Stern

17. EAN 978-1-59513-039-6 $17.00

One might say there has been a slow poison brewing inside me, bubbling, and churning, and threatening to erupt for the major portion of my life. The only reason it's been contained for so long is that I did not have every ingredient I needed. I now have them all and I am ready for Jackson Winkerson. By the time I'm through with him, he'll regret what he did to me.

This brew has been gathering itself for over twenty- three years. Never once, not for one day, not for one hour, have I left my brew unattended or unwanted. Three months ago, it reached its most potent stage. My husband, Coleman Cottumn, died. I would have delivered my brew the day after he was buried, but I had to wait the standard ninety days before my attorney, Marshall Evans, declared me in full control over everything my deceased husband left behind, which to my delight, is far more than I ever imagined. He could have given Bill Gates a fair run in financial genius.

Better Off Dead

Fighting Fate, Round One
Peggy Poe Stern

18. EAN 978-1-59513-038-9 $17.00

A strange feeling overcame me. It was as though I would never see this man, who was my almost invisible boss, again. My life flashed before my eyes as a sudden premonition hit. A cold shiver ran up my backbone and puckered my flesh. He knew 771-0001 would not return.

The shiver turned to hot anger. He was sending me to my death!

19. EAN 978-1-59513-037-2 $17.00

Better Off Gone

Fighting Fate, Round Two
Peggy Poe Stern

My biggest problem was that I was coming out of being brainwashed and I didn't know how to protect myself. I had miraculously received unexpected freedom. If I blew this opportunity for a new life, and the Special Forces of Homeland Security found out I was still alive, I would be dead for real.

No Candy Tilless would die in my place ever again.

This rogue group who referred to itself as the Special Forces of Homeland Security wouldn't make the same mistake twice.

For me to be safe, I had to find all the answers to my questions, and I needed to know them now.

I poured myself another cup of coffee and sank down on the sagging sofa. Slow down, think, I told myself. The research I had done on brainwashing hrlped me to realize I had traits that made it possible for me to easily become brainwashed. Impatience to know all the answers right now, in black and white with no gray areas, was one such trait. So was gullibility, disillusionment, and naïve idealism. I didn't think I had naïve idealism. I suspected that quality died in me soon after birth.

20. EAN 978-1-59513-036-5 $12.00

Old Barns of Ashe

Along Came a Stranger, a short novel

Peggy Poe Stern

Mother's secret treasure was hidden deep inside the old mattress she had slept on for seventy years. Twenty of those years she'd slept on it alone – after Dad's death.

Here's an excerpt from her journal of a cherished affair:

I had come from the springhouse carrying a half-gallon jug of cold milk when I heard the sound of a truck. I almost dropped the jug when Alfonso's truck pulled up.

"Now who could that be?" Frank asked as he met me in the yard.

"I wouldn't know," I told him and then rushed inside the house as though I was afraid of strangers.

Through the kitchen window, I saw Frank stride to the open window of the driver's side of the truck.

"You lost or something?" I heard Frank ask.

"Is this the Frank Ledford place?" Alfonso asked as he opened the truck door and got out, even though Frank hadn't invited him to do so.

"Could be," Frank drawled. "Who wants to know?"

"I'm Alfonso Cohan. I take photographs of old barns and then paint pictures of them."

Frank gave him a look as though he were an alien from Pluto.

Alfonso ignored the look as though it wasn't obvious. "A man in town told me you had a dandy of a barn and I was wondering if you'd mind me snapping a photo of it."

"You take pictures of old barns and then paint paintings of them?" Frank said in disbelief.

"I do."

"You tetched in the head or something?" Frank questioned with sincerity.

"Most likely." Alfonso grinned that grin I had learned to treasure. I nearly broke into a flood of tears from the pain I was feeling. It didn't seem right that my husband and the man I loved stood out there in the yard, and they weren't the same man.

21. 978-1-59513-035-8

Wanted

Blue Ridge Bounty Hunters - One
Peggy Poe Stern

From Chapter 18:

When we reached the sheriff's department, I went in to get two of the officers to help get Ray Dean out of the hearse. Neither Ella May nor I were up to another round with him.

There were questioning looks as they dragged him out in his underwear. Both of them pretended not to notice that Ella May was wearing his clothes, until curiosity got the best of the new officer.

"What's with . . ." the new officer finally said as he nodded toward Ray Dean and then Ella May.

"Don't ask," the other officer interrupted him. "Most of them are upset with Scottie Adams once she gets them here. It's becoming her trade mark. Even the night shift is becoming familiar with her bounty hunting abilities."

I cringed knowing Manning Woodring worked the nightshift.

I followed them inside with the keys to the cuffs. I didn't want to leave my cuffs behind, plus I knew Ray Dean would be put into the shower and given a pretty orange jumpsuit to wear.

When I got back to the hearse with the cuffs and body receipt, I asked Ella May if she wanted to try for number three.

"I'm getting' kinda hungry," she said. "Let's go back to the office, fix us a peanut butter and jelly sandwich, and then file for a while. I'm tuckered out."

I had no arguments.

22. 978-1-59513-034-1
A young mountain woman copes with a second husband, running her farm, raising children, and a developer trying to take her land.

Mountain Gorilla

Laine's Beech Mountain Story, Book 3

Peggy Poe Stern

From Chapter 22:

"Let's see if you're really pregnant first," Jonas sounded rather bored and a lot sleepy. "Then I'll see what you can do about prevention. In the meantime, I'm going to bed early. I have a heavy workload tomorrow."

"You work too hard," I told him. "Why don't you take a few days off and stay here with me and our babies?"

Jonas almost laughed. "Surely your mountain gorilla is getting enough work done for you without you wanting me to forget about my patients and help you."

This surprised me. I hadn't been thinking about farm work. I was thinking about Jonas being tired from working too long and hard.

"Barnabus doesn't need help," I told Jonas. "If he did, I'd get him to send for his older brother. He says his brother is bigger and can do a lot more than he does. I didn't expect you to take off and work on the farm," I added. "Andy told me a doctor needs soft hands so he can detect folk's problems, such as lumps and growths. Farm works calluses up hands until they're hard and unfeeling. I don't want that for you."

23. 978-1-59513-033-4

The Rising Sun

Brutally assaulted and threatened, Hannah fears for her life. She's seeking conviction and Benlee's out on bail.

Seeking Justice
Peggy Poe Stern

From Chapter 1:

Hannah was terrified, her nerves unsettled. That's why she wore her prettiest jeans and favorite T-shirt to work. Her hair was freshly washed and her makeup put on thick. It had to be thick in order to cover up the bruises. She also smiled too much. It was her effort to hide what was going on inside her, as was her efforts to look good. She needed to look good on the outside as camouflage for what was happening to her on the inside. She knew only too well a troubled woman would draw attention. A brave one would draw admiration. She wanted neither.

What she really wanted was a pistol, a small one she could carry with her and conceal.

"How are ya, Sugar?" Norman asked as he took a seat at the counter.

"Better," she lied. How would he react if she told him she was going out of her mind with fear with every tick of the clock?

He looked her face over just as he did every morning. She didn't want him looking in her eyes; he would see too much. She turned her back on him, grabbed the coffee pot, poured him his morning coffee, and handed him extra … .

24. 978-1-59513-032-7

Sweet Lendy

An Appalachian Whodunit
Peggy Poe Stern

During the seventies, most everyone in our small Appalachian town of Mountain View had some indiscretions. Even as town police chief and deacon of the church, I had mine too – I just pretended to go fishing every Saturday night. Our fooling around seemed tolerable – until a pretty, young woman showed up one summer.

From Chapter 7:

"What gave you such an idea as that?" I tried to ask innocently, although I knew she was right.

"I've got ears, Hank. I also heard talk that Walter Smith was trying to catch you red-handed with his wife tonight. Everybody knows you go fishing on Saturday nights although not in the same spot each time. I took a chance on you being here and got Will Bennett to drive me out and drop me off. I've been here about ten minutes."

"In ten more minutes, I'll have you back home."

"Don't think so," she said.

"And why not?"

She reached for her blouse and started undoing the buttons. I reached out and grabbed her hand to stop her. "Unless the talk I heard is nothing but stupid gossip, you'd better take off your shirt and start making out with me."

Talk about being stunned. "What on earth . . ." I questioned.

"Any minute now you're gonna have company. Smith hired some men to track you down and see how many fish you've caught. Since you've not got a string of fish, I'd better become what you've caught."

25. 978-1-59513-031-0

From Chapter 5:

Last of the Summer Wine

Home Comfort
Peggy Poe Stern

A strange feeling took hold as I watched the landscape before me. Part of me wanted to run through the snow, leaving my tracks in the world of unmarred beauty. Another part of me didn't dare make tracks in the perfection only God could create.

"Not yet," came a voice that made me jump a good foot although the voice was familiar. "Don't go down there yet."

"Where are you?" I asked as I looked around. I hadn't seen any tracks other than mine.

"Over here, under the pine tree."

Five feet from me stood a towering pine tree with its branches weighted down with snow. Someone was beneath the branches that hung to the ground, but I didn't see any tracks.

"If you walk around back of the tree, the branches aren't as thick and you can come inside."

I made my way around the tree. He was right, that side of the tree was shaded by other trees and the branches hadn't grown as vigorously. I saw his tracks in the snow leading up the mountain to where he had also stood to view the beauty.

"Come on in, you'll be amazed."

I stepped into his footprints and eased my way between branches, while trying not to dislodge the snow by keeping my head lowered. Underneath the shelter of the large pine was a thick carpet of brown needles. Adam was sitting on the ground with his back leaning against the trunk of the tree. The drooping branches made a kind of sheltered cave that was extremely cozy.

"Come here," he said as he patted the needles beside him indicating for me to sit down. "If you sit right here, you can see the beauty through the branches. It's . . . amazing."

I moved to the tree trunk and sat down. He was right. The branches I was looking through formed a frame for the beauty, making it even more enchanting.

"Oh, my," I whispered.

What in Sam Hill

Pursued

Peggy Poe Stern

Novel #26

26. 978-1-59513-064-8

Tailing her cheating husband, Jim Barrington, Nadine witnesses the torture and murder of two men by members of the Barrington Society. While reporting the murders, she realizes the Society has people working within the FBI. Pursued by the Society so she can't testify against them and the FBI so she can, she vanishes.

From Chapter 6:... she needed to talk to him, give him some kind of explanation for her tears.

"My parents were killed in an accident when I was five years old. ... My Aunt Lucy took me in and raised me all by herself. She wanted me to go to college and make something of myself. I became an attorney. When I graduated, I managed to get a job in Raleigh at a law firm. I took on a pro bono case and was forced to resign because of it."

From Chapter 2: Nadine had lost her job because she tried to help a woman in need. In her opinion something wasn't right in the cosmic universe and she wanted to fix it in the best way she knew how. ...

She went running home to Aunt Lucy and Louisa Mae.

"You did the right thing," Aunt Lucy said. "Mind you that making a living is important, but a person is supposed to help their fellow man once in a while. It's the Christian way and should never be denied. Do what's right, child. Always do what your heart and mind tells you is right." ...

Nadine applied for a job as a public defender in a little town in upper Tennessee called Barrington - named after the man who'd made the nearly deserted piece of land into a prosperous town. ...

The one thing that puzzled her most was that one of the doctors who worked at the small, local hospital took an interest in her. It just so happened, his name was James Samuel Barrington III, the grandson of the original James Samuel Barrington, but everyone called him Jim. He was pushing forty and had never been married.

From Chapter 19: "They won't be convicted," Nadine said from the backseat as though she was talking to herself. "They'll have me killed before I can testify against them. The Society couldn't have existed all these years without loyal members and their families. There's no way the FBI will be able to arrest everyone or protect me from them.

Jonas Jones

Laine's Beech Mountain Story, Book 4
Peggy Poe Stern

27. 978-1-59513-029-7

Jonas has changed from the man I married and I don't know what I'm going to do about it. I'm racking my brain trying to figure out what to do. What makes a good man change into a troubled one? How in this world am I going to help him change back? I'm more alone with him here than I was when he was gone off to the war.